Cornish Clouds and Silver Lining Skies

Ali McNamara

SPHERE

SPHERE

First published in Great Britain in 2022 by Sphere

1 3 5 7 9 10 8 6 4 2

A CIP catalogue record for this book
is available from the British Library.

ISBN 978-0-7515-8101-0

Typeset in Caslon by M Rules
Printed and bound in Great Britain by
Clays Ltd, Elcograf S.p.A.

Papers used by Sphere are from well-managed forests
and other responsible sources.

Sphere
An imprint of
Little, Brown Book Group
Carmelite House
50 Victoria Embankment
London EC4Y 0DZ

An Hachette UK Company
www.hachette.co.uk

www.littlebrown.co.uk

For those living every day with
invisible disability.

One

'But how do I get over there?' I ask, staring across the sea at my new home.

The island I'm gazing at appears to float on the water like a tall ship stationary in its port. Currently, it's cossetted by a calm and inviting sea. The waves are barely gentle ripples on the surface as they caress the island on this clear, sunny day. But I can easily imagine on a day when the wind is gusting fiercely, the waves might look a little less friendly as they batter the grey craggy rocks that surround the island.

The young man who is my designated guide for today looks at me with a bemused expression.

'By boat, of course,' he says in his broad Cornish accent. 'You do right now, anyway. When the tide is out, you can use the causeway.'

'I was under the impression there was a permanent path over to the island. I'm sure that's what it said in my email.' I reach into my bag for my phone, but my guide shakes his head.

'No, Aurora is a tidal island. When the tide is out there's a stone causeway, but when the tide is in,' he gestures down the

1

side of the harbour wall towards a white and purple motorboat moored there, 'you take *Doris* here.'

'But ... Fisher, isn't it?' I ask, double-checking I've got his name right.

The young man nods.

'Fisher, I don't know how to drive a boat.' I look in horror at the small motorboat bobbing about on the water.

Fisher grins at me.

'Sorry, I mean sail,' I apologise.

'No, you were right the first time – it's drive.'

'Then why are you smiling?' I'm becoming more anxious about this new job by the second. I so need everything to go well this time. It's my chance to prove that I can cope with minor assignments. Otherwise, I'll never be given the big ones again.

Earlier – when everything was going smoothly and to plan – I'd felt a little more comfortable. Fisher had met me and my little dog, Fitz, off the train after our long journey down from London to the most southerly tip of Cornwall. He'd proceeded to load all my luggage into a Land Rover without a single complaint. As we'd driven towards my temporary new home, Fisher had told me all about the busy little harbour town of St Felix. And for the first time since I accepted it, I'd begun to feel that this new assignment might actually be a good thing. It was once we'd arrived at the harbour to cross over to the island that things began to go downhill.

'Look,' I say now, trying to pull an email up on my phone with one hand, while holding Fitz's lead with the other, 'it says here the weather station is on an island a few hundred metres out to sea, but you can easily walk across from the town of St Felix using the causeway.'

'And your message there would be right,' Fisher says cheerily. 'At low tide you can indeed walk or drive across to the island, but it's not low tide right now, is it?'

'Clearly not,' I mutter, staring at my email as my heart sinks further.

The offer to come to Cornwall had come completely out of the blue. Due to ill health I'd been on an extended leave of absence from my position as a senior meteorologist at Met Central in London. Now I was feeling much better I'd assumed I'd be returning to my old job. But my boss had phoned and suggested this opportunity might be just what I needed to get back into the swing of things – 'a little more gently' had been her exact words.

As she'd gone on to explain what this new job entailed, I'd had a gut feeling it might be trouble, but I had little choice in the matter. Either I took this temporary position and proved I was capable again, or the career I'd worked so hard for over the years was just going to slip away from me, like so much else in my life had recently. At least this way I was still clinging on to some sort of career. Much like the barnacles on the harbour below me, it might be easier to let go, but there was no way either I or they intended to release our grip just yet.

'Look ... *Sky*, isn't it?' Fisher asks, imitating me.

I glance at him to see if he's trying to be clever, but I just see a kind, tanned, handsome face looking back at me. His dark chocolate eyes are wide, and his expression completely innocent. It's hard to imagine Fisher ever deliberately ridiculing anyone. 'Do you mind if I call you Sky?'

'No, of course not,' I say, still peering down apprehensively at the boat.

'If you want to, we can wait until later and head across to the

3

island when the tide turns,' he suggests. 'Then I can drive you over in the Land Rover, no worries. But you seemed so keen to get over there and get cracking when you arrived. I thought you'd want to go immediately.'

At least I appeared keen, that's something. 'Yes, you're right, we should go now. I suppose Fitz and I are going to have to get used to travelling by boat if I'm going to be living and working over there.'

I glance back at the island. The sun is now shining directly above it, and fluffy white clouds are providing the perfect backdrop to show the island at its very best.

Cumulus congestus and *cumulus mediocris*, I think automatically as I watch the white clouds float across the sky. *Formed by the upward convection of columns of warm moist air on sunny days such as this.*

'You could only travel back and forth at low tide, if you wanted to?' Fisher suggests, breaking into my cloud spotting. 'But as someone who has spent a fair amount of time on Aurora, I have to say that would be very restrictive.'

'No, you're completely right, we should get going as soon as possible. You can teach me how to drive this boat, I assume?'

'Of course. I've been sailing across to Aurora since I was a nipper.'

'I thought *you* said it wasn't sailing just now,' I reply, allowing myself to break into a smile.

Fisher winks at me. 'Call it what you like, it's still the same thing. Right then, Miss Sky, let's see if we can make a sailor out of you and your little dog!'

Once we've got me, Fitz and my luggage on board the little boat, there's just enough room for Fisher to clamber aboard.

After a quick lesson in boat safety, Fisher unties the mooring and we set off. I have to admit Fisher is a very good teacher; he makes everything about driving the little boat seem very straightforward. Basically, once you start the engine there are only three options – forward, neutral and reverse, and I soon have my hands gripped tightly on the steering wheel as I guide *Doris*, our surprisingly zippy little boat, across the sea towards the island under Fisher's watchful gaze, and Fitz's excited barking.

I'm surprised at how incredibly free I feel as I cross the waves. The fresh breeze blows not only my hair temporarily away from my face, but my misgivings too.

'This feels amazing!' I tell Fisher as we speed across the waves. 'I had no idea it would be so much fun!'

Fisher grins. 'I'm glad you're enjoying it. Now, follow the route I told you a few minutes ago. Remember, that's the best way across to Aurora. You avoid hidden rocks and swells in the ocean that way.'

'It's a good job you're here,' I tell him. 'I would have simply driven across in a straight line.'

'And you'd have damaged the boat and possibly yourselves as well if you did that. This is your safest route by far, any other way can be very dangerous – like I said, there's rocks around the island that you can't see until the tide is out. Only an expert or someone very familiar with the area would attempt to cross any other way.'

'How do you know the island so well?' I ask him, watching the waves in front of me through the windscreen of the boat.

'My grandad used to be a part of the Wave Watch team here. He'd often bring me across when I was small and he was on duty.'

'Wave Watch – that's like a sort of Coastguard, isn't it?'

'Kind of, except they're all volunteers and they don't do any rescuing, only observing. They keep a watch over the sea in the area. They look out for craft and people swimming, and keep an eye on them to make sure they don't get into any trouble. They monitor the weather, too – a bit like you're going to – and report back to the fishermen, so they're aware of any severe weather that might prevent them going out in their boats. The island was the Wave Watch headquarters until recently, when it was decided you should move in.'

'Oh, I'm sorry about that, I didn't know. It wasn't my decision to come here, my company just asked me to take the job. They didn't say anything about moving anyone off the island.'

'No need to worry, the Wave Watch have been moved to Tregarlan Castle. It's not really a castle, just a really big house up on the hill, it's been here for centuries, but it looks out over the same bay as the house on Aurora, so they still get a good viewpoint. You might have noticed it as we drove in?'

'Yes, I did, it's very impressive. I read about the house when I was looking up St Felix before I came here. Isn't it owned by National Heritage?'

'It's *run* by them, but it's owned by a couple of locals – Poppy and Jake Asher. She also owns the local flower shop, and he has the nursery up on Primrose Hill. It's down to them that the Wave Watch got permission to move into Tregarlan temporarily.'

'I'm glad I don't have the added worry of watching out for boats in danger as well as watching the weather,' I say, narrowly avoiding a collision with a seagull bobbing about on the waves. Luckily the seagull decides at the last minute to fly away, giving me a disdainful look as it soars up away from the boat's path. 'That's quite a lot of responsibility.'

6

Fisher nods. 'It is. But they do a great job, and they've saved a lot of lives as a result. My grandad was sad when he had to leave.'

'Why did he have to leave?'

'Long story,' Fisher says, quickly. 'Look, we're nearly there.' He suddenly stands up from where he's been squeezed in-between my pieces of luggage and comes over to the controls at the bow of the boat. 'Let me show you how to guide *Doris* into Aurora's own little harbour.'

Once we've navigated our way into a small natural harbour created by the nearby grey and black rocks that jut out of the sea, Fisher shows me how to moor the boat to a worn wooden jetty.

He helps first Fitz and then me on to dry land, then he glances at my luggage still piled high in the boat. 'Now, we just need to get all that up to the house.'

'I probably should have packed a little lighter,' I say apologetically, 'but I wasn't really sure what to bring.'

'Don't be worrying about it,' Fisher says with a shrug. 'You need what you need. Just give me a minute, I'll be right back.'

He probably assumes this is all my clothes or things for Fitz, I think as I watch Fisher head up a narrow path and disappear around a bend. What he doesn't know is that a lot of what's concealed in my cases are things that make my life easier – items most people wouldn't ever need to think about bringing with them to a Cornish island. But things I need in case this trip doesn't go as well as I hope.

While I wait, and Fitz is having a good sniff of everything close by, I take a look around at the island. Now I'm here I can see that Aurora's terrain is actually quite lush – there are leafy plants, soft areas of moss and grass, and little pink flowers scattered in between the rocks and stones. The gravel path that Fisher has just walked along carries on up towards a tall, whitewashed house at the top of the island. From here I can just make out half of the curved bay window that is going to act as my watch station.

It's not until I hear the growl of an engine that I suddenly realise how quiet the island is, too. The tranquillity is only broken by the occasional call of seabirds swooping across the sky and diving down into the waves to look for fish, and by the lapping of the waves themselves, as they wash against the shoreline.

But all that is interrupted now by the growling noise that's gradually getting louder. Fitz stands to attention and begins his own version of the growling, but he soon realises he has nothing to fear when a bright red, open-top Jeep rounds the bend of the hill, with Fisher in the driving seat.

'Your carriage awaits, madam,' he says as he pulls up next to my luggage and switches off the engine. 'It's a bit noisy, but it goes well. I think they chose quite wisely, all things considered.'

I look at the vehicle in front of me. 'How did this get here?'

'It turned up when all your equipment came. Actually, a lot of your equipment was ferried over in this. It goes much better on the cobbled causeway than the delivery van that brought the rest of the boxes.'

'My company provided it?' I ask in surprise.

'You need something to get you back and forth, don't you? Like I said, when the tide is out you can use the causeway, but when it's in, you use *Doris*.'

'Yes, sorry, of course you did. I just didn't expect Met Central – that's who I work for – to be this generous.' I look at the Jeep again; it looks sporty and fun to drive. 'I don't know why, but I assumed we'd have to walk across the causeway to get back and forth from the mainland. This is a much better idea.'

'You can walk, but it'll take you a while. Take it from me, use this or the boat. It'll be a lot easier and quicker. On some tides the causeway isn't clear for very long. If you're going to be any time away from the island, you need to make sure you can get back all right, otherwise you'll be stranded until the tide turns.'

I nod. It's actually quite a relief to know I won't have to walk every time. Island living is already a lot more daunting than I'd anticipated, and the Jeep is a welcome addition.

'Right then,' Fisher says, 'let's get your stuff up to the house.'

We manage to move my luggage in two trips. The first Fisher drives, while Fitz watches eagerly from my lap; on the second, it's my turn to get used to navigating the winding path and the steep incline up the hill, while Fisher looks after Fitz.

Then we move all my bags and cases into the hallway of the house. Now we're level with it, the house seems a lot bigger than it did when I was standing at the bottom of the island.

'Do you want me to show you around?' Fisher asks.

'I really don't want to impose on you any longer, you've already been so kind. I'm sure we'll be fine from here. Thank you so much for all your help, Fisher. I really appreciate it.'

'Not at all. It's been my absolute pleasure.' He looks wistfully up at the house. 'I've many happy memories of time spent here at the house and on the island. I'm lucky to be the caretaker of the place now the owner only rents it out.'

'Ah, I didn't know that. Who is the owner?'

'I'm not sure. I'm paid by the council, but I've only been

doing it since my grandad retired from the job a few years ago. He loves this island even more than I do.'

He looks away from the house back to me. 'So, any time you need anything while you're here you just shout and I'll be right over to help.'

'Even if the tide is in?' I ask, smiling.

'Course! It's not only *Doris* that can make it over here. I have my own boat too! Fisher McMurray at your service, Miss Sky, or should I call you Captain Sky now that you can sail a boat?' He winks at me.

'Thank you so much, Fisher. I hope you don't regret that offer, I'm pretty sure I'll be calling on you an awful lot in the next few days.'

'It will be my pleasure to be at the service of Captain Sky and Seaman Fitz!' He gives us a small salute.

And Fitz, on cue, gives a bark of approval.

Two

Fisher has arranged for one of his mates to collect him in a fishing boat and take him back to St Felix. As they head across the water, Fisher looks right at home in amongst the fishing nets and lobster pots filled with the catch of the day. However, I don't feel quite so at home as I gaze up at the large white house in front of me.

My job as a meteorologist has placed me in many varied and unusual environments over the years – both in this country and abroad – and until twenty months ago, I enjoyed an exciting and challenging career. But in all that time I've never lived on an island before, not as small as this one anyway. So although part of me can't help but feel like this assignment is a little below my qualifications and experience, I have to accept that living on this Cornish island is going to be enough of a challenge for me right now and one I hope my health will hold up to.

'Come on, Sky,' I mutter as I try to gather myself. 'You can do this. It's only for the summer. Make a success of this and you'll prove you're ready to get back to bigger and better things.'

I'm not going to be totally alone here on the island. Other than Fitz, who is currently exploring every inch of the area around the house, a young trainee meteorologist will be joining me as my assistant, which is both a relief and a worry at the same time.

I was used to having assistants, and I was looking forward to working with someone who was hopefully as keen and excited by the weather as me. But I had also grown used to being on my own lately, and I was worried that living with someone else again might be difficult and awkward.

'No, I'm not going to worry about that right now,' I announce to a surprised Fitz. 'If I've learnt anything lately, it's that life is for living, not worrying about what might happen. I've been given another chance and I'm not going to waste it. Let's start by seeing what our new home is like.'

Fitz doesn't need telling twice; he races into the hallway and I follow him, pausing for a moment to take in my new surroundings. The house is basic, but it's squeaky clean and smells freshly painted. The hallway is white like the outside of the house, and the floor underneath my feet is covered in red-brick tiles. There's a stairway with a long oak banister that leads up to what I assume must be the two bedrooms the house had promised – one for me and one for my assistant.

'Let's look around down here first,' I suggest to Fitz, but he's already ahead of me. I see his furry black tail disappearing into another room at the end of the hall.

Fitz has always been an adventurous, inquisitive little dog. I've only had him about eight months, but in that short time we've become inseparable. He'd come to me as a puppy, when my next-door neighbour's Yorkshire terrier had accidentally got pregnant, and my neighbour was desperate for the six gorgeous puppies to go to good homes.

Fitz, whose errant father is a Jack Russell, is classed as a 'Yorkie Russell', he's a scruffy mix of black, brown and white wiry fur. Even though I'd been wary at first of taking on the responsibility of a dog in my condition, I have to admit that living with Fitz has done me the power of good. He has given me not only new purpose, but also some much-needed companionship, at a time when my so-called friends had become disappointingly absent from my life. Although my health was much improved by the time Fitz arrived, I still had bad times. But even on my darkest days Fitz never left my side.

'I see you've found the kitchen,' I tell Fitz as he stands in front of me, panting. 'Let's get you some water.'

Fitz's food and water bowls are packed away somewhere in one of the boxes, so I open a few of the pale blue kitchen cupboard doors to try to find him a temporary container for his water.

The cupboards are filled with brand-new, white crockery in place settings of four, along with spotless glasses, saucepans with the labels still on, and shiny cutlery in the drawers. I knew household items were being sent for my stay, but I'd assumed I'd have to unpack everything and put it all away. Perhaps Fisher had taken it upon himself to do this for me? He seemed to care an awful lot about the little island and the house that sits upon it.

I find a suitable bowl and fill it with water for Fitz, then I watch him lap thirstily from it for a moment. There's a large fridge-freezer standing in the corner of the kitchen, so I go over and open it, and I'm overjoyed to see a few basic supplies already waiting for me, including some fresh orange juice, which I pour into one of the glasses and drink just as thirstily as Fitz had done.

'I guess we'll have to get used to buying our supplies from the mainland,' I tell Fitz as he drips water on to the floor from his wet chin. I reach for some kitchen towel and give his tiny beard a wipe. 'I don't think we'll be able to get a supermarket delivery out here!'

Not so long ago, when I couldn't leave my house, my weekly supermarket delivery had been a necessity I couldn't have survived without. When I was able to care for myself once more, and my mum had moved back to our family home, a supply of ready meals and easy-to-prepare food was essential to my recovery and energy management.

See, look how far you've come, I remind myself as I stare at the fridge-freezer in front of me. *You're not only looking after yourself and Fitz now, but you're doing it all the way out here, on an island in the middle of the sea!*

Alongside the fridge-freezer, there's a large range cooker, and on the worktops, a shiny kettle and a modern four-slice toaster.

'They really have pulled out all the stops for us,' I say to Fitz as I inspect a fancy coffee maker that grinds its own beans and froths up hot milk. 'I didn't expect all these home comforts, but they're very welcome! I thought the only reason I was offered this job was because they couldn't get anyone else to do it. But maybe they *really* did want me after all?'

Fitz looks up at me, his head cocked to one side.

'You don't care where we are as long as we're together, do you?' I say, lifting him up for a cuddle. 'And you really don't know how much I appreciate your unconditional love.'

Fitz gives me a lick on the cheek.

'Exactly!' I tell him, grinning. 'Right, now we've quenched our thirst, let's go and see what else this house has to offer, shall we?'

Along with the kitchen, there's a bathroom on the ground floor and, unusually, the two bedrooms. *I'll be taking this one*, I think as I look in on a bedroom with a large, king-size bed and a firm mattress – again the bed and the mattress seem brand new. No expense has been spared when it came to setting up this house for us, and yet again I can't help but wonder why.

Fisher had told me that this house had originally been occupied by an elderly couple, but when they both passed away, the house had become quite derelict. Everyone thought the couple had owned the house and the island, but it turned out that they'd only rented it. When the Wave Watch volunteers had showed an interest in setting up a station here on the island via the local council, permission had been granted immediately by the mystery owner. No one lived on the island once it became a Wave Watch station, not until now that is.

'Shall we go upstairs?' I say to Fitz as we finish our exploration of the ground floor.

Fitz doesn't need asking twice as he races ahead of me to the top of the stairs. I pause for a moment at the bottom, grateful as always that I can actually do this again. Never do I want to go back to those dark days when a flight of stairs felt like a mountain to be climbed, while carrying a backpack filled with bricks.

But thankfully today I'm able to follow Fitz, even if I do take the stairs a little more carefully and slowly than my companion.

'Wow!' I exclaim as I reach the top, and I'm greeted by a huge open-plan room with an enormous bay window at one end. 'This is amazing.'

The room has clearly been designed to make the most of the view. At one end there's a sofa, two armchairs, a couple of side tables and a TV, and at the other, right in front of the bay window, are the remains of the Wave Watch station.

They've taken all their equipment with them, but left behind a large desk, an office chair and the units that used to house their gadgets and machinery. It looks a lot like someone has moved out of rented accommodation, taking their possessions with them, but leaving behind the fixtures and fittings.

I go over to the window and take my first look out at the view I'm going to be spending the next few weeks, possibly months, looking at.

It's amazing how much you can see from here – not only an incredible view over the town of St Felix, with its quaint fishermen's cottages, winding cobbled streets, solid stone harbour and long sandy beaches, but also what feels like a never-ending seascape, stretching over the waves, and out into the deep Atlantic Ocean.

A house with a view like this, on its own island, must be worth an absolute fortune here in Cornwall, I think as I stand taking in the amazing vista surrounding me. *I wonder why the owner doesn't live here themselves, or at least rent it out as holiday accommodation; they'd make a fortune.*

But for now, I'm glad they don't. I may not have wanted to come here. I may have taken a while to accept the surprising offer to weather watch from this island. But now I'm here, I'm so glad I did accept. It may not be the most glamorous job I've ever done, or a job that's going to further my career in international meteorology circles, but as I gaze out at the beautiful Cornish coastline, I wonder if a view is ever going to take my breath away quite as much as this one is right now.

*

The rest of the day is mainly spent unpacking – not only my luggage but also the many boxes of weather-recording equipment that have been sent over in advance by courier.

As I unpack the scientific instruments, I feel like I'm greeting familiar friends. There are the well-known gadgets like a rain gauge and wind sock, along with a thermometer and barometer for measuring temperature and atmospheric pressure. And the less recognisable – an anemometer for measuring wind speed, a hygrometer for measuring humidity, and a pyranometer for measuring solar radiation.

As I discover each device hidden underneath the polystyrene packing chips, and set it up in the most appropriate place either on the desk in front of me or outside of the house, I begin to feel more and more at home.

When Fitz begins to get a little restless, I take him for a short walk around the island. Short, because it only takes us ten to fifteen minutes to walk the entire circumference of Aurora, and that's over rocky, undulating, narrow paths. It must easily be less than half a mile around the whole island.

'Sorry,' I apologise to Fitz when we arrive back at the house. 'It's not very far around here, is it? We'll have to take you over to the mainland to give you a good walk.'

I'd been quite surprised when I first got Fitz just how much energy he had for a little dog. He was always on the go and I had hoped as he grew older that he'd calm down a little. But Fitz can outwalk me any time – not a huge achievement these days, but I feel like I am getting a little fitter and stronger every day, and much of that recovery is down to him.

As the day draws to a close, I'm totally exhausted. I know I've done too much, and I should have paced myself a little better – ideally the journey and all these jobs should have been spread over a number of days – but there is just so much to do before my new companion, Talia, arrives tomorrow, and I want it to be perfect for when when she gets here.

I'd initially turned down the offer of an assistant, but when it was pointed out that I couldn't, and nor should I be expected to, monitor the weather 24/7 myself, I'd eventually agreed to a housemate. Talia, who has just completed the second year of her meteorology degree, had successfully applied for the position, which would be her work experience for the summer.

The last thing I want is for Talia to begin our time together by thinking I can't cope, or that I need any special treatment. This assignment may appear simple on the surface, but to me the greater challenge is going to be proving I can manage, not only to Met Central, but to myself, and part of that is keeping any weakness hidden from those around me.

I know I shouldn't view my health as a weakness. It takes an awful lot of strength to cope with a chronic illness – I should know, I've dealt with it for nearly two years. But currently I'm feeling so much better, and I just want to forget about it, to move on, to prove to myself I'm back to normal, even if deep down I know I'm not.

'Time for bed soon,' I say to an already snoozing Fitz. We're currently resting on the sofa in the living area upstairs. I'd made the perfectly comfortable seats a little more supportive by adding some of the cushions I'd brought from home, and I'm sitting half-looking at the equipment still waiting to be set up, and half-mesmerised by the view through the window – a calm sea below a clear midnight-blue sky. 'Before we go to bed I'd better check the weather for tomorrow though.' Since all our equipment isn't quite up and running yet, I don't want to get caught out if I have to take the boat over in rough weather. I look at my watch, the news would nearly be over now, so I'm just in time for the weather.

I don't often watch television forecasts. Usually wherever I am I have my own weather equipment close by, so I don't need to. But during my time away from work I've found myself tuning in more often.

'Ah, good,' I say as the forecaster appears on my screen in front of their map. 'This one actually knows about the weather.'

I've made it into a little game for myself – guessing which television forecasters do actually have some meteorological qualifications, and which ones are just weather presenters, as so many of them are these days, and so far I have a 100 per cent correct guess rate.

Tomorrow, I'm pleased to see, we're forecast low wind speeds and high pressure over Cornwall, which should make my first solo boat trip a little easier. Fisher has helpfully pinned the coming week's tide times on a little noticeboard in the 'watchtower', as I'd decided to call the part of the sitting room by the window that holds all our equipment. So, I know it will be high tide when it's time to collect Talia from the station.

I'm not quite sure how I'll get her luggage from the station back to the boat, but I hope we might be able to find a taxi to take us to the harbour. Either that or if, unlike me, she travels light, we might even be able to carry her luggage back ourselves.

'Right, now we can go to bed,' I tell Fitz as I switch off the TV. 'I have a feeling it's going to be a long day tomorrow.'

As Fitz and I lie on my new bed – me in between the new duvet and sheets I've brought with me, with my head resting on my own comfortable, familiar pillow from home, and Fitz curled up on top of the duvet at the end of the bed – I think about the arrival of our new housemate. *Please let her be a nice, easy-going sort of person*, I pray. *I really can't bear the thought of living* and *working with someone loud, brash and full of themselves.* I need a calm, quiet sort of life these days. I don't need someone that will rock my boat too much.

But I'd been assured by the lady from human resources, that Talia was absolutely lovely, and was super keen to come and work with me on this project. Apparently, she knows St Felix quite well because she has family living here, and that's one of the reasons she was so eager to secure the placement.

Talia is a nice peaceful-sounding name, I try to convince myself as I lie worrying in the dark. *I'm sure it will all be absolutely fine, and by tomorrow evening we'll be settled in here together, ready to start work without any bother whatsoever.*

But life so often mimics the weather. However calm you hope it's going to be, there is always the chance of a storm brewing somewhere . . .

Three

The train into St Felix is running several minutes late, which is just as well because I am too.

My first solo trip across the water hadn't exactly gone smoothly. To begin with I'd struggled to get Fitz to stay on the boat. I'd get in with him and get him settled, then I'd have to climb back out again to untie the mooring rope, by which time Fitz had decided if I was getting out again, then so was he. In the end, I'd untied the rope with Fitz still in my arms, then climbed as quickly as I could into the boat before it drifted away from the wooden jetty without us.

The crossing, thank goodness, had been fairly uneventful, but when we reached the harbour, I'd had the most enormous row with a very unhelpful harbourmaster about where my boat should be moored. He was a small, angry sort of man, with overly neat grey hair and a matching moustache, who obviously loved the power his harbourmaster's uniform gave him. I'd been extremely apologetic in the hope he'd understand I was new to all this, but when he found out I'd come over from Aurora, this information seemed to rile him up even more.

Eventually, with the help of one of the local fishermen, I'd found my correct mooring and we'd been allowed to pull up and exit from the boat with the promise we'd be back shortly.

'Don't you worry about Gerald,' my friendly fishermen had told me cheerily. 'His bark is far worse than his bite. Harbourmaster is a serious job, but he takes it a bit too seriously, if you know what I mean. You're doing just fine for a newcomer.'

Gratefully, Fitz and I had then rushed along to the station. There was no time to stop and get to know the town a little better, as I'd hoped we'd be able to. This morning, it's filled with tourists and holidaymakers enjoying Cornish pasties and ice creams in the summer sunshine, so we have to weave in and out of them as we try to hurry through the narrow streets.

From what I see as we pass by, and from what I'd seen when Fisher had driven me through here yesterday, St Felix is a very pretty little harbour town. There are shops aplenty, selling everything from traditional pasties and fish and chips, to crafts, flowers and souvenirs. Old fishermen's cottages have been turned into pretty holiday lets, and the harbour is awash with colourful bunting and red-and-white striped deckchairs for people to rest on and take in the scenery.

But Fitz and I have to race past all this, so that when we finally arrive on the station platform to greet my new colleague, I'm not feeling quite as cool and collected as I'd hoped I might.

I take a few deep breaths as the train pulls into the station, then I watch carefully for anyone disembarking who looks like they might be Talia.

Three families carrying buckets, spades, cool boxes and blankets spill from the train first, followed by a few couples, both old and young. There are some lone travellers, but they look like they might be heading to work in St Felix.

Finally, a slight-looking girl with blonde hair tied in plaits alights from the end carriage. She's wearing frayed denim shorts and a white T-shirt with a yellow smiley sunshine in the centre.

Great! I think as I spot her. This must be Talia, and – even better – she's not carrying much luggage, only a small holdall.

I begin to walk towards the girl, carrying Fitz in my arms. A male passenger wearing sunglasses, smart chinos and a white linen shirt alights from the train behind her, and begins to lift several suitcases down off the train on to the platform.

The girl waves at me, and I'm even more sure this must be Talia. But then she turns back and speaks to the man, they quickly divide the luggage between them and then the man gets back on to the train. But my mind is firmly on greeting Talia, so I don't think too much about it.

'Hello!' I call as I get near to the girl. 'Are you Talia?'

'I am!' she says, smiling warmly back at me. 'You must be Sky.'

'It's great to meet you at last. Welcome to St Felix, although I think you probably know the town better than I do, don't you?'

'Yes, my uncle lives here, so I've visited a couple of times with my mother in the past. Hello, little guy,' she says, reaching forward to fuss Fitz, who's looking with interest at Talia. 'And what's your name?'

'This is Fitz.' A thought occurs to me. 'I hope you're all right with dogs?'

'Oh yes, I love them. Thank you so much for allowing me to come and work with you this summer, Sky. I'm so excited to be actually doing some proper work at last.'

I'm about to answer her, when Fitz suddenly starts to bark and wriggle in my arms, so I put him down on the ground.

I look past Talia, and see that the man she'd been talking to before now has a slim black Labrador on a lead. Unlike Fitz, who's going bananas at my feet, desperate to go and see the other dog, the Labrador simply looks at him and elegantly wags its tail.

The man walks towards us in a manner that mimics his dog – smoothly with a little swagger of the hips – while I desperately try to calm Fitz down.

'Don't worry!' the man calls good-naturedly. 'Comet often has this effect on the opposite sex – a bit like her owner!'

I can't help staring at the man now as we allow our two dogs to get closer to each other; even wearing sunglasses he looks strangely familiar, but I can't pinpoint why. So I concentrate on the dogs instead. There is much tail wagging and sniffing, and then Fitz does what he always does to older dogs, his equivalent of a bow – his front legs stretch out in front of him, so he looks like he's doing the aptly named yoga position of downward dog.

The black Labrador sniffs Fitz, and then playfully nudges him with her nose. Fitz leaps up immediately, happy his elder has accepted him.

'At least we know they get along,' the man says to my surprise. 'That's a good start, isn't it? I'm certain their owners will do too . . . ' He lowers his shades for a second, so I catch a glimpse of two twinkling sapphire-blue eyes and a pair of dark eyebrows raised in a playful manner.

I'm thrown by his comment. Was this stranger coming on to me? I might be a little rusty, but that sounded very much like a chat-up line.

'Sorry to hold you up,' I say hurriedly, hoping this guy, who still looks incredibly familiar, will move along – I really want to talk to Talia again. 'I'm sure you have somewhere to be.'

The guy pushes his sunglasses up on his head now. He looks at me a little strangely before glancing at Talia.

'You two obviously travelled in the same carriage together?' I try, hoping this will move him on. 'That's nice. Thank you for helping Talia with her luggage. I think we can take it from here.'

'I had no idea we were going to be on the same train,' Talia says, smiling at the man now. 'Quite the coincidence, really.'

'Fate!' the man says, winking at her. 'But at least we've got to know each other on the trip.'

There's something weird about this exchange I can't quite put my finger on.

The man is clearly a lot older than Talia, who I know has just turned twenty. This guy looks closer to my age, so must be around the forty mark. He's a good-looking sort of chap – if you like that kind of smooth, overly polished look. He's tall and slim, with short, wavy, jet-black hair, styled with a bit too much product. But surely he isn't hitting on Talia as well, is he? And why would Talia be falling for some middle-aged lothario's chat if he is. She's a bright, smart meteorology student?

'You must be the infamous Sky I've been hearing all about,' the man says, holding out his hand to me.

'How do you know my name?' I ask, shaking his hand reluctantly.

'Er . . . I was told it in an email, I think?' he says, his confident manner clearly a little rattled by my reticence. 'And Talia here was talking about you non-stop on the train, weren't you?'

Talia nods, also looking a little unsettled by our exchange.

But I can't help it, there's clearly something going on here I don't quite understand. 'Why would you be told my name in an email?'

'Because, I'm your new partner, aren't I?' he announces, as if I should know this already. 'Surely you recognise me?' he flashes a set of bright white teeth and a well-practised confident smile in my direction.

I stare at him in utter confusion; he does look familiar, but my brain is currently focusing on the other piece of information about him being my new partner.

'I'm here to help you unravel this mysterious weather conundrum we've all been sent to solve,' he continues when I don't speak. 'Talia and I have come up with some ideas already as to what could have been causing it. Well, Talia has mainly, but I think—'

'Wait just one minute . . .' I say, holding my hand up to silence him. 'None of this makes any sense. I've come to the station today to meet Talia, she's the only assistant I'm expecting to share weather-watching duties with. No one has ever mentioned a third person to me – not once. So, if this is Talia,' I say, gesturing towards her, 'who are you?'

Four

The man hesitates for a moment. He takes a step backwards and looks at me, as if by doing this I'm supposed to recognise him immediately. But the last few minutes have thrown me so much, it could be my next-door neighbour standing there and I probably wouldn't have placed them.

Until now I had everything straight in my head. There was going to be me and Talia and Fitz staying on the island. I knew how it was going to work and who was going to do what. I'd planned for every scenario so it would all run smoothly. Every scenario, that is, except the one standing in front of me right now.

Hesitantly the man steps forward again when it's clear I don't have a clue who he is. 'Sonny Samuels at your service,' he says, introducing himself with a smart salute, reminding me of Fisher. 'Jamie to my friends, which I hope you'll consider yourself to be in the very near future!'

Now I know where I recognise him from! Sonny Samuels is a well-loved TV weather presenter – I think the last time I saw him he might have been on breakfast television – not that I watch it that often, I usually listen to the radio when I'm getting ready for work. But I'm told by those in the know that he's very popular and has quite the following. He is, however, firmly in my weather *presenter* group. I'm absolutely certain he's not a qualified meteorologist.

'Yes, I do recognise you now,' I say politely, 'but I still don't quite understand why you're here.'

'I've been sent by Met Central to help you out?' he says, as if I should already know this. 'I thought they would have told you? Talia certainly seemed to know all about it.'

Talia throws him a 'please don't include me in this' look, but it's too late – I've already turned to her, looking for answers.

'Yes,' she blurts out. 'I got an email telling me Sonny was going to be joining us. That's why I can't stay with you on the island now.'

'What! Since when?'

'They told me you'd only got two bedrooms in the house,' Talia says quickly, looking increasingly worried. 'That's why I'm going to be staying with my uncle in the town.'

'No, that can't be right,' I say, shaking my head. 'You're supposed to be staying with me.' I turn my gaze to Sonny again. 'Is this something to do with you?'

Sonny looks annoyed now. 'Actually, I offered to stay in a hotel or a cottage or something. Let me assure you I have no desire to stay on an island in the middle of the sea. But they're pretty booked up here for the summer, so it was thought best I stay on the island with you, and Talia go to her family. Are you sure you didn't get the email? It seems a bit lax on Met Central's part not to tell you. Maybe it went into your junk file? Where's your phone – shall we take a look?'

'No, that won't be necessary,' I tell him firmly. 'There

definitely wasn't an email.' I sigh. We can't stand here all day debating this, we need to get back to the boat or there won't be time to make the crossing. The train has long departed now, and we're the only ones remaining on the station platform. 'Look, you're here now. I suppose I'm going to have to deal with it for the time being. But I will be checking up on you later with Met Central.'

'That sounds like a threat!' Sonny says, grinning.

I don't grin back. This might be a laugh to him, but I can't cope with unexpected surprises – it's too stressful. I like to know what I'm doing and when, so I can be prepared. An over-exuberant weather presenter was simply not in any of my plans for this summer.

'You're all right with me moving in, aren't you?' he continues, unabashed, when I don't answer. 'I'm a great house guest. I clean up after myself and I don't snore – not that we'll be sharing the same bed or anything . . . ' He winks, in a way that likely allows him to get away with those sorts of remarks in his usual company.

I don't acknowledge his innuendo, but continue to stare at him, not quite believing that this is happening. I'd been worried enough that sharing with Talia might affect my carefully practised routines. But the thought of Sonny Samuels disturbing both the peace of the island and my internal equilibrium is just too much to comprehend.

'Like I said, I'll need to make some phone calls,' I say eventually. 'Even though you both seem to know all about this change of plan, I'm not sure I'm comfortable with it.'

'Many women would be more than delighted to be stuck on an island with me,' Sonny says, playfully. 'I'm sure you'll come round to the idea.'

'I wouldn't bank on it,' I mutter, turning away from him.

'Look, why don't we all go and get a coffee and talk about this?' Talia suggests, trying to lighten the situation. 'There are some gorgeous little tearooms in the town.'

'That's a lovely idea, Talia,' I say, smiling at her. None of this is Talia's fault, and I'm keen for her to know I don't blame her. 'But I'm afraid we don't have time.' I glance at my watch. This was one of those days Fisher had warned me about when high tide wasn't that high, and therefore didn't last as long as it sometimes did. 'We have to get back over to the island before the tide goes out too far and we have to walk across. I guess you both know Aurora is tidal?'

'Of course,' Sonny says, nodding with Talia. 'We take a boat across when the tide is in, and they said there would be some sort of vehicle for us to use on the causeway when it's low.'

How come he knows this and I hadn't?

'That's right. So we need to make the crossing back over in the boat as soon as possible, because our Jeep is over on the island right now.'

'I like a Jeep,' Sonny says approvingly. 'Very cool.'

'Why don't you drop me off at my uncle's house on the way back to the harbour, if there's time?' Talia suggests. 'I can get settled in there while you two sort out what's what over on the island. I'll walk over later when the tide is out; that way you won't need to fetch me.'

'I'm still not happy you've been evicted from your place on Aurora,' I tell her. 'Everything has already been arranged, as far as I'm concerned.' I can't help throwing another disapproving look at Sonny. 'Besides,' I say, grasping at any reason to stop me having to live with him, 'what if our two dogs don't get along – no one has thought of that, have they?'

30

But as I look over at the dogs, I've already answered my own question.

Fitz and Comet, tired of listening to us talk over their heads, are sitting together on the platform. Comet pants as she waits to find out what's happening next, which makes her look like she's smiling, and Fitz sits happily next to her doing the same, except his tongue occasionally extends just far enough to give Comet a friendly lick.

'Looks like that's one problem we won't have to worry about,' Sonny says, smiling at the two dogs. 'Unlike their owners, they seem to be best friends already.'

Luckily, a large seven-seater taxi that's just finished a drop-off at the station is available to take us back to the harbour – there is no way we could have managed all Talia and Sonny's luggage and the two dogs ourselves. We drop Talia off at the prettily named 'Blue Canary Bakery', which her Uncle Ant owns with his husband, Dec.

I'm amused by their names, but Talia says you soon get used to it and forget about their TV counterparts. She also tells us that the Blue Canary bakes the most delicious cakes and pastries, and she promises to bring some over to the island with her later.

The taxi drops me, Sonny and the dogs off at the harbour. I debate whether I've time to make some phone calls before we have to leave, but annoyingly there's just not enough time according to Fisher's list of tide times; it will have to wait until we get to the island.

Between us we manage to load all Sonny's luggage onto the boat. Then we persuade Comet to jump in, and finally Sonny passes Fitz to me, before leaping effortlessly down on to the deck beside the two dogs and his suitcases and bags.

'How many times have you done this before?' Sonny asks as I start up the boat, ready to guide it out of the harbour.

'Not that many,' I reply, not wanting him to know how inexperienced I am.

'I thought not. Perhaps you'd better wait a moment.'

'And why would that be?'

'Because we've not untied the boat from the harbour yet,' Sonny says, grinning as he points to the mooring rope still attached to a ring on the harbour wall.

I feel my cheeks flush.

'Oh yes,' I reply lightly, as if it's just a minor matter. 'Perhaps you'd be so kind?'

'Since you ask so nicely.' Sonny deftly climbs back up on to the harbour.

We don't quite manage to depart before Gerald the harbourmaster spots us and immediately heads our way.

'I was wondering when you were coming back,' he calls down to me. 'It's about time you left for the island, otherwise there's a chance you'll run aground.'

'Thank you, yes, I'm aware of that. Fisher, the caretaker of the island, left me strict instructions on how long the tides will last for the next few days.'

'Fisher . . . ' he says, smirking. 'That'd be about right.'

'What's that supposed to mean?' I ask, biting when I don't want to. I just want to get over to the island as quickly as I can and sort out this Sonny mess. 'Fisher has been very helpful to me.'

'I bet he has. Fisher and his grandfather put the welfare of that island above anything else.'

'What's wrong with that?' The last thing I need right now is another argument with this jobsworth. But Fisher had been nothing but patient and kind with me and Fitz, and I feel like I owe him a defence.

'It doesn't matter,' Gerald says, shrugging. 'Wacky Walter Weather wants to have a bit more loyalty to his colleagues and less towards an island, that's all.'

I stare at him for a moment, knowing I should probably leave it, but I can't help myself. 'And just who is Wacky Walter Weather?' I ask.

Gerald grins, but not in a pleasant way. It's mean and mocking, which makes me dislike him even more.

'Wacky Walter Weather is your friend Fisher's grandfather – that's what folk around here call him on account of his weird and wonderful ways of forecasting the weather.'

'Nothing wrong with that,' I say through slightly gritted teeth. I know of those who like to use old wives' tales and suchlike to try to predict the weather, and there's nothing wrong in it. But I also know how much better and more reliable it is to use the scientific formula that we choose. 'Each to their own.'

'You clearly haven't met Walter then,' Gerald continues, 'he's trouble. Always trying to stir up problems for us folk just going about our day-to-day business. Bloomin' good job they threw him out of the Wave Watch when they did.'

Fisher had mentioned something about this, but I'd much rather hear his version than Gerald's.

'Do I know you?' Gerald demands, suddenly turning to Sonny, who is watching our altercation with interest. 'You look familiar?'

Sonny's eyes light up, clearly happy to be recognised. 'You may know me from Breakfast AM?' he says, turning on his TV smile. 'Until recently I presented the weather there.'

'Nope,' Gerald says stoutly. 'Never watched it.'

'Er . . . newspapers, then? I'm featured in the gossip columns a lot with my wife?'

Gerald just stares blankly at him.

'No, not a gossip sort of guy, eh?' Sonny continues unabashed when Gerald doesn't respond. 'What about an advert I did for Sunshine Cruises last year? That was shown at peak times quite a bit.'

Gerald turns his head a little. 'Yeah, the dumb boat advert – that's it. You were dressed as a sea captain – now I remember. Your uniform wasn't correct – it was really annoying.'

'Ah well, that's not down to me, I'm afraid. But there, we have it at last. Now don't treat me any differently because of my fame, I'm new here too, and eager to learn just like Sky.'

'Hmm . . .' Gerald eyes him suspiciously. 'Well, you'd best be getting over to that island if that's where you're heading. Are you getting paid to sit and watch the weather too?' he says, smirking again. 'Just like this one?' He nods his head derisively in my direction.

Sonny stiffens, and I see his whole demeanour change from chilled and relaxed to steadfast and determined in a second.

'I can assure you, Gerald, we're here to do much more than sit and watch the weather. We're here to record some very unusual collisions of charged particles in the solar wind. They've been colliding with molecules in the earth's upper atmosphere, and it's resulted in some particularly extreme circumstances.' Sonny says all this with an airy confidence. Even though I'm pretty sure he has no idea what he's just described, it sounds like he does and even I'm taken aback. 'Sky here is an extremely well-respected and highly qualified meteorologist. She wouldn't have been sent here if this work wasn't of the utmost importance.'

34

Gerald looks similarly shocked for a moment, but then he folds his arms defensively across his chest. 'Don't try and fool me with your clever language and long words, you're just talking about clouds, sun and rain. There's nothing new you two can tell me about the weather; I sit in that office over there day after day watching it change. You don't need some fancy degree and a silly title to teach you how to do that.'

'No, you don't,' Sonny says quickly. 'Just as I'm sure you don't need any qualifications or too much brain power to sit and watch boats come in and out of a harbour all day long . . .'

I grin, knowing exactly what he's getting at.

Gerald nods in agreement, then his expression slowly begins to change as he realises what Sonny's inferring. But luckily for us, at that moment a holidaymaker comes over to ask Gerald a question about the harbour, so he's immediately distracted.

Sonny takes this as his cue to escape. 'Chocks away!' he calls as he throws the rope on to the deck, then follows it by leaping athletically down there himself.

'I think you'll find that's anchors away,' I say, smiling to myself as I look through the windshield and begin guiding the boat out of the harbour. 'We're not flying.'

'I don't know,' Sonny responds swiftly. 'We might experience some extreme turbulence on this crossing – if our past conversations are anything to go by.'

I quickly turn my head to look at him, but he's already sitting back in the boat with his arm around Comet on one side of him, and Fitz on the other.

I sigh as I look back out to the island.

When I'd agreed to this, I knew if I created a calm environment, got enough rest and had a peaceful regular routine, I would be able cope with this assignment and prove myself to

Met Central. I'd had it all planned out and I was confident of what the weeks ahead would be like.

But now Sonny Samuels has been thrown into the mix, I get the feeling that dealing with the over-exuberant weather presenter sitting in the back of my boat is going to cause me more trouble than anything else this island could ever throw at me.

Five

'We did send you an email,' Gemma in Met Central's HR department repeats for the second time. 'I can only apologise if you didn't receive it.'

I sigh into my phone. I wasn't getting anywhere with this conversation. It seemed like I was stuck with Sonny, however hard I tried to get rid of him.

'But it's unfair on Talia to have to stay in the town,' I try. 'This is supposed to be her work experience.'

'Talia seemed perfectly happy to stay with her uncle,' Gemma says, clearly beginning to get frustrated as well. 'I really don't see what the problem is, Sky. Unless you're uncomfortable sharing the house with a man? Which would be completely understandable, of course, and in which case we would obviously need to *rethink* things.'

Even though I've taken my phone outside to make this call, I look carefully around me just in case Sonny is close by. I get the feeling from the conversation so far and Gemma's current tone, that I might be the one to be re-thought in regards to this job, not Sonny.

'It's not the fact he's a man I have an issue with,' I say, choosing my words carefully. 'It's the fact I'm sure he's not a ... *qualified* meteorologist.'

'Of course he's not qualified,' Gemma says, an amused tone to her voice now. 'He's a presenter, isn't he? As you well know, Sky, not all weather presenters are such experienced and qualified meteorologists as you.'

'Then why is he here? We're not presenting the weather from the island; we're doing scientific observations and research.'

Gemma sighs. 'I'm going to be honest with you, Sky, you're not stupid, you know when something's not on the level.'

I wait for her to continue. *I knew something wasn't right about this.*

'The reason Sonny has been sent to the island with you is that he needs to get away for a bit.'

'Why? What's he done?' I demand.

'Clearly, I can't go into all the details – that would break employee confidentiality – but Sonny is a very popular weather presenter; Met Central don't want to lose him from our TV screens. The viewing figures for his forecasts are more than double some of the other presenters.'

'So why isn't he keeping to what he does best? Why send him here to annoy me?'

'Personal reasons, is all I can tell you, I'm afraid. We need him to get away for a while, so when this opportunity came up, a remote island off the coast of Cornwall seemed like a great idea to ...' She hesitates.

'To who?' I ask, desperate to know more. Something about this just isn't adding up. 'Who has suggested this?'

'I can't talk about it, I'm afraid,' Gemma repeats to my intense irritation. I hate not knowing the whole story, especially about someone I'm being asked to live with. 'You know Met Central are fully behind you and your recovery, Sky, and I'm sure you're aware that if you are successful in this assignment many more exciting opportunities will await you. But for now, we just need you to trust us. Sonny Samuels *will* be staying in Cornwall, that's not up for debate. But for your sake, Sky, I really hope you can try to make a go of it with him. We wouldn't want to lose you . . .'

And there it is, the truth laid out. It wasn't a case of Sonny's place here on Aurora being up for debate. It was mine.

While we've been talking, I've been gazing back over the large expanse of golden sand that has been uncovered now the tide has begun to ebb. Fisher was right – the tide changes very quickly here, and already in the place of the waves we'd crossed over not long ago, there is a large expanse of shiny wet sand, and the first appearance of the much-talked-about brick causeway that leads from the island back to St Felix. As I'm watching, there is movement just below the rocks at the bottom of the island, and Fitz races around on the damp sand with Comet and Sonny hot on his heels.

Fitz looks happier than I think I've ever seen him. He's such a ball of energy that I've often felt quite guilty I can't give him as much exercise as he probably needs.

But I could give him this – a playmate, who even in the short time they've known each other has clearly become his new four-legged friend.

Sonny sees me watching them and lifts his hand in acknowledgement, then he quickly uses it to run his fingers through his wind-swept hair, which blows over his face as he turns with his back to the breeze.

My hand reaches instinctively to my own hair – tied back

tightly as always in a neat ponytail the wind barely daring to disturb it.

Would having Sonny on the island with me really be that awful? I wonder for the first time as I watch him playing with the dogs. He obviously adores Comet, and he seems to have taken to Fitz already. Could someone that clearly loves dogs as much as him really be that bad? Maybe it was time to give the little dog that had helped me so much something in return. If he was prepared to deal with Sonny, then I would have to as well.

'Sky?' Gemma calls. 'Have I lost you? It's gone awfully quiet this end.'

'No, I'm still here,' I reply hurriedly. I'd almost forgotten I'm still on the phone. 'Gemma, I'm not happy about this – I'd like that noted. But I am prepared to give it a go. But Sonny has to accept that I'm in charge of this weather station, not him. I assume he knows that already?'

'Oh yes,' Gemma says quickly, but not entirely convincingly. 'Both Sonny and Talia know exactly who's boss. Right, I'm so pleased that's sorted. I'm sorry but I have to dash, Sky, I have a meeting in five minutes. I'm sure you'll all have a blast down there – I'm almost jealous. Wishing you lots of luck!'

Thanks, I think as we say goodbye and I end the call. *I'm sure I'm going to need it.*

'All sorted?' Sonny asks, as he meets me with the dogs back at the entrance to the house.

'Looks like I'm stuck with you,' I reply, as light-heartedly as I can. I've decided I have no choice but to make a go of this, and I'm going to try to remain as positive as I can about the situation. Could it be possible I've misjudged Sonny in the short time I've known him?

'I'm not that bad,' Sonny says, grinning in that same annoyingly energetic way he does everything. 'I'm wonderful company once you get to know me – so I've been told many times before.' He lowers his sunglasses in the same salacious way he had earlier and his eyes twinkle with mischief.

Or perhaps my first impressions had been correct after all?

'Let's wait and see, shall we?' I reply diplomatically. 'Fitz seemed to enjoy playing with Comet on the sand just now. If he can adapt to living with a stranger, then I guess I can give it a go too.'

'He has a lot of energy, doesn't he, for a small dog.'

'Too much sometimes!' I say, turning to head back inside.

'Why Fitz?' Sonny asks as he follows me into the hall.

I pass him one of the dog towels I've purposely left by the door, so he can wipe the sand off Comet's feet. Then I take one to do the same for Fitz.

'What do you mean?' I ask, carefully wiping four small paws, then giving Fitz's back a rub too. It doesn't need it, but he loves it when I do that.

'Why call him Fitz? It's unusual, but it really suits him.'

'It's after Robert Fitzroy,' I say, deliberately leaving out the necessary detail.

'Oh, the guy who started the Met Office – cool!'

I'm surprised. I hadn't expected Sonny to know that.

'Did you name Comet after the machine that generated the first operational computerised forecast?' I ask hopefully. *Might we have more in common than I'd first thought?*

'Nah, I didn't name her at all, my wife did. I think she just liked it. Comet was her dog originally.'

Oh yes, Sonny had mentioned a wife to the harbourmaster. I think I might have seen the odd photo of them online and in newspaper gossip columns. It's not an area of the media I usually dwell on, but I seem to remember them being quite a glamorous couple as they were photographed out and about amongst the London nightlife.

'Why have you brought Comet here if she's your wife's dog?'

'Because my wife is about to become my *ex*-wife,' Sonny says, folding his towel and tossing it back in the basket. 'We've been separated for some time, despite a few futile attempts to patch things up. Our divorce should be finalised any day now.' For the first time since I met him earlier, Sonny doesn't sound like his name as he speaks. There's a hint of bitterness and perhaps melancholy to his voice. 'Comet here is one of the better parts of my divorce settlement.'

He ruffles Comet's head before she and Fitz trot happily into the kitchen together to get water, leaving us on our own in the hallway.

'I'm sorry to hear you're divorcing,' I say, meaning it. I know how painful a break-up can be – especially if one of the parties involved doesn't really want it – and for the first time I feel some sort of connection to Sonny.

'Happens, doesn't it?' Sonny shrugs. 'That's life.'

'I suppose so.'

'Are you married?' he asks, glancing at my left hand. 'Or in a relationship?' he continues when he doesn't see a ring there.

'No.' I answer firmly, not wanting to tell him any more.

'That's a very firm no,' Sonny says, grinning, and I watch him begin to return to his usual chipper self once more. 'I sense a story there?'

I hear the sound of two dogs eagerly lapping water. 'They're thirsty,' I say. 'We'll have to make sure we keep their bowls filled up. It's all the salt water; they're not used to it.' I follow the dogs through to the kitchen, hoping this will be the end of the conversation.

'So,' Sonny says, not far behind me. 'Why don't you tell me the story of why you've ended up here on this Cornish island with only me for company?'

'Why does there have to be a story?' I say, reaching down to refill the dogs' already empty water bowls. 'Maybe I simply wanted to do it.'

'*Come on*,' Sonny says, pulling out a chair and sitting down at the kitchen table. 'I don't believe that any more than you do.'

I fill one bowl and put it back down on the kitchen floor.

'Really, it's not at all interesting,' I insist.

'Everyone thinks their story isn't interesting to others – the *best* people do, anyway. In my experience, those that think everything they do is fascinating, and want to share it with everyone – usually on social media – are usually pretty pretentious and extremely dull.'

I glance at Sonny for a moment as I finish filling the second bowl with water. When his full-on TV persona dips occasionally, there's something about him that I find quite intriguing, much to my annoyance.

'Have you unpacked yet?' I ask, changing the subject, as the second dog bowl almost overflows with water. I tip a little bit out and hurriedly put it down on the floor.

Sonny shrugs. 'I'll do it later. I think it's important we get to know each other a little better since we're going to be housemates for the summer. I'll put the kettle on, shall I? And we can have a good old natter.'

Sonny and I sit up in the living room drinking our tea, looking out over the incredible view through the bay window. Sonny is

43

casually reclined on the sofa and I'm sitting bolt upright in one of the armchairs; the dogs are curled up at our feet.

'So, when do we start weather watching properly?' Sonny asks, nodding towards the equipment. 'It's the clouds that are the problem, isn't it? That's what Talia suggested on the train.'

'Tomorrow morning. The clouds aren't a problem, though – no weather is a problem. Not if you're equipped to deal with it.'

'*Really?*' Sonny asks with interest. 'What about a tsunami – that's a problem caused by freak weather. Very few people are equipped to deal with that.'

'If you knew anything about meteorology, you'd know a tsunami isn't usually caused by inclement weather, but more likely by a movement of the seafloor associated with an earthquake. Either that or by landslides, volcanic activity or, very rarely, meteorite impact.'

I take a sip of my tea, and try not to look too smug – I've been proved right. Sonny doesn't know anything about the weather.

'Ah, well that told me,' Sonny says, taking a long drink from his own mug.

'It isn't just the clouds we're here to observe, though,' I say, feeling like I should speak again. 'All the weather here has been … unusual of late. There've been some forecasts and readings taken that simply haven't added up. We've been brought in to look at that, as well as the unusual cloud formations.'

Sonny nods, and looks over at the equipment again.

'Will you need me to talk you through all this?' I ask, testing the water again. 'I imagine you don't use too many anemometers or hygrometers when you're reading an autocue.'

'For reading wind speed and humidity, you mean?' Sonny

answers straight away, bouncing back with a grin. 'I might not know about tsunamis, but I know what those instruments do.' He pauses for a moment before saying, 'You don't think much of me, do you?'

'What makes you say that?' I ask innocently. I reach down and lift Fitz on to my lap. Comet is sound asleep by Sonny's feet.

'I just get that feeling. You don't try too hard at keeping it hidden.'

'Sorry,' I say, trying to sound apologetic. 'It's just I'm not good with surprises – and you've come as a pretty huge one. I like to know what's going to happen so I can be prepared and adjust if necessary.'

Sonny looks quizzically at me, and I wish I hadn't said quite so much. 'Some would see me turning up on their doorstep as a rather pleasant surprise . . .' He grins.

'Perhaps. But I'm not one of them, I'm afraid – nothing against you,' I hurriedly add.

I'm trying here, really I am, but Sonny is the sort of person I usually do my best to avoid. He's loud and chatty and a bit too full of himself, and every time I think he might have calmed down just a little, he springs right back into full Sonny mode – like a jack-in-the-box enthusiastically popping up again when he's been compressed in his box a little too long. I find him totally draining, and these days I try to avoid anything that might sap my energy.

'What you see is what you get with me,' I continue, trying to explain. 'I'm a very honest person, and I'm proud of it too. I can't bear two-faced people who are nice to your face then go behind your back. Or fake people who pretend to be something they're not . . .' My voice fades a little. I'm talking about someone else now, and I know I shouldn't judge Sonny by their standards, but I can't help it. 'You're just not my cup of tea, I'm afraid,' I add, and to try to soften this last part, I jokily lift up my mug of tea.

'Golly!' Sonny clasps his hands dramatically to his chest as if I've wounded him. 'That hurts! Seriously, though,' he says, dropping his hands again, 'I can't be that bad! Am I supposed to fall into one of these aforementioned categories?'

'You tell me?' I ask, hoping above all he'll be honest. That would be one thing in his favour.

'Okay . . . ' Sonny thinks for a moment. 'Well, I'm not fake – so there's a plus on my chart to start with. I don't talk behind people's backs – there's another. Am I doing all right so far?'

I nod.

'I do have a couple of little secrets, though, that I should probably tell you about.'

'Go on.' I wonder what he's going to say.

'My first secret is that my name isn't really Sonny.'

'You mentioned that when we first met.'

'Did I?'

'Yes, at the station. You said your friends call you Jamie.'

'Ah, so I did. Good memory!' he says, tapping his head. 'My parents christened me Jameson Samuels, but I think that makes me sound like a whisky!' He pauses, as though this is usually where people laugh at his joke, but when I don't, he simply continues unabashed. 'It's also quite a mouthful. So when I went into TV, I shortened it to Sonny. Sonny Samuels has a better ring to it, don't you think?'

'For a weather presenter, perhaps. But I prefer Jamie.'

'Really?'

'Yes.'

'Why?'

'It doesn't sound as silly as Sonny.'

Sonny laughs. 'You said you were honest.'

'I did.'

'Then why don't you call me Jamie?'

'All right, I will.'

'Is Sky your real name? It's very fitting for a meteorologist.'

'It is, actually.'

'Cool. Did you always want to work in weather?'

'For as long as I can remember – yes.'

'This is the bit when you embellish on what I've just asked.' He smiles encouragingly at me. 'You know, tell me something about your life.'

'Why?'

'Why what?'

'Why do you need to know?'

'Because I'm interested.'

I sigh, I don't want to be rude, but I'm tired, really tired, and my head is beginning to feel fuzzy and like it's stuffed with cotton wool where my brain should be. But I know he won't let it go if I don't tell him something.

'All right. Er, I've been interested in the weather since I was a child. A meteorologist was all I ever wanted to be from a really young age. It was my grandfather that got me into weather watching properly, though. He built a home weather station on his house, and we used to record the weather together when I visited him.'

Some of my happiest memories, I think to myself.

'That's nice,' Jamie says approvingly. 'I was always jealous of people who knew what they wanted to be from a young age. I kind of fell into weather presenting accidentally.'

'That doesn't surprise me,' I say before I can stop myself.

Jamie's head tilts to one side and he looks at me with a part-amused, part-puzzled expression.

'You're a funny one, aren't you?'

I'm not sure how to take this. 'What's that supposed to mean?'

'I don't know, you're just different to anyone else I've ever met – you're direct, you say what you think, even if it's not what people want to hear.'

'You mean I'm different to the TV types you probably hang around with. I told you before I was honest.'

'You're definitely that.' Jamie smiles at me. 'I like you, Sky. I think we're going to get on just fine when you learn to loosen up.'

'Loosen up!' I exclaim in a voice loud enough to wake Fitz on my lap. 'I am perfectly fine the way I am, thank you. I have no intention of loosening anything.'

'Now that's a real shame,' Jamie says suggestively, looking me up and down. 'I'm kidding! I'm kidding!' he cries when I glare at him. 'It's just a joke.'

'I'd appreciate it if you'd keep your suggestive jokes to yourself. You might get away with them in your normal place of work – although how I'm not sure. But we're here to do a job, which I intend to perform in an efficient and professional manner, and I expect you to do the same.'

Jamie is about to respond when we hear a voice from downstairs. 'Hello! Anyone home?'

'We're up here, Talia!' I call, relieved to have a distraction from Jamie's constant chit-chat. 'Come up.'

Talia appears at the top of the stairs.

'Wow! This is so cool,' she gasps, looking around. 'Look at all this equipment – and that view!' She rushes over to the window.

'Not bad for Cornwall, is it?' Jamie says, standing up and joining Talia by the window. 'I have to say I've been quite pleasantly surprised by what I've found since I arrived here. Usually, I'd save my plaudits for the more foreign and exotic climes.'

You would, I think, but I don't say anything.

'But I count myself extremely lucky to be spending my summer in such an amazing place, with two equally amazing women.'

Talia smiles bashfully at Jamie. 'That's very kind of you, Sonny. I can't wait to work with you too.'

'Please, call me Jamie,' he says, smiling warmly back at her. 'All my best friends do. Don't they, Sky?' He winks at me.

I can only nod.

Clearly living with both Jamie and Sonny this summer would be like living with my own version of sunshine and showers – both absolutely necessary in nature, but one was usually a lot more welcome and easily tolerated than the other.

Six

Monday afternoon, and I find myself heading across the causeway with Jamie in the Jeep to the mainland, to pick up supplies for the house and to give the dogs a much-needed run-around on the beach.

We left Talia happily sitting in front of the bay window, watching and recording the weather. She is so eager to learn that I'm really enjoying spending time with her. Our first morning together as a threesome had been spent going over exactly how we were to record our observations, and checking both Talia and Jamie knew how all the equipment worked. Talia, as expected, knew pretty much everything I needed her to. Jamie, as I'd also correctly anticipated, was a little slower at picking things up, and needed a fair amount of time and explanation to understand how the weather-recording equipment worked.

'What did I just say?' I asked Jamie at one point when, yet again, he appeared to be distractedly gazing out of the window, this time when I was patiently trying to explain to him the sort of readings we needed to record on a regular basis.

'Er ... something about wind speed?' he guessed, clearly without the faintest idea.

'Nice try, that was a few minutes ago – this time it's humidity. Am I just wasting my time here?' I asked, more than a tad annoyed. What was the point in him even being here if he wasn't going to at least try to help? Talia was easy, the perfect student, but Jamie was constantly trying my patience and making me use up extra energy I didn't have, explaining the same stuff over and over again.

'No, you're not wasting your time. But can't we just pick it up as we go along?' Jamie asked with his usual laid-back attitude. 'It might be easier than trying to learn all this at once?'

'Do I need to remind you you're not actually supposed to be here?' I countered. 'I should only be explaining this to Talia, who as you might have noticed doesn't really need me to tell her anything.'

Talia looked half pleased at my praise, but at the same time concerned for Jamie.

'I don't really know everything,' she said diplomatically. 'You're teaching me ever such a lot, Sky. How about if I try and show Jamie how everything works once you've told me? Then I can be sure that I've absorbed it all too.'

Immediately I felt bad. Talia was showing much more patience and kindness than I was. I needed to try to remember that not everyone absorbs knowledge as quickly as I'm able to – or I used to be able to. My physicality isn't the only thing to have suffered during my illness; my memory isn't quite as sharp as it used to be, either. I often suffer from what is known as 'brain fog', which pretty much prevents me from doing anything that requires mental cognition, until like its meteorological counterpart it disperses, and my mind can see clearly again.

'That's kind of you, Talia, thank you.' I turned to Jamie. 'I'm sorry if I snapped. I think the last two days have taken it out of me more than I realised.'

'That's okay,' Jamie said, shrugging. He leant back on the desk chair and swivelled to and fro. 'I know I'm not the best student. Never have been, really. I learn much better by doing than by being told how to.'

I nodded. 'Okay, I'll try and remember that.'

'You do look a bit tired, though,' Jamie said, tilting his head to one side. 'Do you want to postpone our trip over to St Felix?'

The truth was I felt far from perfect. The dramas of yesterday and travelling and setting everything up the day before had totally wiped me out. Once Talia had headed back to her uncle's last night, I'd immediately gone to bed, exhausted, without even waiting for Jamie to return from dropping her off in the Jeep.

Jamie hadn't said anything this morning about my abrupt early night, but I felt the atmosphere was a little frosty over breakfast. I was used to that, though – people often assumed things when it came to me, and most of the time I didn't have the energy to correct them.

In my experience, only the most patient and supportive of people understood when you kept cancelling on them, and I was keen not to start off this new relationship by immediately cancelling this afternoon's planned trip.

'No, I'll be fine,' I told him confidently. 'Besides, it will do the dogs good to have a long walk.'

Even if it won't do the same for me.

'You sure you're all right?' Jamie asks now as I drive carefully across the bricks of the causeway towards St Felix. 'You're pretty quiet.'

'I'm just trying to concentrate. I'm not used to driving over uneven bricks with water either side of me, and two dogs in the back of an open-sided vehicle.'

The tide is on its way out at the moment, so the causeway is clear, but there are still some shallow waves lapping either side of us as we make our way across.

Jamie nods and goes quiet.

'It's just you've been a bit subdued since our teaching session this morning,' he pipes up again a minute or two later. 'Not that you're ever that chatty – not with me, anyway. But even taking your intense dislike of me into account, you're still very quiet.'

'Like I said earlier, I'm just a bit tired, that's all. It's been a busy couple of days.' I glance across at him, then quickly return my gaze to the front. 'And an *intense* dislike of you is a little strong.'

'My apologies; shall we call it a mild dislike, then?' Jamie says, and I know he's grinning at me without even looking.

'Sure,' I agree, determined not to fall for his charms. 'Let's call it that.'

'You're a tough cookie, you know?' Jamie continues as I make my way to the end of the causeway and change gear to enable me to drive up the beach towards the road.

'Am I?' I ask, not really listening, but concentrating hard on my driving instead. I've never driven on sand before, and it feels weird, even in the Jeep.

'I think so. As far as I'm aware I've done nothing to you, and yet you've decided for some reason I'm a bad egg.'

'Actually, that's where you're wrong. I don't think you're a bad egg, as you put it.' I change right down into first gear to enable us to climb the last part of the sandy beach up on to a

53

stone jetty that runs parallel to the harbour wall. 'I don't know you well enough to make those sorts of assumptions.'

'Shouldn't I get the benefit of the doubt, then, until you do?'

I pull up along the harbour front in the parking space that has been reserved for Aurora Island – a godsend, Fisher had informed me. Apparently parking spaces are like gold dust in St Felix during the summer months. I turn off the engine and turn to look at Jamie.

'It's not *you* I dislike . . . Well, it is a little bit, I suppose, but it's not all your fault.'

'You'll have to explain a bit better than that, I'm afraid,' Jamie says, looking bemused.

'I mean, it's not the only thing I have a problem with. I don't like change, you see. I thought I knew exactly who I was going to be sharing this job and the house with. I'd got it all straight in my head, and I thought I could cope with it all. Then suddenly you show up and everything changed in an instant. All my carefully laid plans out of the window.'

'I know I was a surprise to you, but I'm not that bad a surprise, am I?' He raises his eyebrows.

'You don't understand . . .' It's no good; I'm going to have to try to explain. 'My whole life has to be planned out to prevent . . .'

'Do you have some sort of OCD?' Jamie asks, without waiting for my reply. 'I had a mate with that once. If he set a table, he actually had to measure how far apart the cutlery was so it was exactly the same on each place setting. If you so much as moved a fork he'd go nuts.'

I sigh. Jamie isn't listening. But this is nothing new – most people don't listen properly when I confide in them, and even when they do, few truly understand, even those closest to me . . .

Jamie is just like all the others.

'No,' I say shortly, 'I don't have OCD.' I open the Jeep door and climb out. Then I slam it shut again. 'Are you coming?' I ask as Jamie remains in his seat, watching me. 'The dogs are raring to go.'

I open up the little door at the back of the Jeep and two excited dogs bound out. While Jamie climbs out of the vehicle I slip on their leads, and then, without saying another word, Jamie and I set off to explore St Felix together.

'It's a charming little place, isn't it?' Jamie says when we've been walking for a while. 'Very Cornish.'

So far we've ambled up and down narrow cobbled streets, past whitewashed cottages with brightly painted wooden doors that had once been fishermen's homes but were now holiday lets. We've got supplies from one of the little supermarkets and taken the laden shopping bags back to the Jeep. We've walked past several long beaches with golden sands and cheerful-looking beachside cafés, and stopped to let the dogs run over the soft sand and paddle in the sea – which I'm pleased to see is still quite a long way out. Now we're heading back into the main part of the town.

A lot of holidaymakers are out on the beaches enjoying the early-summer sunshine; most sensibly shelter from the cool wind behind stripy windbreaks. There are a lot of people like us, out walking their dogs. But unlike the people who chat amiably to each other as they explore the town together, since we left the Jeep Jamie and I have only spoken to each other a maximum of three or four times, to politely enquire which way the other wanted to go, what we should do next, or what to buy in the supermarket. So I find myself jumping when Jamie suddenly strikes up this conversation.

'Yes . . . it's very pretty. I like it,' I reply quickly, relieved he's broken the silence, which was becoming more than a little awkward.

'Talia said we should stop by the bakery and pick up some bread and pasties. She said her uncle will be looking out for us.'

'I think that's just along here,' I say, pointing to a narrow street filled with quaint little shops that leads up off the harbour front. 'We dropped her off along Harbour Street yesterday, but everywhere looks quite different when you're not driving through the busy streets. It's taken me quite a while to get my bearings.'

'Yes, I know what you mean,' Jamie agrees. 'It's much better exploring the place on foot. There's the shop over there.' He points to a bright and cheerful bakery a little way along the cobbled street, with delicious-looking cakes and pastries displayed in the window. 'The Blue Canary.'

'Shall I wait with the dogs while you go in?' I offer.

'No, I'm fine waiting outside. I'm not bothered what we get as long as you get a Cornish pasty or two. It's been years since I've had a genuine one of those. You still have the purse, don't you?'

Last night Jamie and I had agreed to have a kitty between us to cover food and household expenses. 'Yep, it's still in my bag from when I paid at the supermarket,' I say, passing Fitz's lead to Jamie. 'Right, I'll be back shortly then.'

There's a small queue waiting to be served as I enter the shop, so while I wait, I enjoy the delicious sweet and savoury aromas of freshly baked goods.

But the short queue, which I had expected to move quite quickly, takes longer than it should, and as I stand there waiting, with people now crowded into the shop behind me and the queue filtering out on to the street outside, I feel myself start to sway a little.

Oh God, not now! I think, beginning to lift my legs up and down as if I'm marching on the spot. But the movement only helps a little, and all too quickly the inside of the bakery starts to swim in front of my eyes, as if someone is washing liquid over a watercolour painting and all the detail is beginning to blur.

I can still hear the woman complaining in front of me about the amount of meat in her chicken pasty as my body starts to crumble and I feel the hands of the person behind me on my back – either trying to catch me as a I fall or, more likely, trying to prevent me crashing into them.

'Are you all right?' is the next thing I hear, as a sea of worried faces look down on me from above.

'Should we call an ambulance?' another voice asks keenly.

'I'm fine,' I say, my head still swimming, and I attempt to sit up.

'Give her some space,' a third voice joins in. 'She needs air, not interrogation.'

The crowd moves back a little, and I see that one of the bakers, who had been serving behind the counter, is now kneeling next to me. 'How are you feeling?' he asks. 'Here, let me help you.'

'Thanks,' I say as he slowly guides me into a sitting position. 'I'll be fine now.'

'Let us at least get you a glass of water. Dec, can you get some water please!'

'Sure, Ant, I'll be right back!' a much smaller and thinner man calls, as he hurries away.

So this must be Talia's Uncle Ant next to me. He looks very much like you'd expect a baker to look – quite round, with a kind, cheerful face. 'Really, I'll be fine,' I try to reassure him. 'I just need some air, that's all.'

'At least rest for a few minutes,' Ant says anxiously. 'We've a lovely little courtyard out the back; it's tiny but very quiet. You can get some fresh air and have that glass of water.'

I nod, and allow him to help me to me feet.

'Oh,' I say, remembering Jamie and the dogs. 'My ... er ... my friend Jamie is waiting outside with our two dogs.' My heart sinks at the thought of him seeing me like this. It's exactly what I wanted to avoid happening.

'Not to worry. We'll get word out to him.' He looks across at the other customers still watching our exchange with interest. 'Amber, could you possibly find a Jamie outside with two dogs and tell him what's happened. Ask him to come around to the back gate.'

A woman with long auburn hair and a friendly smile nods. 'Sure, Ant,' she says with an American accent. 'I'm on it!'

The crowd of people parts a little, and Ant guides me through the bakery to the back of the shop, and then through a short hallway to a door that leads outside to a small but cosy courtyard. It's filled with colourful flowerpots and equally colourful flowers, and a couple of comfortable seats, which Ant guides me towards.

'Now take a seat, and I'll see if we've located your friend. Ah, here's Dec with that water.'

The smaller of the two men appears with a glass of cold water. 'Thank you,' I say, taking the water gratefully from him, while Ant opens up the back gate and pokes his head around it.

'My pleasure,' Dec says. 'Are you feeling better now?'

'Yes, thank you. I'm sorry to have caused such a commotion in your shop.'

'It's fine, please don't worry. Louise and Harry – our other staff – will hold the fort.'

'Are you Jamie?' I hear Ant call to someone in the street outside. 'Oh, I do beg your pardon, of course you're not! I recognise you, now you're that bit closer – you're Sonny Samuels, aren't you?'

'Guilty as charged!' I hear Jamie's cheery voice reply. 'On both counts. Jamie is my real name; Sonny is simply my alter-ego. Is Sky all right? Someone just told me she'd passed out in your shop?'

'Yes, do come through,' Ant says and he stands back to let Jamie and the dogs in. *It's Sonny Samuels!* he mouths to Dec, thrilled.

Jamie, looking surprisingly worried, appears at the gate with Fitz and Comet.

I'm mortified that he should see me like this. It's not that I'm bothered by what he thinks, but it had been so important for me not to show any weakness on this job, and I'm failing at that already.

Fitz immediately pulls towards me, so Jamie lets go of his lead so he can scamper over and jump up on my lap.

'Hello, you,' I say, stroking him.

'What happened?' Jamie asks, coming over. 'Are you okay?' He kneels down next to me and gently touches my arm. He looks genuinely concerned and I feel terribly guilty for causing such a fuss.

'I'm fine, I just got a little hot waiting in the shop and must have fainted, that's all. Nothing to worry about.' I try to say this with as much bravado as I can muster, when really this happening again, and so soon after we've arrived here, has knocked the wind from my sails.

Since Jamie appeared at the gate with the dogs, neither Ant nor Dec is taking much notice of me; their focus is completely on Jamie. I don't mind, though; I don't like being the centre of attention at the best of times, let alone like this.

'What brings you to St Felix, Sonny?' Ant asks, virtually fluttering his eyelashes at him. 'Work or play?'

'Work,' Jamie says matter-of-factly.

'Will you be broadcasting from here?' Dec asks keenly. 'We do so love your forecasts, don't we, Ant?'

Ant nods eagerly.

'Not this time, I'm afraid,' Jamie says, the only one of the three seeming to remember I'm still here. 'I'm working with Sky. We're here to watch and record any unusual weather patterns over St Felix.'

'You're the meteorologists working with my niece Talia!' Ant says, putting the pieces together. 'She mentioned there were three of you, but never said one of you was *Sonny Samuels*!'

I roll my eyes. I don't know if I'm more irritated that they think Jamie is a meteorologist, or that simply saying the name *Sonny Samuels* seems to put both of them in a frenzy.

'We are indeed,' Jamie says, not correcting them. 'Talia is a lovely young girl, a credit to her parents. One of whom is your sister, I believe?' he says to Ant.

Smooth, I think, watching 'Sonny' in full flow.

'Yes, my sister Julianna,' Ant says, looking shocked that Sonny would know this.

'You . . . you must come round and have tea with us one day,' Dec offers almost bashfully. 'We'd love to get to know you a little better . . . I mean, so we can *all* get to know each other.'

'That would be great,' Jamie says, grinning. 'I'm not going to say no to afternoon tea with two famous bakers!'

'Oh no, *you're* the famous one, not us,' Ant insists, blushing a little.

'I won't hear of it!' Jamie insists. 'The Blue Canary Bakery is renowned throughout Cornwall, if not the whole of the West Country!'

Both Ant and Dec pull coy expressions.

'I think we've probably taken up enough of your time,' I say, standing up and handing Dec the empty glass. 'Thank you, I feel much better now.'

'Oh ... not at all,' Dec says, seeming to suddenly remember I'm here. 'It's our pleasure. Are you sure you're okay now? You're very welcome to stay a little longer.'

Even though they've both been very kind, I get the feeling 'Sonny' might be the real reason they want us to stay. 'Thank you so much for your kindness, but we really must go. We've left Talia in charge at the island and we have to get back before the tide turns, otherwise we won't be able to cross the causeway in our Jeep.'

'Let us at least send you off with some goodies,' Ant says. 'What did you come in for originally?'

'Pasties!' Jamie says with relish. 'I was just telling Sky here – I haven't had a genuine Cornish pasty in years!'

'Well, you've come to the right place. Our Cornish pasties are legendary – even if we do say so ourselves.' Ant and Dec look proudly at each other.

'I'll just pop through to the shop and get you some,' Dec says. 'I'll be back in a jiffy!'

'So,' Ant says, glancing bashfully at Jamie, 'what is this unusual weather you've come here to watch?'

'It's mainly cloud patterns, isn't it?' Jamie asks, looking at me. 'Sky here is the expert; I'm just some bloke off the telly.'

I appreciate his honesty. 'We're recording all the weather,' I explain, 'but it's the clouds that have been showing some very unusual activity. It seems—'

'You definitely won't be broadcasting while you're here, then?' Ant asks forlornly, still gazing at Jamie.

'Nope. Like I said before, that's not what I'm here for this time.'

'Shame . . . I mean, it's good you have more strings to your bow than just TV work.'

Jamie nods. 'Yes, it is. I'm sure Sky will be able to teach me a lot, though.' He turns and smiles at me, and for the first time, it feels genuine. 'I'm definitely Jamie while I'm here in St Felix. I've decided to let Sonny go on vacation for a while.'

'Oh, is it a secret you're here?' Ant asks excitedly. 'All hush-hush?'

'Er, no, not really.'

'Don't worry, my lips are sealed!' he says, putting his finger on his lips. 'We won't tell a soul.'

Somehow, I find that hard to believe, but I'm pleased to hear Jamie is intending on distancing himself from Sonny. Although I've yet to notice any major difference, he surprised me just now with his genuine concern.

'Here we go!' Dec says, reappearing with a large white paper bag of goodies. 'I've popped a few things in here for you. You'll have to let us know what your favourites are, then we can save you a little something every day you're here.'

'That's very kind of you,' I say, taking the bag from him before he can move towards Jamie. 'What do we owe you?'

'Oh no!' Dec says, looking horrified. 'It's our treat. We know Talia is over the moon to get this job. It's the least we can do to look after her co-workers.'

I'm about to tell them we can't possibly accept, when Jamie pipes up.

'Cheers, fellas,' he says, smiling with what I now recognise as a 'Sonny special'. But Ant and Dec simply melt at the sight of it. 'I'm sure it will be the best feast we've ever had!'

'Are you sure you're all right now?' Jamie asks as we leave through Ant and Dec's back gate and find ourselves on a quiet little side street that runs parallel to its livelier cousin, Harbour Street.

'Yes, totally. I'm just a bit tired, that's all. The last couple of days have been pretty hectic, and I didn't sleep too well last night.'

'Hmm . . . ' Jamie looks intently at me. 'That's what you said earlier – just a bit tired.'

'Well, I am. Honestly, I'll be fine, please don't fuss.'

'Okay,' Jamie says, sighing. He pulls out the Ray-Bans he'd been wearing earlier when it was sunny, and puts them on as we begin to walk. 'Right, should we head back to the Jeep now?'

'Yes, I think we should. We don't want to get caught out by the tide. Why are you putting those back on?' I ask, looking at him. 'Even I'm not wearing sunglasses, and I always wear them in bright light. Right now it looks more like rain with all the nimbostratus that's suddenly appeared above the sea.'

Jamie lifts his glasses back up. 'Nimbostratus?'

'Layers of dark cloud to you. You'd see them more clearly without the sunnies.'

'Sunglasses aren't only to block out bright light.'

'What are they for, then? Oh wait, are you trying to disguise yourself from your many fans?'

I can't help smirking. Who does Jamie think he is? Yes, Ant and Dec had fawned all over him, but I'm sure the average St Felix holidaymaker isn't likely to bother him.

'Mock all you like, but they do help if you don't want to be noticed. And since we want to get back over to the island as quickly as possible, it's best if we get to the Jeep without any hold-ups.'

I shake my head scornfully.

'Fine!' Jamie says, pulling off his glasses with a flourish. 'Have it your way.' He folds his glasses and puts them back in his top pocket. 'Don't say I didn't warn you, though.'

We continue to walk back in the direction of the Jeep. The town is busy this afternoon, the streets packed, and we have to weave in and out of the many holidaymakers. It's not long before Fitz and I find ourselves separated from Jamie and Comet.

I stop walking and look back to see where they've got to. Eventually I spy them both quite a way back along the harbour front. Jamie is posing for a selfie with a lady wearing a straw sunhat, who looks overjoyed to be getting a photo with 'Sonny'; she thanks him profusely and then walks away, beaming happily at her phone. Jamie begins to walk in our direction again, but someone else pops up holding out their phone, so Jamie smiles again, has a few words with them, and then encourages Comet to move on. It happens twice more as he tries to walk Comet along the harbour.

Clearly Jamie must be more well known than I'd first thought. *Just because I don't watch breakfast TV, read gossip columns and scroll through social media*, I remind myself, *doesn't mean to say other people don't.*

'I did warn you,' Jamie says as he finally catches up with us. He pulls out his sunglasses again. 'Now can I put them on?'

'Do what you like,' I say, shrugging, and I begin to walk back to the Jeep with Fitz.

'All right, what's the problem now?' Jamie calls, jogging to catch up with us. 'I can't help it if people recognise me. It's one of the hazards of the job.'

'Hazards!' I repeat, as we reach our parking space and I unlock the Jeep doors. 'Don't make me laugh. You love all the attention!'

Jamie appears to consider this for a moment, 'Okay, I'll admit sometimes I do like it. But I promise you, Sky, most of the time I really don't.'

I shake my head as I walk around to the back of the Jeep. 'If I believe that, I'll believe anything,' I say as I pour the dogs some water from a bottle. They both lap thirstily from the bowl as soon as I put it down on to the ground.

'Believe what you like, but it's the truth,' Jamie says, watching them. 'I really don't know what your issue with me is, Sky,' he says, looking up accusingly. 'As far as I'm aware I've done nothing since I met you to provoke this level of scepticism and antagonism.'

He's partly right, of course; he'd not deliberately done anything to me. But I couldn't help but be irritated by him. Watching him converse with total strangers when he'd been accosted by his adoring fans just now made me realise that's likely how Jamie sailed through all of his life – effortlessly, easily, and with total control.

The complete opposite to how I now lived my life. Every day was a battle for me; there were no 'easy days', days when life just happened without a fight, without a struggle, and without the constant worry that I'll end up back in my own private hell hole.

But it isn't Jamie's fault I feel this way. I must stop comparing the apparent ease of his life to my own – it's not fair. I'm about to apologise, but Jamie speaks first – 'Perhaps at some stage, Sky, you'll step down off your perfect pedestal and deign to share what your real issue with me is. Then I might have half a chance at putting right whatever it is I've done wrong!'

I stare at Jamie. I don't blame him for snapping, but 'perfect pedestal'! How wrong he is. If only he knew the truth, then maybe he'd understand.

But how was he ever going to do that, when I had no intention of sharing the truth with him, or anyone else here in St Felix?

Seven

The journey back to the island is a quiet one.

Jamie is obviously sulking, and I simply haven't got the energy after our eventful excursion over to St Felix to attempt to put things right.

We reach the island, park up, then we carry our shopping back up to the house, where we unpack it in the kitchen still mostly in silence.

'Ah!' Talia says as I climb to the top of the stairs to see how she's getting on. 'Here you are. I saw you driving across, but when I didn't hear much noise downstairs, I wondered if something had happened?'

'Yes, we're back,' I say quickly. 'How are you getting on here?'

'Great! I've had a lovely time watching everything going on outside. You can see it all from here – there's been people swimming and bodyboarding in the bay. A few fishing boats bobbing about in the waves and casting out nets, and some lovely seabirds passing by and landing on the island.'

'But the weather?' I ask her. 'What about that?'

'Oh, nothing unusual, really. I've been taking readings, and recording everything like you said.'

'Ah, okay, good.'

I'm beginning to wonder just why we've all been brought here. I've been here a couple of days and I haven't seen anything out of the ordinary yet.

'How did you get on in the town?' Talia asks. 'St Felix is a lovely little place, isn't it?'

'Yes, it is. We went into the bakery and met your Uncle Ant and his husband.'

'Lovely, aren't they? Been running that bakery together for years. They make some delicious cakes; the smell in that shop is to die for.'

'Or to faint for?' Jamie says, arriving at the top of the stairs.

Talia looks puzzled.

I glare at Jamie, but turn back to Talia. 'I may have fainted just briefly in the shop,' I tell her. 'But it's nothing to worry about – honestly.'

'That's what she said to me,' Jamie says, walking over to the desk. 'I didn't believe her either.'

'All right, all right.' I sigh. 'Look, I sometimes feel a bit off if I have to stand for very long in one place. There was a queue in the bakery that got held up by someone complaining. I felt a bit dizzy and then I fainted – really, nothing to worry about.'

Talia and Jamie exchange concerned looks.

'If it's happened before you should probably see a doctor,' Talia says anxiously.

'I have, and I've been diagnosed with something called Orthostatic Intolerance.' I attempt to say this as reassuringly as I can. Part of me hates myself for not being completely honest with them, but I just can't. If I can get through this experience with them not knowing anything else is wrong, then I've at least achieved that victory. 'I'm okay if I keep moving, it's just if I stand for too long – the blood doesn't quite pump to my brain fast enough, it's partly to do with my blood pressure. It can happen if I get up suddenly as well.'

'Oh, I see,' Talia says, still looking concerned.

'Don't worry; I'm not going to suddenly pass out on you.'

'Only on me, apparently,' Jamie says wryly.

I ignore him. 'Now show me the readings you've taken this afternoon,' I ask Talia, hoping to change the subject. 'Let's see if there's anything unusual.'

I glance out of the window at the dark nimbostratus cloud lying heavily in the sky – *It's definitely going to rain shortly.* I'm about to look back at Talia's weather recordings, when I take a second look. *Where has that tiny white cumulus cloud come from?* It floats across the sky like a fluffy white duck swimming across the surface of a pond. *Those two types of cloud almost never appear together*, I think, still watching it – *and this one looks like a . . . no, don't be daft it can't be . . .* But there's no doubt about it, the cloud has now formed into a circle, and separated a little in the middle to form three triangular gaps so it looks very much like a peace symbol.

I turn back to the others.

'Did you see that?' I ask them, spinning back to the window.

'What?' Jamie asks, behind me.

But the cloud has now reformed back into its usual fluffy shape as it begins to merge into the rest of the bank of dark cloud.

'Oh, it's gone. It was just a cumulus cloud, that's all.'

'What's special about that?' Jamie asks.

'You almost never get cumulus and nimbostratus together!' Talia says excitedly. 'I wish I'd seen it!'

I smile at Talia; it was good to be working with someone who clearly shared my enthusiasm for the weather.

'She knows her stuff!' I say proudly.

'Unlike me, I suppose,' Jamie says with a wry expression. I get it, Sky, I'm not as qualified as you are, or even as knowledgeable as Talia here. But it doesn't mean I'm not as interested in the weather as you two.'

I think about the cloud that has just passed by outside.

'I'm sorry,' I say, meaning it. 'Perhaps I have been a little hard on you since you arrived.'

Jamie looks surprised, but nods graciously. 'Apology accepted. I'm still not sure why, though?'

I hesitate for a moment, which is just long enough for someone to knock hard on the door downstairs.

We all look at each other as if to say – *Everyone on the island is here in this room, so who can be knocking on the door?*

'Hello!' a familiar voice calls out. 'Anyone home?'

'Fisher!' I call happily, rushing to the top of the stairs. 'Yes, we're here. Come up!

'Fisher is the caretaker of the island,' I quickly explain as Fisher climbs the staircase. 'He helped me a lot when I first arrived.'

'Greetings!' Fisher says as he reaches the top of the stairs. 'I thought I'd pop over and see how you're all getting on?'

'Great, thank you,' I say, pleased to see him. 'Let me introduce everyone. Fisher, this is Talia, she's a trainee meteorologist here to help me out with the watch.'

Talia smiles shyly at Fisher, who nods his head in greeting. 'Pleased to meet you, Talia.'

'And this is Jamie. He is also here to ... well, to help out.'

'Very gracious of you, Sky,' Jamie says, giving me a brief glance. He moves to shake Fisher's hand. 'Pleased to meet you, Fisher. Already heard a lot about you.'

'I thought it was just going to be two of you?' Fisher asks, as he shakes Jamie's hand warmly. He stares at him for a moment, clearly trying to work out where he's seen him before.

'It was originally,' I explain. 'But Jamie is a last-minute addition to the watch.'

'Have we met?' Fisher asks Jamie. 'You look familiar. Have you holidayed in St Felix before?'

'No – not that I recall, anyway,' Jamie says, grinning. 'You probably know me from ...' He hesitates and looks across at me.

It's clear it's going to keep happening, and there's nothing I can do about it. 'Go on, get it out of the way,' I say lightly. 'You know you want to.'

Jamie eyes me for a moment, a stubborn expression developing on his face.

'Perhaps I just have one of those faces,' he suggests casually to Fisher, but I know it must be paining him to say this.

'Could be that,' Fisher says matter-of-factly. 'They say everyone has a doppelgänger – maybe you have a face similar to a lot of others that have holidayed here in St Felix.'

As I grin at him, Jamie looks mortified by this thought.

'So, you're all getting on all right?' Fisher asks, looking around. 'You've mastered the boat, have you, Captain Sky?'

Now it's Jamie's turn to grin at me.

'Yes,' I say hurriedly, ignoring Jamie's obvious amusement. 'I've been across to the mainland once in the boat and once in the Jeep.'

71

'Good stuff. And the rest of your party,' he says, turning to Jamie and Talia. 'You guys are all okay? Anything you need?'

'I have everything I could ever want here,' Jamie gushes. 'Two beautiful ladies to work with, and a fridge full of pasties downstairs.'

'Oh my goodness, the pasties!' I say, looking with dismay at him. 'Did you put them away when we came in?'

'Er ... no. Don't think so,' Jamie says. 'Why? What's the problem?'

'I remember taking the cakes out of the bag from the bakery and putting them away in the fridge. But I left the pasties on the side because they were still warm.'

'So?' Jamie asks.

'Where are the dogs?'

'Still downstairs,' Jamie says, suddenly realising what I'm suggesting. 'But you don't have to worry about Comet, she won't touch them.'

'I'm more worried about Fitz,' I say, heading to the top of the stairs. 'I don't think he'll be quite so restrained if there's fresh pasties left within his reach!'

I go down the stairs as fast as I can, and then I hurry to the kitchen where I find a pair of happy-looking dogs in the middle of a pile of ripped paper and broken bits of pastry. Their demeanours immediately turn to guilt when they see me.

'Fitz!' I cry. 'You bad boy!'

Fitz puts his head down.

'Oh, Comet,' Jamie says, as he joins me in the kitchen. 'Have you been led astray?'

'That's a bit harsh,' I snap. 'How do you know it wasn't Comet that took the bag first?'

'She wouldn't,' Jamie insists. 'She's too well behaved to do that. She was probably joining in with Fitz. I don't blame him; he probably hasn't been trained to the same high standards.'

'It can't have been Fitz,' I lie, part of me annoyed with Jamie's assumptions, and part wanting to defend my friend at all costs. 'I distinctly remember putting the bag on the counter. There's no way he could reach up there. Comet must have pulled the bag off first.'

Comet looks reproachfully at me with her big brown eyes, and now it's my turn to feel guilty.

'Oh,' Jamie says, 'if that's the case, then I guess you must be right. But it's *very* unlike her.' Jamie and Comet both stare hard at me now. But I don't give an inch.

'Perhaps we should just say both of them are at fault, and leave it at that.'

Jamie shrugs. 'Perhaps we should.' He bends down and begins picking up the discarded paper, so I pull a dustpan and brush out from the cupboard under the sink and silently begin sweeping up the remains of pasty.

'What happened?' Talia asks, breaking the silence after a few minutes of us cleaning up without speaking.

'The dogs got the pasties,' I reply diplomatically.

'Oh no! You were so looking forward to them, Jamie.'

Jamie shrugs again. 'There'll be other days. At least they didn't get to the cakes.'

'Can I be of any help?' Fisher asks, popping his head around the door next to Talia. I see Talia's face flush at his proximity, and I have to hide a smile. Fisher's muscular appearance and chiselled features obviously haven't gone unnoticed by my young apprentice. I can't blame her; he's a very handsome young man. There might have been a time a few years ago when I would have been interested in him too. But my days of dating handsome men – any men, in fact – have long passed. Not only do I not have the energy required for dating now, but there's no way I'm ever going to allow myself to be let down again.

'Depends if you can produce a meal for four from a few basic provisions,' I reply jokingly. 'I'd have invited you to stay for dinner, Fisher, but that was when I had something to give you.'

'What have you got?' Fisher asks, to my surprise. He pushes the sleeves of his well-fitting long-sleeved T-shirt up his fore-arms and begins looking in our fridge.

'You have eggs!' he says, lifting them out like a trophy. 'And you have milk. You'd be amazed what delights I can rustle up with these little beauties.'

'Then you go for it,' I say, smiling at him. 'I'm sure we'd all be grateful for anything you can provide. Won't we, Talia?'

Talia jumps at her name. 'Oh ... oh, yes please, Fisher. I'm sure whatever you cook will be delicious.'

Fisher smiles at her, and it's all Talia can do to stop herself melting on to the floor.

'Good man,' Jamie says encouragingly. 'I have to admit I'm a terrible cook. If you hadn't offered, we'd have had to ask Captain Sky here to sail *Doris* back over to collect fish and chips!'

'Your vehicle!' I say, suddenly remembering that Fisher must have driven across the causeway. 'How will you get back?'

'Don't worry, I walked over,' Fisher says, smiling at me. 'But I'm glad to hear you're taking the tide times seriously, Sky. If one of you can pop me back over in *Doris* later, that will be grand.'

'Absolutely,' I say. 'I'll be taking Talia back later, so you can go together. Maybe you could walk Talia back to her uncle's for me when I drop you both off?'

Fisher nods. 'Of course. Not a problem.'

I glance at Talia. I'm sure if she'd just witnessed the Northern Lights from the watch-station window, she couldn't look any happier than she does right now.

'Who taught you to cook like that?' Jamie says, putting his cutlery down on his empty plate and pushing it forward. 'They need a medal! Or a knighthood.'

'Or even a damehood,' Fisher says, smiling. 'Any culinary skills I have are solely due to the patience and teaching skills of my grandmother. I'm glad you enjoyed it.'

Fisher has masterfully produced four delicious omelettes – flavoured and seasoned with the few provisions we'd purchased at the supermarket.

'Yes, it was delicious,' Talia says shyly, glancing across at Fisher.

Fisher smiles. 'I'm pleased you liked it.'

During the course of dinner, we'd discovered that Fisher not only looked after the island as part of his caretaking duties, but several other buildings around St Felix, including Tregarlan Castle.

'I thought you said National Heritage looked after it,' I'd said when he told us.

'They do, but I'm the onsite caretaker; I look after the place when there's no one else there.'

'You live at Tregarlan!' Talia had exclaimed. 'That's amazing.'

'I only watch over it.' Fisher had shrugged. 'It's no big deal. I have a little apartment there.'

But Talia had thought it a very big deal, and had spent a good while talking to Fisher about the castle and its history, while Jamie and I had simply watched on, occasionally exchanging knowing glances with each other.

Jamie wasn't all bad. I was gradually beginning to realise that. If only he'd spend a little more time being Jamie, and slightly less being Sonny, I think I could begin to warm to him even more.

'So, we've talked plenty about my job, and what I do here in St Felix,' Fisher says now. 'What exactly are you all doing here? I know you're here to watch the weather – but why? What's wrong with what the Wave Watch are doing?'

'Sky,' Jamie says, nodding at me, 'you must be the best person to answer that.'

'There've been some extremely irregular readings taken here over the last few months,' I say, wondering quite how to explain the rest. 'But it's not only the readings, there have been some rather strange observations reported, too.'

'What sort of observations?' Fisher asks.

'Meteorology is a science,' I begin in practised form, ignoring Jamie, who chooses this moment to feign a huge yawn. 'Different types of weather occur due to very specific changes in temperature, air pressure, cloud formation, wind humidity and rain. There are patterns and mathematical equations that have been established and proven over many years. You see—'

'What Sky is trying to say in her roundabout way,' Jamie says, cutting in, 'is that some weird clouds and peculiar weather has been noted over St Felix that don't quite make sense to the bods that record all this stuff. We've been sent here to take a look and to see if we can work out why it might be happening. What?' Jamie asks when I glare at him. 'That's the simple version, isn't it?'

'That doesn't surprise me, actually,' Fisher says, nodding, before I can reply.

'It doesn't?' I ask.

76

'No, there is always something strange going on around here. You only have to ask my grandad; he's witnessed a lot of it. Either that or he's heard about it over the time he's lived here.'

'What sort of things?'

'It's kind of difficult to explain. But there're many folk around here that can tell you stories about the . . . *unusual*, shall we call them, events that have taken place since they came to St Felix.'

'Oh yes,' Talia chips in, when both Jamie and I pull doubtful expressions. 'Both Dec and my Uncle Ant have told me all sorts of stories about the things that have happened. St Felix is supposed to have been blessed by an ancient sorceress called Zethar many hundreds of years ago. It's said that strangers or newcomers who come here with problems have a very good chance of being helped in the same way that the villagers back then looked after and protected Zethar from her persecutors – her magic is said to have cast a spell over the whole town, making it a little bit magical.'

I'm not sure what to say to this, so to be polite I don't say anything. I like Talia and I don't want to offend her by saying what I really think.

But as usual Jamie has lots to say.

'Wow, that's amazing,' he gushes. 'I love old myths and legends like that and Cornwall is full of them, isn't it?'

'It is indeed,' Fisher says. 'Celts, aren't we? Our lands are built on them. If you're interested just go into the pub one night – the Merry Mermaid, by the harbour – and you'll be sure to find someone who'll tell you a tale or two.'

'That sounds like a good plan! What do you say, Sky? Shall we pop over one night and meet a few of the locals?'

'Er . . . perhaps,' I say, again to be polite. Part of me is resistant because I really don't want to sit all night listening to tall tales that are clearly not true, and part of me always struggles in making commitments. I just never know how I'm going to feel when the time comes, and I hate letting people down.

'You don't sound too keen?' Jamie says. 'Come on, I bet even you can let your hair down once in a while.' He gestures at my ponytail.

'Once in a while, yes. But we are here to do a job, remember? This isn't a holiday.'

Jamie shakes his head at me.

'The locals are all very friendly, Sky,' Talia encourages. 'I'm sure you'd feel welcome.'

'I'm sure I would,' I tell her kindly. 'I'm not sure it's my thing, that's all.'

'Don't worry, Talia,' Jamie says, a glint in his eye, 'I don't think Sky is worried how friendly people will be. More that her logical and extremely scientific mind might be challenged by tales of St Felix myth and legend. Is that right, Sky?' he asks, innocently tilting his head to one side.

I give him a withering look, even though he's partly right. 'No, not at all, actually. I'm sure hearing more about St Felix and its history can only help us while we're here. You can never have too much knowledge on any subject.'

'Great! How about tomorrow night, then?' Jamie says keenly, before I can change my mind. 'What about it, Fisher, are you up for a pint or two?'

'I'm always up for a pint, mate!' Fisher says. 'It would be wonderful, though, if *both* ladies would join us?' He looks hopefully at Talia.

'I'd love too, Fisher,' she answers coyly. 'Sky?'

'Oh, all right,' I sigh, 'I give in. But it will have to be after our scheduled shifts have finished, and don't expect me to sit all night listening to fairy stories about a mythical Cornish sorceress!'

'We won't, Captain Science!' Jamie says, mocking me by saluting like Fisher had. 'You never know, you might surprise yourself and actually have fun for once!'

Eight

The Merry Mermaid is a quaint, traditional Cornish pub set right on the front of the harbour. Outside there are wooden benches, which tonight are packed with holidaymakers enjoying the evening sunshine. Inside there is a long bar that runs the length of the L-shaped building, filled with ornate, colourful beer pumps. The seating varies from high stools at the bar to more comfortable banks of plush seating that run along the inside of the pub walls, and a number of tables and chairs dotted about in between.

It is at one of these tables that I now sit with Jamie, Talia and Fisher, while Fitz and Comet lay beside us on the floor in front of a small open fire that, even though it's summer outside, makes the pub feel cosy.

We'd had a good, if uneventful, day on the island. We'd taken shifts to watch St Felix Bay, and we'd recorded the ever-changing weather and anything else we saw that might be considered unusual, which really wasn't much. Even the clouds were behaving themselves today, and I'd begun to wonder if I had actually witnessed anything out of the ordinary yesterday.

I had, though, become a little annoyed with Jamie when I'd gone to take over his shift. Although he seemed to know exactly what had gone on during the time he'd been keeping watch, his notes in our logbook were extremely patchy.

'But nothing much happened!' he'd protested when I pointed out his lack of records. 'What's the point in constantly writing down exactly the same wind speed, or a cloud floating across the sky? It's a beautiful day out there. Shall I draw you a smiling sunshine instead?'

I'd ignored his flippancy. 'We have to record everything, otherwise we won't be able to spot any unusual patterns or configurations that might develop.'

Jamie had rolled his eyes. 'All right, what if I record it on my laptop instead?'

'Why can't you use the logbooks like Talia and I have?'

'It's just so old-fashioned writing everything down, isn't it? The computer is faster and easier.'

'I intend to write everything up digitally at the end of each day. But if we initially record manually, it's quicker and more immediate.'

'Maybe,' Jamie had muttered, but his face had such a look of dismay that I'd been quite shocked.

It was so unusual for him to show any sort of genuine vulnerability, that I'd found myself immediately back-tracking. 'Look, do it your way,' I'd agreed. 'If it makes you happy to take notes directly on to your laptop, then it's fine with me. Just make sure it goes in the logbook afterwards so we have a continuous record.'

'Yes, Sir Captain Sky,' he'd said, saluting with his usual level of playfulness. 'Whatever you say!'

*

'It's a busy old pub, isn't it?' Jamie comments now as we sit sipping on our drinks, chatting to each other while we watch both locals and holidaymakers mix together through the bar. 'They must make a few bob here over the summer months.'

'Yeah,' Fisher agrees. 'There's always a good atmosphere in here, whether its summer or winter, that's much to do with Rita and Richie the owners. They're a lovely couple. Been here years they have.'

'Fisher!' a male voice calls.

I turn as Fisher lifts his hand to a tall, sandy-haired man making his way across the bar towards us. 'Mate, it's been a while,' Fisher says, standing up to greet him. 'How are you?'

'Good. How's things at Tregarlan?'

They have a brief discussion about the castle, and I figure out from what they're saying that this must be one of the owners he'd talked about when I was in the car with him.

'Jake, let me introduce you,' Fisher says, turning to us. 'This is Sky, Talia and Jamie. They're living and working on Aurora for the summer, watching and recording our St Felix weather.'

'Hello,' Jake says, lifting his silver tankard in greeting. 'Nice to meet you, welcome to St Felix.'

'Jake is our local flower grower,' Fisher explains. 'He also owns Tregarlan Castle, where I work.'

'Technically it's my wife, Poppy, who owns it,' Jake explains. 'But it was sort of passed down to both our families. Long story, you know?'

I nod. 'Does your wife own the flower shop too?' I ask. I remember Fisher telling me when I arrived. It's a lovely little shop; I'd noticed it yesterday.

'Yes, she does. She runs it with our friend Amber.' He

glances across at Jamie again. 'I'm sorry, do I know you? You look awfully familiar.'

'I just have one of those faces,' Jamie says quickly, using his excuse from yesterday.

'No, it's something else ...' Jake says with a puzzled expression. 'Oh, I know, you're that weather forecaster chappie, aren't you? Poppy always sits up and takes notice of the weather when you're on the screen; never that interested in it normally. I think I should be jealous.'

'She's probably just interested in the forecast,' Jamie says, looking a tad embarrassed.

'I'll tell myself that next time, shall I?' Jake grins. 'What brings you to St Felix? Are you going to be broadcasting from here?'

I turn my attention away from Jake, while Jamie explains once again that television is playing no part in his visit. Then he has to answer further questions from Fisher about his television career, as this is news to him as well.

I glance around the pub while all this is going on. I really have no interest in hearing more of Jamie's tales about working in TV weather.

There is so much more to meteorology than simply predicting what the weather might do, so people know whether to bring an umbrella when they leave the house or a sunhat. Meteorologists hold many critical positions around the world – vital jobs like working with governments, the armed forces, farmers and aviation.

I'd happily sit and tell people all about what I do. Weather is my passion, and it has been for as long as I can remember. No one is ever interested, though, but mention that you work in television weather and they're hanging on your every word.

As I'm gazing around, trying to block out Jamie's voice, I see a middle-aged man and a woman enter through the pub door. The man is in a wheelchair and he deftly manoeuvres through the crowded pub like he's done it many times before. The landlady, Rita, greets both him and his companion by name so I assume he must be a local.

I notice his wheelchair is one of the small, speedy kinds that tend to be used by people that are permanently disabled. While I'm wondering what's happened to him, he turns to look around the pub and our eyes meet.

To my intense embarrassment, he cheerfully lifts his hand in greeting, so I immediately do the same, hurriedly lowering it when I realise that he'd only done it because I'd been staring at him.

My face is hot as I turn back to my table.

'That's Jack,' Fisher explains, seeing my discomfort. 'He owns the art shop in St Felix. The woman next to him Kate, she owns the craft shop.'

'Do you know *everyone* in this town?' I ask, desperate to change the subject. The last thing I wanted was for Fisher, or anyone for that matter, to think I'd been gawping at someone in a wheelchair.

Fisher laughs. 'St Felix is a bit like that. We get so many holidaymakers that we locals like to stick together.'

'Right, I'd better be going,' I hear Jake say as he finishes up his conversation with Jamie. 'Nice to meet you, Sonny . . . I mean Jamie. I won't let Poppy know you're here in St Felix. I'll let it be a nice surprise for her if she bumps into you.' He winks, and Jamie acknowledges him by lifting up his pint glass.

Jake drains the last of his own beer, and bids us goodbye.

84

He puts his tankard back down on the bar before he leaves, and Rita hurries over to collect it.

'Nice fella,' Jamie says, watching him go.

'Yes, he is,' Fisher agrees. 'Very easy going. Oh, there's Walter; I was wondering if he'd be in tonight.'

We look across at the door Jake is just leaving through, and see him stand aside as an old man wearing a navy-blue fisherman's cap, checked shirt, yellow waistcoat and baggy trousers held up by a brightly coloured scarf comes through the opening. He's using a stick to walk with, but he lifts it to acknowledge the departing Jake, and then makes his way slowly across to the bar.

'Walter is the one you need to speak to about those myths and legends,' Fisher explains. 'What Walt doesn't know about St Felix isn't worth knowing. I'll get him to come over.'

Fisher stands up and heads over to the man at the bar.

'Ready?' Jamie asks me mischievously.

'For?'

'For your very scientific and methodical mind to be severely challenged. If what Fisher says is right, old Walter over there will be able to spin us many a tale about the legends of St Felix.'

'Just because I listen, doesn't mean to say I have to believe it,' I reply defiantly.

'Everyone, this is Walter,' Fisher says, guiding the old man over to our table. 'Walter this is Sky, Talia and Jamie. They're the meteorologists I told you about.' Walter nods his head at us, while Jamie pulls up a chair for him. 'I should probably point out that Walter is also my grandfather,' Fisher says, looking proudly at him. 'Now you sit right here, Walt, and I'll get you that pint I promised. Another round, everyone?' Fisher asks, looking keenly at us.

'I think it's my round next, so I'll come and help you,' Talia offers. 'Same again, everyone?'

Talia takes our requests and she and Fisher head up to the bar together.

'He's a good boy,' Walter says in a deep but gentle Cornish accent as he watches Fisher go. 'But he is prone to fuss – especially over me.' He turns back to us now. 'So, you're staying over on Aurora, are you?'

'Yes, just for the summer,' I reply. 'We're investigating some unusual weather reports.'

'Is that right?' Walter asks, slowly nodding his head. 'And who, may I ask, has filed these unusual reports?'

'The Wave Watch team, I believe. They record most of the weather here, don't they?'

'That's what they'd have you believe,' Walter says mysteriously.

'Are you saying they don't?' Jamie asks with interest.

'Now, I never said that, did I?'

Jamie and I exchange puzzled looks.

'What do you mean?' I'm beginning to wonder if Walter is quite all there.

Walter shrugs. 'They have their ways of recording weather. I have mine. Neither of us is right or wrong. Just different.'

'So you're interested in the weather?' I ask, suddenly remembering what Gerald had told me about Wacky Walter Weather. Now I've met him, the name makes a bit more sense. Walter does seem a bit unconventional, with his colourful dress sense and the slightly odd things he says. But wacky's a bit much. Maybe eccentric would be a better way to describe him.

Walter nods. 'Have been all my life. But I don't use all them fancy gadgets to tell whether there will be rain or the wind is going to change, I use my own methods.'

'Like what?' Jamie asks, clearly intrigued by Fisher's grandfather.

I wait for Walter to refer to things like fir cones, seaweed and other such myths for forecasting weather, but to my surprise he doesn't.

'I use nature,' he says steadily, his beady eyes watching us both to see how we react to this. 'Nature will always tell you what she's up to before she makes her next move. She looks after her own, and prepares them for what's to come.'

'Like when there's lots of berries on bushes in autumn if it's going to be a hard winter?' Jamie asks.

'That's quite basic. But you're on the right track. I use proven methods of calculation that have been passed down through the generations. Before we had all the gadgetry you use today, people were predicting the weather so they knew the best time to harvest their crops. And in these parts fisher-men had to know the best time to head out to sea, to reduce the risk of drowning if high winds should blow in when they were already out in their boats.'

'What's your success rate like?' Jamie asks.

'Pretty high,' Walter says with assurance. 'What's yours?'

Jamie grins. 'Luckily for me I only present the weather; it's people like Sky who do all the hard work.'

Walter turns to me. 'I have a feeling, Sky, that my methods are as far away from yours as Land's End is from John O'Groats.'

I smile. 'You might be right.'

'But the reason you've been sent here isn't. I too have noticed some odd weather patterns that can't quite be explained.'

'You have?' I ask, suddenly eager to hear more. 'Like what?'

'Here we go,' Fisher announces, as he expertly places three pints of beer down on the table. 'One for you, Walt, one for Jamie and my own.'

'Here you are, Sky,' Talia says, placing my own drink – an orange juice and fizzy water – in front of me.

'Thank you,' I say, smiling at her. 'Everything all right?'

'Oh yes,' she says, glancing shyly at Fisher. 'Very much so.'

'Now, Walter, have you been telling my friends here all about the myths and legends of St Felix?' Fisher asks, lifting his fresh pint of beer.

'No, lad, we've been discussing the weather, of all things,' Walter says, drinking from his own pint.

'Ah, I should have known – your favourite subject! Walt here fancies himself as a bit of an amateur weather forecaster.'

'I'll give you amateur,' Walter says good-naturedly. 'I'm as accurate as that lot at Met Central any day. So then, what is it you would like to know about St Felix?'

Walter spends the next half-hour or so telling us tales about St Felix and the supposed magic that's said to surround the town – thanks to the Cornish sorceress that Talia and Fisher had mentioned.

'But I'll tell you something,' he says, just as I've begun to drift away into my own thoughts, 'there is one myth, legend, call it a prediction if you like, that should be of some concern to us.'

'What's that?' Jamie, who has been lapping up every word Walter has been entertaining us with, asks eagerly.

'It's said that before Zethar left St Felix, she had an important warning for the townsfolk, and that warning has been passed down through every generation that's lived here since.'

'What was it?' Talia asks, agog.

'She said, "If winter should fall on a blood-red summer sky, the town will flood and many will die . . ." '

'Gosh,' Talia says, looking worried. 'That would be awful. I wonder what she meant, winter on a blood-red summer sky? How can it be winter in a summer sky?'

Walter shrugs and looks enquiringly at me. But unlike the others I remain completely unaffected by all this folklore.

'Let's hope this summer it doesn't snow during a sunset then,' I say, smiling to myself as I lift my drink from the table. 'Otherwise, we're all doomed.'

'Ooh, do you think it could be that?' Talia asks, still wide-eyed. 'That would fit, wouldn't it?'

'Talia, you're a meteorology student! Pull yourself together. When is it ever going to snow in the summer by the Cornish coast? They barely get snow here in winter, let alone in the height of summer during sunrise or sunset!'

'True,' Talia says ruefully, looking at Walter. 'It's not very likely to happen. But then I guess that's a good thing, isn't it?'

'And I would have agreed with you both until this year,' Walter says nodding. 'But like I said before, I too have noticed some unusual weather activity lately. I've been watching the weather in Cornwall for more years than I can remember. If winter should fall on a blood-red summer sky at any time, I'd lay money this summer is as good a time as any.'

Nine

'What did you think to Walter?' Jamie asks after we've sailed back across to the island.

We'd left Fisher to walk Talia back to her uncle's flat above the bakery, and then we'd set off from the harbour, across a moonlit sea.

Although the small lighthouse at the end of the harbour gave us some light to make the crossing, the full moon added the little bit extra I needed to feel safe.

Jamie had been very good while we were making the crossing. After enquiring if I needed any help, he'd sat quietly in the back of the boat looking after the dogs while I concentrated on getting us safely home.

But now we are cosied up in the watchtower, drinking mugs of hot tea before bed. I'm in my nightclothes, with a dressing gown wrapped tightly around me, and Jamie is in a loose T-shirt and pyjama bottoms, and is quiet no longer as he reverts back to his usual inquisitive nature.

'I quite liked him,' I reply. 'He reminded me of my own grandfather.'

'Oh, yes,' Jamie says, pricking up his ears, 'the home-made weather station you told me about. This must be where you got your love of the weather from.'

'Yes, Grandad and I used to spend a lot of time together in his shed. He had all his equipment in there because my grandmother wouldn't let him have it in the house. But unlike Walter, we used equipment to make our forecasts, not nature.'

I smile now at the memory of sitting snuggled up in Grandad's shed with a blanket over my knees, my hands clutching a mug of hot chocolate to keep warm. I would watch, fascinated, as my grandad took readings from all his 'gadgets', as he called them, taking the time to explain to me what they all meant, and how that would affect what would happen next in the skies outside.

'Nice,' Jamie says. 'You don't speak much about your family.'

'Do I need to?'

'No, but I'm interested. Do you still see your grandfather?'

'He died a few years ago.' *Not long before I got ill*, I think to myself. *I'm glad he never saw me at my worst. He would have worried far too much.*

'I'm sorry,' Jamie says, looking it. 'You have other family?'

'Yes, my parents live not far from Oxford. No brothers or sisters, though, before you ask.'

'Only child, eh? Me too.'

I nod.

'What do your parents think of you being here?'

'They're fine with it,' I reply carefully. The truth is they were overjoyed when I told them I was taking this job. They had been used to me travelling the world with my career, and wouldn't have thought anything of me taking a job down here in Cornwall. Compared to some of my previous postings, this was local. But things had changed, and they knew now if I was going to be working again my health must definitely have improved. I'd rung Mum a couple of times since I'd arrived to let her know how I was getting on, and I could tell by her voice how happy she was that I was coping and things were going well.

The pressure to make a success of this was everywhere. But nowhere was that pressure greater than in my own head.

'Just fine?' Jamie asks quizzically.

'*Yes* . . . What else do you want me to say?'

'Nothing.' Jamie holds up his hands in surrender. 'Nothing at all.'

'You have family?' I ask, trying to make amends for closing him down. But if I opened up any more about my family, who knows what else might escape?

Jamie nods. 'Not a large one, though. My dad walked out on us when I was young, so Mum brought me up alone. I'm still very close to her.'

'She must be very proud of what you've achieved.'

'She is. It wasn't easy for her back then; she had to work two jobs, and I wasn't exactly an easy child to look after, as I'm sure you can imagine.'

I smile as I visualise Jamie as a young boy – full of cheek and likely getting away with all sorts of mischief.

'To have a son on television must be very special for her.'

'I think so.'

My opinion of Jamie has begun to change. Before, I'd assumed everything he'd done in life must have come easily to him. He certainly exuded the sort of charm that made you think everything he did was smooth and effortless. But now I know a little of his background I realise that patter has probably come from years of having to stand on his own two feet a tad more than most children did.

'Coming back to Walter,' Jamie says when we've sat for a moment or two with our own thoughts. 'What did you think to what he told us – about the sorceress's premonition?'

'Not a lot,' I reply calmly, sipping from my mug.

'What do you mean *not a lot*? He virtually told us that St Felix was doomed to flood if there was some freak weather here.'

'Exactly. Freak weather. It rarely happens – contrary to what the media would have you believe. Over the last few years, as a result of global warming, the world *has* been experiencing more unusual weather, and there've been some terrible floods and fires as a result. But to the extent Walter is suggesting, in this country?' I shake my head. 'Nope, not going to happen.'

Jamie smiles.

'If you were expecting me to come away from that pub believing in Cornish pixies, and some fairy story about a sorceress and a prophecy,' I continue, 'then I really haven't been showing you my true personality since we met.'

Jamie studies me for a moment, which I find a little unnerving, so I look away from him out towards the bay window.

'You've tried to show me the side of you that you think people should see,' Jamie says, to my surprise. 'But I don't think you've shown me the real you – not just yet, anyway.'

Feeling even more uncomfortable, I go over and pretend to be studying the instruments on the desk. In addition to our manual observations and readings, we also have some automatic weather recording equipment set up for when we aren't officially 'on watch' during the night, or for the occasional times during the day when someone isn't able to be in the watchtower.

I glance up and watch the few clouds that are occasionally floating past the bright full moon. They keep forming into the shape of those theatre masks – the happy and sad ones – and they cover and uncover the moon over and over again so the moon looks like a face popping out from behind its chosen mask.

'Nothing was unusual in the automated readings when we got back,' I say, pretending to thumb casually through the logbook while I watch the night sky in amazement. But as quickly as it had begun, the clouds soon return to normal as if nothing has happened, and continue their gentle meandering across the sky.

Am I imagining this? I wonder. *First the peace symbol and now the masks?*

'Don't change the subject,' Jamie says from behind me.

'I'm not,' I say, turning around now. 'I was just remarking that nothing unusual happened.' *When we were out, anyway.*

'So even you're expecting it to at some point, then?'

'No, not really.' I move away from the window. 'But something odd must have been happening for them to have sent us here in the first place. I don't know if you're aware, but most weather recording is done automatically these days; it's rare for Met Central to station one person at a weather centre, let alone three.'

'So why you?' Jamie asks.

'What do you mean?' I sit back down on the sofa next to Fitz.

'I mean of all the people that could have been chosen, why were you picked to come here? From what I've heard, you are a well-respected, eminent meteorologist at Met Central. Why did you want to come to Cornwall of all places and watch the weather? Lovely though the view through that window is.'

'I felt like doing something a little quieter for a change.'

This wasn't that far from the truth. I did need to do something peaceful and calm right now. It just made everything that little bit easier.

'Sure . . .' Jamie says, looking at me with disbelief.

'What's wrong with that? Why do you have to question what I say all the time, like I'm lying or something?' I stroke Fitz so vigorously he wakes up and looks at me with a confused expression.

I can't help it, Jamie gets to me. He's always pushing for more. Part of me wants to tell him – tell him everything. But I know if I do that any authority I might have here would immediately disappear, and instead be replaced by sympathetic looks and, worse still, pity. And I've had enough pity to last me a lifetime.

'I don't think you're lying as such,' Jamie says earnestly, 'but I do get the feeling you're hiding something from me.'

The room is suddenly quiet, so all we can hear as we sit in the watchtower is the waves lapping gently against the rocks at the base of the house, and the clock ticking rhythmically on the wall.

'Something you don't want to tell me,' Jamie suggests when I don't say anything. 'Am I right?'

'You might be,' I hear myself saying in a quiet voice, thinking of the clouds I saw out of the window a few moments ago. *Maybe it was time I lifted my own mask just a tad and was a little more honest with him.*

'I know you think I'm just some buffoon who stands in front of a weather map,' Jamie says, watching me. 'But just because I didn't spend years passing all sorts of exams like you did, I'm not a bad person. I can be quite a good listener if you try me?'

'Do you ever stop talking long enough to listen?' I ask, attempting to lighten the moment. *Part of me is wavering, I can feel it, and I'll try any diversion to stop what I'm desperate to keep hidden from spilling out.*

But instead of seeing the funny side as I expect him to, Jamie simply looks hurt by my comment. 'For someone who is meant to be good at observing, Sky, you really haven't bothered to look that deeply with me, have you? Perhaps if you tried a little harder you might see there's more to me than you think.'

I stare at Jamie for a moment.

'I think we both might be a little tired?' I suggest. This was not the reaction I was expecting at all and I'm momentarily confused by my thoughts, and by my feelings too. 'Maybe we should go to bed now?'

'Sure,' Jamie says, turning away to stroke Comet. 'If that's what you want.'

'Golly!' I say, feigning surprise, still desperate to break the tension in the room. 'No, raising of your eyebrows or suggestive comments? I suggest us going to bed and you say absolutely nothing?'

'You hate it when I do that,' Jamie says, still not buying into my fake joviality.

'Yes, but that's you, isn't it? You always make light of everything.'

'Like I said just now, try looking a little harder, Sky. You might be surprised by what you find.'

Still feeling bewildered by this new version of Jamie sitting in front of me, I lift Fitz and head towards the door. 'Goodnight, Jamie,' I say, pausing there for a moment. 'I'll see you in the morning?'

'Goodnight, Sky,' Jamie says, still not looking at me, but staring out of the window now. 'Sleep well, won't you?'

I nod as I leave the room and head quickly downstairs to my

bedroom, still feeling bad not only that I haven't been more honest with Jamie, but that I seem to have upset him as well.

And that strange mix of feelings keeps me awake far longer than I want once I actually get into bed.

Jamie is everything I try to avoid in people – loud, confident, energetic and a bit full of himself. But there's something about him that gets to me, another side that I'm just beginning to discover. And until I figure out how to deal with the mixed feelings that he seems to conjure up within me, I know I'm going to spend many more restless nights thinking about him.

Ten

The next morning I'm on the early shift.

Even though last night's conversation is still playing on my mind, I'm glad I went to bed when I did. As I go about the hourly tasks of registering the wind speeds, air pressure, rainfall, humidity and anything else worth noting, I already feel weary. *You're going to have to be careful, Sky,* I tell myself. *You need to get enough rest; otherwise you're going to be in trouble.*

But my early-morning start is more than made up for by the sight of a beautiful sunrise over the bay. As I pause to watch it for a moment or two, my attention is caught by a little red motorboat heading out around the bay.

Nothing unusual in that – we often see craft, mainly fishing boats heading out and returning with the day's catch. There's also a regular stream of larger passenger boats taking day-trippers when the sea is calm enough, but they tend to head the other way around the bay. This boat is heading towards the choppier waters that surround a large group of rocks not far from the island, and it's already bouncing and bobbing around in the waves.

'I hope you know what you're doing,' I mutter as I begin typing up yesterday's notes from our logbook, looking out every now and then to check on the boat. 'It's hard enough crossing from the mainland to here, let alone around that way. Damn, what have you written here, Jamie? Your handwriting is terrible, no wonder you prefer writing on a computer.'

The boat disappears around the base of the island so I can't see it any more from the watchtower, and I carry on with my work.

I glance up occasionally to look out of the window, and at the equipment, and I'm surprised to see some of the dials suddenly dancing around.

'What *are* you doing?' I say, tapping the side of the barometer. 'You shouldn't be reading that in this weather?'

The dials return to normal, so I watch them for a moment to make sure they're working normally, and then I'm about to return to my laptop, when I glance out of the window again. Salmon-pink clouds have begun to form against the backdrop of the paler blossom-coloured sky. It's not the striking colours that make me continue to watch the clouds, but their shape. One cumulus cloud in particular seems to be forming into the shape of a boat as it moves across the sky. Not just any boat, but a small motorboat, much like the one I just saw on the water. The wispy stratus clouds below it are also changing to look more like stratocumulus and now almost resemble . . . *No, they can't be*, I think, staring even harder. But they are, the clouds are making themselves look like the crests of waves, so the boat can bob along on top of them, just like the motorboat had been doing a few minutes ago.

I stare at the incredible cloud formations, but they only last a few seconds before the detailed picture the clouds have created begins to change and fade away.

'Well,' I say, still staring out of the window. 'How very odd, Fitz.'

But Fitz is snoozing at my feet, not bothered in the slightest that anything out of the ordinary has occurred.

When Jamie makes his first appearance of the day up in the watchtower, still wearing his T-shirt and pyjama bottoms, I feel immediately uncomfortable.

'All right?' he says affably, looking bleary-eyed and unshaven. His dark hair is tousled and unkempt, very unlike the way it usually appears. 'I made you a cup of tea.' He passes me a mug.

'Thank you.' I take the tea, immensely grateful not only for the hot beverage now in my hands, but also that Jamie doesn't seem to want to discuss what was said last night.

'Much been happening?' he asks, looking out of the window and then down at my notes.

'You missed a rather lovely sunrise.'

'You were here *that* early?'

'I didn't actually see the sun rise, but the sky was a beautiful colour early this morning ... and there were some *interesting* cloud formations, too.'

'Really, like what?'

'Oh, nothing you need to worry about,' I say, changing my mind. If I share with Jamie what I've just seen he'll probably only mock me, and I don't want to create animosity between us again. 'There was a little boat that went the other way around the bay, which is unusual.'

'The rocky way?' Jamie asks, perching on the edge of the desk.

'Yes.'

'They must have known what they were doing. Didn't you say Fisher had warned you not to go that way?'

'He did, and all his advice to me so far has been spot on.'

Jamie nods, apparently considering this. 'Do you think Fisher likes our Talia as much as Talia seems to like him?' he asks suddenly.

I'm surprised by his question. 'Er, I'm not sure. I hope so. She seems pretty keen.'

'He's a good-looking fella, why wouldn't she be? The guy is in good shape and he has a great personality. He's a catch, as the young folk would say.'

I laugh. 'I'm not sure the young folk, as you call them, would say that!'

Jamie shrugs. 'I'm not really that up with the latest lingo. What do they say now, then?'

'How would I know? It's a while since I've considered myself young. He's hot, perhaps? Fit? That kind of thing.'

'Yeah, that's probably more like it. You said you're not young, but you must be younger than me – those stairs were a killer on my knees this morning, and I thought I was fit – fit in the work-out sense, you understand. Not in the context you just mentioned.'

I grin now; it's quite refreshing to hear Jamie talk about himself in a more downbeat way. 'They are quite steep; I struggle with them too.' Although it isn't just my knees that suffer every time I climb the stairs, but my weak leg muscles too. 'How old *are* you, then? Your real age, I mean, not your stage age!'

Jamie grins. 'Ah, you know me too well. I'm closer to forty than fifty, if that helps. What about you?'

'I'm also closer to forty . . . than thirty,' I say, smiling.

Jamie thinks about this. 'Very clever. So, we're practically the same age. I guessed as much.'

'Technically I'm a little younger. But yes, I suppose so. Does that surprise you?'

'Your need for sleep and rest gives you away,' Jamie says. 'It comes to us all eventually.'

'I can't lie. I do need my sleep these days.'

'Nothing wrong with that. It's obviously working.'

'Working?'

'Your beauty sleep,' Jamie says, grinning. 'That's a compliment, by the way. You seem to have trouble spotting them.'

'Oh . . . thank you,' I reply, choosing not to inform him that my need for sleep has little to do with a beauty regime.

'So,' Jamie asks, 'is there a Mr Sky in the picture? You told me a little about your family last night, but you haven't mentioned a significant other since we've been here.'

I feel myself stiffen, and not just because he's mentioned last night. 'No, there's not, actually.'

'A Mrs Sky, then?'

'No. There was a boyfriend, but I'm single now . . . and much better for it,' I add before I can stop myself.

'Nasty break-up, was it?' Jamie asks sympathetically. 'We've all had them.'

How does he know . . . ? I'm just beginning to wonder when Jamie continues: 'Did you dump him or the other way around?'

'Look, I'm really not comfortable talking about this.' I turn away from him on the swivel chair, hugging my tea closely to me.

'Sure, I get the picture; I won't say anything further on the matter. You really aren't happy discussing your personal life with me, are you? How about we converse on the weather and nothing else?'

I feel bad; it isn't Jamie's fault I'm a bit touchy on certain matters, but he does keep pushing me on topics I'm not comfortable talking about.

'Look, if you must know I haven't been in a relationship for some time, and I don't intend to be either. I'm past all that; relationships are far too much trouble, cause too much hurt, and use up too much energy. There,' I say, turning back just enough so I can see him again, 'is that sufficient information for you?'

'Sure, no worries. I totally get it – I'm getting a divorce, remember? That isn't exactly plain sailing. I promise I won't say another word.' He pulls an imaginary zip over his lips, then he drinks silently from his mug.

I sigh, and turn back to the window.

'Have you had breakfast yet?' he asks after a moment or two.

I have to smile. 'That zip isn't very strong, is it?'

'I didn't say I wouldn't speak, just I wouldn't try and converse with you about relationships.'

'Fair enough, I'll take that. No, I haven't. Are you offering to make me some?'

'Of course! Cooked breakfast it is, then!' He jumps up off the desk with his usual zest. 'We got more eggs, didn't we?'

'We did.'

'Great, even I can scramble eggs. I'll give you a shout in a few minutes.'

'You better bring it up here. I can't leave the watchtower until Talia gets here at ten.'

'Righty-ho, Captain!' Jamie says, saluting. 'Down to the galley it is for me then. See you in a bit.'

That man is irrepressible, I think as I hear him bounding back down the stairs whistling.

But as I look out of the window again, I realise I actually kind of like it.

'Are you okay?' I ask Talia as she settles herself into the seat in front of the window. 'You don't need anything before we go?'

'Nope, I'm absolutely fine,' Talia says happily, arranging herself in front of all the recording equipment.

'Did Fisher see you back to your uncle's house okay last night?' I ask as casually as I can.

'Yes, thank you,' she replies coyly. 'And he's asked me out on a proper date!'

'No, really?' I say, unbelievably pleased for her. Her face is a picture of happiness as she recounts what happened outside the bakery last night.

'He seems like a lovely chap,' I reassure her. 'I'm happy for you. I hope it goes well.'

'So do I,' she says, her cheeks pink. 'Oh, I almost forgot, I bumped into Walter on his way out of the bakery this morning. He wondered if you'd pop in and see him some time at his house.'

'Did he? Why?'

Talia shrugs. 'I don't know? Maybe he has something else to tell you about the prophecy.'

'Please don't call it that. It's hearsay, that's all. A tall tale passed down and embellished through many generations, I have no doubt. This Zethar likely never even existed.'

'Ooh, don't say that when you're in St Felix,' Talia says, looking shocked. 'You'll be thrown out of the town. Nearly everyone believes in Zethar and her happiness spell. Did you know that Felix means happy? That's where the name for the town originally came from.'

'Really?' I reply, not sounding entirely convinced.

'Yes, just ask my uncle or Dec about it if you want to know more. They know all about the magical things that have happened in St Felix's past.'

'I might just do that sometime. Right, our plan this morning is to take the dogs over to the mainland for a longer walk and then pick up a few things. If you think you'll be all right here we might be able to call in on Walter before the tide changes.'

'Yes, you do that. I'll be absolutely fine. Ooh,' she says, looking at the logbook, 'you had pink stratocumulus this morning? That must have looked incredible from up here?'

'Yes, it was pretty special,' I reply, thinking again of the red boat. 'Talia, you know a fair bit about this area. Is it ever safe for boats to go out of the bay and around the rocks the other way? I mean, opposite to the way Fisher told me to go.'

'It's unusual, and I'd say pretty dangerous, but I guess it can be done if you know the area well enough. Why would you attempt it, though, when you can go the other way safely? It only takes a little bit longer.'

'Yes, that's what I wondered too . . . ' I shake my head. 'Never mind, it doesn't matter now. Right, we'll see you later then. Have fun.'

'Oh, I will do,' Talia says, already picking up the binoculars and looking out of the window. 'I don't need encouragement!'

I smile as I make my way downstairs and outside.

It is really lovely to be working with someone as young and keen as Talia. In recent years I've worked with a lot of older, more experienced meteorologists and as clever and knowledgeable as they are, they lack the pure joy and enthusiasm that Talia has for the role.

'What are you smiling about?' Jamie asks as I meet him by the boat.

'Talia,' I say, lifting Fitz up into the boat, and encouraging Comet to follow. 'It's so lovely to be working with someone so keen and passionate about the weather.'

'That reminds me of someone . . .' Jamie says, untying the mooring and climbing aboard beside me.

'Who?'

'You, of course!' He sits down with the dogs while I manoeuvre the boat out of the little harbour. 'I can imagine you living and breathing everything weather when you were first at university.'

'I can't recall a time I wasn't interested in it,' I reply, steering the boat away from the island and out into the waves. 'It's been my whole life for as long as I can remember.'

'Can I get a turn at steering *Doris* today?' Jamie calls from the back of the boat. 'I'm sure the dogs would be more than happy for us to swap.'

'Sure, it's not difficult. Come up here and I'll show you.'

I give Jamie a quick lesson in how everything works and then I stand beside him while he steers. Fitz and Comet are happily sitting in the back of the boat, their ears flapping in the wind as we travel across the waves. *It must be like an extreme and probably better version of your head out of a car window*, I think, watching them with their eyes half closed and their tongues lolling out of their mouths.

Jamie, too, looks incredibly happy as he steers the boat over the waves.

'This is fun!' he calls, his own hair blowing in the breeze. He turns to me, smiling, and I easily return his smile. It's always lovely to make others happy, and I'm grateful that this weather project is bringing so much joy to those around me.

*

When we arrive at St Felix, I help Jamie steer the boat into the harbour and then because the tide is only halfway in I have to climb up the little ladder on the side of the harbour wall to tie the rope to our mooring post.

Then we all alight from the boat and head to the beach, where we run the dogs around for about half an hour, throwing balls along the sand.

'So, where to next?' Jamie asks when we've all had enough of the sand.

'First we need some supplies – so we'll have to pop to the supermarket as well as the bakery.'

'Yep, I definitely need some more of those Cornish pasties,' Jamie says longingly.

'You mean you *want* some.'

'No, I *need* them!' He grins. 'Where else?'

'Talia said Walter would like to see us. Actually, she said me, but I think she meant both of us.'

'Really – why?'

'Don't know,' I say, shrugging. I look at my watch. 'The thing is we don't have that much time before the tide turns. We can't be all day.'

'How about you take the dogs and go and visit Walter, and I get the shopping today?' Jamie offers.

'Are you sure? You loved listening to Walter's tall tales!'

'Maybe if you spend a little more time with him, you'll take him more seriously? I think he has a lot to offer us. Sure, his weather forecasting methods are a little different to ours, but he certainly knows his stuff. It might help us to understand the weather here a little more.'

I look doubtfully at him, but I appreciate his offer.

'All right then, I'll go and see Walter, you get the

107

shopping.' I reach into my bag. 'Here's the list,' I say, holding out a piece of paper. 'Try not to get too carried away in the bakery!'

'As if!' Jamie says, shaking his head. 'Don't worry, I don't need the list. I heard what you and Talia were saying earlier when you wrote it, I'll remember.'

'Are you sure? Why not just take it to be sure?'

Jamie takes the paper from me and shoves it in his pocket. 'And here's the purse.'

Jamie hesitates again. 'Do I have to carry a purse?' he asks, taking it from me warily. 'Can't I just use my card and then you reimburse me later?'

'Count yourself lucky,' I say, assuming he doesn't want to carry a woman's purse, 'that I picked up my Kipling purse this morning – it's a nice plain navy, it could have been my Cath Kidston one that has flowers all over it.'

Jamie looks at the purse the same way he looked at the list, but he takes it reluctantly and hurriedly stuffs it in the pocket of his jeans.

'Will Comet be okay with me?' I ask as Jamie clips on her lead.

'Yes, she knows you now, she'll be fine. Won't you, girl?' he says, ruffling her head. Comet looks up at him lovingly as he feeds her a treat, then Jamie reaches down and gives Fitz one too, which he gobbles up immediately.

'I'll meet you back by the boat in an hour?' I say, looking at my watch again. 'Hopefully that should be enough time.'

'Great, I'll see you then,' Jamie says and he sets off in the direction of the town.

Comet watches Jamie for a moment as he departs without her, then she looks up at me. 'It's all right,' I tell her, ruffling her ears. 'He won't be long. Right, come on, you two,' I say, giving a little tug on both their leads, 'we're heading this way.'

We walk around the outside of St Felix, following the coastal path. Talia has told me where to find Walter's cottage, and this seems like the best, if not the shortest, way to get to it without taking the two dogs through the busy part of the town.

'Imagine living here permanently,' I say, chatting to the dogs as we go. 'The views here are stunning, and there's some lovely walks for the two of you. London will seem a very poor alternative after we've spent our summer here.'

As we follow the path – the sea on one side of us, and mostly holiday properties on the other – we come to a hill with a large area of short mown grass on one side. There's a little path that cuts through the centre of the hill; it isn't strictly on the way to Walter's, but it looks so pretty I decide to take it. This is an area that Jamie and I haven't yet reached on our walks, so I'm keen to explore further.

The hill seems to be popular with dog walkers, and there are already a number of dogs running about off their leads on the grassy mound.

Comet pulls towards them keenly. 'I'm not sure I should be letting you off your lead when Jamie's not here?' I tell her. 'You might have to stay on it this time, I'm afraid.'

But Comet has other ideas and begins to pull hard up the hill towards the other dogs. Fitz takes her lead and does the same. So suddenly two dogs – a big strong one, and a much smaller, but just as determined one – are tugging me up the hill.

'Hey, slow down,' I call as they bound up the hill together, pulling me faster then I want to go. Suddenly, a golden Labrador races past us on the path, and as Comet pulls just that little bit harder to keep up with him, I feel her lead slip from my hand.

'Comet – no!' I call as she bounds up the hill without me. 'I don't think so,' I tell Fitz as he tries to do the same. 'I can keep hold of you!'

'*Comet!*' I call again, this time more breathlessly, as Comet, her lead trailing behind her, bounds towards the Labrador, who is now running around on the grass. I have to stop for a moment to catch my breath. *Damn, why am I so unfit these days? Years ago, I could have chased both dogs up this hill without any difficulties whatsoever.*

'Are you all right?' a male voice asks, as a man in a sporty-looking wheelchair comes alongside me. I recognise him as the man from the pub, who Fisher had called Jack. It's clear he takes his fitness seriously, because now he's closer to me I can see along with the sporty wheelchair and exercise clothes, he has a well-defined chest, strong shoulders and huge biceps, on which several military-looking tattoos are etched.

'Yes,' I say, slightly less breathlessly. 'I'm fine. Thank you.'

'Would you like me to fetch your dog?' he asks, looking across at the dogs playing together.

'Oh no, please don't put yourself out. She's not actually my dog; I'm looking after her for someone. Fitz,' I say, looking down at him, patiently watching the others having fun, 'is mine.'

Jack puts his finger to his lips and produces a shrill whistle. 'Barney!' he calls. 'Come here!'

Barney stops what he's doing, and pricks up his ears, so Jack whistles again.

The dog then comes racing back towards us with Comet following close behind.

'Good boy,' Jack says, giving Barney a treat from his pocket.

'Comet!' I say in a stern voice as she arrives beside us with her lead still trailing on the ground. 'That was naughty.' I grab her lead and she looks remorsefully up at me.

'No harm done,' Jack says pleasantly. 'Not to me, anyway. You look like you've had better days. Are you sure you're all right? You look a little pale.'

'I'm fine, really. I'm just a bit tired.'

Jack looks perceptively at me. 'There's a bench over there; why don't you take a seat? I'd join you, but as you can see I already have my own!'

I nod gratefully at him and we make our way to the bench.

'Why don't you let them off their leads so they can play with Barney?' Jack suggests, looking at Comet and Fitz gloomily settling down beside me. 'Can you trust them normally?'

'Yes, they're both usually really good.'

'Well, then? Barney won't stray too far away, I promise.'

I unhook Comet and Fitz's leads and they both bound off with Barney down on to the grass while Jack and I watch them from the top of the hill.

'Barney isn't really my dog either; he was my partner's before we moved in together. We've been together a couple of years, so I guess it's okay if I call him mine now.'

'Kate is your partner, isn't she? She runs the craft shop and you run the art shop in town.'

'Yes, that's right, I'm Jack. How did . . . ? Oh, I saw you down the pub with Fisher the other night, didn't I? Yes, I remember you now. You're one of the people over on Aurora watching the weather. Don't look too surprised; things don't stay quiet around here for long.'

'Yes, I am one of the meteorologists on the island. I'm Sky, by the way.' I hesitate for a moment. 'I'm sorry if you thought I was staring at you in the pub,' I say, feeling suddenly awkward. 'I really wasn't, you know?'

'It's fine; I'm used to it. I've been in a wheelchair long enough not to be bothered by people having a good gawp.'

'But I wasn't. I mean, not like that. I was actually admiring your chair, it looks ... nifty,' I try, not really finding the right word.

'Yes, she's certainly nifty,' Jack says, smiling. 'Why the interest?'

I hesitate again. I really don't like talking about this, but I wasn't likely to see Jack again, was I, so what did it matter for once if I did?

'I had to use one for a while,' I tell him quickly. 'It was more an electric wheelchair really; I wasn't strong enough to push one around like you are.'

Jack nods, not appearing to be thrown by this confession like most people are if I ever have to mention it, which I rarely ever do. 'And why was that?'

'I had ... no I *have* an illness. It was so bad that until about ten months ago I had to use a chair to get around. When I first had Fitz, I had to have a dog walker because I wasn't strong enough to take him out on my own.'

'Bad luck,' Jack says, so matter-of-factly it's refreshing. Usually people become over-sympathetic if I share that information with them, and there will be comments like *You poor thing!* and *How awful for you.* 'At least you're not in one now, though – how come?'

'I got better—' But I have to correct myself again. 'Let's just say it's under control at the moment.'

'Good for you. What is it – cancer, MS?'

'ME, actually,' I say, assuming he won't have heard of this. People rarely have, and even if they do know of it, they usually don't understand exactly what it is.

'Oh, that's a tough one,' Jack says to my surprise. 'Hidden illnesses always are. It's okay for me – people can see I'm disabled. There's no messing around, here I am in my chair. But when you have a hidden disability its tough, no one knows. You can't see it, even though it can be just as bad, sometimes even worse than a physical impairment.'

I stare at him. No one I've ever met outside of my occupational therapist and my immediate family has ever got it quite as quickly, or summed it up quite so succinctly. Even my so-called boyfriend at the time, who on hearing my diagnosis had not even attempted to understand. In fact, he left me not long after, telling me he couldn't cope with illness. It 'wasn't his thing'.

I feel tears springing into my eyes so I hurriedly look away at the dogs.

'They're having a great time,' Jack says, following my gaze. 'I said they would. Is that why you were so out of breath on the hill?'

I turn back to him. 'Yes, I used to be really fit – running, the gym, etc. That hill wouldn't have fazed me at all. But now . . . '

'Bit like climbing Mount Everest, is it?' Once again Jack hits the nail on the head.

I nod.

'I get it. I was super fit too before I stupidly stepped on a landmine when I was in the army and ended up in this.'

'You still look pretty fit to me,' I say, admiring his muscular arms.

'Thanks, I've tried to keep in shape, but I'm not the person I was before.'

'That's what I hate the most – not being able to be *that* person.'

'I hate to sound like I'm preaching,' Jack says, suddenly serious, 'but people told me what I'm about to tell you, and I didn't believe them. But now I understand they were completely right.'

'Go on,' I say when he pauses.

'Until you fully accept you'll never be *that* person again, you'll never move on, not properly.'

I think about this.

'Are you still trying to be the same person you were before you got ill?' Jack asks.

'Probably,' I admit. 'I think I put far too much pressure on myself trying to be what I consider "normal".'

'There you go, then. Trust me; it's not easy, but once you let the old you go, and move on with the new version of you, it gets a lot easier, believe me.'

'I do believe you. But it's so hard . . . '

'I know it is. But you'll come to it in your own time, you can't rush it.'

Jack's phone begins to ring, so he pulls it from his pocket.

'Sorry, got to take this – it's the missus! Hey, Kate, what's up?'

I watch the dogs running around on the grass, while Jack takes his call.

Fitz has given up trying to compete with the other two big dogs, and is doing his own thing, investigating some little rocks not far away from them.

You know when it's time to move on to something new, don't you, Fitz? I think, watching him happily sniff the rocks on his own. *Do you think you can teach me how to let go, so I can move on too?*

114

Eleven

'Did you manage to get everything?' I ask as I meet Jamie back at the boat. I'd never got to Walter's after meeting Jack, but I hoped it might wait until another day now. I'm still feeling pretty exhausted and I just wanted to get back to the island and have a rest.

'Most of it,' Jamie says, looking slightly flustered as he bends down to fuss Comet.

'Why only most?'

'I got a little held up . . .'

'Why would you— Oh, wait, were your many fans out in force this afternoon?'

'I can't help it if I'm popular, can I?' Jamie says, grinning as he stands up again.

'Don't give me that,' I say. 'You love all the attention.'

'Sometimes. Sometimes not so much. But I can't just ignore people, can I? They'll think I'm an arrogant arse if I walk away when they ask for a selfie or an autograph. I've been called a few names before when I've been in a hurry and haven't been able to stop.'

'Really?'

'Yeah, one time I'd just left the dentist. My mouth was all numb and a bit swollen and I was trying to get to my car and go home. But some woman cornered me in the car park and asked me for a selfie. When I mumbled that I was sorry but I couldn't do it that day, she went off on a right one.'

'What is wrong with some people?' I say, shaking my head.

'It can actually be quite scary suddenly being approached by complete strangers who think they know you because they've seen you on TV. Especially when you're surrounded by a crowd,' he continues. 'No wonder really famous people employ a security guard. One polite lady wanting a quick selfie with me is usually fine, but a gang of drunk women on a hen night can be pretty terrifying!'

'I can imagine,' I reply quietly, not really knowing what to say to this. Yet again Jamie has surprised me, and made me think differently about him. 'So, getting back to our shopping, what *did* you manage to get before you were bombarded by fans?'

Jamie runs quickly through the list from memory.

'Sounds like you got everything,' I say when he's finished. 'Did you use the list in the end?'

'Nope, all up here!' Jamie says, tapping the side of his head.

'One thing you forgot. You didn't go to the bakery.'

'I know!' Jamie cries with a look of anguish. 'And that's my favourite part! I was on my way there when a few people began to recognise me.'

I look at my watch. 'We might just have time if you hurry.'

'Can you go?' Jamie asks with a pleading look. 'What if I get held up again?'

I sigh. I really don't want to have to track all the way back to the bakery. I'm exhausted, not just physically, but mentally

116

too. But I can't tell Jamie that, otherwise I'd have to explain why. 'All right,' I sigh, giving in. I hold out my hand. 'Give me the purse. Is there still enough money in there?'

'Yeah, plenty. I used my card.'

'What is the point of us having a kitty for household expenses if you don't use it?' I reply with annoyance.

'Cards are just easier.'

I haven't got the energy to argue. I grab the purse and head as fast as I can towards the bakery. If I don't hurry, the tide will soon be getting too low for us to make the crossing safely.

'Young lady!' I hear being called behind me as I move as quickly as I can manage through the crowds of holidaymakers – which isn't very quickly at all. 'Miss Sky!'

I stop and turn around. Walter is moving even more slowly than me along the street. He waves when I spot him.

'You heard me,' Walter says with relief as he eventually arrives beside me.

'The one good thing about having a slightly unusual name is when it's called in a crowd, you kinda know it's you.'

'Yes, indeed. The perfect name for a student of the weather.'

'What can I do for you, Walter?' I ask. 'I was on my way to see you earlier but I got ... waylaid. I'm sorry if I seem a bit rushed, but I have to get to the bakery and then back to our boat or we'll miss the tide.'

'You will be ruled by the tides living over on Aurora,' Walter says, losing his train of thought in favour of thoughts about the island. 'Beautiful place ... I spent much time there when I was on the Wave Watch team. I miss it.'

'Fisher told me you were once a part of that,' I reply politely.

'When it started there were a lot of us, you know?' Walter continues, still firmly in reverie. 'You volunteered either for

117

that or for the Lifeboat if you lived in St Felix. But numbers have thinned considerably over the years as people left and weren't replaced.'

'That's a shame ... Why was that?' I add when Walter doesn't immediately continue.

He gives a wry smile. 'Lots of reasons, I suppose. But it seems Lucinda Clarkson is the most common reason lately.'

'And she is?' I ask, glancing towards the bakery. I just hope there isn't too much of a queue when I get there.

'Lucinda was in charge of the Wave Watch when I was there; she still is now, I believe.'

'You believe?'

'I don't have anything to do with it these days – we fell out, you see.'

I couldn't imagine anyone falling out with Walter, he seemed such a polite, mild-mannered gentleman.

'You fell out with the Wave Watch or they fell out with you?'

'A little of both, perhaps,' Walter says diplomatically. 'Lucinda didn't take kindly to my unusual methods. She thought everything had to be by the book – or the gadgetry, to be exact. When I started at the Wave Watch our aim was to keep the seas around us safe; recording the weather was just a part of that safety protocol, so as well as taking recordings from the basic equipment we managed to raise funds to buy, I used my own methods for predicting the weather. No one had a problem with it until she came along.'

'Lucinda?' I ask, trying to follow all this while standing in the middle of a busy street with holidaymakers bustling past us, and the constant screeching of the local seagulls looking for easy prey in the form of an unguarded ice cream or a Cornish pasty.

118

Also, I've been standing a few minutes now in one place, and I'm already weary. I just pray that Walter will get to the reason he wants to see me. I need to rest, and I need to do it soon.

'Yes, what with her and Gerald . . . You'd think they owned St Felix the way they carry on.' Walter looks like he has a sour taste in his mouth.

'Do you mean Gerald the harbourmaster?'

'Yes, you've met him, have you?'

'Small chap, grey hair, pointy nose over a silly moustache?'

Walter smiles. 'That's the fellow, and yes his moustache is very silly, but sadly he is not. He used to be with the Wave Watch too, but he's turned into a real jobsworth since he took over the harbour. He takes his role very seriously – too seriously, if you ask me.'

I nod, remembering my encounters with Gerald. But as I think about the harbour my mind is focused sharply back on the time. 'I'm sorry to hurry you again, Walter, but you wanted me for something?'

'Oh yes, so I did my dear . . . Hmm . . . now it's slipped my mind. What was it again?'

While he looks down at his hands resting on his stick in front of him, I look towards the bakery again.

'Nope, it's gone!' he says with a shrug. 'Perhaps it wasn't that important in the first place.' He smiles and touches the brim of his cap. 'I won't keep you any longer, Miss Sky. Good day to you.'

And with that he hobbles back along the street.

I shake my head. *How very odd!*

The bakery queue is long, but not too long when I finally get there, so I take a chance and join the steadily moving line. When I get to the front, I'm pleased to see it's not Ant or Dec serving but someone else behind the counter, so at least I won't be held up with idle chitchat, or enquiries as to the whereabouts of a certain weather forecaster.

I place my order, wait for it to be bagged up, and then I quickly pay and dash out of the shop, again moving as quickly as I can back along the harbour to a waiting Jamie, who is sitting in the sun on one of the benches that run along the harbour wall with Fitz and Comet lying by his feet.

'You took your time,' he says as I rush along the harbour towards him. 'I was getting worried.'

'Worried about me or worried about your pasties?' I ask breathlessly as I pass him the paper bag from the bakery.

'The latter, of course!' he says, grinning.

But his grin doesn't last long. We're about to climb down into the boat when I notice how much lower it is in the water than when we'd arrived. The rusty metal ladder barely reaches the deck.

'The tide is awfully low already,' I say, looking down into the water, 'I don't think we've got time to get back over to the island.'

'You worry too much,' Jamie says confidently. 'We'll be fine.'

'No, I really don't think we will. If the water is too shallow, we'll run aground.'

'We'll what?'

'The boat will get stuck.'

'But it looks fine from here.'

'Not if we hit a sand bar or a rock or something.'

'She's right, you know.' I recognise the familiar nasal voice of Gerald, the harbourmaster, behind us. 'You go across there now and we'll be sending out a rescue boat for you, and I'll have to justify the cost.'

120

'But how are we going to get across, then?' Jamie asks irritably.

'You'll have to wait until the causeway is clear, then you can walk. Either that or wait until the tide is in again so you can take your boat, but that won't be until ...' He makes a performance of pulling his shirtsleeve back to look at his watch. 'Twenty-two hundred hours at the earliest.'

'How long before the causeway is clear enough to walk over?' I ask dejectedly.

Gerald shrugs. 'Maybe an hour, if you're lucky.'

I sigh. 'Looks like we'll have to wait, then.'

'Looks like you will,' Gerald says, looking pleased with himself. 'I'm afraid I'll have to charge you, though.'

'For what?'

'For outstaying your permitted time. The agreement the harbour has with boats from Aurora is they are not allowed to moor for longer than three hours in the day without prior permission.' He looks at his watch again. 'And by my calculation you're just about to go over that time.'

'Couldn't you make an exception just this once?' Jamie asks. 'We are quite new to this.'

Gerald shakes his head. 'This harbour may look like a lot of boats casually moored to you, but I can assure you it runs in a precise and orderly fashion. There are rules for a reason.'

'To make you feel superior?' Jamie mutters under his breath, but I'm too exhausted to smile.

I'm hot from rushing around and hungry too, neither of which is helping my general energy levels. 'Fine us then!' I snap at Gerald. 'I really don't care any more, but I'm sure it will make your day. Walter was right about you. You're just a ... a glorified traffic warden, but with boats instead of cars.'

I flop down on the bench where Jamie was sitting just a few minutes earlier and fold my arms.

'Did I hear you say you'd been gossiping with Wacky Walter Weather?' Gerald asks, seemingly ignoring the rest of my insults. 'What has that old codger been saying about me now?'

'Nothing, only the truth,' I counter, glad at least the mention of Walter's name has riled Gerald.

'Ah, that old fool knows nothing about nothing.'

'He knows how to speak the English language correctly,' I reply, pleased with myself for another witty retort. 'Unlike some . . .'

Jamie grins at me, while Gerald glares.

'I'll be sending you that fine,' he says, his voice changing back to its formal tone. 'Expect it within three to five working days. And I'll be keeping an eye on you from now on,' he continues in a much more threatening voice. 'A very close eye indeed.'

We watch Gerald march back down the cobbled harbour with his nose in the air, and his arms swinging by his side in military fashion. He stops to inspect the parking ticket on one of the cars as he passes, and then he unlocks the door of his little office and slams it shut behind him.

'We'll be on his list from now on,' Jamie says.

'What list?' I ask in a quiet voice, which sounds weak even to me.

'People like that always keep a list, don't they? And I'm sure we'll be right at the top now. Are you all right?' Jamie asks as he turns back and sees me slumped on the bench.

'Yeah, I'm just a bit tired from rushing around this morning. Perhaps if I have some food and a drink, I'll feel a little better.'

'Luckily we already have food,' Jamie says, looking down at the shopping bags. 'Shall I get us something to drink – coffee? Juice?'

'Coffee and some water would be great, thanks.'

'I'll be right back. You take it easy,' Jamie says, regarding me with concern. 'You look a little pale. Shall I take the dogs to make it easier for you?'

'They seem happy here. I'll give them some water while you're gone.'

Jamie nods and sets off along the harbour back towards the town.

While he's gone, I pour some water from the bottle we'd brought for the dogs into their bowl and they both lap gratefully from it.

'Sorry you have to wait,' I tell them as Comet sits next to me, and Fitz sits up on my lap. 'None of us wanted to be delayed like this – especially me.'

I text Talia to tell her what's happened, and she texts back saying everything is fine on the island and not to worry. I'm about to text back and ask if she could bring the Jeep over to collect us when the tide goes out a bit further, when I remember Talia had told us on the first day how she hadn't passed her driving test yet. So we have no choice but to wait and walk back across when the causeway is clear enough, and then drive back over and pick up the boat before it becomes impassable again.

'What a pain,' I say to the dogs. 'We're going to have to be a lot more careful in the future so this doesn't happen again.' It's not just the inconvenience of having to leave our boat and walk back over to the island that's bothering me. I know I've already done too much; the signs are there – I'm getting really weary, which will very rapidly change to exhaustion if I don't rest properly soon. Jamie told me I looked pale, and I've noticed my voice is weak. I'll be slurring my words soon if I'm not careful – that one is always fun to try to explain to people.

I close my eyes and rest my head against the harbour wall; maybe if I can just get a few minutes' peace and quiet I can get through this without it getting too bad.

''Ello 'ello, what are you doing here?'

I open my eyes and find Fisher standing in front of me.

'Fisher! Hi,' I say, blinking in the sunlight even though I already have on sunglasses – there's another sign, the light is getting painfully bright on my eyes. The dogs wag their tails excitedly at Fisher, and he fusses both of them. 'I'm waiting for Jamie to come back.'

Fisher looks down at *Doris*. 'You know the tide is going *out*, don't you?'

'Yes, I'm afraid so, we missed our slot – so to speak. We're stuck here now until we can walk over the causeway in a little while.'

'Do you want a lift? I've got the Land Rover nearby; I've just come from a shift at the castle.'

'Could you?' I say eagerly, sitting up. 'That would be ever so kind.'

'Hey, anything for Captain Sky!' he says, saluting me. 'If you and Jamie are both over here. Does that mean—'

'Yes, Talia is over on the island. I'm sure she'd be over the moon to see you.'

'Oh ... er ... well, yes, that would be an added bonus, I suppose,' he says, his cheeks pinking a little. 'I don't want you to think that's the only reason I offered, though,' he adds hurriedly.

'Of course not,' I say, grinning.

When Jamie returns, we share an al fresco late lunch on the harbour with Fisher, while we wait for the tide to go out far enough for the causeway to clear. The benefit of having Fisher's Land Rover to travel back in is we're able to make the crossing much earlier than if we'd had to go on foot. The large vehicle is able to splash through the shallow water and grip the wet cobbles much more easily than if we'd been walking across carrying shopping bags and walking two dogs.

Talia is there to meet us. I'd surreptitiously texted her to let her know Fisher was bringing us back earlier than expected, and as I'd anticipated she is waiting on the little jetty looking as fresh and buoyant as one of the red and white buoys that bob around in St Felix harbour. In comparison to her energetic youthfulness, I feel like one of the crumpled fish-and-chip papers that fill the harbour bins.

'Hello!' Talia calls happily as we climb out of the car. 'I hear you came to my friends' rescue, Fisher.'

'I wouldn't call it that,' Fisher replies in his usual chilled way. 'But I told Captain Sky here if I could ever be of help, she should give me a shout. Just so happens I stumbled upon her in her hour of need.'

Jamie and I exchange a knowing look over the bonnet of the car.

'Do super heroes carry shopping bags?' Jamie asks Fisher. 'Because there's quite a few of them in the back of your vehicle that need taking up to the house.'

'Don't worry, I've got them,' I call, about to make my way back towards the boot.

'No, you don't!' Jamie says. 'You need some rest – look at the state of you. Much as I like women falling at my feet, in your case I'll make an exception.'

'Goodness, Sky, you don't look at all well,' Talia says, dragging her gaze away from Fisher for the first time. 'Have you fainted again?'

'No, I'm just a bit tired,' I reply. 'I'll be all right when I've had a rest. I'll just get the dogs sorted first and check the watchtower to see what's been going on.'

'No you won't, I'll do that,' Jamie insists. 'Bed, now!'

'No innuendo again?' I ask, finding the energy from somewhere to smile weakly. 'How very disappointing.'

Twelve

I awake later that afternoon not feeling a lot better than before I'd gone to bed. But that's nothing new; sleep rarely makes me feel better, it's the rest that comes from doing it that helps to counterbalance my exertions.

I lie in bed and stare at the ceiling.

People are beginning to notice.

They are noticing that I have a problem, and I don't want that, I want to be treated the same as everyone else. But I'm not like everyone else, am I? Not underneath it all. I have a disability. I'm disabled.

Urgh, I hate saying it, even to myself. But I can't get away from it, however much I want to. My illness is there all the time – hiding, just waiting for me to weaken so that it can be unleashed once more. It's like a monster inside me, that unless I'm very careful, once unleashed, won't be controlled again for quite some time.

It's simple really – to keep my own personal monster locked away; all I have to do is not use too much energy. Sounds easy, until you realise that everything you do uses energy. From the moment you wake up in the morning to the moment you go to bed, you're constantly using up your body's stores of energy. Even just lying in my bed thinking like this, my brain is using energy.

The way I try and explain my fatigue to anyone who shows an interest, is by using an analogy about a faulty phone battery that constantly needs charging. It seems a bit strange to begin with, but they usually understand by the end.

And my battery is getting really low right now, I think to myself. I'm going to have to do something about it, and soon, or things will just get worse.

But this is good, I try to convince myself as I lie in the fuzzy warm light that a room with curtains drawn on a sunny afternoon has. When my monster escaped last time, it was so much worse than this, so much harder to get it back under control. At least I want to have a life now; last time it was so bad I wanted my life to be over.

However, if I don't want the others to discover that I'm hiding a monster, I will have to be more careful. I must pace myself so I don't leave any sort of escape route, any way the monster can overpower me again and ruin what I have here.

Pacing. I roll my eyes and sigh. So much easier said than done. *Just don't do more than your energy levels are capable of and stop before you need to* – I hear my occupational therapist saying over and over again. But when there's so much to do here, and so many things to oversee, I can't just lie down every time I feel I've pushed myself a little bit too hard.

Yet if I don't want to go back to being imprisoned in my bed twenty-four hours a day, lying in a darkened room barely able to bathe or feed myself, that's just what I am going to have to do. There's no magic cure for my monster, no pill that will keep it at bay. *Pacing* is the only word you'll see on a non-existent doctor's prescription for the monster that is ME. So pacing myself and my energy levels is what I'm going to have to find a way of doing, as secretively and covertly as I can.

I think about what Talia and Jamie would say if they knew about my illness. Talia would probably be super sympathetic and supportive, and Jamie would probably make light of it, like he does most things – which on this occasion actually wouldn't be that bad. I never want a fuss.

But I can't tell them. They'd treat me differently if they knew, and I don't want to be different, I want to be the same as everyone else.

Jack said I wouldn't be able to move on with my life if I didn't accept my condition. But I wasn't ready to do that. Not yet, anyway.

I do a few gentle stretches on the bed, to try to ease my aching muscles, then I get up and pull back the curtains, and I'm surprised to see that the tide has already begun to turn.

I must have been in bed longer than I'd thought.

I head along to the kitchen to get a glass of water, and then I carefully climb the stairs to see what's going in the watchtower.

'Ah, it's Rip Van Winkle,' Jamie says from the seat at the desk in front of the window. 'Feeling any better?'

Fitz rushes over to me, his tail going nine to the dozen, so I pick him up for a cuddle, while Comet lazily wags her tail from her basket in greeting.

'Where are Talia and Fisher?' I ask, looking around the empty room.

'Gone for a little walk,' Jamie says, winking. 'Not that there's far you can walk around here, but perhaps they're finding other things to amuse themselves . . .'

'Perhaps . . . ' I choose not to bite. 'I see the tide has started to turn. Is Fisher still going to take one of us back to get the boat?'

'Yes, I've said I'll go. Fisher is going to take me a for a pint until it's high enough to bring *Doris* back over.'

'Sounds like your sort of plan.' I put Fitz down and wander over to the desk. 'Will you be all right bringing her back on your own?'

'Yeah. Don't worry, Captain, I'll only have the one drink – I'll be in total control, I promise!' He salutes me.

'Anything exciting been going on outside?' I ask, trying to look over his shoulder at his laptop.

'Nah, not really,' Jamie says hurriedly closing the lid. 'I did see quite an interesting cloud, though.'

'Oh yes?' I ask, my ears pricking up. 'What type?'

'If you want technical names, then you're going to be disappointed, I'm afraid, but it looked a bit like a monster.'

I jump at the word. 'How do you mean . . . a monster?'

'It was sort of big and had its arms in the air like this.' Jamie demonstrates. 'It looked a bit how the abominable snowman is depicted – that kind of big hairy monster. Silly really, I probably imagined it after too long staring out of this window.'

'No, not silly at all,' I say, trying to sound objective. 'Clouds often resemble things if you watch them for long enough.'

'I didn't expect that reaction from you,' Jamie says, grinning. 'I thought you'd poo-poo anything like that in favour of purely scientific clarifications.'

'Actually, I've seen one or two things myself when I've been on watch.'

'Really, like what?'

Feeling a little silly, I tell him about the peace symbol and then the boat, but not the moon and the masks – that was a bit too personal – and then what had been going on when I'd seen them.

'How odd,' Jamie says. 'Are we going to see a big hairy monster coming up the stairs in a minute?'

'No, only me!' Fisher calls as he appears at the top of the stairs. 'Will I do?'

'Where's Talia?' I ask, looking behind him.

'Making us all a cup of tea. After we've had that we'd better head off, Jamie.'

'Sure, mate,' Jamie says, nodding. 'I'll finish up my shift here and then we'll go.'

'Not too much beer, please,' I say, going over to the sofa and sitting down. 'I want *Doris* back here in one piece.'

'Never mind about me!' Jamie calls over his shoulder. 'I can perish at sea as long as the boat is all right.'

'I reckon you'd survive anything!' I reply. 'It would take more than a choppy sea to take you out.'

'You're probably right,' Jamie agrees. 'So where did you and Talia get to?' he asks Fisher with a surprisingly straight face.

'Ah, we just took a quick tour around the island, then sat and watched for dolphins and seals off the north-west side.'

'I didn't know we'd see any of those around here,' I say, delighted to hear we might see such things on Aurora. 'Are they common?'

'Oh yes, there's quite often a pod of dolphins and occasionally you'll get seals basking on the rocks.'

'How wonderful.'

'Is Fisher telling you about the dolphin we saw?' Talia has appeared at the top of the stairs with a tray of tea things.

Fisher rushes over to help her.

'Thank you,' Talia says, beaming at him as he takes the tray.

131

'Yes, we were lucky enough to spot a dolphin,' Fisher continues, 'weren't we, Talia?'

'Yes, it was magical . . . ' Talia says happily, holding Fisher's affectionate gaze.

'So, what else can you tell us about this island?' Jamie asks Fisher as we all take a mug of tea from him and sit down to drink it. 'Don't worry, Sky,' Jamie says, seeing me glance anxiously over towards the window, 'I put all the automatic recording equipment on before I left my post.'

'Aurora has a fantastic history,' Fisher says, his eyes lighting up. 'Obviously you know about its name?'

I shake my head.

'Really? I thought someone would have told you about that by now?'

'You've told me more than anyone about this island, Fisher – you and your grandfather.'

'Yeah, Walt knows even more than me.'

'Why do you call him Walt if he's your grandfather?' Talia asks.

Fisher shrugs. 'Dunno really, just always have. Everyone calls him Walt or Walter. Some even call him Wacky Walter Weather because of his unusual, but usually accurate, ways of predicting the weather. That's what got him thrown out of the Wave Watch, you know, because he wouldn't conform to their way of doing things. Walt is a pioneer. If they don't want him, then I say he's better off without them.'

Talia nods her agreement.

'You were telling us about the island's name, Fisher?' Jamie prompts.

'Ah yes, that's a good one. Aurora, as you might have guessed, was named because of the lights.'

'The Northern Lights?' Jamie asks. 'Aurora borealis?'

'Yes, our Aurora is named because of the show of lights that happens here occasionally.'

'You see the Northern Lights down here?' Jamie asks in astonishment. 'I had no idea that was possible.'

'Yep, apparently it's been seen many a time over the years.'

'Have you ever seen it, Fisher?' Talia asks in awe. 'That would be amazing to witness.'

'I wish I had, but no, I've never seen them. I would love to witness them with you, though, Talia, it's supposed to be awesome.'

They share another doe-eyed look.

'I hate to be the bearer of bad news,' I say, trying to sound apologetic, but knowing I have to correct them, 'but it would be almost impossible for anyone to see any sort of Aurora here – borealis or australis. They only take place in high-latitude regions like the North or South Pole, which is why they are often referred to as polar lights. The chances of seeing one off the west coast of Cornwall is extremely unlikely, if not impossible.'

Fisher considers this, and looks across at me like he's deciding how best to proceed. 'I don't want to disagree with you, Captain Sky, because I know you know your stuff, but they have been seen, in all their wonderful glory.'

'By who?'

'By many folk, including Walt.'

'Your grandfather has seen polar lights, *here*, in Cornwall?' I ask doubtfully.

'Now they wouldn't be *polar* lights, would they? They'd have to be near the North or South Pole to be that,' Fisher replies innocently.

'He's got you there, Sky!' Jamie cries in delight.

'That is my point exactly – they occur in bands around the polar regions – they do not take place here in Cornwall – it's scientifically impossible.'

'Then what *has* been seen here?' Talia asks. 'There must have been something, or why would the island be named Aurora?'

'Sleeping Beauty?' Jamie suggests, attempting to keep a straight face. 'I can't see why an island would be named after a princess, though?'

I shake my head disparagingly. 'I do hope that's one of your jokes, and you actually know the name Aurora comes from the Roman Goddess of the Dawn, who was supposed to have travelled from east to west announcing the coming of the sun?'

'Of course I do,' Jamie says, pulling a face at the others.

'That reminds me of the meaning of your name,' Fisher says, looking adoringly at Talia. 'Talia means due from heaven, doesn't it?'

'It does! Gosh, how clever of you to know.'

'Joys of the internet, eh?' Jamie says, with just a hint of sarcasm.

He rolls his eyes at me, and I grin back.

But Fisher doesn't appear to hear, he's too busy gazing at Talia.

'Anyway, back to these lights,' Jamie says, bringing everyone to attention again. 'Clearly there seems to be no proper explanation for them?'

'Perhaps it was just a very intense sunset or a particularly vibrant sunrise?' Talia suggests. 'They can be very colourful, can't they, Sky?'

'Well ... yes, but I don't see how you'd mistake them for an aurora?'

'Best ask Walt next time you see him,' Fisher says, shrugging. 'I can't really tell you anything more, but as far as I know that's why the island is called Aurora.' He looks at his watch. 'I think it's probably time to head over to the mainland – you two ready?' He looks at Jamie and Talia.

'Will you be all right here on your own?' Talia asks me.

'Yes, of course, I'll be fine. I was on my own during my first night here and I survived.'

Talia nods. 'I'll just get my things,' she says to Fisher.

'Just give me a minute to get my wallet and my waterproofs in case the crossing is a little choppy on the way back,' Jamie says.

'Is it forecast to be rough weather?' I ask anxiously. Both Jamie and I were so inexperienced with the boat, I didn't want him taking any risks.

'No, the equipment suggests the sea should be extremely calm tonight,' Jamie says confidently. 'There's nothing in the data to suggest otherwise.'

'Good. You should be fine then.'

Jamie glances at me, like he's going to say something, but thinks better of it. 'I'll get my waterproofs just in case, though,' he says heading for the stairs. 'Always be prepared – that's what the Scouts say, isn't it? Not that I was ever a Boy Scout, of course; I got thrown out of the Cubs for misbehaving!'

'Now that's something I can believe!' I say, smiling.

Even if I can't believe much else of what I've heard this afternoon.

Thirteen

Ah, peace at last, I think as I put my feet up on the sofa in the watchtower, after having a long hot soak in a bubble bath.

I munch slowly on my dinner – a simple, but tasty plate of cheese on toast – while I listen to the gentle sound of the waves lapping around the rocks at the base of the island.

I so need this – a quite night to myself with no distractions, no one chatting to me or asking me questions, nothing for my brain to compute, or my body to do other than sit here and relax.

The dogs are both fed and happily curled up together in the corner of the room, and I'm already in my pyjamas, comfortable and cosy.

I finish my toast and pop the plate on the coffee table in front of me, then I pick up my mug of hot chocolate and sip on that – more relaxed and comfortable than I've felt in a long time.

After I've drunk my hot drink, I put the mug down next to the plate and I sit back on the sofa and close my eyes. The rhythmical rolling of the waves, in and out, is like my very own mindfulness soundtrack, and soon the comforting sound begins to lull me into an exceptionally relaxed state. I'm not concerned, though; I know I won't fall asleep resting here – it usually takes a strong sleeping tablet or several antihistamines to produce the sort of effect that's going to induce sleep in me at this time of night.

But surprisingly I do fall asleep and quickly, so that when Fitz nudging my arm wakes me, I jump, just for a moment unsure of where I am.

'Oh, we're here on the island,' I say to a bemused-looking Fitz as he gazes up at me. 'I didn't know where I was for a moment.'

I pull him on to my lap. Then I sit back again so I can wake up properly.

'Wait, where is Comet?' I ask, looking across at her basket. Fitz jumps off my lap and runs to the top of the stairs.

'She's down there, is she? Perhaps she wants to go outside.'

I follow Fitz to the top of the stairs and I'm about to make my way down them when suddenly I become aware of the strength of the wind. Before I'd fallen asleep it had been barely noticeable, a gentle breeze at most, but now there are strong gusts battering the side of the house, and I can hear the waves crashing against the rocks outside.

'That sounds like a storm,' I say to Fitz, and then I hear Comet bark and scratch at the front door.

'I'm coming, Comet!' I call, making my way downstairs as quickly as my stiff, fatigued muscles will allow.

I get to the bottom of the stairs just as another gust of wind hits the front door and it rattles on its hinges.

'Blimey, that is some storm out there,' I say, heading towards Comet, and then I remember Jamie and the boat. 'Gosh, I hope

Jamie hasn't tried to come over in this weather.' Comet whines and scratches on the door again.

My heart sinks, as suddenly everything pieces together and I realise what's happening. Fitz hardly ever wakes me, he knows better than that, but his nudging is what had woken me just now. He was obviously concerned for his friend, down here whining and scratching, and Comet in turn is more than a little concerned for Jamie.

Surely, he wouldn't have set off in weather like this? I wonder, trying to think quickly. *He'd have stayed on the mainland until the storm passed*.

My phone is in my bedroom charging. 'Hold on a moment, Comet. Let me just get my phone.'

Comet watches me dash to my room, where I grab my phone and dial Jamie's number. The phone goes straight to answerphone, so I hang up. I try Fisher next, but his does the same.

'Damn!' I glance at my watch as I realise I've no idea of the time – it's eleven fifteen. If Jamie was going to come back over in the boat he'd have left by now, surely ... Unless he spent longer at the pub than he'd said he was going to because of the weather?

I try ringing his number again, while I head back into the hallway to try to calm a very agitated Comet. Again, the call goes straight to answerphone.

'Jamie, you're probably already aware there's a storm raging around the island and I guess around St Felix too, so on no account try and bring the boat over until it's passed. It's not safe.' I think for a moment and add, 'If you get this message before you leave the mainland tonight, please call me back, Comet is very worried about you.' I hesitate, before saying quickly, 'And I'm worried about you too.'

I hang up.

'Right,' I say, knowing Comet is not going to settle until she's been outside. 'We'd better go out and take a look.'

I grab my yellow mackintosh – that Jamie had laughed at when he'd first seen it because according to him it was so generically seafaring – putting it on along with a cap and my walking boots. Finally, I help both Fitz and Comet into their harnesses and attach their leads. 'Now,' I say to Comet, 'on no account are you to pull me around out there, do you understand?'

Comet glances at me as though she's wondering why I don't just get a move on and open the door.

'I mean it!' I say sternly. 'No pulling or we'll come back inside immediately and we won't find Jamie.'

Comet tilts her head to one side at the mention of Jamie's name. Then to my astonishment, she moves away from the door and sits down calmly so I can open it.

'Good girl,' I say encouragingly. 'Right, let's do this.'

Before I venture outside, I quickly tighten the hood of my coat around my head. If I step outside with it loose, I'll definitely lose my hat in the strength of the wind. Finally ready, I pop the house keys in my pocket, open the door and we all head outside.

The wind immediately hits us hard with a strong gust from the side.

Comet and I manage to keep contact with the ground, but Fitz is blown over on to his side. I quickly pick him up and hold him close to me. Then Comet and I make our way slowly out into the night.

The area around the house is well lit by both outside lights and the lighthouse-style lamp that sits on top of the watchtower, next to some of our weather-recording equipment. We can see where we're going around the island, but not too much further out into the sea.

'It's worse than I thought,' I say, the wind blowing my words straight back at me. 'This is a dreadful storm.'

Every time we stop, Comet looks hopefully into the darkness trying to spot Jamie, but neither she nor I can see anything, we can only hear the sound of huge waves crashing against the rocks around the island.

Where are you, Jamie? I wonder, and my hearts sinks further with every minute we spend outside. *Please let this be one of those times you've agreed to stay for 'just one more' in a pub.*

'We better go back,' I tell the dogs, as Fitz shivers in my arms, and the rain pelts down on us from above. 'Us being out here isn't going to help anyone, let alone Jamie.'

A soaking-wet Comet looks mournfully up at me. 'Come on,' I say, tugging on her lead a little. 'We'll be more use inside than out here.'

Comet dejectedly follows me back to the front door, where I let us in and close the storm firmly outside.

After I've whipped off my raincoat, hat and boots and quickly dried the two dogs, I check my phone – still nothing – so I pace about the kitchen while the kettle boils. Then I quickly make a cup of tea to warm me up, and take it upstairs to the watchtower with Fitz, while Comet waits by the door.

I sit at the desk and look hard through the bay window. I can still hear the wind howling outside while the waves crash against the rocks below. The light on top of the watchtower casts a reasonable beam out around the island, making us visible to others, but not really helping me to see much further than about twenty-five to thirty metres out to sea. And a night sky filled with storm clouds and rain pelting down isn't making the task any easier.

I check the equipment and it's definitely registering everything going on right now, but how did we not forecast this earlier? Jamie had told me before he left with Fisher that the weather was due to remain calm tonight. Did he make a mistake?

I quickly check the notes that he'd printed off before he left, and everything seems correct and completely normal – no signs of an approaching storm at all.

But how is that possible? If the instruments are working now, telling me exactly what is going on outside, why didn't they pick anything up sooner? It's as if this storm came from absolutely nowhere.

My phone rings, making me jump – it's Fisher.

'Sorry to bother you this late, Sky,' Fisher says apologetically, 'but I noticed you tried to call me a little while ago? I was just on my way to bed when I saw your missed call.'

'Do you know where Jamie is, Fisher?' I ask, hearing the desperation in my voice. 'Is he with you, by any chance?'

'No, he left ages ago. He only had the one pint like he said he was going to, and then as soon as the tide was high enough he left to take *Doris* back over to you on the island.'

My heart sinks.

'Do you know if he actually left there and then?' I ask hopefully. 'Is there any chance he might have gone somewhere else, and didn't actually leave the town?'

'I don't think so,' Fisher says, beginning to sound a tad uneasy. 'He wanted to get away because he was worried about leaving you alone too long.'

My heart sinks even further. If it wasn't bad enough that Jamie had left when it wasn't safe, he'd done it because of me.

'Clearly he's not with you now, then?' Fisher asks when I don't reply.

'No,' I say quietly. 'He's not back yet. I don't know what to do, Fisher. What if something has happened to him? He's only made a couple of trips in the boat before, and never in weather like this. He's such a novice with the boat – we both are – and I know I wouldn't cope in this storm.'

'I'm at Tregarlan at the moment,' Fisher says, an air of authority to his voice that I'm relieved to hear. 'I'll head up to the tower they use for the Wave Watch and see if I can see anything from there. If I use their binoculars and telescope, I should be able to see if *Doris* is still moored at the harbour. If not, I'll hopefully be able to see across to you on the island too. If Jamie's anywhere near, perhaps I might be able to spot the boat. Give me a few minutes, and I'll call you back, okay?'

'Sure. Thank you, Fisher.'

'No worries, and don't you worry too much either, I'm sure he'll be absolutely fine. He's that type, isn't he?'

'Yes, I suppose he is.' I try to say this with positivity, but I can still hear the fear in my voice, and I'm sure Fisher can hear it too.

'He probably stayed on in the town until the storm passed, and we're worrying about nothing,' Fisher tries to reassure me. 'I'll call you back in a few minutes.'

Fisher hangs up and I turn back to Fitz, who is sitting behind me looking vexed. His head is cocked to one side, and his ears are pricked up. Comet is still downstairs waiting patiently by the front door in case she can hear Jamie returning.

'Oh, Fitz,' I say to the little dog as I pick him up and pull him close to me. 'That silly man has made us all so stressed. He'd better have a good reason for causing all this worry.'

I sit in the office chair, swinging Fitz and me back and forth, allowing the rhythmical movement to calm me a little, and Fitz, who always enjoys a cuddle, is more than happy to stay put on my lap.

I hadn't liked Jamie at all when we first met – but that wasn't really his fault. He'd been thrust on me when I hadn't been expecting him, and I never cope well with surprises. My life these days is like a military operation – I always know what I'm going to be doing, how long I'm going to be doing it, and who I'm going to be with. It's just the way I deal with living with this dumb illness day in, day out. To have a stranger suddenly turn up and throw all my carefully arranged plans into chaos, like Jamie had, was never going to put them in my good books.

But Jamie has changed since he's been here. The person I first met had been much more Sonny than Jamie – like he had a sort of alter-ego he swapped between. I didn't care for Sonny at all, but I kind of liked Jamie now I'd got used to having him around. I might even go as far as to say I'd miss him if he wasn't here ...

My phone rings— I snatch it up.

'Fisher!' I cry. 'Any news?'

'I'm afraid not.' Fisher says, sounding agitated. 'I've taken a good look around the area as far as I can see with the gadgetry here, and I can't see any boats in trouble.'

'That's good, isn't it?'

'I can't see *Doris* down in the harbour either,' he adds. 'So no, not really.'

'Jamie definitely left the harbour, then. You're sure about that?'

143

'He must have done. Where else would the boat be? I'm going to go down there now and check – just to make sure.'

'Thank you, at least we'll know then. Maybe he was about to set off and the storm came in and he turned back, but he had to moor the boat somewhere else?'

'That's possible,' Fisher says, not sounding very hopeful. 'Let me get my waterproofs on and I'll head down there. If I don't see the boat, though, you know I'm going to have to call the Coastguard and report him missing.'

'Yes . . . ' I reply quietly. 'I know.'

'You keep an eye out around the island for now,' Fisher says, and I can hear him already walking towards where his waterproofs are kept. 'I assume you're already in your watch room?'

'Yes, I'm here now.'

'Good. I know you probably can't see all that much in this weather, but if Jamie did head back over to Aurora, you might be one of the first to spot him. If you do see anything let me know, won't you, otherwise I'm definitely calling the Coastguard as soon as I get to the harbour.'

'Sure, I'm on it,' I say, swinging back around and looking intently through the glass. 'Call me immediately if you find anything out, won't you?'

'And you me,' Fisher says. 'Speak soon.'

Fitz and I spend the next ten minutes or so watching intently through the window while we wait to hear from Fisher. But the storm is still making it extremely difficult to see anything at all out of the watchtower windows.

'What we could do with right now is a break in the clouds and that full moon we had last night. Then we'd have a lot more light to see by.'

My phone rings again – Fisher!

'Sky,' Fisher says in a solemn voice I don't like the sound of. 'I'm at the harbour. *Doris* is not here. I'm going to call the Coastguard.'

I'm about to agree, when suddenly I notice the rain isn't pelting against the window any more, and not only that, the clouds are on the move.

'Hold on a moment,' I say to Fisher. 'It's stopped raining. The storm must have passed; we might get some light from the moon in a moment.'

'Yes, it's easing up here, too,' Fisher says, 'but I really don't think—'

'I can see something!' I cry, cutting him off as the clouds part and a beam of moonlight so strong it looks like it's coming from a lighthouse beacon is cast across the waves. 'I'm putting you on speaker phone!' I say, grabbing the binoculars.

I focus the binoculars on the small moving image that's illuminated by the moon. And as the image comes into focus, I almost drop the binoculars in excitement.

'It's a boat!' I shout to Fisher. 'I think it's *Doris*.'

'Where?' Fisher cries.

'Er . . . just off the mainland, under where the castle is. It's coming across the sea in the moonlight.'

I can hear Fisher running – I assume along the harbour to the end where the little lighthouse is.

'Yes, I can just about see it,' he says, his breathing fast. 'I'm looking through my binoculars.'

'I really think it's *Doris*!' I exclaim. 'It looks a lot like her.'

'You must have a better view than me,' Fisher says, and I can hear the frustration in his voice. 'I can't tell.'

I keep my binoculars trained on the little boat, and

amazingly so does the moon. It's as if it's guiding the boat back safely across the waves to the island.

'It *is* Doris!' I shriek gleefully. 'And I can see Jamie, too.'

'Thank the Lord!' Fisher says, and I can hear the relief in his voice. 'Thank. The. Lord.'

'I'm going to go down to the jetty to meet him,' I tell Fisher. 'I'll call you and let you know what's happened in a bit.'

'No, I'm going back to the castle and my bed,' Fisher says, sounding much more like his usual chilled self. 'Call me in the morning and tell me what happened. As long as he's back safe and sound, that's all I care about.'

'Okay,' I say, grinning from ear to ear. 'I'll do that. Thank you so much for your help tonight.'

'Oh, I didn't do anything,' Fisher says. 'You wanna thank Mother Nature. It seems it's the clouds moving when they did that has brought him back safely – that and the power of the moon.'

With Fisher's words still ringing in my ears, I rush down the stairs with Fitz at my heels.

'He's coming back!' I tell a worried-looking Comet waiting by the door. 'Jamie is coming home!'

Comet barks, and it's all I can do to stop her breaking down the door while I pull my coat, hat and boots back on.

Then I harness both dogs up and we set off down towards the little jetty.

Jamie and *Doris* are just coming into view as we wait with anticipation for them to arrive.

When Jamie gets close enough, he waves at us, then he steers *Doris* into the jetty while I try to control a very excited Comet.

He throws the rope out to me and I tie it to the mooring post, then a very bedraggled Jamie climbs from the boat and makes a huge fuss of a very agitated Comet.

He looks so exhausted and drained, that without thinking I lean forward and give him a hug.

'Gosh?' he says, looking a little startled as I gaze expectantly at him, waiting for answers. 'You've obviously had a good evening. Anything exciting happen?'

Fourteen

'Now are you going to tell me what happened?' I ask impatiently, as we sit in the watchtower a lot drier and warmer than we'd been half an hour ago.

Jamie and I have changed from our wet clothes into warm ones and we're drinking from mugs of hot tea, while the dogs sleep in front of the little electric fire we've put on for the first time – its ruby and amber flames make the room seem even cosier than it was before. The storm has now completely disappeared. The wind has dropped, and the sea, lit only by the bright moon in an inky cloudless sky, is like a millpond.

Jamie has been very quiet since he got back, and I've not pushed him into telling me anything so far. I've waited patiently for him to have a hot shower, and for us to make tea and get settled in the watchtower. But now I'm eager to hear what happened to him.

'How did Fisher know I was missing?' Jamie asks, skirting my question again.

I've told Jamie a little of what had happened tonight

with Fisher, but what he hasn't told me yet is what had happened to him.

'Because I called him when you didn't arrive safely back here. It was Comet that first alerted me something might be up, and that's when I realised how late it was and you should have returned. So, what did happen to you? You were gone ages.'

Jamie takes a long gulp of his tea and puts his mug on the table in front of him.

'What I'm going to tell you now is going to sound very strange – weird, even. But just hear me out before you comment, all right?'

'Sure.' I nod.

'I mean it, Sky.'

'*Okay*! I'll be quiet, I promise.'

'As you know, it was a perfectly calm and clear night,' Jamie says, not looking at me, but concentrating on his story. 'Just like we'd forecast it would be earlier. After I left Fisher in the pub and got down to the harbour, I noticed that the wind had picked up just a little bit, and the clouds were beginning to move with more speed across the sky. I didn't worry, though, as I knew I was only going to be out at sea for a few minutes. Fisher had given me some extra guidance about sailing over at night, so I was perfectly happy with what I was about to do.'

He pauses for a moment, and glances at me. But true to my word, I don't say anything.

'I set off from the harbour with no problems at all, but when I was about halfway across, the storm hit. The wind came from nowhere – it was like a tornado spinning across the sea.'

'Tornados are usually land based,' I have to interrupt. 'Unless they are tornadic waterspouts – which would be almost

149

impossible to see here in the UK. A cyclone is more likely to occur over the sea.'

'Okay, so it was a cyclone, then.'

'But it can't have been a cyclone, either – we don't get them here; they only occur over tropical or sub-tropical waters.'

Jamie rolls his eyes. 'What do you want me to call it, then – a hurricane?'

I shake my head. 'You may have experienced strong gale-force winds – were the waves high?'

'What?'

'The waves – using the Beaufort wind force scale you can estimate the strength of the wind by measuring the size of the waves.'

'Funnily enough, I was in the middle of the sea, in a small boat, with a storm coming towards me. My first thought wasn't measuring the waves! Anyway, you promised you wouldn't speak!'

'Sorry,' I say apologetically. 'I can't help myself when it comes to weather. Please continue.'

'*Thank you* ...' Jamie says firmly. 'As I was saying, I could see this *strong* wind coming towards me, and also the rain and the clouds moving rapidly across the sky. I knew I couldn't get to the island before it got to me because of the speed it was travelling at. I thought about turning back, but that seemed too far to make safely as well. Then suddenly, like you witnessed as I arrived back just now, the moon appeared from behind the clouds and it was – okay, this is the first silly bit – it was like it was guiding me to safety.' He pauses to note my reaction, but I just nod calmly for him to continue; this is exactly what I'd thought, too.

'So, I took a chance and followed the beam of light, and

150

it led me around the rocks that Fisher has told us to avoid, and into this tiny bay on the north-west side of St Felix, which would be south-west of here, I guess?' He pauses for a moment to think. 'Yes, that's right. Amazingly, it was completely sheltered there and I was able to navigate the boat safely into this tiny water-filled cave, where I stayed until the storm passed, when yet again the moon incredibly led me safely back here.'

He waits for my reaction.

'You're right,' I say, choosing my words carefully. Jamie has clearly had a distressing experience and I don't want to diminish his ordeal by saying the wrong thing. 'It does sound pretty inconceivable. But nature and the weather can work unusually from time to time. I mean, our readings said it was going to be calm tonight, so where did that storm come from?'

'That is not the only strange part of this story,' Jamie says, his eyes wide. 'There's more. When I was first in the cave, I attempted to call for help on my phone, but there was no signal. So I decided I had no option but to wait for the storm to pass before I ventured out again. But just after I'd sat down to wait, the light from another boat suddenly came into view. The boat navigated itself into the cave, but without the moon's help, which by this time had disappeared behind all the clouds.'

'Had they got caught out by the storm as well?'

'I have no idea, because when their lights fell on *Doris* and me, they reversed straight back out and left immediately.'

'What, without saying anything?'

'They didn't stop to chat, if that's what you're asking.' Jamie grins.

'Surely they must have wondered what you were doing there?'

'I guess they thought I was sheltering from the storm.'

'So why didn't they stay until it was safe to leave? Was there enough room for both of you in the cave?'

'Yes, easily. They simply headed back out again into the wild weather.'

'That's odd.'

'Yep, I said it was.'

'Did you see anyone on the boat?'

'Not really; like I said, this was still in the middle of the storm, so their windscreen wipers were moving fast, and the rain was pelting down as they entered and then left. I could barely see them.'

'*That* is very strange. Why would you head back out into treacherous weather and risk your life, when you could shelter safely until it had passed? It makes no sense.'

'Maybe they were in a hurry to get somewhere?'

'Where? They were out on the sea at night in a raging storm! They were hardly on a mercy dash to a hospital.'

Jamie's phone beeps several times in succession, so he lifts it from the table in front of him.

'Just notifications coming in now there's a signal to tell me that I've several missed calls, and also two voicemails from Fisher and yourself. You really were concerned.'

'Of course, you'd barely driven the boat and you were missing at sea in a storm. What are you doing?' I ask as Jamie holds his phone up to his ear. 'You don't need to listen to them. You know exactly what they're about.'

'You really *were* worried about me,' Jamie says, nodding as he listens to my message. 'I'd have thought you'd have been glad to see the back of me if I'd drowned at sea.'

'That's not fair,' I protest. 'Of course I was concerned …

and there was the boat to think about too . . . ' I say hurriedly, when Jamie grins at me.

'You didn't say anything about *Doris* in your message,' Jamie says, clearly enjoying my embarrassment. 'You said you were worried about *me* . . . '

'Time for bed, I think!' I say quickly, standing up. 'It's been a really long and tiring night.'

Jamie just watches me as I gather our empty mugs and walk towards the staircase with Fitz at my heels.

'I'm glad you're okay,' I say, pausing for a moment before going downstairs to the kitchen. I turn to look at him. 'It wouldn't have been the same here without you.'

Fifteen

The next morning, I awake to an unusually bright light flooding into my bedroom.

Gosh that sun is strong this morning, I think as I turn over and gingerly begin to stretch my body, which is always stiff and sore first thing. *It must be a lovely day out there.*

I glance at my watch on the bedside cabinet. 'What? It can't be!' I gasp, grabbing the watch and looking more closely at it.

But it is. It's just after midday.

I realise then that, unusually, Fitz is not at the end of my bed either.

As quickly as I can, I perform the series of lying and sitting stretches I do every morning to ease my body into movement, and then I pull on my dressing gown and head slowly upstairs.

'Ow!' I whisper as I attempt to climb the stairs. 'Eh . . . ah.' Each step is painfully sore on my leg muscles, as my body attempts to transform from still and sleeping, into moving and awake.

'You all right?' I hear from the bottom of the stairs.

'Yes, absolutely fine,' I reply, turning around to Jamie,

using his question as a welcome relief to stop for a moment. 'How are you?'

'Good actually, considering. We thought we'd let you sleep in.'

'We?'

'Me and the dogs. I took them out for a bit earlier when Talia got here. You don't mind, do you?'

'Of course not. I'm sorry I slept so late.'

'Don't be daft, after what I put you through last night, it's fine. Look, I've just made some coffee for Talia and me; do you want some?' he asks, holding up two mugs.

'Yes, that would be great. Thank you.'

'I'll be up in a bit, then,' Jamie says, heading back to the kitchen, while I climb the last few painful steps up to the watchtower.

'Good morning!' Talia calls from her post by the window. 'Actually, no,' she says, glancing at the clock on the wall, 'it's afternoon now, isn't it?'

'Yes, sorry about that,' I apologise. 'I completely over-slept.'

'Don't worry about it,' Talia says. 'Jamie told me what happened last night. You must be exhausted.'

I nod and flop down on one of the comfortable chairs. 'Yes, it does seem to have taken it out of me a bit. Has anything exciting been going on out there?' I gesture to the window.

Talia shrugs. 'Not really. Just the weather we expected for today. Unlike last night; that was very odd, wasn't it?'

'Yes, I think I'll need to check over the equipment this morning ... I mean, afternoon. Something must have been malfunctioning for us to get it so wrong.'

'I've had a quick look and I can't see anything that's faulty. But it would be good to get a second opinion.'

155

'Your expert Aurora barista has arrived!' Jamie calls as he appears at the top of the stairs. 'With three frothy cappuccinos – courtesy of our wonderful coffee machine.'

'Thank you,' I say, taking a warm mug of coffee from him.

'My pleasure.' He smiles. 'And for the lovely Talia – the same, but made with oat milk, of course!'

'Thank you, Jamie.' Talia smiles at him. 'We were just talking about last night and how the equipment could have got it so wrong.'

'The equipment got it wrong, but I have to admit that I might have had a little warning that rough weather could be ahead.'

'What sort of warning?' I ask, already beginning to feel more alive after a couple of sips of coffee.

'Now don't laugh, Talia,' Jamie says, holding up his hand to her. 'I know this is going to sound weird to a scientist like yourself.'

'Why would I laugh and not Sky?' Talia asks, looking at me.

'Because Sky already knows about this, don't you, Sky?'

'Do I?' I ask, wondering if I'd had enough caffeine yet for my brain to be properly awake.

'Yes, we've both experienced it now, haven't we? *The clouds?*' he prompts when I stare blankly at him.

'Oh yes – the clouds! Wait, are you saying the clouds told you that there was going to be a storm last night? Please tell me this is one of your jokes?'

Jamie shakes his head. 'Wish I could. When I was on duty yesterday, I noticed some unusual cloud shapes forming in the sky. I noted them down as cumulus clouds – because they were white and cauliflower like. That's right, isn't it?'

Talia and I both nod, and I'm secretly pleased that Jamie is beginning to learn something while he's with us.

'But then they began to change ... I'm not sure how to describe it but they almost reversed so the bumpy parts of the cloud dropped, and then this huge tower thing appeared over the top of them – it looked a bit like a space ship to begin with and then it formed into what looked like a tornado shape – don't start,' he says sharply, addressing his comment at me. 'I know we don't get tornados here.'

'I wasn't going to say that,' I retort quickly. 'I was going to say ... Wait, what do you think, Talia?'

'They sound like they probably started as cumulonimbus clouds and then formed into cumulonimbus incus,' Talia says expertly. 'And the reverse bumps sound like mammatus.'

I smile at her. 'Yes, I agree. It sounds like what you're describing,' I turn to Jamie now, 'are what are commonly known as anvil clouds – where the top spreads out to look like an anvil or sometimes a space ship, and mammatus clouds – they look a little bit like a cow's udder or ...' I hesitate, this *was* Jamie I was talking to. 'Some people think they look a little like breasts.'

Jamie raises his eyebrows at my second description, so I cut him off before he can comment.

'They are both associated with thunderstorms, though. Why didn't you note that, then we might have been forewarned of what was coming?'

'*Because,*' Jamie says, his amused expression quickly changing to one of annoyance, 'they both disappeared as soon as they arrived. But not before the ... *anvil*, let's call it, had drifted away. I say drifted, but it looked more like a boat fighting its way across the top of the clouds. Then they went straight back to the white fluffy ones – cumulus? Or are you saying they were cumulonimbus now?'

'No, you're right with cumulus.'

'And you're saying you've seen something similar happen while we've been here?' Talia asks, looking at both of us. 'Why didn't you say?'

I look at Jamie.

He shrugs.

'I can't speak for Jamie, but I was embarrassed,' I say, looking down at my coffee. 'I know unusual cloud activity is one of the things that was reported before we came, but it was nothing like this – only groups and types of cloud appearing when they shouldn't. People often see shapes in the clouds, that's nothing new, but the shapes I've witnessed here are like nothing I've ever seen before. They're so clear, so defined, you really can't mistake what they are.'

I tell Talia what I'd told Jamie before about my experiences with the clouds, and what had been happening when they'd appeared.

Jamie nods. 'I agree. I'm not an expert on clouds like you two are, and I've only witnessed it a couple of times, but you can't mistake what you're seeing.'

'Or what they're trying to tell you by appearing?' Talia says, looking at us both. 'It seems to me that these clouds are trying to help you with their messages.'

'Talia,' I say, looking at her disapprovingly, 'put your scientific head back on, please. As you well know, clouds are formed through water vapour and particles in the air. How are they able to tell us anything?'

'I don't know,' Talia says uncomfortably, 'but you can't deny it's happening, can you? It's you two who are seeing these . . . *messages* in the sky, for want of a better description, not me.'

'I'm sorry,' I apologise. 'I didn't mean to take it out on you.

But, no offence to Jamie, you're my fellow meteorologist here, Talia. We see things scientifically, not,' I hesitate to use the word, 'not spiritually.'

'Can't we see both?' Talia asks. 'If you have an open mind – and I like to think I have – then perhaps some things can be explained from a scientific perspective, and some might have a very different explanation.'

I turn to Jamie, hoping for support.

'Don't look at me,' he says, shrugging. 'I have no idea what's going on. If you two can't explain strange cloud behaviour, then I don't know who can. Like you're always inferring, Sky, I'm just a television presenter, you two are the experts!'

'Well, there's definitely *something* strange going on,' I say. 'I can't explain the unusual cloud ... *formations*, shall we call them, rather than messages. But I do know that our equipment can't be working properly, otherwise it would have allowed us to predict there was going to be a storm. And yet when the storm was raging it was picking everything up perfectly, I saw it with my own eyes.'

Talia nods. 'I had a look at the records this morning; I thought that was strange.'

'I haven't actually taken my turn at the helm yet today,' Jamie says. 'Unlike Sky here, the last thing I was thinking about last night was checking to see if the barometer or ane-mometer was working properly.'

I smile. Again he's surprising me with his knowledge.

'What?' he asks when he sees me smiling. 'Don't tell me, I suppose I named them incorrectly.'

'No, not at all. I was smiling because it's lovely to hear how much you've learnt since you've been here. You're really begin-ning to pick things up.'

'Oh . . .' Jamie looks unusually self-conscious. 'Well . . . that's good, isn't it?'

'Very good.' I nod, holding his gaze for a moment, and the dart of excitement that shoots through me makes me physically jump in surprise.

'You all right, Sky?' Talia asks.

'Yes, absolutely fine,' I say hurriedly. 'I think I might have had too much caffeine on an empty stomach. Lunch, anyone?'

'Sounds good,' Jamie agrees. 'I meant to say – when we were in the pub last night, Fisher asked if we'd like to go over and visit Tregarlan Castle sometime.'

'Yes, that might be nice,' I reply, my mind still dizzy by what I've just felt. It's so long since I've felt anything like this, that it isn't just the feeling of what's happened, but the strength of it that's thrown me off-kilter.

'I thought while we were there we might be able to call in on the Wave Watch and see if their equipment picked up anything odd last night. At least we'd know then if it's our equipment that's faulty.'

'That's actually a very good idea,' I reply, a tiny bit stunned by his suggestion. 'You surprise me again.'

'Twice in one day!' Jamie says, grinning. 'Whatever is going on?' But he looks secretly pleased, and again we hold each other's gaze.

'Would you like me to make lunch while you get dressed, Sky?' Talia asks, looking with interest between Jamie and me. 'Or do you two want to make it together while I carry on here?'

'No, no, we'll stick to the rota,' I insist hurriedly. 'Jamie, it must be your shift now, isn't it?'

'Yes, sir, Cap'ain!' Jamie says, jumping to attention and heading towards the desk. 'Reporting for duty, ma'am.'

Talia smiles as she stands up and stretches. 'Great, I'll start getting the lunch then, shall I?'

'Let me get a quick shower and I'll help you,' I insist.

'Nah, you're all right; take your time, I've got it. I brought stuff over with me this morning from the bakery. After what happened last night, I thought neither of you would be going very far today.'

'How did you know what had happened before you came over this morning?' I ask.

'Fisher!' Jamie and I say in unison.

'Yes, Fisher did call and tell me what had happened,' Talia says, blushing a little. 'I hope you don't mind?'

'Why would we mind when you've brought delights from the bakery with you?' Jamie says. 'That's a result in my book.'

'As long as you get a Cornish pasty, you're happy!' I say, smiling at him.

'Too right.' Jamie grins, swivelling around in his chair to face the window. 'Now shush, boss, stop distracting me, I'm supposed to be working!'

After a delicious lunch of pasties, crispy red apples and a slice of millionaire's shortbread each, we sit in the watchtower with Jamie still at the desk and Talia and I on the sofa and one of the chairs.

'How did you get over here this morning?' I ask her. 'Did Jamie collect you in the boat?'

'No, I walked over, before the tide covered the causeway.'

'But that must have been super early.'

'Yes, pretty early, but I didn't want to put either of you out by making you get up earlier than you needed to. Besides, I enjoyed the walk. The town is very quiet then. It felt like

I'd gone back in time, making the crossing on foot. It was quite magical.'

I smile at Talia. Even though she has a very scientific mind like me, unlike me, she also has a very open and imaginative one.

'I wonder how many people have travelled over to this island before us?' Jamie says, thinking. 'No motorboats and Jeeps for them, only rowing boats and on foot. This island must have quite the history.'

'Fisher was telling me some of it the other night,' Talia says. 'Apparently, the island has been used for many things over the years.'

'Like what?' I ask. I've never really thought much about the island's history, so concentrated am I on its present use.

'Other than housing domestic accommodation like it does now, it's been used as a lookout post, a B&B, and there's a rumour that it was used in the Second World War for secret missions.'

'What sort of secret missions?'

'I don't know, that's what Fisher told me. It was used as a smugglers' hide-out, too, back in the day.'

'Really?' I ask. 'What sort of smugglers?'

'You'd have to ask Fisher – probably alcohol and tobacco, I should think.'

'Cornish smugglers are known for smuggling quite a variety of things,' Jamie says. 'I watched a Netflix documentary on it a while back. They were pretty wily when dealing with the customs and excise men.'

'I can imagine this island being used by smugglers,' I say, thinking about it. 'It's separated from the land by the sea, but not so far that they couldn't easily carry their contraband across the causeway at low tide.'

'They'd have had to disguise it, though, or they'd have been caught straight away,' Jamie says knowingly. 'Especially if there was a harbourmaster like Gerald keeping watch over them day and night!'

We all smile as we imagine one of Gerald's ancestors over-zealously patrolling the harbour.

'There is something else I should probably mention,' Talia says, looking a little worried.

'What's that?' I ask.

'Fisher said that . . . Oh, I feel silly saying it now.' Her pale cheeks flush.

'Come on, Talia, we're all friends here,' Jamie encourages.

'Well, Fisher said that the bay is supposed to be haunted, and sometimes in bad weather people say they've seen the ghost of a smuggler's boat. Apparently, it sank due to some foul play at the time. It's usually seen sailing on the sea in the area you were in last night, Jamie.'

Jamie just stares at Talia.

'A ghost ship?' I ask incredulously.

'No, just a boat with some men in it. Like I said, it was something to do with the custom master at the time and,' she smiles wryly, 'a bad weather forecast.'

'Are you suggesting that the boat Jamie saw in the cave was actually a boat full of ghosts?' I ask, trying to humour Talia, who obviously believes everything Fisher tells her.

She shrugs. 'It might be. Why else would a boat be out in that dreadful weather?'

'But it wasn't supposed to be dreadful, was it? That's how Jamie got caught out – the forecast was good.'

I look at Jamie, who's been unusually quiet while we discuss this.

'Was the boat that you saw in the cave full of ghost smugglers?' I ask him with a straight face.

'Well ...' Jamie looks equally serious, and for one tiny moment I think he might actually say yes. 'No, of course it wasn't! This was a motorboat for one thing; I hardly think Cornish smugglers of old drove motorboats with full-throttle engines.'

Talia lets out a huge sigh of relief. 'You almost had us then, Jamie! Didn't he, Sky?'

'I doubt Sky would ever believe in such a thing as ghosts, would you?' Jamie asks me, still grinning.

'No, I'm afraid not. But I do think it's good these old stories are passed down through the generations, Talia,' I say kindly. 'It keeps things ... lively.'

'Wait until I see Fisher!' Jamie stands up, gathering the lunch things on to a tray. 'Filling your head with all his nonsense. I'll be having words with him!' He winks at Talia. 'Just keep an eye on the desk for a few minutes, boss, will ya?' he says to me as he heads towards the staircase with the tray.

'It will soon be my time to take over anyway,' I say, getting to my feet. 'I'll just start my shift early if you like?'

'Whatever you say, Captain!' Jamie calls in his usual cheery way, not looking back. But as he turns and begins to head down the staircase, his expression doesn't quite match his happy-go-lucky voice at all; he looks a tad anxious, possibly even afraid.

Surely Jamie doesn't think he really saw ghosts in that cave last night? I wonder as I watch him leave. *Even he's not that daft.*

But his uneasy expression only suggests the contrary ...

Sixteen

Sadly, our plans to visit Fisher at Tregarlan have to be put on hold for a few days. The predominantly calm weather we've been blessed with is suddenly replaced by low pressure and a cold front, which brings with it high winds and periods of fog, mist and heavy rain.

Not wanting to risk the boat in the bad weather, Jamie and I decide to stay on Aurora, while, much to her annoyance, Talia remains over on the mainland. Even the sturdy Jeep is battered from side to side as we attempt to cross the causeway on the first rough day. We decide at that point to batten down the hatches, and remain in the house until the weather front moves on.

As a much more experienced sailor, Fisher kindly brings us across supplies in his boat. He also confirms that as novices we've done the right thing in keeping away from the rough sea during this weather.

It's an interesting time Jamie and I spend holed up in the house together with the dogs. We try to take Fitz and Comet out the best we can around the island, but not only is Aurora far too small to walk two energetic dogs, it's also quite steep and gravelly, and there are parts of it we just don't feel safe walking around when gale-force winds are gusting around its rocky perimeter.

While one of us is on watch duty, the other prepares meals, tidies up or plays with the dogs to try to use up some of the energy they have left after their short walks. In the evenings, we settle down in the watchtower to play the odd board game or watch some TV together. Sometimes I read one of the many books I've brought with me, while Jamie is happy to watch things on his iPad with earphones.

I also spend some of our time teaching Jamie a little bit more about how to read and forecast the weather – he not only seems to pick this up very quickly when he's one-to-one with me, but he is eager to learn more, and I'm more than happy to converse with him on my favourite subject.

In return, on our walks, Jamie shares everything he knows about the nature of the area with me – the rock pools, seabirds and plant life, which he tells me he knows so much about from holidays spent by the coast with his aunt and uncle when his mum was still working.

The whole experience is an extremely pleasurable one for both of us. Jamie is good company – when he's being Jamie and not Sonny – and it turns out he can not only be wise and insightful about many subjects, but also quiet and peaceful when he wants to be.

'Do you ever read at all?' I ask him one night when we're sitting together in the watchtower after dinner. I'm reading a book about the solar system and a chapter about how it can influence weather around the world, and he is watching a comedy show on catch-up.

'Hmm?' Jamie asks, pulling out one of his earphones.

'Do you ever read books?'

'Sometimes.'

'Fiction or non-fiction?'

'Er . . . both. I didn't think to bring any with me, though.'

'You could download an app to your iPad and read a book on there?' I suggest, in what I think is a helpful manner. 'I know it's not the same as a real book in your hands, but it would be better than nothing if you wanted to read while you're here.'

'Nah, I'm fine watching this, thanks.' Jamie puts his earphone back in and goes back to his screen.

I return to my book, but find I'm not absorbing the words any more. For some reason Jamie's reaction has bothered me, and I'm not sure why.

In the first few days Jamie and I had spent together on the island, I'd found his constant cheeriness and never-ending supply of jokes – often at my expense – and questions about my life extremely wearing, and I'd often been glad to escape to the quiet of my room at night when it had been time to go to bed. But tonight, for some reason, I find myself missing his banter as we inhabit our own very different worlds, and I realise my questions had been a weak attempt to engage him in conversation.

'You okay?' Jamie asks, jolting me from my thoughts.

'What? Oh, yes, yes, I'm fine.'

'Only you've been reading the same page of that book for the past five minutes.'

'Have I? I was just thinking, that's all.'

'Want to share?'

'Not really,' I say automatically.

'What's new?' Jamie says, shrugging, and he turns his attention back to his screen.

'No wait!' I say, realising that for once I really do want to talk. Jamie looks up.

'I'm sorry I haven't been very chatty since we arrived here – about myself, I mean. I'm not very good at sharing things.'

Jamie looks at me with curiosity. 'Go on . . .'

'That's it, really. I don't find it easy to talk about myself.'

'Why?'

'I just don't. Not everyone wants to share every detail of their life – especially with strangers. That's why I don't have social media.'

'I know,' Jamie says. 'I looked you up before I came here.'

'Did you?'

'Yeah, I thought I'd find out a bit about you – social media is usually great for that. But you don't even have Facebook.'

I smile. 'No, I don't. I bet you have all of them, though!'

'I may have a few followers on Instagram and Twitter.'

'Good for you.'

'The only thing I could find out about you online were some scholarly articles about the weather.'

I nod. 'Yep.'

'No photos or anything.'

'That's the best way.'

Jamie studies me for a moment and I feel unsettled under his intense gaze.

'You're a strange one, Sky Matthews.'

'Am I?'

'Yes, I think so – strange in a good way, though.'

'Er . . . I'll take that as a compliment, I think.'

'You should,' Jamie nods slowly, as though he's absorbing this revelation himself. 'I like strange.'

I'm not sure what to say to this.

168

'Just as well you came to Aurora, then,' I reply hurriedly, 'cos we're definitely seeing some strange things here.'

'You can say that again!' Jamie says, looking towards the window. 'This was not what I expected when I said I'd come here.'

'Why did you say you'd come? I've been wondering that since we arrived. You think I dodge questions about myself, but you do too when it comes to the reason for your stay here.'

'I see what you're doing,' Jamie says, waggling his finger at me. 'Switching the subject away from you to me.'

'And I see what you're doing – avoiding the subject altogether! How about we agree to stop questioning each other – and then we'll both be happy?'

Jamie thinks about this. 'All right – for now,' he says begrudgingly. 'You've got me cornered. We'll go back to our mundane yet safe topics, as dictated by you. But I hope we will talk properly one day. I want to get to know the real Sky, not the one *you* think we should know. Because I think those two people are very different indeed.'

He's right, of course. I am hiding so much from both him and Talia. The only difference between us is that Jamie is a lot more confident that at some stage I'll be ready to share my secrets. Whereas I'm not sure the day will ever come when I'll feel brave enough and strong enough to tell him everything he wants to know.

The weather finally calms, and a warm front settles over the south-west of Cornwall. Talia enthusiastically returns to Aurora and insists on making up for the last few days by taking on some extra shifts.

Jamie and I accept her offer, and head over to visit Fisher

at Tregarlan at the soonest convenient time for him and the Wave Watch team.

Much to the dogs' displeasure, we leave them with Talia and drive over at low tide, taking the Jeep, so we're able to drive it through the town and onward to Tregarlan Castle.

Tregarlan is a beautiful and grand stately home. It sits majestically at the top of the hill that overlooks St Felix Bay, and as we drive up its lengthy gravel path, it isn't hard to picture the carriages pulled by horses and the vintage cars that must have made the same journey in the decades and centuries before us.

But unlike the lords and ladies that would have alighted from their rides at the grand main entrance, I drive slowly around to the back of the house, to a private car park that Fisher has arranged for us to leave the Jeep in.

'Servants' entrance for us, I see!' Jamie says as we pull up in the space Fisher is now guiding me towards.

'It does feel a bit like that,' I say, smiling. 'But at least we don't have to pay to park with the visitors.'

'Hello,' I say to Fisher as we climb out of the Jeep. 'How are you?'

'I'm very well, thank you, Captain Sky,' Fisher says, doing his usual salute 'How are the two of you after your few days hunkering down together on Aurora?'

'Well, we didn't kill each other, which is the main thing!' I glance at Jamie, expecting him to make a similar joke.

'I actually found it very enjoyable,' Jamie says, making me sound terrible. 'I never once wanted to harm you, Sky, even if you felt differently about me.'

Great! Now, I feel even worse.

'Yeah, right!' I say, deciding humouring him is the best way to respond.

But Jamie just shrugs.

'Okay...' Fisher says, looking a tad uncomfortable. 'Shall we go? I said we'd speak with the Wave Watch team in about half an hour, so would you like a quick tour around the castle first?'

'That would be fab, thank you,' I tell him. 'Lead the way!'

We follow Fisher around the house while he tells us all about the history of the building and the restoration project that went on a few years ago when National Heritage got involved in the running of Tregarlan.

We pause in front of a portrait of a jolly-looking man wearing a flat cap and a tweed suit. He sits at a table with a silver salver of Cornish pasties beside him.

'The owners, Poppy and Jake, inherited the building from this man,' Fisher says, gesturing to the portrait. 'The previous owner, Stanley Marrick, was distantly related to them, I believe. Stanley was known as Mad Stan the Pasty Man in this area, because of his ability to eat a dozen giant Cornish pasties in one sitting.'

'Now that's the kind of history I'm interested in!' Jamie says, his eyes lighting up.

'Even *you* couldn't eat that many!' I tell him.

'Perhaps not, but I'd enjoy giving it a go.'

Fisher continues our private tour, stopping occasionally to inform us of an interesting fact about Tregarlan or to let us view a particular room. The ballroom is particularly impressive.

'Wow!' I exclaim as we enter a huge ornately decorated room with an enormous crystal chandelier hanging from the ceiling. 'It's beautiful.'

'Tregarlan is often the venue for weddings throughout the spring and summer, and they usually hold the main reception in here.'

'I'm not surprised,' I say, spinning around so I can take in the full 360-degree view. 'I'd have my wedding here. If I was actually getting married, that is . . . ' I add hurriedly as Fisher and Jamie look quizzically at me. 'Which is very unlikely, I can assure you.' *Not now, anyway . . .*

'I think it's probably time to head up to see the Wave Watch,' Fisher says, looking at his watch. 'Lucinda said to bring you around now when they're changing shifts.'

'Who's Lucinda?' Jamie asks as we leave the magnificence of the ballroom and follow Fisher down a long corridor, past the entrance to the kitchen we'd visited a little while ago.

'She's the captain of the St Felix branch of Wave Watch,' Fisher says, unhooking a burgundy red rope that's blocking access to a carpeted staircase. 'Everyone who's a part of the Wave Watch is a volunteer, but there has to be someone in charge, I guess.'

A mobile phone rings and Jamie grabs for his pocket.

'Sorry,' he says, glancing at the screen before he answers. 'I need to take this, it's my agent. Hey, Rach, yes, can you just hold a moment? I'm in a bad area; I'll need to go outside.'

He turns to us. 'Apologies. Can I follow you up in a minute? Just up there, is it?'

'There's only one door at the top of the stairs,' Fisher says. 'It's marked "Wave Watch"; you can't miss it.'

'Great, I'll be along shortly.' Jamie heads backs down the corridor towards the entrance, already talking into his phone.

'So, how does Lucinda feel about us?' I ask as Fisher hooks the rope behind us and we continue up the stairs together. 'I remember you telling me when I first arrived that the Wave Watch were not too happy about having to move off Aurora to make way for us.'

'Difficult to say. Like I told you, I don't think any of them were that happy about moving. Some were just more vocal about it than others.'

'Your grandfather doesn't think much of this Lucinda, does he?'

'He told you about that?' Fisher turns back and looks at me. 'I'm surprised.'

'Yes, I'm not really sure why myself. But I get the feeling she's pretty formidable.'

'That's one word for it,' Fisher mutters. 'There are others . . .'

'As long as she's polite enough to answer our questions, that's all that matters to me. All we need to know is if our equipment is working correctly. Although it seems to have been fine through all the recent weather – spot on, in fact.'

We reach the top of the staircase, and Fisher knocks on a door with a sign that says –

ST FELIX WAVE WATCH.

PRIVATE.

PLEASE KNOCK BEFORE ENTERING.

'Just a minute!' a female voice calls from the other side of the door.

Fisher rolls his eyes at me. 'That's Lucinda,' he whispers.

'You may enter!' the voice calls now.

Fisher turns the handle on the door and holds it open for me.

'Ah, Fisher.' A tall, middle-aged woman with her blonde hair pinned tightly to the back of her head comes towards us. She's wearing a uniform of black trousers, a white shirt with black epaulettes, and a black tie with a gold compass badge pinned to it. 'These must be our visitors.'

'Yes, these are the people currently stationed over on Aurora, weather watching,' Fisher says. 'But it's only Sky for the moment. Jamie is just taking a phone call, but he'll be along shortly.'

I desperately want to correct Fisher and tell Lucinda that what we're doing is so much more than simply watching the weather. But I realise that to an outside observer, that's exactly what it looks like, so I leave it, and instead I shake Lucinda's outstretched hand.

'Pleased to meet you, Sky,' she says. 'Fisher says you're having some difficulties with your equipment. What can I do to help?'

'Thank you. I wouldn't call them difficulties, exactly. It's just we had some odd readings last week. Our equipment forecast calm, dry weather, and then we had that unexpected but severe storm, which really caught us out. I know you have weather-reading equipment here as part of the Wave Watch, and I wondered if you'd managed to predict the storm yourselves?'

I'm sure I see Lucinda's smile stiffen slightly at my question.

'I'm certain we did,' she says, not moving. 'In fact, I was on duty that day and I remember noting the readings down that predicted inclement weather.'

'Could you possibly check?' I ask. 'Then I'd know for sure if our equipment is malfunctioning.'

'I really don't need to,' she insists, folding her arms across her chest. 'My memory for these things is incredibly good.'

'I don't doubt that,' I say, trying to remain polite. 'But if you

174

could just check the readings then I could compare them to my own and see how they differ.'

I'm pretty sure by the stony look on Lucinda's face she is going to refuse, but then the door behind me swings open a little.

'Hi, sorry I'm late,' Jamie says, not following the formal instructions and simply poking his head around the door. 'What have I missed?'

'Ah, here is our errant weather watcher,' Fisher says, opening the door fully so Jamie has no choice but to come in.

Lucinda glances briefly at Jamie, then does a double take.

'Do I know you from somewhere?' she asks, looking with much more interest at him this time.

Here we go ... I think, trying hard not to sigh out loud. *We only came here to check on their readings, not pose for selfies.*

'I really don't think so,' Jamie says, to my surprise. 'I'm sure I would remember if we'd met. So then, what's been happening—'

But he's cut off mid-sentence.

'I have it!' Lucinda suddenly calls out in glee. 'You're that weather forecaster chappie, aren't you?'

Lucinda has become much more animated since Jamie arrived. When I'd been talking to her before, she'd remained firmly rooted to the spot, now she moves companionably towards him.

And Jamie looks more than a little uncomfortable.

'No one told me *you* were going to be moving on to our island,' Lucinda continues, unabashed. 'All kept hush-hush, was it, so as not to cause a stir? Minor celebrity, and all that?' She taps the side of her nose 'Don't worry, your secret is safe with me.'

'Er ... yes,' Jamie says, looking wildly at me for assistance while he backs away from Lucinda's advancing presence.

But I just grin back at him.

Fisher also seems to be finding this encounter highly amusing.

'*So*, how can I help *you*?' Lucinda asks Jamie, disregarding Fisher and me for the time being.

With Lucinda's back now to me I nod encouragingly. *Go on!* I mouth silently to Jamie.

'Er, Sky may have already explained, but we think some of our weather recording equipment might be on the blink, and we wondered if we could possibly see your readings for the night we had that awful storm.'

'I don't see why not,' Lucinda says, smiling sweetly at Jamie. 'Let me just see if I can find those *particular* records.'

She floats towards a filing cabinet, pulls a set of keys from her pocket, unlocks the top drawer, and then begins to thumb through the files inside while Jamie scuttles over towards Fisher and me.

I give him the thumbs-up. 'You got further than me,' I whisper.

Lucinda swivels arounds and glares at me. 'Is there something else?' she asks.

'No, not at all. I was just saying what a lovely station you've turned this part of the castle into. Wasn't I, Fisher?'

'Yes ... you've done very well in the circumstances,' Fisher gabbles.

'Hmm ...' Lucinda says. 'Yes, well, when you're evicted from the station you've spent years building up from nothing, it's not easy. But we're doing our best in the limited environment of Tregarlan.'

As she turns back to the filing cabinet, Fisher pulls a face behind her back. He pushes his finger to the end of his nose so it points up in the air like a piggy.

I have to repress a giggle.

'Here we are!' Lucinda says, pulling a manilla file from the drawer. 'This is the one.' She opens up the file and reads from one of the papers in there.

'Yes, nothing unusual here; we correctly predicted there would be rough weather at sea that night. It must be your equipment that's faulty.' Even though she uses the word *equipment*, her expression suggests she actually means me.

I ignore her implication and decide to remain polite. 'How very strange; all our other readings have been spot on since we arrived. Our equipment has been working very well. It's just that one night that's odd. Would you mind if I took a look at your observations?' I reach out my hand, but Lucinda presses the closed file tightly to her chest.

'Like I said, *we* got the forecast exactly right.' She turns and thrusts the file back into the cabinet and slams the drawer shut. 'I suggest you go and take a look at your own equipment and see if it's been set up incorrectly. It can often happen to an inexperienced forecaster.'

Inexperienced! I open my mouth to respond, but luckily Jamie speaks first.

'Of course we'll be doing that. Won't we, Sky?' He looks at me. '*Sky?*' he prompts.

'Yes,' I say through gritted teeth. No wonder Walter doesn't like this woman; I'd only been in her presence for a few minutes, and I was already wound as tight as one of the little horn shells Jamie and I had found on the island's beach yesterday.

'This observation tower seems so much better equipped

than ours,' Jamie says now, to my absolute horror. 'I'd love for you to give me a tour around it sometime, Lucinda.'

While I glare at him, Lucinda smiles. 'Of course, when would be a good time for you? It's, Sonny, isn't it?'

Jamie nods. 'Yes, Sonny Samuels at your service, ma'am!' He puts his arm on Lucinda's shoulder and guides her gently towards the front of the tower, where a desk filled with equipment I recognise only too well is housed in front of a large window. 'No time like the present. Now, let's take in this beautiful vista first . . .'

I'm about to storm out of the office, when Jamie glances quickly back at us, and nods his head briefly in the direction of the filing cabinet.

I look at him with a puzzled expression, but luckily Fisher understands.

While Jamie keeps Lucinda occupied with conversation about the view and what they can see from the castle, Fisher moves silently, a few paces at a time, towards the cabinet.

Then Jamie asks a few more technical questions about the equipment, all the while making sure Lucinda's gaze is firmly directed away from us.

When Fisher begins to ease the drawer open and it makes a tiny squeaking sound, Jamie calls out, 'Was that a sea eagle?' in such a loud voice that even I jump and look out of the window with them, allowing Fisher to silently remove the file from the drawer and gently push it back again.

He stuffs the file under his Tregarlan fleece jacket.

'Yes, receiving loud and clear!' he says suddenly into his walkie-talkie. 'Yup, I'll be right along. Over and out. Gotta go,' he says as Lucinda turns around. 'There's a boy stuck in the . . . fountain. Can you see yourselves out?' he asks me and Jamie.

'Yes, thank you so much, Fisher,' I say in an equally unnatural voice. 'It's been so kind of you to show us around. Hasn't it, Jamie?' I nod ferociously, in a way I hope makes Jamie understand we've got the file.

'Yes, absolutely marvellous,' Jamie says as Fisher backs quickly through the wooden door. 'And thank *you*, Lucinda. I'll be sure to drop by again sometime so we can finish our tour together.'

'Oh, do you have to go?' Lucinda asks, making no attempt to conceal her disappointment. 'We've only just got started.'

'I'm afraid I must.' Jamie takes Lucinda's hand and kisses the back of it. 'But I shall return to the tower, fair lady. Don't you fret.'

I purse my lips together tightly to stop myself from laughing.

'Yes, thank you, Lucinda,' I squeak, my control over my voice not as great as my control of my laughter. 'It's been . . . enlightening.' And I dash for the door, before my laughter explodes all over the office.

'It's funny,' I hear Lucinda say through the open door as I head down the stairs after Fisher, 'I didn't even realise there was a fountain at Tregarlan?'

'Did you get the right one?' I ask Fisher as I reach the bottom of the stairs and he lets me back through the rope again.

'Of course,' Fisher says, tapping his fleece. 'Let's go up to my apartment, though, before we look at it; I don't want madam up there catching us in the act.'

'I hope Jamie can get away,' I say, as we head to Fisher's apartment on the other side of the house. 'She was pretty full-on with him.'

'That man is a hero,' Fisher says as we hurry back through the long corridors.

'You didn't see him kiss her hand!'

Fisher stops. 'Really?' he says, pulling a face. 'Now that is beyond the call of duty!'

We reach Fisher's apartment – a small but cosy little flat at the top of the west wing of Tregarlan.

Fisher looks down at the file in his hand. 'Let's wait for Jamie, shall we?'

I nod. 'Wait, does Jamie know where your apartment is?'

Fisher pulls his phone from his pocket. 'You made it out alive then, mate?' he says as Jamie speedily picks up at the other end. 'Yes, you're nearly here. Turn right along the corridor then it's the third door along on the left. See you in a minute.'

'He's on his way,' he says to me.

'This is a lovely little flat,' I say, looking around. 'What a view!' I move towards one of the leaded windows. 'You really can see everything from here, can't you?'

'Like I told you before, this isn't the worst job I've ever had. There are some perks.'

There's a knock at the door. Fisher goes to open it and Jamie comes bounding into the room.

'Phew, I didn't think I'd get away. Lucinda was very insistent I come back and visit her . . . *alone*.'

'Looks like you've made another fan!' I grin. 'She won't be so keen on you if she discovers this file has gone, though.'

'I'll put it back tonight when everyone from the Wave Watch has left,' Fisher assures us. 'I have keys to everywhere here.'

'Have you looked yet?' Jamie asks me, gesturing to the file on the small coffee table at the centre of Fisher's open-plan living area.

'No, we were waiting for you.'

'Go on then,' he says. 'Let's see what this big secret is that Lucinda doesn't want us to see.'

I reach down for the file, open it up, then quickly scan the typed pages of information.

Then I look up at the two men, both eagerly awaiting my verdict.

'What is it?' Jamie asks impatiently. 'I can tell by your face something isn't right.'

'According to this file, all the readings taken here at Tregarlan on that day suggest there was very little chance of there being a storm. Their forecast should have been for calm, dry weather, like ours was. I've studied our readings for that night enough to know these are almost identical.'

'But,' Jamie says looking puzzled, 'if we and the Wave Watch both took readings that predicted calm weather, how did there end up being such a violent storm that night? Both sets of equipment can't be wrong, can they?'

'Very unlikely,' I agree. 'But what I'm even more interested in is why Lucinda deliberately lied to us. If these are the Wave Watch readings for that night – and it would seem very likely they are from what I'm seeing – then why would she tell us they'd correctly predicted a storm, when their data suggested otherwise? What possible reason could she have to hide it from us?'

Seventeen

We leave Tregarlan none the wiser after having a cup of coffee with Fisher at his apartment. None of us can think of a reason why Lucinda would lie about the readings – unless it was just to cover up a blunder someone had made.

But for anyone who knew anything about reading weather equipment, to make a mistake of that magnitude would be pretty hard to do. We had predicted calm dry weather because that's what our equipment had told us. The Wave Watch had taken very similar readings, and yet according to Lucinda, and a couple of local fishermen who Fisher had checked with, the Wave Watch's forecast had been spot on that night – stormy weather, with strong winds and high waves. So to keep safe, the fishermen hadn't taken their boats out that night, and had stayed home instead.

'It just doesn't make sense,' I say as Jamie and I pull up in our usual parking spot by the harbour so we can pop into town and get some shopping. 'We both registered the same readings. Why would the Wave Watch say it's going to be stormy if they thought it wasn't?'

Jamie shrugs. 'I have absolutely no idea. But what is interesting is however they went about it, they actually got the forecast right, didn't they? It was stormy that night, so whoever made that judgement call probably saved a few people from going through what I did.'

'Yeah, I know it worked out for the best, but I still want to know how and why that happened. And also why Lucinda was so defensive about it?'

'Maybe she just didn't want to admit they got it wrong.'

'But that's the thing – *they* didn't get it wrong, did they? However they went about it, their actual forecast was right. It was ours that was wrong.' I hated saying it, but it was true – somehow, we'd messed up.

Jamie grins as we climb out of the Jeep. 'I think that's what you're more concerned about – the fact you were wrong. I'm guessing it doesn't happen to you very often, does it?'

'I don't know what you mean,' I say as casually as I can. I knew exactly what he was suggesting, but I wasn't going to admit it.

'I mean, you don't like the fact that you got the forecast wrong and the Wave Watch got it right.'

'Technically, it was *you* who got it wrong,' I tell him as we begin to walk together along the harbour front. 'You were the one who said the weather was going to be calm that night.'

Jamie shakes his head. 'Ah, I see where this is going ... you can't blame your equipment – which we've discovered in a roundabout way isn't actually faulty – so you're blaming me instead. You checked those readings, Sky, you know what they said. I didn't get anything wrong, did I? Admit it, go on; you know you can if you try.'

'Perhaps when you typed your readings on to your laptop

you made a few mistakes? It's easily done, an odd digit here and there can change readings quite considerably.'

As far I'm concerned this has all been light-hearted banter. The sort of teasing Jamie enjoyed. But for some reason my last statement seems to rile him, he stops walking and simply stares at me.

'What?' I ask, still playing along. 'You can hand it out but you can't take it, huh?'

Jamie sighs and shakes his head. 'I'll never get away from it, will I?' he mutters, looking over my shoulder towards the sea. It seems a long way out right now, but I know it's just beginning to turn.

'What do you mean?' I ask. 'Get away from what?'

'Nothing. Nothing at all. Do you have the purse?' Jamie asks, clearly irritated about something.

'Er, yes, I think so.' I open my bag to look.

'Good, then I'm going for a walk. I'll see you back here in an hour. If I'm not back by then head back to the island in the Jeep. I'll find my own way later.' He thrusts the Jeep keys at me and for a brief moment our eyes meet and I see a mixture of hurt and disappointment in the bright blue of Jamie's, before he swiftly turns and marches away, leaving me staring after him.

As I walk towards the centre of town, I wonder what I'd said to upset him so much. I'm very aware diplomacy isn't my strong point, and I can often come over a little bluntly, but I wouldn't deliberately say something to offend. I truly thought we were just having a bit of fun with each other.

But the look in Jamie's eyes before he left suggested otherwise. I don't want to be the cause of anyone's hurt or distress, especially not Jamie's.

I'm so caught up in my thoughts that I don't really look where I'm going, and I'm about to step off the pavement to cross the road when I hear a shout – 'Hey!'

I look down and see I'm about to collide with Jack in his wheelchair. He is forced to brake hard.

'Gosh, sorry!' I call apologetically. 'I didn't see ...' I pause, not wanting to cause even more offence today.

'Me there?' Jack finishes as he turns back from where he's skidded across the road to avoid me. 'It's fine, don't worry about it. You're not the first and you won't be the last – it seems I'm invisible to some people all the way down here in the gutter.'

I look down at Jack grinning up at me. I know he's only joking, but I can't help myself. 'But I don't want to be one of *those* people,' I wail, as I burst into tears. 'I know, you see. I get it. We shouldn't be invisible, but to most we are.'

'Whoa!' Jacks says, looking up at me with concern. 'I was only joking. Kate is always telling me my sense of humour will get me into trouble one day. Please don't cry.'

'I'm sorry.' I try to pull myself together. 'It's been a weird sort of day.'

Jack looks at his sports watch. 'Would you like a coffee?' he asks. 'I guess it's too early for a pint?' he suggests hopefully.

I manage a half-smile. 'I'm driving, but I'm happy to accompany you to the pub if you'd like?'

'I'm driving too,' Jack says, looking down at his wheels. 'But it never stops me!'

So Jack and I head to the Merry Mermaid, which as usual is already surrounded by holidaymakers, none of whom seem to think it's too early to sit outside in the sunshine sipping pints of beer.

'What can I get you?' Jack asks.

'No, let me,' I reply. 'After all, I'm the one who nearly collided with you.'

Jack nods. 'Well, there is that, I suppose. Pint of best, then, please. I'll see if I can get us a seat out here.' He looks around to see if any are free. 'Lucky we'll only need the one!'

I head into the pub, and find inside is a lot quieter than outside, with most of the Merry Mermaid's lunchtime trade preferring to sit outside admiring the harbour view.

'A pint of best, please?' I ask Rita as she comes over to take my order. 'And I'll have a fizzy water, please.'

'Ice, lovely?' Rita asks.

'Yes please.'

While Rita busies herself with our drinks, I stand at the bar and look around the pub.

'Morning!' a voice calls from the corner, and I see Walter sitting at a small table drinking from a ceramic tankard. He pulls a small pocket watch from his waistcoat. 'No, I stand corrected, it's just the afternoon.' He tucks the watch safely back.

'Oh, hello again,' I say, smiling. 'I didn't see you there.'

'That's just how I like it. I prefer to tuck myself away in a corner; I speak up only if I want to talk to someone then.'

'I'm honoured,' I tell him.

Walter looks at the two drinks Rita is lining up on the bar.

'Are you with your weatherman friend today?' he asks.

'Er, no, I'm not actually. Another . . . friend.'

Walter nods slowly. 'I see. I heard the other fella had a spot of trouble out at sea the other night?'

For a moment I wonder how Walter knows this, then I remember.

'Did Fisher tell you?'

Walter nods again. 'He did indeed. Strange course of events, if you ask me. I understand the weather forecast was clear that night?'

'Yes and no. We forecast it calm and dry from the readings on our equipment, but apparently the Wave Watch somehow managed to forecast the storm.'

'Somehow?' Walter asks.

'Yes . . .' I'm not sure what to say now without dropping us in it. I doubt Walter has seen Fisher since this morning's escapades. 'Did you see the storm coming?' I ask, suddenly remembering Walter is an amateur forecaster on the side.

'I did, as it goes.'

Damn, this made us look even worse if both the Wave Watch and Walter had forecast the bad weather.

'But you'd not have picked it up on any of your fancy instruments.'

'How did you know, then?'

'It was in the clouds,' Walter says, taking a sip of his pint.

'Most storms are,' I reply, half joking.

'I mean, I saw the signs in the clouds – they told me.'

Something about what Walter is saying strikes a chord – hadn't Jamie said something similar about that night? Had they both seen the same thing?

'But they don't trust my methods at the Wave Watch,' Walter continues, 'so I find it very odd they knew, if your instruments were telling you otherwise?'

'I thought our recording equipment might be faulty, but we've had it . . . checked and it seems to be working fine now. It forecast and recorded all the rough weather we've had over the last few days absolutely fine. It's very odd.'

'And you're sure the Wave Watch gave out a storm warning?'

'Apparently.'

'Hmm …' Walter appears to be thinking deeply about something.

But I don't get to find out what as Jack appears at the open pub entrance. 'Just checking you hadn't stood me up!' he says cheerily. 'But I can see you've got caught up talking to Old Walter Weather here.'

'Hello, Jack!' Walter greets Jack with a brief touch to his cap. 'I didn't know you were this young lady's waiting friend?'

Jack glances briefly at me when Walter uses the word friend, but goes with it.

'I am indeed. I should have guessed you were in here – all the ladies would stand me up for you!'

Walter smiles. 'Back in the day, perhaps. Not so much now. Don't let me hold you up any longer, Miss Sky. I'm sure young Jack here has many more interesting stories to tell than me.'

'Won't you join us?' I ask, eager to hear more about Walter's weather forecasting methods, and how he might have predicted the storm.

'Oh no, I won't cramp your style,' Walter says. 'I'm more than happy sitting here with my own thoughts. You two go ahead.'

'Perhaps I can catch up with you another time, then?' I say, quickly paying Rita and lifting our drinks. 'I'd be very interested in hearing more about how you predict weather.' *Gosh, this place is really changing me. I'd never have wanted to learn about alternative ways to forecast the weather before I arrived here.*

'Of course,' Walter says, lifting his pint. 'It would be my absolute pleasure to talk to you any time, Miss Sky.'

Jack and I head outside and quickly grab a small table that a young couple have just vacated.

'Nice old fella,' Jack says, gesturing back towards the pub with his glass. 'I've a lot of time for Walter.'

'Does everyone know everyone in St Felix?' I ask. 'It often seems that way when you speak to anyone.'

Jack laughs. 'Yes, it can seem a little odd when you first come here. I remember when I opened my art shop, I couldn't fathom how either everyone knew everyone else, or they were related or something. You soon get used to it, though; the locals of St Felix are a tight-knit bunch, but they're very welcoming to newcomers.'

'I'm only here temporarily. So sadly, I won't be here long enough to experience that.'

Jack nods knowingly.

'What does that mean?'

'It's easy to think you're only here as a visitor, but this town has a way of getting under your skin and into your heart in the strangest of ways. Take it from me – an ex-soldier – this town will have you believing in things you never thought possible. I still don't believe some of the things that happened to me when I first came here, but they led to me finding a completely new path in life, and to a wonderful woman who I still can't quite believe feels the same way about me as I do about her, and for that I'll be forever grateful.'

Jack, looking quite emotional, hurriedly takes a gulp from his pint.

'Now, don't tell anyone I just told you that,' he says quickly, wiping one of his eyes. 'It's not good for my image!'

I nod, but I wonder what he means? What sort of things could have happened to this ex-soldier here in St Felix that would make him say the things he just had?

'Let's talk about you, shall we?' Jack suggests, clearly keen to move on. 'What made you burst into tears just now?'

189

'I'm sorry about that,' I say, still feeling mortified. 'It's not like me at all.'

'I figured that,' Jack says. 'Are you having a bad day with your illness?'

I shrug. 'It's partly that, I guess. I know I'm probably pushing myself too hard right now, and I'm exhausted as a result. But there's so much we need to do.'

'Strangely, after I met you the other day, I happened to read an article in the paper about ME. It's being linked to Long Covid, isn't it?'

I nod. 'Some of the symptoms of Long Covid are very similar to those of ME because it often begins after a virus.'

'Is that what happened to you?'

'Yep, I managed to contract glandular fever – at my age!' I gave a half-smile; it still seemed silly even now. But that one illness had totally changed my life. 'I got through all my university years without catching anything like that, and then in my thirties I contracted a nasty bout, and just never fully recovered. I say never recovered, but some of my worst times with ME are ten times worse than my worst time with glandular fever.'

'Sounds grim. Was there nothing they could do?'

'Not after the glandular fever had subsided. They called it post-viral fatigue to begin with and said I'd recover eventually and it might take some time. But when six months had passed and I still wasn't getting any better, that's when it became ME – in medical terms, anyway. To me it just felt like my life was over, and I'd never feel well again. I was virtually bedbound at that stage. I could barely look after myself I was that ill.'

'I can relate to feeling like your life is over,' Jack says knowingly. 'When I had my accident, I couldn't see the point of even trying to go on without my legs. But things eventually change, and you begin to realise there is light at the end of the tunnel if you look hard enough.'

'Our disabilities are so different, and yet in some ways they're very similar.'

Jack nods. 'You mentioned before you had to use a wheel-chair for a while?'

'Yes, I was very weak then, my leg muscles just wouldn't support me, and I was in so much pain when I tried to walk any distance, even using crutches. That's the thing – most people think that having ME is just about being tired all the time. But it's so much more than that, it affects your whole body.' I take a sip of my water. 'But you don't want to hear about my problems all day.'

'Actually I do, I'm interested. When I was in rehab after my accident I was with a lot of other people in the same boat. I wasn't very good at polite chit-chat back then, I'm not that great at it now,' he pulls a wry face, 'so I didn't try and under-stand what they were going through, it was all about me. I regret that now. People can be sympathetic to your issues, but it's only someone who's going through something similar who can truly understand what it's like to have any sort of disability.'

I look at Jack and suddenly realise he's not simply being polite listening to my woes, he actually wants to talk about them. He's getting as much out of this conversation as I am.

'Like I said before,' he continues, 'the people around here are great, but I haven't met many like me. Probably because they're not daft enough to try and live in a town full of cobbled streets and steep Cornish hills!'

'That's true. It's not exactly easy getting around here, is it?'

'Nope, but I like a challenge. I'm guessing you do, too – otherwise why would you have taken a job stationed on a remote island? There must be easier meteorological jobs in a cosy office somewhere? My guess is you wanted to prove everyone wrong. It's often that that pushes people on to better things.'

I smile; he'd got it spot on.

'You could be right. I was off work on sick leave a long time; perhaps I do want to prove to everyone I'm still capable of doing my job.'

'Not at the detriment of your health, though? It's not worth that.'

'No, I know I can't push myself too hard, otherwise I'll suffer. I'm trying to pace myself while I'm here, but it's so difficult. We have some stuff going on right now at the station.'

'Is that why you were upset before?'

'Partly, and partly because I think I've upset one of my colleagues – Jamie.'

'Is he the TV weatherman I've heard about? His presence in St Felix seems to have caused quite a stir with the ladies of the town.'

'Yes, that's him, and he does seem to have that sort of effect on people.'

'But not on you?'

'Good Lord, no! He's a bit too full of himself for my liking,' I say automatically. But immediately I realise I don't think that at all now.

That had been my first impression of Sonny, but since I'd got to know Jamie a little better, I'd discovered that really wasn't him at all, it was all a front. I'm about to correct myself but Jack continues.

'I know the sort,' he says, nodding. 'So why have you upset him?'

'Truth is I don't know. He stormed off a little while ago and I'm really not sure why.'

'Sounds a bit temperamental to me.'

'He's not usually like that,' I say, keen to make up for what I said before. 'He's usually very chilled and relaxed. It's really quite out of character for him.'

'You must have said something pretty bad, then,' Jack says, and as I stare at him in dismay, I realise he's joking again.

'Don't worry, I'm only teasing you,' he says hurriedly. 'I'm sure you've done nothing wrong. He'll come back with his tail between his legs, like a dog who's been up to no good. And talking of dogs, here comes mine.'

I follow his gaze and see a pretty woman walking towards us with a golden Labrador on a red lead.

'Hello, Barney,' he says to the dog, who I recognise from the hill, 'Hello, love,' he says to the woman, who bends down to kiss him. 'Kate, this is Sky – she's one of the meteorologists staying over on Aurora. I nearly hit her with my wheelchair, so I'm buying her a drink.'

'Nice to meet you, Sky,' Kate says, smiling. She sits down on a spare seat next to the table.

'And you, Kate,' I say. 'But Jack is being very gallant. The truth is I nearly walked into him, so it's me buying him a drink by way of apology.'

'That sounds more like it!' Kate says, laughing. 'Jack has never been known to turn down a free pint! How are you getting on over on Aurora?'

'Good, thank you.'

'Have you recorded anything unusual? I hear that's why you're staying with us this summer.'

I like the way Kate describes this, as if we're guests staying in a friendly B&B, not simply strangers staying in the town for a few weeks.

'This and that,' I reply vaguely.

'That doesn't surprise me – if anywhere is going to have unusual weather it would be St Felix!'

'Jack was saying something similar before,' I say, intrigued by Kate's statement. 'Why do you think that?'

Kate glances at Jack. He gives a small shrug.

'Let's just say St Felix is known for its – how can I put this? – *curious* happenings. Anyone who stays here for any length of time usually experiences something or other.'

'What kind of curious happenings?'

'It's different for everyone,' Kate says, not sounding at all like she's making this up, but that she totally believes everything she's saying. 'But there's an awful lot of us that have experienced something magical.' She glances at Jack again, and the look that passes between them only confirms to me the validity of what she's saying.

'Something none of us can quite explain, but something that changes us, changes our circumstances, and always brings about good.'

Eighteen

I stay a while outside the pub, chatting with Kate and Jack. They're a little guarded when I ask more about these strange happenings they've both talked about, but I understand it's something to do with the craft shop that Kate owns. However, I decide not to push them any further, and eventually after a pleasant half-hour or so in the sunshine we go our separate ways.

Goodness, I think, looking at my watch, *I'll need to get a move on if I'm to get all the shopping on the list we made this morning.* I don't want to get stuck like last time if the tide comes in quickly.

I look out across the harbour, and even though the sea is much further in now, I should just have enough time if I hurry.

I set off towards the bakery, but just as I'm turning into Harbour Street, I bump into Jamie carrying a lot of shopping bags.

'Oh! You're back,' I say, a little surprised to see him. 'And you've been shopping too?'

'I have,' Jamie says calmly, putting the bags down on the

ground. 'I felt bad leaving you to do it all, so after I'd cleared my head, I came back. I was going to call you, but then I saw you at the pub . . . '

He leaves this statement hanging in the air as though I should add something to it.

'I was there for a bit,' I reply, wondering why he'd done that, but pleased he seems to be in a better mood now. 'You'll never guess who I bumped into and what he was telling me,' I say, intending to tell him about Walter.

'I saw who you were with,' Jamie says a little coolly.

I stare at him, perplexed, wondering why he might have an issue with this.

'I was actually talking about Walter, who was inside the pub, but I did have a quick drink with Jack and Kate too. I don't know if you know, but they both own shops in St Felix and they were telling me all sorts about the town.'

Jamie looks thrown for a moment, and then he quickly pulls himself together.

'I didn't see Kate when I passed by, I only saw you and Jack having a drink together.'

'And you immediately assumed what?'

'I just assumed, that's all. Wrongly, it seems.'

'Not that I should have to explain, but this is the second time I've bumped into Jack in St Felix, only this time we went for a drink. We have a lot in common.'

'Do you? Like what?' Jamie asks with a puzzled expression. 'Isn't he in a wheelchair?'

Again, I stare at Jamie. But this time I'm speechless.

'What?' Jamie looks just as perplexed with me as I had him a moment ago.

'If you don't know then I can't help you, I'm afraid,' I say, shaking my head. I turn and march smartly away, leaving him standing on the pavement just as he had left me earlier.

'Sky!' he calls. 'What have I said? Aren't you going to help me with this shopping?'

But I don't turn back; I just keep walking towards the Jeep.

I walk quickly and steadily until I reach the vehicle and then I open the driver-side door and sit inside, staring out of the windscreen.

Jamie soon catches up. He silently loads the shopping bags into the back while I wait. He then comes round to the passenger side of the Jeep and climbs into the seat next to me.

'What was all that?' he asks, staring at me.

I debate whether to reply, but sulking isn't my style, so I decide to confront him.

'How would you like it if every time someone saw you, they described you as that weatherman off the telly?' I say, looking at him for the first time.

'That's usually what they do say,' Jamie replies innocently. 'You might add handsome or hot to that description. But I don't mind it.'

'You wouldn't.' I sigh. 'But some people would. Jack is more than just his disability,' I say, hoping he'll understand.

'Ah, I see now. You're cross because I mentioned his wheelchair.'

'No, it's not that. People who have disabilities don't mind you noticing their issues, but they don't want to be seen as only that. In the same way as people who are ginger are more than just the colour of their hair. Or people from ethnic minorities are more than just their skin colour. It's a *part* of who they are, not *all* of who they are. Do you understand?'

Jamie nods. 'Yes, of course I do. I'm not prejudiced.'

'Good.'

'But what I don't understand is why you're so touchy about it? Do you have a friend who's in a wheelchair, or a family member, is that it?'

'No,' I say hurriedly before he can ask more. 'Too many people make rapid judgements about others without knowing their full story. I just don't like it, that's all.'

Jamie stares out of the window, deep in thought.

'I do understand, you know. Even though you think I don't,' he says, turning back to me with a solemn expression. And I'm surprised by the earnest look in his eyes.

'What do you mean?' I ask quietly.

'It doesn't matter.' He shrugs. 'It's not something you need to worry about. We should head back.' He looks through the windscreen again likes he's willing the Jeep to move forward and set off across the causeway by itself.

'You're right when you say your problems aren't something I need to worry about,' I tell him. 'But you're my friend and I'd like to know. That is if you'd like to tell me?'

Jamie looks at me in astonishment that I've used the word friend. But his expression quickly changes to quiet pleasure as he says softly. 'I like that you called us friends.'

'Well, we are, aren't we?'

'Yes.' He nods. 'I think we are now.' He holds my gaze for a tad longer than usual.

'So?' I ask gently, making him jump.

'Really, it's nothing,' Jamie says, and I can see him thinking quickly. 'It's . . . it's my divorce, that's all.'

'Oh?' I say, a little surprised. 'What's wrong?'

'The tabloids have been all over Carrie – that's my ex – and me since we announced we were splitting up. You might have seen some of the – let's call them salacious – stories they've printed. Mainly about me.'

'Not really.' I shrug. 'I tend to stay away from gossip.'

'Good. That's good. Let's just say our split isn't exactly amicable, and some of the stories that have come out in the press are blatant lies – but they're all credited to a source. That *source* is likely my ex-wife.'

'Nasty.'

'Yes, it is. She's also sadly one of the main shareholders at Met Central, so she's making things very difficult for me there too. If it was up to her, I think I'd have been fired by now. But luckily, it's not her decision. TV is all about viewing figures and I get pretty high ones for a weather forecast.'

'Yes, I did know that,' I tell him.

'I thought you might. Anyway, to keep Carrie sweet, it was agreed they'd take me off screen for a while. I think sending me here was the ideal opportunity to hide me away, but keep me on the payroll until things calm down a little. So,' he says, holding out his hands, 'here I am.'

I nod, waiting for more. But when Jamie doesn't continue, I ask, 'Is that it?'

'Er, yes, I think so.'

'But you said you understood about being judged without people knowing the full story? I'm sorry that you're having difficulties with your ex, really I am, but I don't get how it's the same?'

'Because people judge me by what they read in the newspapers and online,' Jamie says, although even he doesn't sound that convinced. 'They don't know the real story, do they?'

'Right, I see.'

'Don't you believe me?'

'Yes, of course. I just don't think it's quite the same as being judged for a disability that people can see.' *Or one they can't*, I think to myself.

Jamie nods, taking the point. 'No, of course it's not. The two are not comparable at all.'

'Is there something else you want to share?' I ask hopefully. 'I got the feeling earlier there was.'

Again, we hold each other's gaze.

'I get the feeling there's something you're not sharing with me either,' Jamie replies. 'Maybe we're both hiding a secret?'

'Gosh, look at that tide?' I say, looking out of the window. 'We'd better get a move on. We don't want to get caught out like last time!'

I quickly start the Jeep's engine, put it into gear and pull away towards the causeway before Jamie can question me further.

I still don't think he's telling me the full story. But then I'm not exactly being honest with him either, am I?

Nineteen

The next few days pass uneventfully, and I'm surprised how relieved I feel.

I'm able to get plenty of rest in between my weather-watching shifts, and this allows me to accompany Jamie and the dogs for several longish walks across the sands over to St Felix when the tide is out. Sometimes we stop for cups of coffee in the sunshine and occasional pasties, which are eaten while sitting on one of the wooden benches that are dotted about the town, overlooking some of the more attractive viewpoints.

It's lovely and relaxing and I find I'm enjoying Jamie's company more each day I spend with him. Underneath the bravado and swagger that is TV personality Sonny Samuels, Jamie appears to be a very different sort of man. He's intelligent, astute and often very sensitive, and he has a wonderful knack of making me laugh at the tiniest of things that we notice as we sit watching the fascinating and curious world of St Felix pass by in front of us.

I don't like Sonny one bit. But I have to admit his alter-ego, Jamie, is really starting to grow on me.

'Wouldn't it be wonderful to live in a place like this,' Jamie says to my surprise on one of these days when we're resting after walking the dogs. It's a gorgeous afternoon in St Felix – the sun is shining and the town looks particularly beautiful from our view-point, high up on one of the hills overlooking the bay. 'I've always loved living in the city, but now I'm starting to wonder if those happy times I spent with my aunt by the coast when I was young might actually be something I'd like to return to in the future.'

'St Felix is a far cry from London, that's for sure.'

'Can *you* imagine yourself living by the sea one day instead of in the hustle and bustle of the city?'

I think about this. 'I've been stationed in weather stations all over the world, so I've lived in lots of places over the years. It's not difficult to imagine living somewhere new.'

'I know, but St Felix isn't just new, is it? It's special . . . '

'I see you're falling for its charms, then. Jack warned me about that.'

'What do you mean, he warned you?'

'He said . . . Oh what was it again? Ah yes, St Felix has a way of getting under your skin and into your heart in the strangest of ways.'

'That's quite poetic.'

'Yes, I thought so.'

'Bit of a strange thing to say, though?'

'Maybe. But it seems to be casting its spell over you already.'

'And not you?'

'I never said that. St Felix took a special place in my heart the first time I looked out of the watchtower window and saw that view. Now *that* is magical.'

'It is indeed. We're very lucky to see it every day, aren't we?'

'Yes,' I reply, for once agreeing with him. 'We definitely are.'

*

One rainy morning when the weather isn't quite so pleasant outside, we're having coffee with Talia in between shifts at the watchtower.

'I was talking to Dec and Uncle Ant last night,' Talia begins, looking at us a little apprehensively over the top of her cappuccino.

'Oh yes?' I reply. 'Everything all right?'

'Everything is fine. It's just that the town's arts festival is coming up in a few days, you might have seen the posters?'

I had noticed some brightly coloured flags and banners appearing in and around St Felix advertising a festival. 'Yes, I've seen them.'

'There's several craft competitions for locals that take place on the Saturday to kick it off. You know the kind of thing – arts, crafts, baking, etc.'

I glance at Jamie; I could see where this was heading, even if he couldn't.

'Yeah, I know what you mean,' Jamie says. 'I've presented prizes at these types of village events before. I do hope there's not a bonniest baby competition! I loathe those. Judging kids on the way they look at that young age – it's bad enough when they're older and they have social media to do it for them.'

'Oh no, there's nothing like that,' Talia says quickly. 'It's all based around the arts. The Blue Canary sponsors the baking competition, the craft shop the craft categories, the flower shop the floral displays, and the art shop the paintings. The thing is, Dec was saying how they didn't really have anyone to present the prizes this year, and they wondered if ... ' She pauses, hoping Jamie will fill the gap for her.

'Me?' he asks, looking shocked as his hand goes to his chest and Sonny Samuels makes an appearance again.

'Would you mind?' Talia says, looking apologetic. 'It would be a great coup to have a celebrity doing it this year, and it would probably attract a lot more people to the tents – it's all for local charities, you see.'

'Then how can I refuse?' Jamie says, smiling at her. 'Of course I'll do it. On one condition, though. I do want something in return.'

'What?' Talia asks, obviously dreading the mention of a fee or something similar.

'I want to take part in the pasty eating competition I've seen advertised,' Jamie says with a grin. 'I hear the record is twelve, and I reckon I could break that easily.'

The weather, as we correctly predict, is fine and dry for the St Felix Arts Festival. In fact, all our predictions since 'the storm' incident have been spot on, and even though I've tried to let it go, it still bothers me that we'd got that particular night's forecast so very wrong.

The town, always pretty even in the rain, is even more attractive today, festooned in brightly coloured bunting and flags. There are white marquees dotted around the town anywhere large enough to house one, and even more people are milling about the place than usual, enjoying not only the festival but the beautiful weather it's been granted.

Jamie had been very quickly advertised as the festival's 'celebrity' guest, and when we arrive on Saturday afternoon for the first day of the three-day celebration, he's quickly whisked away to get ready to present the various prizes.

I hadn't really intended on spending very long at the festival. I've been left in charge of the two dogs while Jamie – or should I say 'Sonny', as he morphed into as soon as we arrived – was on presenting duties, and even though both of the dogs are being extremely well behaved, it's a trial attempting to weave in and out of all the people with them on their leads.

'Captain Sky!' a voice calls and I see Fisher coming towards me, hand in hand with Talia. 'You made it over, then?'

'We thought we'd come and support Jamie since he's presenting the prizes today.'

'Hello, you guys,' Fisher says, bending down to fuss the dogs. 'How you doing?'

Fitz and Comet lap up the attention.

'You've dared to leave the station unattended, have you?' Fisher says, looking up at me from where he's squatting down next to the dogs. 'I didn't think you were allowed to abandon your post?' He winks at Talia, who immediately looks embarrassed.

'Just occasionally,' I say, smiling at Talia. 'Hopefully we won't miss anything major – we have our automated equipment to let us know what's been going on while we're away.'

'Would you like us to take the dogs for a while to allow you to look around?' Talia asks, obviously trying to make amends for Fisher's comment. 'There's a lot to see in the tents; I wouldn't want you to miss out.'

'I don't want to put you to any trouble,' I say, looking at Fitz and Comet. 'We'll be just fine if we get away from the crowds and head out for a walk.'

'Miss Sky.' I hear Walter's gentle voice wafting through the crowd and turn to see him steadily making his way towards us. 'I'm so glad you managed to come along; there's a lot here that might interest you.'

'Hello, Walter,' I say, smiling at him. 'Lovely to see you again.'

'And it's even lovelier for me to see you and your two beautiful dogs once more,' Walter says, as Fitz and Comet sniff around his feet.

The two dogs look keenly up at Walter when he produces two dog biscuits from his pocket. 'Would you mind?' he asks me. 'I always keep some about my person in case I bump into any canine friends. I'd run out the other night at the pub when I saw you and I'd like to make amends to them.'

'No, of course not,' I reply, watching the dogs hungrily gobble down their biscuits after Walter has asked them to sit first.

'Now, what are you going to look at first?' Walter asks. 'There's a very interesting exhibition about the history of St Felix in one of the tents, and another has a very thorough exploration of the art of Cornish smuggling.'

'I thought it was just amateur work that was being displayed?' I say, looking around. 'You know, the classes Jamie is presenting the prizes for.'

'Yes, there is that going on. But there's so much more to see and explore if you're interested.'

I get the feeling Walter is keen to show someone around, but he hasn't been able to find anyone yet. 'Why not? It sounds fascinating,' I say politely, wondering what I've let myself in for. 'If you really don't mind taking the dogs?' I ask Talia and Fisher.

'Of course we don't!' Talia says with delight. 'You know how much I love these two beauties.'

I pass her their leads and we agree to meet back here later. Then I allow Walter to guide me in the direction of the exhibitions he'd been talking about.

'It's very kind of you to let me show you around,' Walter says as we walk slowly towards one of the marquees. 'As you've probably guessed, I don't really have anyone to do this sort of thing with. Young Fisher is off with his new lady friend today, and to be honest even if he wasn't, I don't think he'd be that interested. He already knows quite a bit about the history of the area.'

'Do you have any other grandchildren that live locally?' I ask.

'No, Fisher is my only grandchild. My son and his wife were sadly killed in a skiing accident when Fisher was a young boy. My wife and I brought Fisher back to St Felix and raised him together. He's turned out to be a fine young man. Even if I am a little biased.'

'Gosh, I'm so sorry,' I say, meaning it. How awful for Walter, and for Fisher.

'That's one of the reasons I began to study the weather in more detail,' he continues, clearly glad to have an opportunity to talk about his loss. 'David and Hetty were caught out in a freak snowstorm that wasn't forecast by the Swiss authorities at all. They were competent skiers so had gone off-piste for the afternoon. When the storm hit, we think they must have been caught in the subsequent avalanche. We were grateful that at least their bodies were discovered so we could give them a proper burial.'

Walter pauses as he takes a moment to reflect.

'Little Fisher was only four at the time. We hardly knew him, because David and Hetty lived in London and we didn't see them all that often – what with their careers and everything, they were quite busy. They didn't get down to Cornwall as often as my wife and I would have liked.'

I'm not sure what to say, my heart is breaking for Walter.

'But what a wonderful job you and your wife did on bringing up Fisher,' I say, trying to think of something positive to add.

'He's a wonderful young man – very useful to have around. He's certainly helped me a lot since I've been here.'

Walter nods. 'Yes, he is. I'm very proud of him. *We* were very proud of him. Fisher might have told you my Doris passed away a few years ago now.'

Doris! Of course. I'd thought it a strange name for a boat. Fisher must have named her after his grandmother.

'Yes, he did mention it. Again, I'm really sorry, Walter. At least you still have Fisher.'

'I do, and he's a godsend to me. He's taken over where I left off around here. I used to be the caretaker of the island, you see, before he took over. In fact, I used to have my hand in many pies around here, but age comes to us all eventually, and you have to slow down a little. The Wave Watch was my passion until I had to leave. I was one of its founding members here in St Felix.'

The knowledge that Walter had been forced to leave the Wave Watch makes me even crosser now I know about his unfortunate past. He'd clearly loved his time there very much. Damn Lucinda, with her snobbish attitude and superior ways.

'Anyway, that's past history,' Walter says with a shrug. 'Why don't we go and look at some much more interesting history in the marquees.'

I would have been more than happy to stand and listen to Walter's tales about his own life, but I nod amiably and we carry on our way.

The first tent Walter takes me to tells the story of St Felix using paintings, sketches, photos and books open at specific pages.

I wander round the displays, pausing occasionally to read some text or look at a picture in more detail. Most of the exhibits concentrate on St Felix's fishing history, and it's interesting to see some of the old black-and-white photos of the town and match them up with the buildings and streets I know today. There's also a section covering some of the shipwrecks that took place around the coastline, and the Wave Watch also have their own exhibit, complete with a display of photos and some text about what they do and why.

But as I'm about to head over to the exit where Walter is sitting patiently on a wooden chair, I'm drawn to another exhibit.

The photos in this particular display depict some carvings that are said to be inside a cave somewhere along the St Felix coastline. One carving is of a woman's face, another of a horse, and the third is a verse, all intriguingly carved into rock inside the cave.

The verse reads –

> Mar not my face but let me be
> Secure in this lone cavern by the sea
> Let the wild waves around me roar
> Kissing my lips for evermore

I read the verse again, and then the accompanying text.

The carvings were apparently discovered by a St Felix resident in the nineteenth century. He was out walking his dog across the sand during an incredibly low tide, when the dog ran inside the cave, the man followed and was astonished to find not only pictures carved there, but an interesting verse too. The man returned to the town, excitedly telling tales of the mysterious carvings he'd discovered. But it was some time later before the tide was low enough again for anyone else to access the cave and take a look for themselves. As the years passed and more people were able to witness the carvings, the tales of how they got there became ever more fanciful and complex. But it wasn't until the early part of the twentieth century that any photographic evidence was produced. A Cornish photographer took a camera and tripod down to the cave, where he documented the carvings for the first time; his black-and-white photos were subsequently published in a local newspaper. In the decades that passed, on the rare occasions when the tide was low enough to allow access to the cave, many people visited and photographed the carvings for themselves They were fascinated by both the carvings and the many possible stories as to who might have created them.

The story that survives as the most popular and commonly told is that of a beautiful woman who was riding her horse along the beach one day. As the horse and rider explored the open sands, the tide crept in around them at such a devastating speed that they were left no choice but to take shelter. However, the tide rose so high, that sadly they were both trapped and subsequently drowned inside the cave.

The woman's lover was so distraught at the loss of his soulmate, he could often be seen wandering the shore around the caves hoping to find her and take her home.

One day, again during a particularly low tide, it's said a part of the cave appeared to him that he had not been able to reach before. While the man explored deeper into the cave, he sensed the presence of his lost lover. He chose to leave a lasting reminder of his love for her by carving a poem nearer the entrance of the cave, worn smooth over the years by the constant pounding of the waves; he also carved a portrait of his lost love and her horse.

'Romantic, isn't it?' Walter says over my shoulder.

'Oh, I didn't know you were there!' I say, surprised to see him. 'Yes, it is. Do you think it's true?'

Walter shrugs. 'Whether that part of the cave exists? I'm pretty sure that's true – there are many small caves and caverns situated at the bottom of the cliffs around St Felix, and some are only accessible during a very low tide. I don't think there's been a tide low enough for some years for anyone to check whether the carving still survives. If the sea continues to batter it, eventually it will erode away, never to be seen again with human eyes, only through these photos.'

I look again at the pictures.

'But as to the validity of the story,' he adds, 'that's up for debate.'

'How do you mean?'

'I don't doubt that someone carved the rock as a memorial to a lost loved one. But I wonder whether it was quite as simple as the woman and her horse simply getting stranded in the cave.'

'What else could have happened to them?'

'I wonder whether the woman was led there under false pretences. I've done a bit of research into this story, and about the time this was likely to have been carved, there was a small resurgence in the smuggling trade in this area.'

Walter looks at me as if I should be putting two and two together by now.

'I'm so sorry, Walter, I'm not really following you.'

'Come over here,' Walter says, beckoning me across to another display. 'Maybe this will help.'

I look at the display that Walter has led me to. It's all about Cornish smuggling, and in particular, smuggling in St Felix.

'Do you want me to read all this?' I ask, looking at the

lengthy text that accompanies some of the visuals – mainly paintings and prints of Cornish smuggling boats, often depicted fighting a rough sea and a much larger customs ship.

Walter shakes his head. 'Try this,' he says, pointing to a particular section of text with his stick, before settling himself down on the chair next to the exhibit.

I do as he suggests, more out of politeness than my own curiosity.

The article is all about how sailors and fishermen would rely on amateur weather forecasters to tell them when it was safe to head out to sea in their boats. This would usually work very well – that was until a group of local crooks started to pay off some of the forecasters to give out clear, calm forecasts, even when they thought bad weather was approaching. The criminals would then wait for the boats to hit bad weather, often capsizing or grounding on rocks, then like pirates they would board the boats and take whatever cargo was aboard – sometimes that would be fish if it was a fishing boat, or if the boat was bringing in cargo to the town, they might be lucky enough to get foodstuffs, alcohol or even tobacco.

'Yes, I did know that happened,' I say to Walter when I've read the article. 'One of the reasons Robert Fitzroy founded the original Met Office in 1854 was to put in place more official and reliable weather forecasts – especially for those at sea.'

'What if one of those forecasts had been given out the day the woman rode her horse out on to the sand?' Walter says, raising his eyebrows as he leans forward on his cane.

'One of the dodgy ones, you mean?'

Walter nods.

'It's possible, I suppose. She could have been caught out as the tide raced in much faster than she'd expected. The waves

212

would have been higher and stronger if the weather was bad. Are you suggesting she was deliberately led there?'

'It's possible, isn't it?'

'I suppose so, but I guess we'll never know now, will we?'

'Probably not,' Walter says, his voice sounding laidback and relaxed, but there's something in his pale blue eyes that makes me think there's something else going on.

I'm about to question him further when we're interrupted by a loud Tannoy announcement, informing us the prize giving is about to take place by celebrity weatherman Sonny Samuels.

I can actually hear squeals of delight coming from outside the marquee.

'You'd better hurry,' Walter says, smiling at me. 'You don't want to miss it.'

'I can hear Jamie – I mean, Sonny – speak any day of the week,' I tell him. 'I'm much more interested in what you're trying to tell me right now.'

'It will all come to you in time,' Walter says knowingly, 'of that I'm certain. But I mustn't take up any more of your time. So for now, I bid you farewell.'

Walter pulls himself to his feet and salutes me, in much the same way Fisher does sometimes, then he sets off slowly across the marquee towards the exit.

'What will come to me in time?' I whisper to myself as I stare after him. 'Walter, what is it you want me to know?'

Twenty

I stand in the crowd and watch Jamie present the prizes to the St Felix locals with enthusiasm, proficiency and total ease, and I realise how often he must have done something similar before. The prize winners all eagerly get their photo taken with Sonny Samuels, and Sonny produces the same dazzling smile for each photograph. He flirts with the women, compliments the men, and jokes with the children. He does all of this in pure 'Sonny mode', loudly, exuberantly, and with a confidence that only someone used to the limelight can turn on when needed.

Yes, Jamie can be confident and self-assured, but Sonny is ten times so. It's like Jamie has an internal switch that he flicks when he needs to turn Sonny on and Jamie off. I know now that 'Sonny mode' is all an act. But it can't be easy pretending to be one thing, when really you're something else.

A split second after this thought has occurred to me, I realise I could be talking about myself. I've been pretending since I arrived in St Felix too. Pretending to the others there's nothing wrong with me, pretending to myself that I'm coping.

The only difference between me and Jamie is I can't turn

off my charade at the flick of a switch. Until I'm prepared to admit to the others that I have a problem, my switch is firmly stuck in the on position.

'Hello again, Sky,' a voice says, making me jump, and I turn to see the smiling face of Kate, Jack's partner.

'Hi,' I say, smiling warmly back at her. 'How are you?'

'Good, thank you. He's certainly drawn quite the crowd.' She nods in the direction of Jamie.

'Yes, he's quite the crowd-pleaser.'

'I can't imagine he's like that all the time or he'd be very difficult to live with.' She gives me a knowing smile.

'Indeed. Luckily, when Sonny is switched off he becomes almost bearable.' I wink at Kate.

'How are you feeling now?' Kate asks. 'I hope you don't mind but Jack told me about your ME. That's a tough illness to live with. Molly, my daughter, has a friend who has it. She had to drop out of school and missed all her important exams; she's a little better now, thank goodness, but she's still not the same girl she once was.'

'It's not easy, but I'm coping, thanks,' I reply, not knowing whether to feel embarrassed or flattered that Jack has talked about my problems with Kate.

'Good. I hope your colleagues at the island are ensuring you get plenty of rest. Molly says the only way Emily can cope is to pace herself thoroughly and stop before she gets too tired. But that's not easy, is it?'

'No, it's not. I'll get there, though. Is Jack not here today?' I ask, looking around.

'He's back at the art shop. I'll have to get back to my shop soon too, I'm only on a quick break. St Felix is busy enough in the summer, but the festival attracts even more people

215

to the town – great for our tills, but it's just so hectic!' She checks her watch. 'Right, I really had better get back. I've left Anita and our Saturday assistant in charge. I'll see you again soon, I hope?'

'Yes, I hope so,' I say, as Kate disappears back into the crowd.

The prize giving is now complete, but Jamie has got caught up having more selfies taken, so I take a wander past some of the stalls. I wave to Ant, who is manning a little bakery stall with produce from his shop.

'Sky!' he calls, beckoning me across. 'How are you, darling? No more fainting, I hope?'

'No, I'm good, thank you,' I say hurriedly. 'You look like you've been busy here.'

'I have, we've almost sold out! Luckily, we've got the pasties put aside for this afternoon's competition or I don't think there would be one. I'd easily have sold all of them if they'd been on the stall.'

'Oh yes, the pasty-eating competition. Jamie – I mean, Sonny – is going to have a go at that.'

'Don't worry, Talia calls him Jamie all the time; we've got used to it. She said our local celebrity was going to take part. I for one can't wait to see Sonny . . . ' He rolls his eyes. 'I'm doing it now! I can't wait to see *Jamie* eating my pasties.'

'He's had plenty of practice; he's had at least one every day since we arrived. Even when we were stranded over on the island because of the weather, we still managed to get some sent across.'

Ant looks thrilled. 'Talia said he enjoyed them, but I had no idea to that extent. I'm honoured. Truly I am. Perhaps Dec and I could get a photo with him sometime . . . You know, for the bakery?'

'You'll have to ask him but I'm sure he'd be more than delighted.'

'Fabulous, darling! Sorry, customers,' he says, looking behind me. 'I'll see you at the competition, yes?'

I nod and move on, browsing a few more stalls as I go.

I buy myself a coffee, and find a bench to drink it on away from all the crowds, and I'm just starting to wonder when Fisher and Talia will get back with the dogs, when I see them coming towards me.

'How did you get on?' I ask, as the dogs make as much of a fuss of me as I do them.

'Great, they were absolute angels,' Talia says. 'Weren't they, Fisher?'

Fisher nods. 'How's things here? Ditch Walt, did you?'

'No, I didn't ditch him! We parted ways after he'd spent a good while showing me round the History of St Felix marquee.'

'Nice.' Fisher grimaces. 'Sorry about that.'

'It's fine; it was quite interesting, really. It's just ...' I hesitate.

'It's just what?' Fisher asks.

'I got the feeling Walter wanted me to know something. It's silly really, but he said it will all come to me in time. What do you think he meant by that?'

'No idea,' Fisher says, shaking his head. 'The old fella is usually quite articulate when he wants to tell you something. He'll tell you straight, no messing about.'

'What were you talking about?' Talia asks.

'At the time we were looking at a display about smugglers, and before we'd been looking at some old photos. They were of the carvings that are down in a cave at the bottom of the cliffs in St Felix Bay.'

'The Lost Love carvings?' Fisher asks. 'The woman, her horse and the verse?'

'Yes, you know them?'

'Fisher was telling me all about those the other day,' Talia says. 'It's so romantic, yet so very sad at the same time.'

'Isn't it?' I agree.

'Walt has always had his thoughts about those,' Fisher says. 'He seems to think the woman was led there on purpose so she would drown.'

'Oh no, really?' Talia gasps. 'You didn't tell me that. How awful. Why does he think that?'

'Something to do with a dodgy weather forecast,' Fisher says. 'Is that what he was telling you, Sky?'

'Something like that.'

'Again, I'm sorry. You just have to humour him sometimes.'

'It's fine, honestly, I like Walter, and I find his stories really interesting. I think there's more to it than that, though.'

Fisher opens his mouth to speak, but Jamie's voice is the first we hear.

'How's my favourite gang?' he calls as he heads our way. 'All good, I hope?'

Jamie still sounds very much like Sonny as he bounds up next to us and flings his arms around Fisher and Talia's shoulders.

'Having fun?' he asks eagerly, his eyes shining with excitement. Talia smiles happily up at him, while Fisher just glances at the arm now casually slung around his shoulder.

'Looks like you're the one who's been having fun,' I reply calmly. 'Has Sonny left the building yet?'

'What do you mean?' Jamie asks, looking confused.

'Nothing.' I shrug.

'Are you going to come and watch me win the pasty-eating competition?' he asks. 'Apparently, the record is twelve – which will be a breeze. I haven't eaten all day in preparation for this.'

'Of course we are,' Talia says keenly. 'We'll be cheering you all the way, won't we?'

Fisher and I mumble slightly less enthusiastic replies.

'Do the dogs need walking first?' Jamie asks, leaning down to pat Comet.

'All done. Fisher and Talia kindly took them while I had a look around the festival.'

'Great, well done, you two. Right, I'll head over to where the comp is being held and see what's what. See you guys over there!'

We watch him bound away, still full of the same vigour as when he'd arrived.

'You know what?' Talia says, voicing my thoughts and probably Fisher's too. 'I much prefer Jamie to Sonny. Does that sound odd?'

'Not at all,' I reply, smiling at her. 'I think we all feel exactly the same!'

Jamie sits in the middle of the long line of trestle tables all set up for the pasty-eating competition. There are eleven other participants sitting alongside him, and next to each competitor is a huge pile of Cornish pasties.

Jamie had been looking quite confident until a few minutes ago when his plate of pasties had been delivered by Ant and Dec, proud sponsors of the event.

It seemed the record that Jamie was so confident about breaking was indeed twelve pasties, but twelve *giant* Cornish pasties, not twelve regular-sized ones as Jamie had initially thought.

I can't help smiling as I see the over-confident façade of Sonny slip away under the table, to be replaced by a very apprehensive-looking Jamie.

'On your marks,' Dec calls, holding up a Cornish flag, 'get set . . . go!'

The competitors all grab their first pasty and begin eating it as fast as they can, and then some of them quickly move on to their second, and then a third.

'Hey, Poppy,' I hear Fisher say behind me as I watch Jamie look ever more anxious as he quickly falls behind. 'Another year, another pasty-eating competition, eh? Stan would have been so proud it's still going.'

'Yes, he would be,' a woman's voice answers. 'No one has ever beaten his record – only equalled it, and that was Jake's son Charlie a few years ago now.'

I turn around and smile at the woman.

'Sky, this is Poppy, my boss from Tregarlan,' Fisher says, introducing us. 'Poppy, this is Sky, my other boss from over on Aurora.'

'I wouldn't call myself that,' I say quickly. 'Fisher has been a lot of help to me since I arrived on the island. I don't know what we'd have done without him.'

'He's a godsend, that's for sure,' Poppy agrees. 'But don't tell him that,' she whispers, knowing Fisher can hear her. 'We don't know what we'd do without him at Tregarlan either.'

I glance back at the pasty eaters, one or two of whom have already given up, but Jamie is still going, albeit a little more slowly than some of the other competitors.

'The Stan you mentioned just now, is this the same Stan Fisher told me about when we visited the castle?'

'Yes, Stan was a relative of mine,' Poppy says. 'Well, he wasn't actually a relative, but it's a very long story; he's actually related to my stepchildren, Bronte and Charlie. He started this competition, and he still holds the record for the most giant pasties eaten . . . well, eaten without subsequently throwing up, anyway.'

I look back at the trestle tables, some of the competitors, including Jamie, are beginning to look a little green.

'If you've visited Tregarlan,' Poppy continues, 'you will have seen Stan's portrait hanging in the great hall.'

'Yes, I did. The house is beautiful; you're very lucky to own it.'

'Thank you. Much of that is to do with National Heritage, though; I can't take all the credit. But we're very proud of it and its history. Some of which could be linked to your island, actually.'

'Really – how?'

There's a groan from the crowd. I look over and see that Jamie has thrown in the towel – literally, he's ripped the paper bib that all the contestants are wearing from around his neck and thrown it as a scrunched-up ball on to the table.

'Apparently, once upon a time smugglers used to land on the island. They'd wait there before venturing across to the little beach that's directly opposite, over on the mainland. There's a secret tunnel that leads up from the beach to Tregarlan. They used it to transport goods into St Felix and then onward into the rest of Cornwall.'

'How very exciting. I love old legends like that.'

'Oh, it's not just a legend,' Poppy says matter-of-factly. 'The tunnel is definitely there – I've walked along it myself.'

'Gosh, really?'

'Yes, it starts in our cellar and goes all the way down through the rocks to the beach. Nothing else it could have been used for but smuggling back in the day. We were considering making it part of the tour around Tregarlan, but it was going to cost too much to make it safe enough to take visitors through regularly. So, for now, we've shelved the idea.'

'That's a shame; it would have been great to experience that.'

'If you ever want a tour just let me know, or even Fisher here. I'm sure he could take you through there safely enough.'

'I could indeed,' Fisher says, nodding. 'Not a problem.'

We watch the end of the pasty-eating competition – a young holidaymaker is declared the winner, with a total of eight and a half giant pasties. Jamie begrudgingly (although he puts on a good show of being in awe of his competitor's achievement) presents him with his trophy and they both pose for photos looking rather pale and a little green, rather like they've been at sea a bit too long in rough weather.

Even when he had actually been caught in a storm at sea, he hadn't looked as green as he does now, I think, smiling to myself. But as I stand politely applauding, something clicks in my mind.

It's like fixing several pieces of a jigsaw puzzle together at once, and suddenly seeing the picture in front of you finally coming together. The many pieces of information I'd gathered this afternoon begin to form into one singular thought.

No, I say to myself, trying to shake the thought from my mind. *Surely not?*

While the crowd around me begin to disperse, I remain completely still. I vaguely hear Poppy say goodbye to me, and I hope I respond appropriately. But I simply can't shake this thought, banging against the inside of my head, like it's trying to break the glass on an emergency alarm bell.

What if the wrong forecast had been given on purpose the night Jamie got caught out in the boat? Just like the smugglers had arranged in days gone by, so they could steal from the cargo of boats washed up on the rocks. And what if what Walter thought was correct, too, and the innocent woman riding her horse *had* got caught up in one of those dodgy forecasts, just like Jamie had?

Except in this case the Wave Watch had said it was going to be stormy when they clearly must have thought it was going to be dry like us. Their incorrect forecast was the reverse of trying to wreck ships on the rocks, it was almost as if they told everyone there was going to be a storm to prevent anyone being out that night.

But why would they do that? What possible benefit would there be from giving out a stormy forecast when dry weather was clearly afoot? What could you gain from doing that?

Unless . . . There it is again, the nagging thought that just won't go away. It taps persistently on the inside of my head, desperately trying to make itself heard.

What if they didn't want anyone to be out at sea that night for a reason? To go to so much trouble, the reason must be a dishonest one.

I think about the boat Jamie said he saw in the cave. It had arrived after him, and instead of taking shelter like Jamie had, it had quickly backed away and left, heading back out into the storm.

Why would you do that? You'd have to be either incredibly stupid or up to no good.

I try again to shake the thought – there must be some other

explanation? But for now, I can't think of one. The one word that ties all these strange happenings together is the same one I've heard mentioned to me so often this afternoon.

Smugglers.

Twenty-one

'Are you mad?' Jamie asks incredulously when we're back over on the island. I'd asked Fisher and Talia to join us for dinner, which they had agreed to, and Fisher had brought his boat over so they could safely return to the mainland together later.

Jamie had now made an amazing recovery from his earlier queasiness. He'd claimed after the competition he'd felt perfectly fine, and could have gone on eating pasties if he'd tried, but he didn't think it was fair to outshine the other competitors.

After we'd all taken the mickey out of him for about ten minutes following that statement, we'd decided to get ice creams all round, which Jamie had, unsurprisingly, politely declined.

But now the four of us have returned to the island, and we are currently sitting around the dining table – which we've recently moved upstairs, so we can enjoy the fabulous view while we eat – tucking into plates of spaghetti bolognaise that Fisher insisted on cooking for us all.

'I know it sounds a little crazy when you first hear it,' I say calmly. 'But think about it before you completely reject the idea.'

I've just finished telling them everything that had sprung into my mind earlier, and my reasoning behind it all, and Jamie's reaction isn't too far from what I'd expected.

'Smuggling, though,' Jamie says. 'Don't you think it's a bit far-fetched?'

'Not necessarily. When I went to my bedroom earlier, I had a little search on the internet and I found a few reports about this sort of thing still going on around the British coastline. Yes, the type of goods might have changed from hundreds of years ago, but it's still smuggling.'

'I thought you were having a rest?' Jamie asks a little accusingly.

'I was. But I did this first.' I look at Fisher and Talia. 'What do you two think – am I completely mad?'

Talia shrugs. 'I don't think you're mad, Sky, far from it. But this might be a little ... out there, shall we say, for St Felix.'

'Fisher?'

'You might be on to something,' Fisher says to my relief and also my surprise. 'I've suspected something might be going on for a while now. I just couldn't be sure what.'

'Have you seen something?'

'No, not really. But I've noticed that the Wave Watch have been getting more and more forecasts wrong lately. That's why I thought you guys might be here to begin with.'

'We were sent to investigate unusual weather patterns being recorded – rather than forecasts being incorrect. But it might be related. Have you asked anyone about it?'

'I have, actually. One of the volunteers said they thought their equipment might be getting old and need replacing. But another was very coy about it all, and wouldn't say much at all.'

'Did you ever ask Lucinda?'

'No, I try to avoid Lucinda if I can. She was the cause of Walt having to leave the Wave Watch. I've never really forgiven her for that.'

'Do you know why she caused him to leave? Walter suggested it was something to do with them not liking his forecasting methods – that they preferred to rely on modern equipment.'

'Yeah, that's what he said to me, too, but I suspect from things he's let slip that there was more to it.'

'Like what?' Talia asks, looking concerned. Talia has taken quite a shine to Walter, like we all have.

'Do you think Walter suspected something similar to what I'm suggesting?' I ask. 'From the little he's shared with me, I wouldn't be surprised. I knew he was trying to tell me something. I wish I'd taken him a bit more seriously now.'

'I'm not sure,' Fisher says, looking perplexed. 'If Walt had suspected something like smuggling was going on, I can't imagine he'd keep quiet about it.'

'What if he didn't have any proof, though?' I suggest.

'Like we do, you mean?' Jamie says, raising his eyebrows. 'We only have your suspicions, Sky. Nothing concrete to go on at all.'

I think about this. 'Can you remember anything about the boat that came into the cave after you during the storm?'

'Not really, it was dark and they had their lights on full, so I was bit blinded. All I know is they didn't hang around when they saw me.'

'Exactly – why wouldn't they if a storm was raging outside? Why risk going out on the sea again? It doesn't make sense.'

'And a group of modern-day smugglers working off the coast of this little Cornish seaside town does, I suppose?'

'You explain everything that's been going on, then?'

Jamie shakes his head. 'I can't – that's the problem. I can't disprove your theory, Sky, but you can't prove it, either. Unless we actually see some smugglers in their boat pulling into the harbour at night and offloading their wares, we have absolutely nothing to go on.'

'Although,' Talia says, waving her hand in the direction of the bay windows, 'if anyone is going to spot anything untoward going on around St Felix, we're in the best place to do it.'

My eyes follow her hand towards the window.

'You're absolutely right,' I say. 'If anyone is going to see anything strange, then we will. We'll have to start making a note of all the boats that pass by and when, just like the Wave Watch do … Wait, there was an odd little boat one morning, not that long after we first arrived. I thought it was strange at the time, because it went the wrong way around the rocks – the dangerous way.'

'Might be something to go on?' Talia says encouragingly.

'Or it might just be a boat out early one morning?' Jamie says. 'Please don't let us get carried away with this. If I'm going to be a part of it – and I don't think for one minute you two are going to let me get away with not being! – then we are going to register cold hard facts, not supposition.'

'You sound like a television police detective now,' I say, smiling at him, pleased he's on board.

'Sky, if what you're suggesting turns out to be in any way correct, then this is not a game we're playing here. This is a serious matter, and it won't be some bumbling police detective that will turn up in St Felix to save the day, it will be a whole swarm of police cars, boats and probably helicopters too. Smuggling, in whatever form it comes, is taken extremely seriously today. If you think this is going to be some Famous Five adventure, with jolly japes and ginger beer, then you need to back out right now.'

My smile fades. 'No, I don't think that at all. I know how serious it could be. But if it is going on, and we have a chance to make it stop, then we have no choice but to do everything we can to protect the people of St Felix.'

Over the next week or so, we step up our surveillance through the watchtower windows. Fisher, after he's spoken to Walter and is unable to get anything further from him about his suspicions, also joins us in our observations, so we are able to have someone on lookout nearly twenty-four hours a day.

I take my turn with the others at both the day and the night shifts. But it's tough, and my body does not take kindly to having its sleep routine messed with.

But what can I do? I can't ask the others to do night shifts if I'm not. This is all my doing, my idea, and I have to step up and take charge.

'Are you all right, Sky?' Talia asks me early one morning when I've just come off night shift and she's taking over. 'You look awfully pale.'

'Yes, I'm fine, nothing a good sleep won't fix.'

'I hope you don't mind me saying, but even when you have slept you don't look a lot better.'

'I don't do very well when my sleep is messed with,' I reply quickly. 'But who does, eh? Thanks for this cuppa, Talia. I'll drink it and then I'll head off to bed.'

But Talia still looks worried.

When I do eventually head downstairs to my bedroom, I glance in the bathroom mirror while I'm cleaning my teeth.

Oh no, my eye is doing that weird thing it always does when I'm getting too tired.

There are many ways I know if I'm doing too much – over the time I've been ill, I've learnt that my body will give me lots of little warnings to slow down, before it gives me the big one, and makes me rest whether I like it or not.

It can be as simple as my muscles and joints beginning to hurt that little bit more, or I'll tweak something in one of my ankles so it's painful for me to walk around – anything to make me slow down and rest.

The eye thing is one of the weirder ones that other people often notice before I do. One of my eyes becomes larger than the other, giving me a strange, crooked appearance. It can look a little like one side of my face has fallen – like I've had a stroke. But it's not that, it's simply one of my warning signals. My body's way of telling me to stop.

I can't stop now; I have to see this through with the others. But I know if I don't listen to my body soon, it won't be lots of little things that are happening, it will be one big thing. And if the monster strikes badly enough, I'll end up stuck in bed unable to do anything for myself, and that is the last thing I want to happen while I'm here on Aurora.

So I head off to bed, doing everything I can to prevent the monster from getting to me just yet. I take some anti-inflammatory pills to calm my aching joints. I plug in my heated pad to try to ease my sore back while I fall asleep. I take a sleeping tablet from my prescription, and finally I put my ear-plugs in and an eye mask on to try to get an undisturbed sleep.

But even so, it takes me a while to settle. My mind wanders back and forth between what we're doing in the watchtower to what's going on with my body right now, and then on to the worry of what if I do have a major relapse, what will the others think, and how will I cope with it, here on the island?

Eventually, to try to calm my racing mind, I get up for a while, go to the toilet and I then have a few sips of water from the glass next to my bed. The changing light in my bedroom makes me desperately want to go to the window and see what the weather is doing outside. I try to resist, knowing this won't help my circadian rhythm, but it's no good, I have to see. So I go over to the window, pull back the curtains a little, and take a quick peak.

The sky is a bright cornflower blue – which will please the many holidaymakers in St Felix right now – with white fluffy cumulus clouds floating gently across it.

As I watch, the clouds suddenly begin to move with more pace across the sky; I realise that something unusual is happening. But before I can grab my phone from where it's charging to document it, the clouds have already morphed together into what looks very much like an animal – no wait, it's a horse with four long cloud limbs galloping across the sky. I watch, astonished, as the clouds continue to move and change and a new shape appears, and the horse is joined by a woman rider, her long hair cascading down her back.

As I stare in amazement at the pictures forming in the sky, I wonder how many other people might be witnessing this with me from the beaches and harbour over at St Felix. But the clouds haven't finished yet, and as the horse and rider gallop along against the bright blue backdrop, another cloud looking very much like a huge wave comes crashing down over the top of them. The horse and rider immediately vanish as the clouds all pool together again, and carry on about their business as if nothing unusual has ever happened.

I close the curtains and head back to bed. Then I lie staring at the ceiling, trying to piece together what this very clear but strange occurrence could mean.

I knew exactly what that cloud formation was representing – that's not in doubt. The question bugging me is why the clouds have formed themselves into the story of the cave carving that Walter had drawn my attention to at the exhibition. What could it possibly mean?

As I begin to feel drowsy from the sleeping tablet, I replace my earplugs and cover my eyes with my mask, eventually drifting off to sleep. But after what feels like only a few minutes I wake again. Someone is tapping me gently on the shoulder and saying my name.

'Sky, wake up . . .'

'I don't think she's going to,' another voice says. 'It looks like she's taken some sort of tablets . . .'

I push up my eye mask, and pull out my earplugs.

'What's going on?' I ask, looking bleary eyed at Talia and Fisher standing either side of the bed. 'Why are you waking me up?'

The sleeping tablet is still pretty potent inside me, and everything seems a bit floaty and off-kilter.

'We didn't know whether to wake you or not,' Talia says anxiously. 'But Jamie said we should since you'd been asleep for a number of hours.'

'Hours? Are you sure? I feel like I've just nodded off.'

'Are you okay?' Fisher asks, glancing at the various sleeves of tablets on the bedside table.

'Yes, yes, I'm fine. I just took something to help me sleep, that's all. What's going on?'

Fisher nods, but still looks concerned. 'You'd better come upstairs and then we can explain properly.'

'Right.' I yawn. 'Best give me a minute and I'll be up.'

'I'll make some coffee,' Talia says. 'You look like you might need a mug or two.'

I wake myself up the best I can, still unable to believe I've slept for hours rather than minutes. I feel utterly exhausted as I pull on my dressing gown and haul myself up the stairs, my body aching from head to toe, and my head still fuzzy from the sleeping tablet.

'Right, what is all this?' I ask, finding the three of them sitting up in the watchtower, looking like they are ready to head out somewhere. Fisher is in wellingtons, and Talia and Jamie are in their walking boots.

Talia thrusts a mug of coffee in my hand, while Jamie looks at me with a concerned expression. 'You don't look too good, boss,' he says. 'Maybe we should have left you sleeping.'

'I'll be fine when I've had this,' I say, lifting the mug of coffee. I sit down on the sofa. 'Now, tell me what's been happening.'

They all look at each other, then Jamie speaks.

'It's the tide,' he says, glancing out of the window. 'It's really low and seems to be getting lower by the minute.'

'And?' I reply, still not really with it.

'We think it might be the lowest we've seen since we arrived,' Jamie continues. 'If it keeps going out some of the caves around the bay might become accessible, including the one I got stranded in—'

'And the one with the carvings!' I finish, my brain clicking into gear.

'They might even be one and the same,' Fisher says. 'We don't know that yet.'

'How long has the tide been going out?' I ask, glancing

towards the window, although from the sofa I can't actually see that much of the sand, only the sky.

'Long enough,' Jamie says. 'Usually, we'd have expected it to turn by now, but it hasn't, it just seems to be going out further all the time.'

'Then what are we waiting for?' I ask, gulping down my coffee. 'Let's go!'

But the others don't move; they all look at each other again.

'We wondered if it might be better if you stay here,' Talia says, clearly the bravest of the three. 'We need someone to keep watch just in case the tide changes really fast, and we need help.'

'You really look like you might be better resting,' Jamie says, nodding in agreement.

Fisher remains silent.

'Did any of you see the clouds earlier?' I ask, not responding to their suggestion.

'What clouds?' Jamie asks.

'I thought not. My room faces in the direction of the only blind spot in the watchtower. Before I went to sleep, I took a look out of my window, and the clouds did one of their artistic arrangements for me. This time they formed into a horse, a female rider and what looked like a huge wave, which completely engulfed the horse and rider. Since no one else saw it, I'm taking that as a sign that I'm supposed to go to the caves with you.'

'But—' Jamie begins, but Fisher interrupts him.

'Sky's right. She should go. She's the one Walter confided in, the one whose idea this twenty-four-hour surveillance was, and, by the sounds of it, she's the one the clouds want to discover whatever it is they want us to know. I'll stay, if you want someone here?'

'Thank you,' I say, giving Fisher a grateful look, 'but we'll all go to the caves. No one will stay behind. We'll leave the recording equipment going, and we'll keep an eye on the tide. If we think it's turning fast then we'll head back immediately.'

'There used to be some flares in one of the outside storage cupboards,' Fisher says. 'We could take the Jeep for speed and put them in the back, then if the worst happens we could raise the alarm quickly if we need to. There are some spots around the coast here where the signal is non-existent, so I can't guarantee our phones will work.'

'Great idea,' I say approvingly. 'Right, what are we waiting for?'

'You to get dressed?' Jamie says, looking at my attire.

'Ah yes.' I look down at my pyjamas and dressing gown. 'There is that.' I gulp down the rest of my coffee. 'Give me ten minutes max, and we're off in search of our mysterious woman on horseback!'

Twenty-two

Anyone who lives or has spent any time by the sea will know that the weather around the coast can change in an instant. The bright blue skies and fluffy white cumulus clouds I'd seen when I looked out of my bedroom window have now changed into dark, ominous, cumulonimbus clouds – the type that are usually filled with heavy rain. So, as we set off across the wide-open expanse of sand in the Jeep – Jamie driving, me with Fitz on my lap in the passenger seat beside him, and Fisher and Talia squashed in the back with Comet between them – it's inevitable that the clouds are going to burst above our heads and rain is going to cascade down upon us.

Not bothered by this minor setback, we zip up our raincoats and pull on our hats, knowing that the inclement weather will put off a large percentage of people from strolling out this far on to the sand to explore with us. The others had been spot on, the tide has never been this far out before, and it's opened up a whole section of the coastline that I've only ever seen boats sail past from our window in the watchtower. Even Fisher is in awe, telling us several times that he has never seen this part of the coastline without being in a boat.

The low tide allows us access to several caves in the tough, resilient rock face that has supported the town of St Felix for many centuries. We pull up at each one, climb out of the Jeep and explore – taking it in turns for one of us to wait outside on watch, keeping an eye on the tide in case it should suddenly come rushing back in. There's no way we are going to be caught out like the ill-fated woman and her horse.

Each cave is unique in size and shape, but none of them so far have been large enough to house one boat, let alone two. But it's our fifth and final cave that looks the most promising as we pull up outside. The opening is much bigger and on first glance it appears to go further back into the rock than any of the others have so far.

'My turn to wait,' Talia says, looking longingly at the opening. 'Trust me to miss out when it looks like this might be the one.'

'I'll come right out so you can go in, if it is,' I tell her. 'No one need miss out if this is the cave with the carving in it.'

Talia nods. 'Thank you, Sky. Right, I have the klaxon,' she says, holding it up. 'I'll sound it once if I think the tide is getting too close, and three times if you need to evacuate fast!'

Jamie, Fisher and I set off to explore the cave while Talia waits with the dogs by the Jeep. Fitz and Comet had got pretty bored after the first couple of caves, and now much prefer to remain on the sand with whoever is waiting at the Jeep. That way they get to play ball across the huge expanse of sand rather than wandering around in a dark, damp cave.

Like all the other caves, as soon as we move away from the daylight, we switch on our torches so we can see where we're going. The walls are damp and shiny, and there's occasional dripping water where cracks in the ground above have allowed rainwater to seep through. But it's clear by the barnacles that cling tightly to the walls and the ceiling, and the occasional pieces of abandoned seaweed caught on the sharp rock edges above us, that waves usually fill this cavern, and if you were unlucky enough to be caught in it filling with water, there would be no hiding place from the incoming tide.

'This one is much bigger,' I say, shining my torch all around me. 'You could easily get two boats in here. Do you think this is the one you sheltered in, Jamie?'

'It might be,' Jamie says, looking around. 'But it was dark, and I was more preoccupied with the weather than what the inside of a cave looked like.'

'I'd say this is definitely the one,' Fisher says, shining the beam from his torch on a patch of the wall.

'How do you know?' Jamie asks.

'Look,' he says, beckoning us over. 'Paint.'

We go over to where Fisher is shining his torch – sure enough there is a patch of purple paint on the wall of the cave.

'That paint matches the colour of *Doris*'s hull perfectly,' I say, looking at Jamie. 'Do you remember catching the wall at all?'

Jamie considers the marking for a few seconds. 'Yes, I think I did. Like I said, I was so preoccupied with the weather outside I wasn't really thinking all that much about what was going on inside here – not until the other boat turned up, that is.'

'Let's explore further, shall we?' I begin to weave my way through the large rocks that jut up through the sand. 'I tell you what, you'd need a high tide to access this cave in a boat, otherwise you'd catch your keel on the rocks.' I shine my torch up to the top of the cave for a moment. 'The ceiling is pretty high, you could access here with a mainsail raised if you didn't want anyone to hear your motor.'

I shine my torch back on the other two, and see Fisher is smiling at me.

'What's so funny?' I ask.

'Hark at you with all your fancy boating terms,' he says. 'I remember a time when you didn't know your port from your starboard.'

'Well, times change,' I say, smiling back at him. 'And so do people.'

Slowly we make our way a little further into the cave – me leading the way, with Jamie following and Fisher bringing up the rear.

Even though I'm enjoying our expedition, I can't say I'm finding any of it easy. I'm still exhausted from being on the night shift last night, then not catching up with my sleep properly this morning. Add to that the fact I only took a sleeping tablet a few hours ago, so I'm still feeling quite drowsy. My joints hurt, and my muscles are starting to feel like jelly as we trudge into the depths of the cave. I also feel a tad light-headed, and my brain is slowly turning to mush, making thinking about anything increasingly difficult. But if I can just keep the fast approaching 'monster' at bay, I won't have to miss any of this.

Please keep going, I silently urge my body. *Just until we get back to the house; then you can rest, I promise.*

'Wait!' Jamie shouts as I'm about to manoeuvre myself around another cluster of rocks. 'I think I see something on the wall.'

I turn back to where Jamie is aiming his torch, and Fisher close behind him is now doing the same so we have twice the light on the wall.

239

'It's the carving!' I hear Fisher whisper in awe. 'It's the woman and her horse.'

I head back towards them and shine my torch on the wall too.

In front of us is a large, but simple carving of a woman riding a horse across the waves, and next to it is carved the verse, which Fisher reads – 'Mar not my face but let me be. Secure in this lone cavern by the sea. Let the wild waves around me roar. Kissing my lips for evermore.'

We stand quietly for a few seconds, taking this in. Even though I've seen a photo of the carving, standing here in the cave witnessing it for real is really quite moving.

'Sad, isn't it?' I say. 'I thought that when I saw the photo, but seeing it for real has really brought the poignancy of it home.'

'Yes,' Jamie says quietly. 'You feel for all of them. The woman and her horse must have been terrified being trapped here together in the last few hours of their lives. And the grief her broken-hearted lover must have felt in order to carve this . . . It doesn't bear thinking about. No one deserves that.'

I turn towards Jamie, touched by his words. He glances back at me, and in the dim light cast off the damp walls, he holds my gaze.

'If he did grieve for long,' Fisher says, interrupting us.

We both quickly turn our heads back to look at the carving.

'There's another school of thought that he came back to the cave, carved this, then waited for the tide to return so he too would drown, hoping to be reunited with his lost love once more.'

'If that's true, it's even more romantic.' I sigh, not sounding like my usual self at all. But there was something about this story that had really touched me. 'Very *Romeo and Juliet*.'

'Sorry to spoil the moment,' Jamie says, 'but we still have

the rest of this cave to explore, and if we don't hurry up then we might end up with the same fate as the woman, the horse *and* the grieving lover.'

After we've taken a few photos of the carving, we head on further into the darkness. Now the opening of the cave has fully disappeared, we really can only see by torchlight. I'm glad Jamie and Fisher are with me on this adventure; I wouldn't have wanted to be in here on my own.

'What's that?' I say as we come to a solid mass of rock in front of us, and my torch catches on something up ahead. 'It looks like a door?' I wait for the other two to catch up and we all shine our torches on the wall up above us. 'It *is* a door,' I say as the light reveals a small wooden arch-shaped door, being held together with rusty nails and black wrought-iron bars.

'There's a mooring ring next to it,' Fisher says, moving his torch along the wall. 'Looks like boats have been tied up here at some point. Probably to offload their cargo to whoever was going to come out of that door.'

'Where do you think it leads?' I ask. 'Do you think it goes up to Tregarlan, like the tunnel you and Poppy were telling me about?'

'I don't know. I've been down that tunnel a few times; it leads out on to the little beach. Maybe there's another one we haven't found before that comes out here.'

'Probably hasn't been used in years,' Jamie says. 'It was likely used to offload supplies for the castle in the past.'

'Or was it used as a smuggling tunnel?' I suggest, still looking at the door. 'In the past – and more recently, too.'

'I'd say it's definitely been used quite recently,' Fisher says, moving a little closer to the wall and shining his torch up to the door. 'Look where the barnacles are clinging. They're around the frame of the door and in the centre. There's none on the edge; that means the seal of the door has been broken recently and they've been disturbed, otherwise they'd be all over it.'

'Now do you believe me?' I ask Jamie. 'Why would someone be opening this door if not to receive smuggled or stolen goods? What other possible reason could there be? It's clearly covered with water when the tide is high; anyone opening this door would have to know exactly how high the sea was on the other side, otherwise water would pour through it.'

'But we don't know where it goes yet,' Jamie says. 'If we knew that, *maybe* we could try and find out who has been down here and why. But until then this jury is out, I'm afraid.'

Suddenly we hear a loud wailing sound reverberating through the tunnel – the alarm!

'That's Talia,' Fisher says, looking round. 'The tide must be heading in. We'd better go; we can discuss this later.'

Fisher and Jamie immediately turn and begin to head back through the cave. I'm about to follow them when I decide to try to take a quick photo of the door, just in case we want to look at it again. The camera on my phone takes a while to focus in the dim light, but I manage to get a couple of half-decent photos.

As I turn to follow the others, the beam of my torch catches on something shiny on the ground below the door. *What's that?* I wonder, shining my torch directly on it. I move closer to the object and pick it up. It's a metal badge of some sort; it's a bit rusty so I quickly put it in my pocket to look at later. I'm about to turn away when something else catches my eye – a dark mass at the back of the cave. Whatever it is has barnacles clustered on it so it blends easily into the rocks, but instead of being sharp and jagged, it looks a lot smoother and more rounded.

'Sky!' Jamie calls, and the beam of his torch blinds my eyes for a moment. 'Are you coming?'

'Yes, I was just taking some photos!' I call back, quickly pointing my phone in the direction of the strange object. I press the shutter on my camera again and shove my phone back in my pocket.

I manage to take a couple of steps in Jamie's direction before it happens.

'Ow!' I suddenly cry. 'Oh no, not now,' I moan under my breath.

'What's up?' Jamie calls, and I see the light of his torch coming towards me. 'Are you okay?'

I try to take another step, but the pain in my foot shoots up my leg with such force that I jump in the air, and when I land awkwardly, my other ankle starts to hurt too.

I fall against a rock, and use it for support.

'What's up?' Jamie says, shining his torch on me. 'Have you hurt yourself?'

'Kind of, it's my ankle.'

'Which one?' he asks, coming closer.

'Both,' I say quietly, looking up into his anxious face.

'Both?' Jamie asks. 'How have you hurt both – did you fall?'

'No, I just caught one awkwardly, and then the other sort of came out in sympathy.' I feel stupid even saying it.

Jamie looks at me with a puzzled expression now.

'Can you walk?' he asks.

'I'll be all right. Just give me a minute or two.'

The klaxon sounds again. Three short blasts . . .

'I'm not sure we have a minute or two, by the sound of that. Here, put your arm around my shoulder.' Jamie puts his left arm around my waist, then he takes my right hand and feeds it around his neck. 'Hold on tightly,' he instructs as we attempt to move forward.

'Ouch. Ow, Aargh!' I cry as each step is total agony.

'Damn it,' Jamie mutters. He looks towards the opening of the cave, which is a tiny white spot in the distance. 'This is going to take far too long with you like that. I'll have to carry you.'

'No you will not,' I insist furiously. 'I'll be fine.'

'Sky, I am not leaving you here like this, neither am I prepared to drown alongside you so your female pride can survive intact. Now, put your arms around my neck.'

I look at him, not moving.

'This will be a lot easier for both of us if you do. Or would you rather I put you over my shoulder in a fireman's lift?'

Regretfully, I put my arms around his neck.

'That's better,' Jamie says, putting one arm behind my back and the other under the back of my knees. 'Now, one, two, *three*!' he says, swooping me up into his arms, in what might be misconstrued at any other time as a romantic gesture. Today, in a dark cold cave, with my whole body exhausted and in pain, it just feels like utter relief.

'Keep moving your torch back and forth in front of us – to the ground and up again – so we can navigate our way out of here safely. The last thing we need is for me to fall over as well.'

I do as he says and we move forward at a surprisingly quick pace. Jamie is obviously a lot stronger than he looks.

But it's not just the pace of our exit that surprises me as we move towards the daylight. What's even more unexpected is how comfortable I feel nestled in Jamie's arms. The closeness and warmth of his body, instead of feeling awkward or strange, feels just right, as if there is no other place I would rather be.

Twenty-three

I open my eyes, and then quickly close them again.

Urgh, it still hurts.

I turn over slowly in my bed, to give the side I've been sleeping on some respite, hoping for a little relief from the pain I've awoken with.

As I lie there wondering how long I can remain in bed before I need to get up and use the toilet, my mind turns back to the events of a few days ago.

After Jamie had carried me heroically from the cave and deposited me safely in the Jeep, there hadn't been time for explanations to the other two. The waves were fast approaching across the sand; soon the sea would surround the island and we'd be trapped the wrong side of it.

Jamie had driven us at speed across the sand, with me in the front and Talia and Fisher in the back holding on tightly to the dogs, even though Fitz was whining and pulling to get in the front with me.

Fitz knew, even if the others didn't yet. The monster had got to me, and now I was going to suffer.

We'd reached the island as shallow waves were beginning to lap at its edges. Jamie had pulled up right next to the house, then lifted me swiftly from the Jeep and carried me inside.

'Bedroom or sitting room?' he'd asked as he'd stood in the hall with me still in his arms.

'Bedroom,' I seem to remember muttering. My brain was starting to deteriorate as well as my body now.

Jamie had then carried me into the bedroom and called Talia, who I think had helped me out of my clothes and into my pyjamas. It all got a bit hazy after that.

All I knew was I'd spent the last few days in bed, with a bucket next to me because I couldn't get up to use the bathroom at the end of the hall. Partly because I didn't have the strength, and partly because my ankles were still too painful.

My meals had been brought to me on a tray, which sometimes I'd eaten, and sometimes I hadn't, and my constant companions had been Fitz, sleep, a hot-water bottle, and several packets of painkillers of varying types.

The others had offered to call a doctor several times. But I'd said no, I'd be fine in a few days, and I truly hoped I would. If I rested maybe, just maybe, the monster would leave easily this time, quickly and without making a fuss.

There's a gentle knock on my door.

'Sky, are you awake?' It's Talia.

'Ah-huh,' I reply, attempting to open my eyes. *At least I can do that today*, I think as I see the hazy light of the bedroom. Two days ago, even daylight was painful.

I roll onto my back as Talia opens the door.

'How are you feeling?' she asks in a low voice. The others have quickly learnt not to speak in loud voices, and to keep the curtains of my room drawn, even though I could tell they desperately wanted me to enjoy some daylight.

'A little better,' I reply, knowing that's what she wants to hear.

'Oh, good. I've brought you a cup of tea.' Talia comes into the room. 'Shall I put it next to you?'

I nod. *Ouch! Even that hurts.*

'Would you like me to pass you your crutches?' she asks, looking at the crutches next to my bed. 'Do you think you might make it to the bathroom today?'

Slowly, I attempt to pull myself up in bed. It's painful, my muscles are stiff and sore, and my joints pulse with the heat that's soaring through them.

'I'll try,' I say, to make her feel better. 'But I'll have some painkillers first.'

Talia has been wonderful looking after me. She's moved into the house and is sleeping in Jamie's room. Jamie gallantly offered to sleep on the sofa upstairs, and the pair of them have become my constant carers.

They had been surprised to learn that I had everything I needed to get through this already here with me. My crutches had been retrieved from where I'd hidden them at the back of my wardrobe. A hot-water bottle, an electric blanket to keep me warm when I had the chills, and a heated pad to place on painful parts of my body had been found in my chest of drawers. I already had my sleeping mask and sunglasses on hand to block out the bright light – so painful to my eyes when I was in this state – and some earplugs and noise-cancelling headphones to block out any unwanted sound. I also had enough pills of varying types hidden away in a small bag in my wardrobe to rival a branch of Boots the chemist.

Talia passes me my tea. 'Do you feel up to talking today?'

she asks. 'I'm happy to leave if you'd prefer to be alone. I just thought you might like some company.'

'Stay,' I say, gesturing to the bed. 'I'm not contagious.'

'I know, you told us that the first night.' Talia sits down on the end of the bed.

'Did I? I don't remember.'

'You said quite a few things, actually. Much of which we didn't understand – you were slurring quite a bit.'

I take a sip of my tea; even the basic movement of holding and tipping the mug is difficult when I'm this stiff and sore.

'Yes, that happens,' I say, looking down into my tea. 'This isn't the first time I've been like this.'

'We worked that out ourselves when you had all this stuff hidden around your room. Why was it hidden, Sky? Why didn't you tell us – or warn us, even – that this might happen?'

Talia looks genuinely upset, and I feel awful.

'I didn't want to worry anyone,' I say quietly. 'I really hoped I wouldn't need any of this stuff while I was here, that it was just precautionary. I hoped I'd be okay.'

'What's wrong with you?' Talia asks. 'Is it serious?'

I open my mouth to speak, but there's another knock on the door.

'Morning, morning,' Jamie says, peeking his head around the door. 'How's the patient today?'

'She's feeling a little better,' Talia replies.

'Good to hear.' Jamie smiles at me. 'Well enough to eat some breakfast this morning?'

I nod. 'Yes, please.'

'Great – fry-up it is, then! I'll be right back.'

'Toast would have been just fine,' I say, pulling a wry expression at Talia.

'Jamie has been really worried about you,' Talia says reprovingly.

'Yes. I'm sorry for worrying you both unnecessarily.'

'Actually, I think it was very necessary,' Talia says brusquely, to my surprise. 'We care about you, Sky. You've had us all very worried, and I'm including Fisher in that, too. He's been back and forth over the last few days to check on you, either that or he's telephoned.'

'Gosh, I didn't realise.'

'No, you probably didn't. Like I said, we've all been worried after what happened at the cave, and in the days afterwards. I think we deserve some sort of explanation?'

'You're right, you do. Look, let me drink my tea, and then see if I can get to the bathroom on my crutches. If I can, I'll try and explain after I've taken some painkillers.'

Talia nods. 'All right. I'm sorry if I came on a bit strong just then, but we really have been extremely worried.'

'Feel better?' Jamie asks as I sit on the sofa with a blanket after I've finished my breakfast.

'Yes, much, thank you. And thank you for insisting I come up here. It's wonderful to see this view again.'

After I'd drunk my tea, I'd very tentatively managed to get to the bathroom on my own, without too much pain, using my crutches. I'd then decided to attempt a shower, and although the effort of that had almost wiped me out, the delicious smell wafting from the kitchen had spurred me on. So I'd tugged on some fresh pyjamas and my dressing gown, and when Jamie had suggested we all eat together upstairs, I'd taken him up on his offer of carrying me up there, partly so I could enjoy the view from the watchtower window once more, and partly so I could see if the memory I had of him holding me close is quite so pleasant when it's recreated.

Jamie smiles at me, and something strange tweaks in my stomach. But it's not a painful tweak like most of the other sensations I've been feeling recently, it's a rather pleasurable sensation, something very similar to what I'd felt while being carried up the stairs.

'It's wonderful to see you almost up and about again. Talia and I were worried.'

'I know, she said. In fact, she gave me quite the telling-off this morning, didn't you, Talia?'

'Oh, I didn't mean to tell you off.' Talia looks dismayed. 'I just wanted you to know how concerned we've been about you.'

'It's fine. I'm only joshing with you. You are completely right; I should have been straight with you both from the start. It's just tough to admit sometimes you have a failing.'

'Ill health isn't a failing,' Talia says, looking cross. 'You can't help it if your body is malfunctioning somehow.'

I nod. 'I know, but it doesn't always feel that way.'

I take a deep breath. It's time.

'I have ME,' I say, feeling immediate relief as the words I've kept buried for so long are finally allowed to escape. 'Myalgic Encephalomyelitis, to give it its full name.'

'I've heard of that,' Talia says, 'but I'm not exactly sure what it is.'

'Sadly, it's a lot more than most people think. It's often called chronic fatigue syndrome – which suggests that it's all about being tired. I wish it was just that; that wouldn't be so bad. Fatigue and exhaustion, they're just the tip of the iceberg.'

'Go on,' Talia encourages. Jamie remains quiet, but he's clearly listening intently.

'Without getting too technical, ME is a chronic long-term illness that affects the whole body. I can only talk about it from my own experience – it affects everyone slightly differently, as many illnesses do. But it causes me extreme fatigue, which sometimes gets so bad it affects me in the ways you've witnessed over the last few days. It's not just a sleepy fatigue, though; it weakens the muscles all over my body, including my eyes, and also my brain, so that it doesn't function quite right, and I can't think straight, and my speech often slurs as a result. In addition to that, I get joint pains – so bad sometimes I can barely walk, just like in the cave. I often have an extreme aversion to light and sound, too – hence my earplugs, eye mask, and the sunglasses I have on right now, even though we're indoors. You may have noticed unless it's a very dull day I often wear sunglasses when I'm outside.'

'Yes, I had noticed,' Talia says. 'I wondered why you did that. Isn't there anything you can take to help, though? Like medicines and things?'

I shake my head. 'Nope, there's no cure and no one drug has been found to stabilise the symptoms. Most people rely on a cocktail of painkillers and various vitamins to try and stave off a flare as we call it. That's a flare-up of your symptoms like you've both just witnessed – that and pacing.'

'What's pacing?' Talia is asking all the questions while Jamie sits quietly listening.

'It's a way of trying to live your life so that you don't overdo it and exacerbate your symptoms. The best way of describing it I've ever heard is in terms of a phone battery.'

As I launch into my battery analogy Talia and Jamie look slightly confused, as most people do when I try to explain this. But, confident they will get it by the end, I continue. 'For

251

instance, imagine that you have a phone battery powering everything you need to do with your body. You two would have perfect, brand-new batteries inside your bodies – they last a long time, and you can do a lot with them before they need re-charging – just like a brand-new phone. It also doesn't take a lot of charging to power your own body's battery up again to full. In your cases usually a good night's sleep will do it, exactly the same as if you had a new phone. Following it so far?'

They both nod.

'Good. Now imagine you are living with a faulty battery in your phone. Every time you use it for something, it drops the charge super-fast, and you can hardly do anything before it needs re-charging again; it would be a right pain and you'd expect more from it. Imagine living with that same faulty battery inside your body. You can barely do anything before it needs to be re-charged, and even when it does go on charge, it never goes past, say, forty to sixty per cent. You would have to limit what you did so you didn't use up the charge too fast, wouldn't you?'

Again, they both nod.

'That's what people with ME live with all the time – faulty batteries that never fully re-charge, and even when they do, they drop power a lot faster than a healthy person. How much charge you get every day depends on how badly you are affected.'

'That's awful,' Talia says. 'I'm so sorry, Sky. I had no idea. I mean, I noticed you had to rest quite a lot. But I just thought that was you being super sensible, you know?'

I smile at her. 'If I was super sensible, I wouldn't have allowed myself to get in the state you've just witnessed me in. I should have known better than to keep pushing myself when my body was giving me signs to slow down. I've been doing too much and this is what happens when I do.'

Even though I've failed at keeping the monster suppressed, I feel so much better now I've told them both, that I wonder why I didn't earlier.

'Is it our fault?' Talia asks anxiously. 'Haven't we been doing our fair share of the work?'

'Oh no, please don't think that. It's nothing to do with either of you. You've both been great since we arrived here. It's me. I should have paced myself better. All the signs that I was doing too much were there; my body was warning me I needed to slow down, but I thought I knew better. I thought I could outrun the monster this time – that's what I call my illness – the monster – but he always catches up with me in the end.'

'Oh, Sky,' Talia says, coming over and giving me a hug. 'I'm so sorry. If it's any consolation, I would never have guessed you had anything wrong, you're always so strong and so together.'

As I hug Talia I glance over at Jamie, but I can't tell anything from his neutral expression.

'Thank you. Right now I take that as a huge compliment, considering how I've been feeling. You see, I'm not good at admitting my failures. I like everyone to think I can cope; I've always been like that. I wanted you two to see me at my best, and to prove to myself and Met Central that I'm strong enough to deal with a fairly simple job like this one. But what I should have remembered is that when you have an illness like this, sometimes you have no choice but to let people help you. When I was first ill, I had to accept help from my family. They cared for me back then when I was at my worst, and now you two have stepped up for me – my St Felix family. I don't know what I'd have done without you the last few days, really I don't. Thank you, both of you, from the bottom of my heart.'

Talia and I are both in tears as we hug again.

But as I glance across at Jamie, I find he's turned away and is looking through the window, deep in thought.

'Right, that's enough about me,' I say brightly, quickly wiping away my tears. I assume Jamie has had enough talk of illness for one day. 'Tell me what's been going on here. Has anything exciting happened while I've been tucked up in bed?'

Twenty-four

Over the next few days things get a little easier. I'm able to get out of bed and move around on the ground floor with my crutches. Jamie lifts me up and down the stairs when I need to move between the two levels of the house, and the feeling I have when I'm so close to him doesn't diminish at all. If anything, I actually begin to look forward to the times when he has to lift me up and assist me.

Now I'm a little more mobile, Talia moves back to Ant and Dec's house, so Jamie doesn't have to sleep on the sofa any more. But she is always here in the morning when I get up, and she stays with us until the evening. I hate being so reliant on them both, but I've accepted now I have no choice. Sometimes Fisher joins us and we have some fun times in between our continued watch over St Felix – which the others will only allow me to take part in during daylight hours, and even then not for very long.

I explained what had happened to Fisher – and apologised – and as usual he was completely relaxed and chilled about everything. And once more I feel bad that I didn't confide in any of them earlier.

I am given no choice in the matter of regular rest periods, either: none of them will take no for an answer. When I complain I just want to carry on with what I'm doing for a little longer, I'm immediately swept up in Jamie's arms and carried downstairs to my bedroom. And it's on these occasions, when I'm left alone with Fitz, I find myself wondering what it might be like if instead of backing out of the door when he's deposited me on my bed, Jamie was to stay with me . . .

I can't deny it any longer – I definitely have feelings for him.

But, as I allow myself to daydream about the looks we've shared, the sparks of electricity between us, and the possibility of us being together, I quickly remind myself of the state I'm currently in. I hardly look alluring at the best of times, let alone right now when I'm recovering from a flare. What possible reason would Jamie have to look twice at me when I'm like this?

And it was very clear he didn't want to talk about my illness, let alone forget about it enough to abandon himself to the throes of passion! He'd made that quite clear over the last few days, when he'd talk about anything except my condition.

I'd dealt with one failed relationship as a result of this illness. I wasn't going to put myself through the pain of another – especially when it might only be one-sided on my part.

But other than my slightly worrying fantasies, and still feeling pretty grotty, life on the island is actually quite pleasant, chilled and relaxed for the time being.

The one exciting thing that does happen over the course of the next week is Fisher and Jamie discovering exactly where the door we'd found in the cave leads to.

They spend one long afternoon and evening searching Tregarlan in case the tunnel, like the one that leads up from the little beach, does indeed lead back to the castle.

And the pair of them are as excited as two kids on Christmas morning when they arrive back on the island to tell Talia and me their news.

'We found where the door leads to!' Jamie says, bursting through the entrance to the watchtower early one morning.

'Where?' I say, sitting up from where I'm drinking a cup of coffee on the sofa. Talia, on duty at the desk, turns too.

Jamie waits for Fisher to appear next to him.

'Has he told you yet?' Fisher asks excitedly as he reaches the top of the stairs. I shake my head.

'You tell,' Jamie says, holding his hand out to Fisher. 'It was your genius that worked it out.'

'Shall I make us all some breakfast first?' Talia asks. 'Then you can tell us all about it.'

Since I've started to feel a little better, I've thought a lot about our visit to the cave. When Jamie and Fisher announced they were going to try to investigate where the door led to, I was excited for them, but at the same time annoyed I wouldn't be able to accompany them.

'The minute we find something I'll let you know, I promise,' Jamie told me before he left last night. 'I know you want to be involved in this, Sky, but you must rest if you're to get back to anything close to how you were before – you know that. Proper rest, followed by proper pacing, is the key to your recovery and future health. If you don't get it right now and push yourself too hard, it could prevent you from ever getting better.'

Even though I hated hearing him say it, I was impressed he'd taken that on board from the little I'd told him, and also relieved he'd actually mentioned my illness for once. It was a start.

While we wait for Talia to bring us up some toast and coffee,

I have to be content with trying to work out from the furtive looks Jamie and Fisher keep giving each other what they possibly could have found out.

'Right then,' Talia says eventually, happy that everyone has a warm mug in their hands and a plate of hot buttered toast on their laps. 'Go for it.'

'Shall I go first or you?' Fisher asks Jamie.

'What if I start and you continue when I get to the relevant bits?' Jamie suggests.

'Will one of you just tell me, *please!*' I cry in anguish. 'This is killing me.'

'Right,' Jamie says. 'As you already know, when Fisher and I left here last night we took the boat back to the cave. The tide was high enough, so we were able to get right to the back of the cave again, but on water this time so we were almost level with the door. We tried to open it from this side but it was locked so we couldn't budge it.'

'That's what we expected, though,' I remind him.

'Yes, but we had to try it first. If it had opened we wouldn't have had to move on to plan B.'

'Which was?' I ask impatiently.

'Give me a chance, Sky,' Jamie says, smiling. 'I'm going as fast as I can.'

'I know, I'm sorry, but when you're stuck here in the house all day you don't have a lot else to think about.'

'So, Fisher and I moved to our plan B,' Jamie continues. 'A little trip to Tregarlan. Fisher had heard a rumour that Lucinda was going away for a few days, hadn't you?' He turns to Fisher.

Fisher nods. 'That's right, there are a couple of the Wave Watch team I get on quite well with, and without too much nudging, they let slip she was going to be away.'

'Gosh, is Lucinda really something to do with this?' I ask eagerly. 'She is, isn't she?'

'All in good time,' Fisher says, smiling at me. 'All in good time. I knew that if Lucinda wasn't around, I'd stand a better chance of exploring more of the castle – she often works late into the night, you see, even when everyone else has left. While you were ... at your worst, Sky,' Fisher says, obviously looking for a way to put this delicately, 'I've been exploring the castle to see if I could find any further tunnels. I also did some basic calculations as to the likely whereabouts of another tunnel's entrance based on where our original smugglers' tunnel is situated, and I decided that place was likely to be in the south tower ...'

'Where the Wave Watch is currently situated!' Talia says excitedly.

'Spot on,' Fisher replies, smiling approvingly at Talia. 'When I heard Lucinda was going to be away, I knew this was the perfect time to strike. So after we'd visited the cave, that's where Jamie and I went – long after the last visitors had left – and we did some exploring ...'

'What did you find?' I ask impatiently when he doesn't immediately fill in the gaps.

Fisher looks to Jamie to continue the story.

'Any tunnel was likely to come out at the bottom of the tower somewhere,' Jamie says, 'so we started on the ground floor – that part of Tregarlan doesn't have a cellar – the other tunnel begins from Tregarlan's wine cellar, apparently.' He looks at Fisher, who nods. 'But we couldn't find anything in the rooms at the base of the south tower. No secret panels or trapdoors – much to my disappointment. Then Fisher suggested we try outside – and *this* is the genius part. Fisher?'

'There's this old coal bunker around the back of the house,' Fisher says. 'It's been used for many things over the years, not just for storing coal and fuel for the house. It's large enough that during the Second World War it was used as an underground bomb shelter, and there are rumours it might have been used to hide spies, too, because of its easy access out of Tregarlan into St Felix and beyond.'

'I remember you mentioning that when Jamie and I visited the house.'

'Yes, the official history is the house was used as a base to train British spies, but there's always been a rumour that German spies were trafficked through here. No one suspected a quiet little Cornish seaside town of harbouring German spies to be let loose into the country.'

'So we decided to try down there next,' Jamie says, clearly desperate to continue. 'And the first thing we discovered was someone had pulled some leaves, moss and earth across the entrance to make it look as though no one had been down there for years. But when we pulled open the door, it opened with such ease that it was clear they had – and recently, too.'

'We found our way down through the bunker,' Fisher says, 'where we found a little door, again one that had been opened quite recently. It wasn't locked so we were able to go straight through it.'

'And?' I ask when they don't immediately continue. It's clear both Fisher and Jamie are revelling in telling this story.

'It was another tunnel,' Fisher continues. 'It's almost identical to the first one that leads out from the wine cellar to the beach – the stone has been worn smooth by feet walking on it over the years, its dark and damp, and, just like the original Tregarlan tunnel, it does actually lead somewhere.'

'Where?' I ask impatiently.

'To another door,' Jamie says maddeningly. 'A locked door.'

'Is it the door that leads out from the cave, do you think?'

'We're pretty sure it is.'

'How can you know? Just because it looks similar it doesn't mean it's the same one.'

'This is the genius part of the story.' Jamie grins, looking at Fisher. 'And I hand over to my friend here for the finale.'

'It's not that special,' Fisher says, shrugging. 'Just common sense, really. The reason we can be certain that it's the same door is before we left the cave in the boat, I drilled a tiny hole through the door with my cordless drill, then I left a long thin screw poking far enough through the wood that I hoped we'd be able to see it on the other side if we were successful in finding the right door.'

'When we *did* eventually find a door at the end of the tunnel,' Jamie says proudly, 'we could just see the tip of the screw poking through on our side.'

'Wow! How clever you are, Fisher!' Talia says, clapping her hands together. 'I would never have thought of that.'

Fisher looks quietly pleased.

'There really is a tunnel leading from the cave up to Tregarlan, then?' I say, hardly believing it myself. 'And not only that, it's been used recently, too.'

'It definitely seems that way.' Jamie nods. 'However, what it doesn't tell us is just what the tunnel has been used for or by whom.'

'It has to be something to do with the fake weather forecasts. You said yourself, Fisher, you'd noticed the Wave Watch getting a lot of forecasts wrong, and that was before we arrived.'

'I did. There's been something odd going on there for a

while, that's one of the reasons Walt left. I don't want to cast aspersions, but it all started shortly after Lucinda took charge.'

'You see!' I say, gesticulating to Jamie. 'Lucinda is at the heart of all this, I know she is. They didn't think there was going to be a storm that night; they thought it was going to be calm – that's why the boat went to the cave. Whoever was on board thought no other boats would be about because a fake storm had been forecast locally, and they'd be safe to enter without being spotted. But what they hadn't counted on was you being in there, and they fled as soon as they saw you.'

'It all sounds feasible, I know,' Jamie says, 'but we have no proof of any of this. We need to find out exactly what the tunnel is being used for, and if it is something dodgy, we need something a lot more concrete to tie Lucinda or the Wave Watch to it – if, of course, they are actually involved.'

I think about this. He's right, of course; if only we had something else, some proof of some kind . . .

'Talia,' I ask, as something suddenly occurs to me, 'could you go downstairs and look in the pocket of my yellow mackintosh, please? I think there might be something in there that could help us.'

Talia nods, and heads downstairs.

Fisher and Jamie look puzzled.

'What have you got, Sky?' Jamie asks.

'I'm not sure, but it might be of help. I picked it up from the floor of the cave when we were there, but because of everything that's happened since I'd forgotten all about it.'

Talia returns with something in the palm of her hand, which she hands to me.

'It's a bit smelly,' she says, wrinkling up her nose.

'I'm not surprised; it's been in my pocket for well over a

week.' I attempt to pull off some of the dried seaweed that's clinging to the tiny object, and eventually I'm able to free it from its camouflage. 'You want more proof,' I say, holding the object up so the other three can see it. 'Here it is.'

'What is it?' Talia peers forward to inspect what's in my hand.

'Is it a badge of some sort?' Jamie asks.

'Fisher?' I ask, turning to him. 'Do you recognise this?'

'I surely do,' Fisher says, sitting back in his chair after he's inspected the metal item in my fingertips. 'It's a compass – a badge shaped like a compass, anyway. A compass is the insignia of the Wave Watch. When you're officially accepted into the organisation you get a silver badge presented to you.'

'But the badge in Sky's hand looks like it was originally a gold colour,' Jamie says, peering at the tarnished badge again.

'It is gold,' Fisher says slowly. 'Every Wave Watch station has a captain, and they're presented with a gold badge to denote their seniority. The last person to be awarded a gold badge at St Felix Wave Watch was . . . ' He pauses for effect, but I'm sure we all know what he's going to say. 'Lucinda.'

Twenty-five

Talia and Fisher depart later that morning, with Fisher promising he will check with Walter about past owners of a gold Wave Watch badge.

Of course, just because we have this new clue, it doesn't take us any further forward in figuring out what's going on. But with each new thing we find out, I feel we're moving that little bit closer to discovering just what's going on.

After Jamie has taken the dogs for a walk and we've had lunch, Jamie is due on weather watch for a couple of hours.

'Shall I take you downstairs for your rest before I get set up here?' he asks.

'I'm fine on the sofa,' I tell him. 'You do your shift, and I'll rest here.'

Jamie looks doubtfully at me. 'But will you, though?' he asks. 'Rest, I mean, if you sit there. I think you'd be better downstairs in your bed.'

'Anyone would think you were trying to get rid of me!' I joke.

'No, not at all. But I don't want you to get ill again,' Jamie says seriously. 'That was scary, Sky, for all of us.'

'I know,' I say solemnly, my smile disappearing, 'I'm sorry about that. But I am improving a little day by day.'

'I can see that. Do you think you might be well enough to take a trip over to St Felix soon? Some fresh air might do you good.'

'I would love to, but I'm still struggling to walk properly – even on my crutches.'

Jamie looks undecided about whether to say something or not.

'What's up? I ask. 'It's not like you to dither.'

'I'm not dithering. I'm just unsure how you'll take something.'

'What?' I ask again, wondering what's going on.

'Wait here,' Jamie says, leaping up. 'Oh sorry,' he says, remembering I'm not going anywhere without him. 'I'll be right back.'

I wait on the sofa while I hear Jamie bound down the stairs, and I wish I could do the same. Then I hear the front door open and close, and then Jamie bounding back up the staircase.

'I have a surprise for you,' he says when he reappears. 'Can I take you downstairs?'

'Sure,' I say, wondering what this surprise is going to be. I'm not a great lover of surprises, but just the thought that Jamie has bought me a gift makes my heart skip a beat. *What if it's something romantic? What if he really does feel the same way about me as I do about him?*

I put my arms around his neck, and he lifts me safely down the staircase. So caught up am I in being this close to him again, I don't actually look at what's waiting for me at the bottom of the staircase until we get there.

'Ta-da!' Jamie says, turning around with me still in his arms.

It's then that I see the surprise, waiting in the hall for someone to sit in it. For me to sit in it.

'It's a wheelchair,' Jamie says when I don't say anything. 'I thought it might make it easier for you to leave the house. We can push you outside in it so you can get some fresh air, and then when you're feeling up to it, we can take you over to St Felix and you'll be able to get around a little easier.'

I just stare at the empty wheelchair.

'Sorry, have I done the wrong thing?' Jamie asks anxiously. 'Fisher and I borrowed it from Tregarlan. They've just replaced the wheelchairs they keep for people to borrow who can't get around easily. So this old one isn't being used. Fisher says they won't miss it.'

I continue to stare silently at the wheelchair. I'm not sure what I'd expected the 'surprise' to be, but it certainly wasn't this.

'I've done the wrong thing, haven't I?' Jamie says when I don't speak. 'Talia said you might not like it.'

I turn and look at Jamie. I was right before, this is exactly how he sees me, nothing more than my disability.

'I think I might need that lie-down now,' I say, desperate to get to my bedroom before I burst into tears.

'I'm sorry, Sky. I really didn't mean to upset you. I just thought you might like to get out and about a bit more instead of being stuck in the house.'

'You haven't upset me,' I lie. 'I'm just a bit tired.'

'Sure,' Jamie says, carrying me towards my room, where he deposits me gently on my bed. 'I'll just get your crutches from upstairs.'

I sit on the edge of the bed, desperately fighting back the tears that are far too eager to pour from my eyes.

I know that Jamie only wanted to help me, and I'm grateful – really I am. But I can't bear the thought of him only seeing me in terms of illnesses and wheelchairs.

'Here you go,' he says, appearing at the door again. 'I'll leave them here in case you want to visit the bathroom or anything.'

'Thanks,' I say, trying to summon a smile.

'Do you want me to bring Fitz down here to keep you company?' Jamie asks, still looking concerned.

'He's happy upstairs with Comet now they've had their walk. I'll be fine.'

'I'm really sorry about the wheelchair,' Jamie says, looking genuinely troubled.

I wave him away. 'It's fine, honestly. The thought was a good one. I'm sure I'll get some use out of it. I just need a rest, that's all.'

I make out like I'm going to lie back on my bed.

'Right, I'll leave you to it, then,' Jamie says. 'Just shout if you need anything.'

'I will.'

Jamie closes the door and I lie back on the bed.

I listen to him climb the stairs, and give him long enough to get settled in the watchtower. Then I sit up again.

I need some air.

This room suddenly feels claustrophobic, and I know I have to get out and breathe in some of the fresh sea air that's just outside my door.

Quietly, I put a hoody on over my T-shirt and jogging bottoms, and then I pull on my trainers and lace them up – all the time moving slowly around the room so I don't make any unnecessary noise.

Then I grab my crutches and hobble slowly towards my

bedroom door, pulling it open just a tad to see if I can hear anything from upstairs. When I'm sure the coast is clear, I creep out of the bedroom and towards the front door, passing the empty wheelchair on the way.

Not just yet . . . I think as I shuffle past it. *Not just yet.*

I open the door as slowly and as quietly as I can, and then I sneak outside on my crutches, praying that the dogs don't hear me and alert Jamie to the movement downstairs.

The sea air hits me as soon as I step outside and I stop for a moment to breathe it in. *Glorious.*

Then I hobble slowly away from the door, keeping as close to the house as I can so Jamie doesn't spot me from the watchtower above. When I'm far enough around the house so I know Jamie can't see me at this angle, I begin to head away from the building and the rocky mound it sits upon, a little further down the hill towards some rocks that I've sat on many times since we arrived here on the island, watching the sea crash against their counterparts down below.

It takes me much longer than usual to reach the rocks, encumbered as I am by my crutches. When I do finally reach them, I throw my crutches onto the grass and ease myself down onto the smooth surface of one of the rocks that protrudes through the ground.

I close my eyes for a moment and breathe. In and out. Rhythmical and steady. Just like the waves washing in and out down on the rocks below me – nature is incredibly soothing.

I open them again a few moments later, feeling a little better.

How free you are, I think as I sit on the rocks, watching seabirds swoop gracefully up and down in the gusts of wind, occasionally diving athletically into the water on the lookout for fish. *At the moment I'd be grateful just to walk freely, let alone perform aerial gymnastics like you are.*

One of the things chronic illness of any sort robs you of is your freedom. You might not actually be locked up in a cell like a criminal, but you are always a prisoner. Whether it's your home that imprisons you because you can't get out and about easily on your own, or even your bedroom – because you are so ill you can't even leave your bed. But most of all it's your own body's failings that shackle you, preventing you from being free to do whatever you want.

And that's exactly how I feel right now – a prisoner in my own body.

I'd arrived in Cornwall feeling better than I'd felt in years. I was finally in control of my life, this project on the island and – most importantly, I thought – my body.

Except I'd taken my body for granted, and once more I'd wound up back here– imprisoned by pain and exhaustion, reliant on others to help me survive.

I sigh.

It is, of course, my own fault. I know exactly how I need to live, to at least attempt to keep the monster safely in his cage. If I'd just listened to the signs, instead of burying my head in the sand, hoping it was going to be all right this time, maybe I wouldn't have got this bad.

Sometimes when I have bad days, or even weeks, I'm able to hide away from life until I feel well enough to join in with it again. Living on my own, no one notices when I'm having a bad day, when I need to go to bed in the afternoon to have a lie-down because my head is fuzzy or my brain has gone on strike. No one except Fitz cares when I don't get up until midday because I haven't slept, or my body just won't cooperate enough to allow me to get out of bed without extreme pain and stiffness.

But being here on the island, living with Jamie and Talia, I haven't been as free. I've had to hide when I'm having an off day, and I haven't been able to go for a lie-down any time I've needed one. I knew eventually I would pay the price for ignoring my body's warning signs. And that price has been my freedom.

I watch two gannets sitting on the rocks. Occasionally they preen each other, and nuzzle into the other one's neck – a breeding pair.

Lucky you, I think, watching them. It's so easy for you, isn't it? There's nothing complex to your mating routines, no hurdles you have to cross, nothing you have to hide that prevents you from being together.

But I'm wrong. As I sit and watch the two birds, a third bird flies down and tries to move in on the male's territory. The intruder gets a sharp poke to his beak, and is immediately on his way again. A few minutes later, happy their mate is safe, one of the gannets flies out to look for food again, leaving the other behind looking after the nest.

As I watch the remaining bird rearrange the nest with its beak and shuffle around on top of it until it's happy, I notice it's only using one leg to stand on, the other, it seems, is injured in some way, and hangs loosely underneath the bird's body.

Maybe life isn't quite as simple for you, I think as the first bird returns with a small fish which he feeds to the other, before flying off again. *Maybe you do need a little help, after all.*

I think about Jamie lifting me up and down the stairs.

Was he doing that because he had to, or because he wanted to?

I already know the answer to that without having to think too much about it. Even though I'd thought Jamie was a self-centred idiot when I'd first met him, since I'd got to know him I'd realised Sonny Samuels was simply a character he portrayed when he was on 'show'. The real Jamie isn't like Sonny at all. The real Jamie cares about people and situations in a way I hadn't expected him to.

And it was that Jamie I'd begun to develop feelings for, much to my surprise, not Sonny.

Jamie is kind and caring towards me, but it is a long way from being anything more than that, and I have to stop kidding myself it ever might be.

Perhaps if I'd stayed fit and healthy on this island adventure, it might have developed into something more? But now Jamie sees me for the burden I really am, why would he want what we have to be anything more than a passing friendship?

Yet again tears spring into my eyes. I brush them furiously away and with them, I hope, my feelings too.

I have to get these silly notions about Jamie out of my head once and for all, otherwise I'm going to make a fool of myself, and I've done enough of that already.

The weather had been dry, if a little cloudy, when I'd made my way out here earlier. But now the banks of stratus clouds have been joined by their relations the nimbostratus and the skies begin to darken.

I'll have to make my way back to the house in a minute, I think, looking up at the sky. But the sea air is so refreshing that I can't bear the thought of having to go back inside just yet. I've spent far too long in there lately.

As I watch the clouds move across the sky, beckoning in

the wet weather, I realise there's more than just some random shapes forming above me.

What is that? I wonder, staring up at a cloud as it begins to morph from a wispy, nondescript shape into something more familiar. 'Are they wheels?' I ask, gazing up in awe. 'Yes, they are wheels,' I confirm to myself; 'two big and two little . . . on a sort of cube . . . and is that two handles?' I fall silent as I begin to realise what the clouds are forming. 'It's a wheelchair . . .' I say eventually.

As always, the clouds don't hold their shape for long. As soon as I identify it the wheelchair disappears as quickly as it's appeared. 'What are you trying to tell me?' I ask, hardly able to believe what I've just seen. 'That I should use the wheelchair? What good will that do, other than making Jamie feel better?'

A sudden gust of wind causes a more dramatic move in the clouds, so now they begin to form what looks like a plume of smoke. The two ends then join to form a circle, which when it dips in the middle at the top and bottom forms a very clear heart shape in the sky.

'The wheelchair was given to me with love?' I ask, not actually believing I'm talking to the clouds, let alone asking them questions. 'Or the wheelchair will bring me love?'

But the clouds have already blended again to make one big dark rain cloud, which now begins to pelt down large spots of rain.

'Damn!' I say, looking around for my crutches. 'I'd better get moving.'

But the rain is getting heavier by the minute, and I'm already getting wet. If I try to get to the house at the speed I'm currently able to move at, I'll be absolutely soaked by the time I get back. I look around and notice that the rocky mound behind me which the house sits at the top of dips in a little here, creating a very small arch. If I can get under there it might give me shelter until the rain passes. By the look of these clouds, it should only be a passing shower.

I pull myself up on my crutches and hobble over to the rocks, then I tuck myself underneath the little arch, glad that the wind is blowing the rain at an angle behind me – my little shelter is keeping me drier than it might have done had the rain been coming from any other direction.

As I lean against the rocky wall for support, I fall back a little.

That's odd, I think, putting my hand back to check what's there. *Surely that should be solid*.

But the mossy grass that I'd assumed was clinging to the rocks behind me gives a little when I touch it. It moves and falls away far too easily to be properly attached to the rock.

'There's wood behind here,' I say out loud, as my hand touches something much warmer than stone. 'Why would there be wood . . . ? Oh crikey, it's a door!'

I pull some more of the mossy grass and leafy plants away to reveal a small wooden door with black iron fixings.

'But why would there be a door in the rock face?' I ask myself, trying to turn the handle, but finding it's locked. 'And even more interesting, why is this door identical to the one we found in the cave?'

Twenty-six

When the rain stops, I take my chance and head back slowly to the house.

I'm about to open the door to try to sneak back inside, when it's opened for me.

'Where have you been?' Jamie demands, looking worried and annoyed at the same time.

'I fancied some fresh air, that's all,' I say, stepping past him into the house.

'I could have come with you if you'd said.'

'I didn't want anyone with me; I wanted to be alone for a while.'

'But ... but it's not safe,' Jamie says, shutting the door behind me. 'Not with you on those things.' He gestures at my crutches.

'I was perfectly safe, thank you. I only went and sat on those smooth rocks on the other side of the house. I've sat there many times before, as you know.'

Jamie stares at me, clearly wanting to say something but not knowing whether he should.

'Spit it out,' I say. 'I know you want to tell me off for doing too much, or going out when I should be resting, so just get it over with.' My legs buckle slightly, but I'm held up by my crutches. The short, but difficult walk has taken it out of my weakened muscles.

'It doesn't matter,' Jamie says, seeing me. 'Are you going for a lie-down now or do you want me to lift you upstairs?'

I glance behind him down the hall at the empty wheelchair, but instead of seeing a love heart around it like the clouds had suggested I should, I simply see red.

I'm angry that Jamie sees my disability first, before he sees me. I'm angry with myself for letting the monster get the better of me, yet again. But most of all I'm angry that I can't fall in love like a normal person can.

'I'm fed up being told what to do and where to go all the time,' I snap, taking my hurt out on Jamie. 'I don't want to be carried anywhere. I'll go upstairs myself, thank you.'

Stupidly, I head towards the stairs and attempt to climb them – not the easiest of things to do with crutches at the best of times, let alone when I've already exhausted myself from my little trip out.

I climb one step successfully, and then I attempt the second, but my right leg buckles again, this time more severely so that I wobble and begin to fall backwards, until I feel a strong pair of arms catch me.

'Enough of that,' Jamie says firmly, supporting me around my waist, whilst removing my crutches from my hands and leaning them against the staircase. 'You're coming with me.'

He scoops me up in the same way he always does, but less gently and with more determination than usual, and carries me quickly up the stairs.

'Now,' he says, laying me on the sofa in the watchtower. 'I think we need to talk.'

My arms are still around Jamie's neck; usually I would have let go by now, but this time I don't, I let my hands continue to rest on the back of his neck.

For some reason Jamie doesn't try to pull away either, he simply looks down into my eyes.

'Oh, Sky,' he murmurs, 'why do you make this so difficult for me?'

'I'm sorry,' I whisper, still holding on to him. 'I know I'm awkward. I—' But I'm not allowed to finish my sentence because I suddenly find Jamie's lips pressed against mine.

'Jees, I'm sorry!' Jamie says, leaping up after we've kissed for a few glorious moments. 'I don't know where that came from?'

'Please, don't worry about it!' I say, hurriedly pulling myself into a sitting position. 'Really, it's fine.'

'No, I . . . I took advantage when you were upset. I shouldn't have. You're ill, for God's sake!'

And there it is. Laid out in front of me like he's written it on the wooden floor in bright bold letters.

You're ill.

Jamie turns away from me; he rests his hand on the back of the swivel chair we sit in when we're on watch, and stares out of the window.

'Yes, I am,' I hear myself saying, but I'm not sure why. 'I am ill. I've been ill a long time, and I'll probably continue to be ill for the rest of my life. It's something I have to learn to live with. But that's the thing – I'm still learning, and I'm not very good at listening to my body when it's telling me to slow down.'

Jamie turns around to look at me.

'But I'm more than just my illness,' I continue, still unsure

276

where the words are coming from, but absolutely convinced they're the right ones. 'My illness is a part of me, but it's not the whole me. I refuse to let it be. ME is just a small part of who I am. It will never be all of me.'

'You see,' Jamie says, looking at me with a strange mixture of anguish and admiration. 'When you say things like that it makes me fall for you even more.'

I stare at Jamie. *What did he just say?*

'Yes, you heard right,' Jamie says, looking me directly in the eye now. 'I said I'm falling for you.'

I shake my head. *Was this some strange dream I was having, brought on by too many painkillers?*

'I'm sorry if you don't feel the same,' Jamie says, misunderstanding the shake of my head. 'But—'

'No, you don't understand,' I say, interrupting him. 'I'm shaking my head because I can't quite believe you've just said that – believe in a good way, I mean; in case you misinterpret that too.'

Jamie looks confused.

'I feel the same,' I tell him hurriedly before this gets any more complicated. 'I just never thought you would. Did. I mean—'

'I know,' Jamie says, coming over to the sofa and sitting down on the edge of it next to where my legs are still resting. 'I get *it*. I get *you*, Sky. Even though you think I don't.'

He pulls me towards him and we kiss again for a few glorious moments. As we do, outside the clouds part for a moment, allowing the sun's rays to shine down on us through the window. Could it be even the weather is happy for us?

'I've wanted to tell you how I felt for ages,' Jamie murmurs. 'But you're so hard to get close to.'

'I know and I'm sorry. It's just I'm scared, you see, of being hurt. I already feel so vulnerable in life, that since I've been ill I daren't even imagine myself in another relationship. Until I met you, that is.'

'I know exactly how that feels,' Jamie says. 'To be scared. The last thing I wanted when I came here was to meet someone new. As far as I was concerned, I'd suffered enough relationship traumas to last me a lifetime. But then you came along with your funny uptight ways, and your little dog, and I think I was smitten with you almost as quickly as Comet was with Fitz.'

For a while we simply sit wrapped in each other's arms, lost in our thoughts, and listening to nothing but the waves outside and the beating of our hearts.

'When you said you get it ... and you get me,' I ask, after I've gone over and over in my mind what's just happened, 'what did you mean?'

'You probably think I don't understand what living with a hidden illness is like – and you're right, I don't understand entirely, because I don't live with something like you have. But I do understand what it's like to have a hidden disability.'

Confused, I wait for him to tell me more.

'Just like you weren't entirely honest with me about your problems,' he continues, 'I haven't been honest with you about mine. I'm not as physically debilitated as you are, but I still live with it every day, and I have since I was a child.' He takes a breath. 'You see, I'm dyslexic.'

I stare at Jamie now. 'But you're so confident, so ... together,' I finally settle on. 'How can you be ...?'

'*Dyslexic*,' Jamie finishes for me. 'You can say it, it's not an insult.'

'No, I know it's not. Sorry, I didn't mean it to sound like that; I'm just a bit stunned.'

Jamie shrugs. 'I know, right? I hide it well, don't I?' He grins.

'Yes, you do . . .' I reply, trying to think quickly. 'Wait, is that why you didn't want to write in our logbooks?'

'Yeah, my handwriting isn't the best, and it takes me a while sometimes to process written information. I often have trouble with numbers too.'

'Hence why you didn't want to use the purse full of cash!' I cry as everything begins to click.

Jamie nods. 'Cards are far easier for me. I guess I'm lazy too – can't really blame the dyslexia for that, though.' He grins, as usual trying to find the light in every situation. 'If the dyslexia wasn't enough, on top of that I also suffer from something called visual stress. That's another of the reasons I find it much easier to type on a computer – if I have one of my special overlays on it, that is.'

'What's an overlay?'

'It's a clear cover that I need to put on any reading mate-rial – like a book or a laptop, for instance. Mine are all blue, but there are many colours that people use to help them. If I wore glasses, I might just have them tinted blue for reading, but luckily even in the advancing years of middle-age I'm still spectacle free.'

That would be why Jamie has always been reticent to allow me to see his computer when he's on watch duty, I think as everything begins to slide neatly into place. *I'd have seen the blue tint over the screen.*

'And this visual stress is different from your dyslexia?' I ask, keen to know more, but at the same time annoyed with myself that I hadn't noticed anything untoward. Maybe if I'd been more honest about my own problems, Jamie might have felt brave enough to share his.

'Yes, visual stress can be a part of being dyslexic, but not everyone who has visual stress is dyslexic. If you see what I mean?'

I nod. 'Was your dyslexia picked up when you were at school?'

'Yeah, but not until later in secondary school, and by that time it was too late – I was already classed as one of the *difficult* kids.' Jamie uses air quotes when he says the word 'difficult'.

'How do you mean?'

Jamie grins. 'Can you remember when you were at school?'

'Yes.'

'I'm pretty sure you would have been one of the high achievers, but think about those kids who were never in your classes – and if they were, they were the ones messing about at the back instead of listening to the teacher or getting on with work. I was one of those kids.'

'But it wasn't your fault you couldn't get on with your work if no one knew about your dyslexia?'

Jamie shrugs. 'Possibly, but by then I was already branded a troublemaker. Even when they did realise I had a problem, I was already way behind the others in my year. By the time I'd had special classes and they diagnosed my visual stress so I could get my overlays, it was too late to catch up properly on my GCSEs so I didn't really bother. I'd already lost my confidence, to be honest. But I got good at pretending otherwise.' He grins, and I see Sonny appear once more.

I shake my head as empathy floods through me for the young Jamie. 'But how did you get into television if you had no qualifications? I assume you didn't go on to do any A levels or go to university?'

'Nope. I'd have had to go back to evening classes or something, and at sixteen more school was the last thing I wanted. I worked for a bit in some dead-end but fun jobs, then I got a position at a local news station working in their canteen. I don't really know how it happened but I kept finding myself in the right place at the right time and I started to climb a sort of career ladder at the station. I went from a job in the canteen to working in someone's office filing and stuff, to a runner on local news programmes. I might not have had any qualifications like some of them by that point, but I had the gift of the gab and that got me a lot further than a few GCSEs would have.

'To cut a long story short, one day I was messing about in front of the weather wall – I was supposed to be testing it was working for the nightly news. Someone saw me and suggested I have a go with an autocue. As you can imagine, I wasn't too good with that, so I threw in a few off-the-cuff remarks to spice it up a little and amazingly they liked it. That led to a proper screen test, which I managed to blag my way through, and eventually an offer of a few shifts doing some of the more obscure forecasts at weekends and late nights, and that's where Sonny Samuels was born.'

'And the rest, as they say, is history,' I finish for him.

'Pretty much. Eventually I landed a job on breakfast TV, and then prime time, and here I am today, probably one of the only weather forecasters who doesn't use an autocue.'

'How do you manage?'

'Luckily I've been blessed with a great memory. I read the forecast through a few times first using my overlay, then I memorise it by watching the VT that's going to accompany the forecast. If I get stuck, I simply throw in a few non-scripted comments. Fortunately, the viewers really seem to like my relaxed style over some of the more formal forecasters.'

'I owe you an apology,' I tell him.

'Do you? Why?'

'I completely misjudged you. I thought you'd had an easy life, but you dealt with your dad walking out when you were young and all this, too. The fact you've managed to achieve so much with no qualifications *and* dyslexia is amazing.'

Jamie shrugs. 'I'm nothing special. Lots of people do it.'

'Perhaps, but you should be telling everyone instead of hiding it. It's really something to be proud of. Imagine all the children in the same position you might inspire if you did?'

'I've thought about it. I suppose I'm worried about people treating me differently. I also don't want kids thinking qualifications aren't important – you know, using it as an excuse not to try hard at school. I mean, look at you with all your qualifications. They haven't exactly held you back.'

'No, but my drive and ambition have probably made my illness worse. Do you know that the personality type most likely to end up with ME are people like me? I'm talking career-driven individuals, perfectionists, the sort who want to be the best at everything and can't stop doing something until it's completed. They won't rest until they finish what they're doing, however weary they are.'

'Sounds like you.' Jamie grins.

'Contrary to popular belief that will have you think people with ME are lazy because they can't exercise and they have to rest all the time, it's actually the opposite. If you're the sort of person that's lazy by nature, doesn't mind flopping on the sofa in the middle of the day when you've got a thousand things to do just because you're a bit tired, you're very unlikely to end up with a severe case of ME because you rest when your body needs it, and not when your conscience tells you it's all right to.'

'I'm safe, then,' Jamie says, still grinning. 'Any opportunity to take forty winks!'

I smile too.

'Does your dyslexia bother you as much now?' I ask. 'I mean, clearly you still have it, but are you embarrassed about your condition? Is that why you didn't say anything to me or Talia?'

Jamie shrugs. 'I'm not embarrassed. I just prefer not to have to mention it if possible. Otherwise it needs a whole lot of explanation and conversation. A bit like your illness – it's not something people immediately understand, and if they do, quite often they make the wrong assumptions about it – in my case because I have dyslexia that I'm not so bright, which like your description of assuming people with ME are automatically lazy is far from the truth.'

'Seems like we have a lot in common.'

'Something I can't imagine you thought you'd ever say,' Jamie says. 'I get the feeling when we first met you thought you were as far removed from me as you possibly could be. Like sunshine is to snow.'

'Was it that obvious? I'm sorry.'

'Pretty much – but what's much more important to me is how you feel now, Sky.' Jamie looks at me with a solemn expression, but there's a twinkle in his eye. 'Have I melted your cold front . . . just a little?'

'First,' I tease, looking at him with an equally serious expression, 'I must point out you can't actually *melt* a cold front. However,' I continue, placing my finger on his lips when he opens his mouth to speak, 'a warm front can replace a cold one, and you've done a damn good job of turning a *very* chilly winter into a very *long*, and very *hot* summer . . .'

'That,' Jamie says, sliding along the sofa so he's right beside me, 'could possibly be *the best* weather forecast I've ever heard . . .'

Twenty-seven

The next morning I awake, and as always I turn slowly over in my bed to assess how my body is feeling after my usual night of patchy sleep.

If this was a romantic novel or a Hollywood movie, I'd have woken up this morning with Jamie lying next to me, I think as I yawn and begin to gently stretch my stiff body. But this isn't a fairy tale, this is real life, and real life has a habit of not quite living up to the dream.

Last night after we'd kissed for a second time on the sofa, it became pretty clear that both of us wanted our affections to progress further.

'Let's go downstairs,' I whispered to Jamie. 'We can get much more comfortable on my bed.'

'There is nothing I'd like more right now – believe me,' Jamie replied, sitting up from where he was still awkwardly perched next to me on the sofa. 'But is that a good idea? I don't want to wear you out too much.'

Immediately I felt the weight of rejection pour down upon me like a horrible heavy tar. But when I looked up at Jamie's

concerned expression, and into his kind, caring eyes, I realised he was right – of course he was. I could barely get about
right now without exhausting myself, I didn't want our first
time together to be fraught with pain and anxiety that I was
overdoing it.

'I hate to admit it, but you're absolutely right,' I said, gently
cupping his face with my hand. 'I'm so sorry. Are you sure you
don't mind waiting until I have a bit more energy?'

Jamie smiled. 'It's not ideal for either of us. But I do like the
sound of a bit more energy in the bedroom.'

'Cheeky!' And I reached up to kiss him. 'It will be worth
the wait, I promise.'

'I'm going to hold you to that!'

We then spent what remained of the afternoon and the
evening together. Jamie cooked dinner, and we sat and
watched the most beautiful sunset over St Felix, followed by
the stars appearing one by one in a velvety black sky.

Eventually, when we could put it off no longer, Jamie carried
me downstairs and placed me on my bed. He kissed my lips,
and then my forehead, then we forlornly said our goodnights.
Each of us knew that this was not how we wanted our evening
to end, but if we wanted our first time together to be special,
that was how it needed to be – for now, anyway.

After I've done my usual morning routine of lying and sitting
stretches, I head for the bathroom on my crutches, and I can't
miss the wheelchair standing empty in the hall.

'Maybe you're not so bad after all,' I say to the chair as I pass.
'And maybe you were right,' I whisper, looking up, as I think
about the clouds' message from yesterday.

Once I'm dressed, I stand at the bottom of the staircase
wondering if I should have a go at climbing them again. But

286

before I have a chance to try, the dogs bark upstairs, and come bounding down the stairs together, just before the front door opens and Talia and Fisher come through it.

'Morning!' Talia says, leaning down to fuss Fitz and Comet. 'How are you today, Sky?'

'I'm doing okay, thanks,' I say. 'You're early, aren't you?'

'Not really.' Talia glances at her watch. 'It's half past ten. I'm here for my shift.'

I look at my empty wrist and realise I haven't put my watch back on from last night, so caught up have I been in my thoughts about Jamie.

'Sorry, I just assumed it was earlier. I must have slept in.'

'I'm sure it will do you good to get some extra rest,' Talia says, smiling at me. 'Now, where's Jamie? Should I put the kettle on?'

'I'm here,' Jamie says, appearing at the top of the stairs. He smiles at me, and my insides lift so high I feel like I could float up the stairs on my own.

I smile soppily back, until I remember that Talia and Fisher are watching us.

'Glad to see you're up at last,' Jamie says, winking at me. 'I thought you were never going to wake up this morning. You must have been having some very pleasant dreams to sleep this long.'

I smile again.

'Right,' Fisher says, making me jump. 'I'll be on my way. Just thought I'd pop in and see if everything was all right?' He looks quizzically between Jamie and me.

'Yes, why wouldn't it be?' I answer a bit too quickly.

'The Wave Watch got the weather forecast wrong again yesterday. They said it was going to be heavy rain and high winds overnight.'

287

'But it was so calm out there last night,' I reply. 'Jamie and I were watching the stars together and—' I bite my lip.

'Were you now?' Fisher says, grinning. He looks up at Jamie with a knowing look. 'Like that, is it?'

'Ooh, what's going on?' Talia asks excitedly. 'Do I spy a romance blossoming on Aurora?'

'Don't be silly,' I say, again far too hurriedly. 'It was a beautiful night, that's all. You said the Wave Watch got the forecast wrong. Do you think something went on last night?'

Fisher shrugs. 'Don't know. I was going to ask if you'd seen anything, but clearly you were both too busy *star gazing* – or more accurately *gazing* into each other's eyes – to notice?'

'Why don't you stay for a bit, Fisher, so we can discuss this some more?' Jamie suggests from the top of the stairs. 'The fake forecast, I mean, not anything else.' He glances briefly at me.

'Can't, I'm afraid. I'm meeting Walt. I'm going to talk to him about Lucinda and the badge you found, Sky.'

'Oh, damn I've just remembered,' I say as mention of the badge prompts my memory. 'I'm so sorry, I forgot to say, did any of you know there's a door on Aurora, just like the one we found in the cave?'

'How exciting! Where?' Talia asks.

'On the other side of the island. It's hidden in the rocks the house sits upon.'

'I've never noticed it,' Fisher says with a puzzled look. 'How did you find it?'

I glance up at Jamie. 'I was getting some fresh air yesterday and it began to rain. I tried to take shelter in what I thought was a small recess in the rocks. But when I leant on it, I realised it wasn't rock behind me, it was wood. I pulled some of the greenery away and there was a door.'

'Why didn't you say anything yesterday?' Jamie asks, coming down the stairs.

'My brain goes to mush when I'm not well, a bit like my body,' I explain, only half telling the truth. 'Also, I had some . . . *things* on my mind.' I glance at Jamie. 'Why don't you go and take a look? It's on the opposite side of the house to the watch-tower. There are some rocks there that are smooth enough to sit on,' I explain for Fisher and Talia's benefit. 'The recess and door are right behind them.'

'Shall we?' Jamie asks, looking at the other two.

Fisher glances at his watch. 'If we're quick I might have enough time before I'm due to see Walt. Do you want to come too, Talia?'

Talia looks at me. 'No, I'll keep Sky company for a bit,' she says knowingly. 'I think we need a catch-up . . .'

After I've been carried upstairs, Jamie and Fisher go in search of the door. While Talia makes some coffee for us, I sit at the desk and look out to sea.

'Ooh, a fogbow,' I say to Fitz on my lap, as through the window I see an arch of mist that looks like a rainbow. 'You don't see many of them.'

I'm about to call Talia to tell her to come and look, but then I notice that the clouds at either end of the fogbow are fast forming into little clusters, and they now appear to be making some very uncloud-like shapes.

Is that a door? I wonder, as the clouds at one end of the fogbow morph into an arch, reminiscent of the wooden door Jamie and Fisher have gone out to look for. *Yup, it's definitely a door, and what's that at the other end of the fogbow?* I watch as the clouds move again. 'It's a house!' I say out loud. 'The door is joined to a house!'

'What's a house?' Talia asks, coming to the top of the stairs with two mugs of coffee.

'Look,' I say, turning back to the window. But the clouds have already started to dissolve and scatter.

'Ooh, a fogbow,' Talia says, looking through the window. 'I've never seen one of those before.' She pulls up a chair, and sits next to me in front of the watchtower window.

'You know how it's formed, I assume?' I ask, testing her.

'Of course, it's the same as a rainbow, but it's made up of smaller droplets of water so it doesn't refract the light in the same way.'

'Spot on, as usual. An A-star student.'

'Now you were saying something about a house before?' Talia asks, sipping her coffee.

'I think the two doors we've found both lead to houses,' I tell her, still looking out of the window.

'We already know the Tregarlan one does. Do you think the door on the island leads up to this house, then?'

'Yes,' I say, putting my faith in the clouds without question this time. 'I'm sure it does.'

'Let's wait until the boys get back,' Talia says, 'then we can go in search.'

'You can, you mean,' I say, lifting my coffee mug. 'I'll be stuck here on watch as usual.'

'I see Jamie gave you the wheelchair in the end,' Talia says carefully, sipping from her own mug. 'That will help you to get out and about a bit more, won't it? I didn't know if he would or not, he wasn't sure how you'd take it.'

'To be honest, at first I didn't take it at all well,' I admit. 'But things are different now.'

'Yes, I noticed that,' Talia says with a knowing smile. 'There were some very secretive – some might even say *flirty* – looks passing between the two of you earlier.'

I look down into my coffee and I know my cheeks are giving me away by flushing.

'I knew it!' Talia cries delightedly. 'Tell me all about it . . . I want to hear everything!'

It's been such a long time since I've had a girly gossip with anyone that I've forgotten quite how much fun it is to share something with another female. So many of my so-called friends dropped by the wayside when I got ill and didn't get better in what they felt was an appropriate amount of time, that I've got out of the habit of sharing.

Talia is thrilled, but not as surprised as I'd imagined she might be when I tell her what happened with Jamie.

'It was clear to me ages ago that he liked you,' Talia says. 'The question was whether you liked him?'

'I didn't until a week or so ago . . . Actually, maybe it was before then?' I try to remember when my feelings for Jamie began to change. 'When he first came here, he did nothing but annoy me. That wasn't entirely his fault – I have to admit I've been pretty uptight lately, and there was no way our two personalities were ever going to be compatible. But I've changed since I arrived on Aurora – for the better, I hope – and so has Jamie. It was Sonny – his TV persona – we first met. Jamie, thank goodness, is a very different person.'

'I think Jamie was always there waiting to escape,' Talia says perceptively. 'It just needed the right person to release him – and that person was you.'

'What made you think he liked me?' I ask coyly, slightly embarrassed but secretly pleased by what Talia has said.

291

'He's always talking about you. Always singing your praises and saying how great you are, how clever and unique.'

'That's what he said?' I ask, thrilled by this compliment. 'That I'm clever and unique?'

Talia nods. 'And then when you got ill – I mean, I know now you're always ill, but *really* ill. He was so worried about you, Sky. I think he'd have camped outside your bedroom if we'd let him.'

I feel a mix of emotions at Talia's words – it's lovely to know what Jamie really thinks of me. But the guilt that he'd felt quite so terrible during my worst days is awful to hear.

I don't want to be the cause of anyone feeling like that, and not for the first time since I became ill with this disease, I feel the heavy weight of blame on my shoulders, guilt that my illness is affecting the people I care about.

'But you're on the mend now, aren't you?' Talia says cheerily, trying her best to make me feel better.

If only it were that simple. 'On the mend' is what people say when you're getting over a cold or an operation. The expectation is that one day you'll be fully recovered and back to normal again. I know from experience that chronic illness doesn't quite work like that. Instead of there being a beginning, a middle and an end to our suffering, we live on a never-ending rollercoaster ride. There are ups and there are downs. If we're lucky, we might occasionally see the end of the ride far off in the distance, but the trouble is we are never able to reach it and exit from our carriage safely.

'I'm feeling a little better as each day passes,' I tell her, attempting to match her enthusiasm.

'Good, that's what we like to hear! Oh, they're back already.'

Jamie and Fisher appear at the top of the stairs.

'You were right,' Jamie says, flopping down in one of the armchairs. 'There is a door there, but as always it's locked.'

Fisher remains at the top of the stairs. 'I really have to go now, guys,' he says, looking at his watch. 'Jamie and I have already discussed this, but I don't remember ever seeing a key for that door. I know this island pretty well and I never knew there was a door buried in the rock there. I can only think it leads up into this house somewhere. I can't imagine it goes under the sea. I'll ask Walt when I see him. But for now, it's adios!'

'I'll see you out,' Talia says, standing up, and they both head down the stairs together.

'You okay?' Jamie asks as soon as they've gone. 'After last night, I mean?'

'Yes, fine. Are you?'

'Never better.' He grins. 'We didn't do a very good job of hiding it from Talia and Fisher, did we?'

'No, Talia and I were just talking about you, actually.'

'Oh yes – all good, I hope?'

'Yes, all good.' I smile a little shyly at him as Jamie gets up and walks over to me. He leans down, about to kiss me, but we're interrupted.

'Who's for some tunnel hunting, then?' Talia cries excitedly, reappearing at the top of the stairs. 'Ooh, sorry, have I interrupted something?'

'No, not at all,' I say hurriedly as Jamie stands up again. 'Why don't you two go and look around the house, I'll stay here and keep a lookout.'

'Don't be silly, you don't have to miss out, I can carry you downstairs,' Jamie offers.

'It's fine,' I say, not wanting to be any more of a burden than

293

I already am. 'I have some paperwork to do, anyway. We're still being paid to record the weather, even if there are more exciting things going on right now.'

'I never thought I'd hear you say that,' Jamie says, grinning.

'Say what?'

'That there is something *more* exciting than the weather!'

'Well, people change,' I reply, my eyes firmly on his. 'You of all people should know that.'

Twenty-eight

'You're still thinking about that tunnel, aren't you?' Jamie asks later that night when Talia has gone back to the mainland.

Currently we're cuddled up together on the sofa, watching yet another beautiful crimson sunset over the sea.

I never thought I could feel as happy again as I feel right now. If you'd told me when I first came here that it would be Jamie that would be the cause of my happiness, I'd have more likely believed in Zethar and her prophecies.

'Yes, aren't you?'

'Not really. I've just accepted it's there now we've found where it goes from and to.'

After a long search, Talia and Jamie had eventually found a small door concealed behind the large fridge-freezer in the kitchen.

This door was also locked, but after some 'DIY' locksmithing from Jamie, they had eventually managed to unfasten it. They'd then headed off together with large torches to explore the tunnel on the other side.

I'd felt mixed emotions as they'd left – excitement and

anticipation that they'd managed to find the entrance that I was certain led to the door outside, and sadness that yet again I was missing out on an adventure.

I was used to it, this sort of thing happened to me all the time. It hadn't been quite so bad before I'd come to Aurora. Yes, I'd had to pick and choose which things I could do, and which I couldn't. Which friend's invite I would say yes to, and which I would have to turn down because it would be too exhausting, or too difficult for me to travel to. But I've also been in exactly the same place as I am right now – feeling guilty if I ask people to do too much for me, but sad when I can't do everything with them.

Eventually, after what seemed like for ever, Talia and Jamie had returned, surprisingly without much to tell. The tunnel had led, as we'd expected, down and out towards the sea. They couldn't open the door at the end of the tunnel because it was locked, but they knew it was the same door because they'd used Fisher's trick of marking the door from the outside.

And that was all we knew, other than what Fisher had told us when he'd come to pick up Talia. He'd spoken to Walter that afternoon, and Walter knew right away of the tunnel on the island. He said he thought it was originally used by the inhabitants of the island so they could receive their goods by boat, then ferry them up to the kitchen with much more ease than carrying them up what would have originally been a steep and rocky track, long before the smooth pathway we now drove our Jeep up and down had been dug and installed.

Fisher had also spoken to him about the Wave Watch badge, and Walter had proudly shown Fisher his own silver badge for comparison, confirming that the one I'd found, if gold, could only have belonged to a captain of the Wave Watch at some time.

So now we knew there was a tunnel on the island, and there was another tunnel that led up from the cave with the carvings to Tregarlan. But what we didn't know was if there really was smuggling going on, and if there was, just who was responsible for it. Even though I suspected Lucinda from what I'd been told about her behaviour, and what I'd witnessed when I'd met her myself, it was hard to imagine her being embroiled in a dangerous activity like smuggling. Still, as I was learning, appearances could be deceptive.

'There is *something* going on here, Jamie,' I say, looking up at him. 'Trouble is, I don't know what exactly.'

'Just as long as you don't wear yourself out thinking about it all the time, trying to work it all out. We don't want you going downhill again.'

I smile at him, but at the same time I hate to think of him worrying about me like this – it isn't right. Even though I really like Jamie, and he clearly feels the same, we haven't known each other that long, and it still feels odd for me to have someone I don't really know all that well knowing so much about me and seeing me at my most vulnerable.

'I know one thing already,' I tell him, attempting to steer the subject away from me. 'The weather patterns here are all over the place at the moment.'

'How do you mean?'

'The readings and observations we're recording are not following any of the regular patterns they should be.'

'Is that such a bad thing?' Jamie asks, grinning. 'Why do they need to conform?'

'Trust you to think that! It's not that they need to conform, it's just they always do. Weather follows certain patterns and trends that have been established since records began. They just don't go random for no reason.'

'What do you think is happening, then?'

'I'm not sure. I'd quite like to talk to Walter about it sometime and see if he's ever noticed anything like this before. Even the reports of strange weather that brought us here weren't anything as extreme as this.'

'No?'

'Did you even read the reports? I mean, I know it's difficult, but with your overlay on your computer you should have been able to access them?'

'Thanks for understanding, but I don't think I was ever sent any reports.'

'No? That's odd, I assumed we'd all have been sent them to help us understand what we were here for.'

'The first I knew of it was when I met Talia on the train and she explained everything. My coming here all happened in a bit of a rush, really. The suggestion came through, and next thing I knew I was on a train to Cornwall. Stationing me down here just seemed like the answer to a lot of people's problems. So I went along with it.'

'Gemma knew all about you when I spoke to her.'

'Gemma?'

'She's from Met Central HR department. Remember I made that phone call when we first arrived here?'

'Oh yeah, when you were trying to get rid of me ...'

'Well, you were very annoying ...'

'But not now?' Jamie asks, pulling me closer.

'Not quite so much.' I grin.

'From you – I take that as a compliment!'

'You should.'

Jamie leans in to me, and we kiss for a few moments.

'I've never wanted to get well quite as quickly as I do right now,' I tell him, hoping he'll understand.

'Let me reassure you, Sky, I've never prayed so hard for anything either!'

'Soon,' I tell him. 'I promise. Now, back to these weather reports . . .'

'Only you could go from *that* to the weather!'

'It's important!'

'Go on, then,' Jamie says, smiling affectionately at me. 'If it makes you happy.'

'The reports we were sent were nothing compared to what we're experiencing at the moment – the weather is all over the place. Walter said he'd noticed some strange things too before we arrived. I can only think maybe the original reports came from him, which is a little strange, don't you think?'

'I really don't know, Sky. As you've reminded me on more than one occasion, I only present the weather. I have no idea what's normal and what's not.'

'I can assure you that nothing that's going on around Aurora right now is normal – weather or otherwise, and I for one am going to get to the bottom of it.'

The next day I'm persuaded that taking the wheelchair over to the mainland is a good idea. It will give me 'a change of scenery', which will in turn 'do me good'. These are both phrases that I've heard numerous times before from people who are only trying their best to help. This time, however, I agree to go along with Talia and Jamie's well-meaning encouragement – partly because I don't want to upset them by refusing, and partly because Jamie says he'll take me to see Walter, so we can have a chat.

I have to admit it does feel good to get dressed and ready to go somewhere other than the watchtower, and I manage to get down to our little jetty using only my crutches, which pleases me greatly.

The tide is high so Jamie and I take the boat over with the dogs, while Talia stays at the house. The sea air is gloriously fresh and zingy on my skin as we zip across the water towards the harbour, and for a few short minutes with the wind blowing my hair and the refreshing spray of salt water on my face, I feel free of the pain and exhaustion that have become my constant companions of late.

As I watch the dogs' ears blow in the breeze and their tongues loll happily out of their mouths, I feel more alive than I've felt since ... Well, for a *very* long time.

'Enjoying yourself?' Jamie shouts from the bow of the boat.

'Yes!' I call back. 'You were right, this does feel great!'

We pull up into the harbour. After Jamie has tethered the boat, he helps me up onto the side, where the feeling of freedom I'd experience as we'd travelled at speed across the waves quickly evaporates, as I reluctantly transfer into the wheelchair.

We leave the boat with Jamie pushing me in the chair and Fitz sitting on my lap. Comet walks obediently on her lead by Jamie's side, and already I hate every minute of it.

'Is it okay?' Jamie asks behind me.

'Yes,' I lie. 'It's great, thank you.'

We stop not far from the boat, alongside one of the beaches that still has enough sand on when the tide is high for the dogs to run around.

We let the dogs off their leads and immediately they race across the sand together.

Oh, how I wish I could join you, I think, watching them go.

'You won't push me on there,' I say as Jamie turns the wheelchair to go across the sand. 'These wheels won't make it. Leave me here, I'll be fine.'

'Are you sure?' Jamie asks, coming round to the front of the chair. He glances at the departing dogs. 'I can try.'

'Believe me, I know,' I say, trying to remain upbeat. 'You need a certain sort of chair with special wheels to tackle sand. You go with the dogs, and I'll watch you. Quick, before they get too far away from us.'

I watch Jamie chase after the dogs, and I can't help feel jealous of him running with ease across the soft pale sand.

Even when I'm at my absolute best, running is not something that I would ever consider, let alone be able to do, and yet years ago it was something I could do for miles and miles, just for the fun of it.

'How things change,' I mutter to myself.

'First sign of madness – talking to yourself,' I hear a familiar voice call, and I see Jack coming towards me. He's wearing fitness clothes and using his lightweight sporty chair, which makes my wheelchair look like an old tank in comparison. 'Get a nice tartan blanket for your knees and you'll be right at home there.'

I stare at Jack with such a desolate expression that he looks quite shocked.

'Sorry, have I touched a nerve?'

'No, it's fine, really. It's just me, I *hate* being in this thing.'

'Can't say I blame you,' Jack says, looking the chair up and down, 'it is a bit grim!'

301

I look at Jack grinning and I have to smile back. 'Sorry, I shouldn't be so fussy. Not with you . . . ' I wave my hand in his direction.

'Stuck in one all the time?' Jack asks. 'No, you shouldn't, but I completely understand. So, what's happened to put you back in a chair?'

I love Jack's directness. There's no messing around with him, he just says what he thinks. It's refreshing.

'I overdid it,' I reply honestly. 'I didn't listen to my body when it was telling me to slow down. I ignored the signs and I had a flare. Quite an extreme one, actually.'

'Happens,' Jack says pragmatically. 'It's not all sunshine and roses for me, either. I'm prone to overdoing it too – just ask Kate. But I'm a stubborn bugger, and I won't listen when she tells me to slow down. At least *I* can get myself about on my wheels, though. I'd probably have a face like yours if I had to be pushed around in that old thing!'

Jack looks at me and winks and yet again I grin.

'It's all that could be found in the circumstances,' I say. 'I should be grateful that I've been given this, really. Without it I'd be stuck in the house on the island. This is the first day I've been out for a while.'

Jamie is currently throwing balls for the dogs. Fitz is racing across the beach with sand flying up all around him as he fetches his ball, and Comet, with slightly more grace, is retrieving her own ball from the sea. Jamie turns and waves, so I wave back.

'Is that who got you the chair?' Jack asks perceptively.

'It is. How did you know?'

'Educated guess. Remember, he meant well. Sometimes the people around us don't know how to help. They need to do *something*, so they just do what they think is best. You can't blame them if they don't really understand; no one truly gets it unless they've been in the same boat.'

'I know. You're right. I just hate being so reliant on others, and this chair makes that feeling twenty times worse.'

'I totally get that. It's not easy, is it, this disability thing – visible or otherwise?'

I shake my head.

'Look, your knight in shining armour is coming back with my four-legged buddies.'

I look over and see that Jamie is making his way back across the sand with the dogs.

'Learn to accept assistance if you can,' Jack says quickly. 'That's my advice. Be grateful you have people that care enough about you to want to help. I tried to push everyone away when I was first disabled, and it did me no good at all. I wasn't going to be beholden to anyone. But you soon realise you're protecting no one, let alone yourself. Let those that care for you help you, Sky. Remember they're not just helping you; you're helping them as well.'

'All right?' Jamie asks, eyeing Jack warily as he arrives in front of us.

The dogs are panting heavily, so I try to reach around to the back of the chair to get water for them.

'I'll get it!' Jamie calls, before I've even attempted to stand up from the chair.

I look knowingly at Jack.

Jack grins.

Jamie pours some water into the dogs' bowl and they lap thirstily from it.

'Jack, isn't it?' Jamie says, holding out his hand in greeting.

'Yep, guilty as charged,' Jack says, shaking Jamie's hand. 'And you're the infamous Jamie – or is that Sonny? – I've been hearing so much about.'

'Just Jamie today.'

'I was admiring Sky's wheelchair,' Jack says, much to my dismay.

'It's not ideal, I'm afraid, but at least she can get out and about with it.'

'It's good she has someone to look out for her,' Jack says, glancing at me.

'I try,' Jamie says, smiling at me. 'Hopefully Sky won't have to be in it for too long though. We'll soon have you up and running again, won't we?'

'Hopefully,' I reply.

'As long as you go at your own pace,' Jack says knowingly, 'you'll be fine. You can't rush these things.'

'Definitely not,' Jamie says. 'We have all the time in the world, don't we, Sky? No rush at all.'

'We'll get there.' I squeeze his hand affectionately. 'Eventually.'

'It seems my work here is done,' Jack says, winking at me. 'I'd better go. These muscles won't work themselves.' He gives us a quick flex of one of his biceps. 'Keep your chin up, Sky. I'm sure things will improve for you very soon, and it seems you've got great care while you recuperate. Nice to meet you at last, Jamie. I've heard a lot about you.'

'Bye, Jack,' I say, smiling at him. 'See you soon, I hope.'

'You can count on it!' Jack says and he begins to wheel himself away.

'Seems like a nice fella,' Jamie says as we watch Jack pick up speed.

'Yes, he is. He has a great way of putting things in perspective for me.'

Jamie doesn't say anything, he just watches Jack thoughtfully until he disappears around the corner.

'Right, if you and the dogs have had enough time on the beach,' I say, bending down to fuss them from the chair, 'then we'd better go and get our shopping before we see Walter. We said we'd meet him outside the tearoom at eleven thirty.'

'Your wish is my command,' Jamie says, snapping back to his usual self. 'Let me just clean Fitz a little before he goes on your lap again. He's covered in sand.'

'I can do that,' I say, about to climb out of the chair, 'just pass me the— Oh, you've already got it . . . ' I continue as Jamie whips the towel from the bag and begins to clean Fitz's feet and fur.

'You just sit and relax,' Jamie says, smiling at me. 'I've got this. Oh, sorry,' he says, seeing my face. 'Did you want to do it?'

'It's fine. You're there now.'

Jamie cleans the rest of the sand from Fitz's paws, then he passes him to me.

'I am trying,' he says, as Fitz settles down on my lap. 'Really I am. I don't mean to take over. I just want to help you to get better, that's all.'

'I know,' I tell him, stroking Fitz's back as I think about Jack's words. 'I know you are. I'll try to be better at accepting help when it's offered.'

We decide it will be easier and faster if I look after the dogs while Jamie goes to get the shopping. Jamie parks the wheelchair in a spot on the harbour where I shouldn't be in anyone's way, and then he ties the dogs' leads to a rusty old metal ring in the ground that would once have been used to moor boats.

'Now you be good dogs for Sky,' Jamie says, patting them both and giving them a biscuit. 'You sure you'll be okay here?' he asks me for the third time.

'Maybe you should give me a biscuit too,' I say lightly, but I hope he gets my meaning. 'Then I'll be sure to behave.'

'All right,' Jamie says, sounding a little irritated. 'Point taken. But you were so good at hiding everything before that sometimes I find it difficult to know if you're just putting on a brave face.'

I nod. 'Perhaps we both just need to be a little more patient and understanding with each other? Look, you go, I'll be just fine with the dogs. Honestly,' I insist when he still looks worried.

'I'll be back as quickly as I can.'

'Take your time, we'll be fine.' I lean forward to stroke the dogs. 'We'll be all right, won't we?' I whisper to them as Jamie departs. 'I know you two will behave. And we can but hope that I do too.'

The dogs immediately settle down and go to sleep. I sit for a while, watching the boats bob around in the harbour, and the constant stream of people passing me as they walk to the end of the cobbles, take a look out to sea and then walk back again.

Eventually, I change my position slightly so I can look back along the harbour up towards the harbourmaster's office and the town.

Gerald has company today, I think as I notice two people inside his tiny office. *And a woman, too.*

I wonder if the permanently irritated Gerald has a wife or a girlfriend. The two people are standing quite close together and they look like they might be arguing. The woman lifts her hand to emphasise her point. *Definitely a wife or girlfriend, then,* I think, smiling to myself. *It must be, the way those two are bickering.*

I'm about to look back out to sea when Gerald moves a little in the office, forcing the woman to move too, and I'm surprised to see the woman arguing with him is Lucinda.

I have to look again to double-check, but there's no mistaking that white-blonde hair pinned tightly to the back of her head, and her rather prominent nose.

What are you two arguing about? I wonder, continuing to watch them.

Now Gerald is gesticulating to Lucinda. I squint to try to see them a little better, but the bright sunlight on the window of the office prevents me from seeing more clearly.

Lucinda looks upset now rather than angry, as Gerald continues his tirade.

I'm about to get up and wander casually over to the office to try to get a better look, when I remember my wheelchair and the dogs sleeping peacefully at my feet. By the time I've woken them up, untied their leads and tried to push the chair with the dogs up to the office, the arguing couple would be long gone, I'm sure of it.

And I'm not far wrong. Seconds later, the door of the office flies open and Lucinda storms out, tears rolling down her face. She hurries away from me along the harbour towards the town. I turn back to the office and see Gerald leaning on his desk looking red and flustered. He glances out of the window – concerned, perhaps, that someone might have witnessed what's going on. He catches me watching him so I quickly turn away and pretend I'm seeing to one of the dogs, but I'm sure Gerald has noticed.

Furtively, I glance back. Gerald is now opening the door of the office and stepping outside. He still looks flushed and sweaty from his exchange with Lucinda, but he begins to head my way.

Here we go! This is all I need right now, grief from Gerald.

But luckily Jamie comes bounding back along the harbour at the same time. He overtakes Gerald, barely noticing him in his hurry to get back to me.

'I'm back!' he calls merrily, giving us a wave. 'How's my favourite threesome getting along?'

'Good, thanks,' I say, looking past him to see if Gerald is still heading our way. But Gerald has clearly thought better of it, and has turned back again towards his office.

'So what's been happening while I've been gone?' Jamie asks. 'Anything interesting?'

Twenty-nine

'So, I wondered what you thought?' I ask Walter, as I finish telling him all about the strange weather we've been recording on Aurora lately. 'Is it something you recognise?'

We're outside one of the many tearooms and coffee shops dotted about St Felix. This particular one is on the harbour front, and we're sitting under a cheerful red-and-white-striped umbrella, sheltering from the extremely hot sun that has made an appearance from behind the clouds.

I didn't mention what had happened between Gerald and Lucinda to Jamie. But as he pushed me back past the harbourmaster's office, there was no doubt in my mind that whatever had taken place in there wasn't supposed to be common knowledge. Because the glare that Gerald had given me as we passed by his window could only be described as venomous.

Walter takes a sip from his cup of tea and nods slowly.

'Yes, it is. As you know, I've been recording my own weather observations around here long before you both arrived, and I've never recorded anything like what we've been seeing lately. That was one of the reasons I wanted you to come here.'

I glance at Jamie, a little puzzled. 'You wanted us to come here, Walter?' I repeat. 'What do you mean?'

'Did I say that?' Walter says, his usually calm persona clearly a little rattled. 'I meant I was pleased when you arrived. Pleased that someone else other than me was going to investigate the unusual weather. People around here don't listen to what I say – they call me Wacky Walter Weather. I'm sure you've heard them.'

'Really? I haven't heard that,' I fib. 'I mainly talk to Fisher about you. What about you, Jamie?' I ask hurriedly.

'Er no . . . not very often, anyway,' Jamie admits.

'It's fine,' Walter says, reverting to his usual laidback style. 'Let them say what they like. I have my ways of doing things, they have theirs. So now, where were we? Oh yes, the weather – our favourite subject, eh, Sky?'

'Sky actually admitted to me that there's more to life than just weather,' Jamie says, grinning. 'It was quite the revelation to both of us, wasn't it, Sky?' He winks at me and I know he's getting me back for the question about Walter.

'I'm not sure I said that,' I say hurriedly.

'*Yes*, you said there were more exciting things going on right now on the island than the weather.'

'Oh, really?' Walter asks. 'What sort of things *are* going on on Aurora right now? Fisher told me about the tunnels you found, and he mentioned something about a lost badge?'

I narrow my eyes at Jamie, before I turn back to Walter.

'Oh, it's nothing really . . . ' I begin, then I change my mind. 'Except . . . look, it's going to sound a bit random if I say this . . . '

'Go on,' Walter says encouragingly. 'What is it you want to tell me?'

I glance at Jamie. He shakes his head.

'We've been wondering if there might be some smuggling going on in the area?' I blurt out before I change my mind. 'Possibly from the cave with the carving of the lady on the horse, up through the tunnel that leads to Tregarlan.'

Walter looks at me. His wise eyes blink a few times as if he's thinking about something, but doesn't want to give anything away. 'I think you might be right,' he says eventually.

'You do?' I exclaim. 'Really?'

Walter nods. 'I've suspected the same thing myself for some time – quite a long time, as it happens. But I couldn't get any proof.'

Is this why Walter steered me towards the smuggling exhibits at the festival, and then the display about the mystery cave, so I could make this connection myself?

'I think Lucinda at the Wave Watch is involved,' I say in a low voice, testing my next theory. 'That's why she's been putting out fake forecasts. She forecasts stormy weather when it's not going to be, so there are no other boats out at sea. That allows the smugglers' boat to access the cave without anyone seeing them.'

Pleasingly, Walter nods as he takes this information in.

'And I found that badge in the cave, the one that only leaders of the Wave Watch get – I bet it's hers. Also, she was very shifty when we visited her and asked to see the report for the night that storm hit a few weeks ago. Wasn't she, Jamie?'

It's Jamie's turn to nod now.

'I know it sounds far-fetched,' I continue, 'but what other explanation can there be? Why else would the Wave Watch give out fake weather forecasts? It's like they used to do in the old days, Walter – giving out fake weather forecasts to wreck the ship, then taking what was on board. Except now it's to

311

allow smuggling to take place without anyone knowing.' I look eagerly at the old man, hoping he'll agree.

'Have you finished?' Walter asks calmly, still watching me carefully.

'I have,' I reply, wondering if he's going to tell me it's all a lot of nonsense.

'I think you're right,' he says to my delight, 'about one thing, but very wrong about another.'

Oh.

'I agree there's likely smuggling going on around here. I was suspicious of it when I was at the Wave Watch – I can't prove it, but I think it was one of the reasons I was ousted by the committee. They said it was because my unusual methods didn't fit in with the way the Wave Watch was doing things now. I always suspected there was something else going on, but I had no way of proving it.'

'If we're right about that, then what are we wrong about?' I ask.

'Lucinda,' Walter says, checking either side of him in case anyone might be listening to our conversation. 'She's not involved – well, she is, but not how you think.'

'What do you mean?' Jamie asks. 'Walter, you're going to have to explain further if you want us to understand.'

Walter nods. 'When I was asked to leave the Wave Watch, we were still using the island as our base. Lucinda had not long joined us, which is why for a while I thought it was her doing that had caused my downfall. She was never that friendly to me, but maybe it was just her way?'

He thinks about this for a moment before continuing.

'But then weeks later information came to my attention that led me to believe it was actually nothing to do with her.'

'What sort of information?' I ask eagerly. I wonder for a

moment if Walter has been getting messages from the clouds like me, but his next sentence firmly dismisses that idea.

'I was out for a stroll one day and found her crying,' Walter explains. 'Up on one of the benches that look out over St Felix Bay. I'm not one to leave a lady in distress, even if it is one that I think might have taken a dislike to me.'

I smile, Walter is such a gentleman.

'I enquired if she was all right, and she said yes, it was nothing. But in my experience of women, if they say something is nothing it's usually everything.'

He looks at Jamie, who annoyingly nods in agreement.

'So instead of leaving, I sat down on the bench next to her, and after asking a few probing questions, suddenly her floodgates opened and she told me everything. I think she was grateful to share it with someone.'

'And that everything was . . . ?'

'That she was sorry I'd had to leave the Wave Watch. She hadn't wanted it to happen, but she and the rest of the committee had been put under pressure to force me out. She said they had no choice; most of them didn't want to see me go but their arms were twisted.'

'You mean they were bribed,' Jamie says. 'Money is always at the root of everything.'

'Perhaps some were,' Walter says. 'But I don't think all.'

'But what possible reason would there be for bribing people to force you out of the Wave Watch – what did you do?'

'*Or* what did you know?' Jamie asks perceptively.

Walter nods. 'Exactly. I didn't actually know anything, but like I said I had my suspicions. Weather forecasts not being quite right, people offering to take the late-night shifts when they weren't rostered on . . . Something wasn't adding up. No one had ever been bothered by my *independent*, shall we call them, ways of predicting the weather before, but suddenly they were, especially when I began talking about unusual weather forecasts. They obviously thought I was getting too close to whatever was going on – so that was it – I was out.'

'But who was in charge of the Wave Watch then?' I ask. 'Couldn't you have gone to them?'

'Lucinda was in charge then.'

'But you said she was new?'

'She came to us from another branch a few months previously and was automatically promoted, because Alfred our previous captain had sadly passed away.'

'That's suspicious in itself, don't you think?' I say. 'That she was automatically promoted? And you still don't think it was anything to do with her?'

Walter shakes his head. 'No, she told me she was *leant on* – to use her exact words – to add her vote to my removal, and I believe her. Lucinda is a proud woman, and she takes her role at the Wave Watch very seriously. I'm sure she's finding this all very upsetting.'

'Hmm . . . ' I say, still not really buying this, but something else is niggling at me.

'But leant on by whom?' Jamie asks, while I'm trying to think. 'Who is behind all this?'

'I believe by the same person that's blackmailing her now to give out fake forecasts – she wouldn't tell me who it was; she's pretty scared of them, though.'

'I can't imagine Lucinda would be scared of anyone,' Jamie says, smiling a little. 'She's pretty formidable. Whoever it is must have something pretty bad on her to make her do this. You really don't know who it might be, Walter?'

'No. Like I said, I've suspected something is going on here for a while, not just to do with the Wave Watch but to do with the strange weather too. Something is brewing in St Felix and I really don't like the feel of it.'

'If we could only figure out who wanted you removed from the Wave Watch and who is blackmailing Lucinda to give out fake weather forecasts, then I reckon we'd have our man. Or woman, of course,' Jamie says hurriedly, looking at me.

'No, you're right with man.' I look earnestly at them both. 'Because I think I know exactly who that person is, and they're not too far away from us right now.'

Thirty

'Who?' Jamie asks, staring at me. 'Who do you think it is, Sky?'

I glance across at the harbour. 'I think it's Gerald,' I say quietly.

'Misery master – I mean Harbourmaster – Gerald?' Jamie says. 'He's a pain in the backside, I'll give you that. But a criminal mastermind, really?'

I look at Walter, hoping he'll say different. But he shakes his head.

'I've known Gerald for donkey's years. Don't like him any more than he likes me, but he's not a blackmailer.'

'What makes you think it's Gerald?' Jamie asks, realising I'm serious.

'I saw him and Lucinda arguing earlier, when you left me on the harbour with Fitz and Comet. They were in Gerald's office, and it looked heated. Gerald was clearly shouting and Lucinda was crying . . . again.'

'Doesn't mean to say he's our man,' Jamie says. 'They could have been arguing about anything.'

'Yes, but what?'

'I don't know. Do those two even know each other, Walter?'

'Well, yes; they do, actually. Gerald is Lucinda's landlord. He owns a few properties in and around St Felix, and she rents one of them from him.'

'So they do know each other!' I cry euphorically.

'Shush,' Jamie says. 'Let's not get everyone involved in this mystery just yet.'

'But they do know each other,' I repeat in a hushed voice. 'So that's a start. Ooh, what if Gerald is threatening to throw Lucinda out of her house? Maybe that's what he has over her. Does she live there alone, Walter?'

'Yes, I think she does.'

'How can she afford that?' Jamie asks. 'Property around here costs a bomb to buy and rent. What does she do outside of the Wave Watch – that's a voluntary role, isn't it?'

'Yes,' Walter says, clearly trying to piece all this together himself. 'All the Wave Watch members are volunteers. You know, now you mention it, I don't really know what she does. I've never thought about it before. Maybe she doesn't have a job.'

'How does Lucinda afford to pay rent on a house in St Felix if she doesn't have a job?' I ask, my eyes wide.

'Maybe someone left her money in a will or something?' Jamie suggests. 'What? It's a possibility,' he says when I roll my eyes in frustration.

'And how come Gerald owns so many properties in St Felix?' I ask, my mind racing. 'They don't come cheap; a harbourmaster can't earn the sort of salary that would enable him to buy a few houses. You said you've known him donkey's years, Walter. What's his story?'

'The first I knew of him was when he came here as a

317

caretaker up at Tregarlan – the same job my Fisher has now. He did that for a while, and then he began volunteering at the Wave Watch – that's really when I got to know him a bit better. Like I said, we never got on that well but he was pleasant enough. Then he managed to get the job as harbourmaster. I always got the feeling that's the job he was after. He said he'd had experience before at a different port and St Felix would be a breeze in comparison. He left the Wave Watch shortly after, that's when Alfred took over as Captain, but as I mentioned it wasn't long after that he passed.' Walter crosses himself.

'Gerald worked at Tregarlan?' I ask, my mind slowing now as the clues begin to drop satisfactorily into place.

Walter nods.

'So he knows the place pretty well, then, like Fisher does.'

'Possibly better. Gerald worked as a tour guide as well to boost his wage.'

'Then he'd have known about the tunnel that leads from the house to the beach?'

'Probably, but so do most people in St Felix if they know anything about the house.'

'In that case he might also have known about the tunnel that leads from the bunker outside the house to the cave?'

Walter's expression changes from slightly confused to razor sharp as he realises where I'm going with this.

'What rank did Gerald hold at the Wave Watch, Walter? You said he left when he became harbourmaster, and Alfred took over as Captain. Was Gerald Captain of the Wave Watch too?'

Walter nods.

'And did he have a gold badge?'

Walter nods again. 'He continued to wear it even when he left as part of his harbourmaster uniform. I'm not sure whether he thought it made him seem more important, or whether he was proud of it, but I'm sure he wasn't supposed to.'

'Anyone like to hazard a guess whether Gerald still has his badge?' I ask, as we all look over towards the harbourmaster's office. 'Because I'd bet you anything in the world he's lost it, and I'm pretty sure we all could have a very accurate guess as to where.'

'So, what now?' Talia asks when we're back in the watchtower and we've told her everything that's happened. Fisher has come back over to the island with us and we're now all discussing what our next move might be.

'What can we do?' Jamie says. 'We have no proof this is anything to do with Gerald. We only think it is.'

'I always wondered why Gerald hadn't spotted anything going on,' I say. 'If what we suspect is happening, then surely as harbourmaster he would have seen something untoward going on at some stage.'

'But if the drops always take place at night in the cave, then it would be quite possible he wouldn't see anything,' Jamie says, trying to remain neutral. 'It's the other side of the harbour, isn't it?'

'I'm still keeping an eye on the Wave Watch forecasts to see if they make any more mistakes,' Fisher adds. 'But I guess if we spot any inaccuracies it's going to be too late by then?'

I nod. 'All we can do is keep an eye on their forecasts and keep making our own from our data, and if they seem too different then we know something is about to happen.'

'And what do we do then?' Jamie asks. 'This isn't some Hollywood movie where we can sweep in with big searchlights and flush them out.'

'No, we can't,' Talia says. 'But what if we spoke to the police about our suspicions? Surely they'd be interested in what we've got to say?'

'They'd laugh in our faces,' Jamie says. 'The evidence we have is only circumstantial, we have no actual proof.'

'I could speak to Woody,' Fisher says. 'He's our local bobby in St Felix. Nice enough chap, but he doesn't have too much to do around here. He might like something more meaty to get his teeth into.'

'Worth a try,' I say. 'But until then I guess we just wait and see if we can spot anything strange going on ourselves.'

Possible smugglers were not the only strange thing I was on the lookout for right now – I was still very concerned about the unusual weather.

'There's nothing you can do about it,' Jamie says early one evening a few days after we've spoken to Walter. 'Just because the weather here doesn't fit into your neat little graphs and charts doesn't mean to say anything is wrong.'

'Meteorology is a science, though, and science doesn't have anomalies. It's full of carefully plotted equations and recognised calculations. That's why I like it – there're no grey areas, everything is black and white with a clear and precise answer.'

Jamie grins. 'But life isn't black and white, is it, Sky? I'd have thought you'd have realised that even more since you came here. We all think we know where we're going and what we're doing, but then life throws us a curveball and we're knocked firmly *off* course – just look at you and me.'

I'm not sure if he's referring to our lives and disabilities, or us as a couple.

'But meteorology isn't like that,' I insist. 'Just like you can't add two plus two and get five, specific weather fronts and systems mean something very exact is going to happen; there might be a slight variant on how strong the wind will blow or how hot the sun will make us, but that wind will blow and that sun will shine.'

'And that's not what's happening right now?' Jamie asks patiently.

'No, there's just too many irregularities. Both you and I have witnessed the clouds apparently trying to send us messages since we've been here. But this is different, it's like that isn't enough, and all the weather is trying to tell me something . . . '

Jamie smiles. 'You can't go from saying how exact and precise the weather is to wondering if it's trying to pass you secret messages!'

'I know. I hear what I'm saying and I'm annoyed with myself for even thinking it. But something weird is going on, and I'm determined to find out what.'

'You've been poring over those books all afternoon,' Jamie says, looking at the logbooks on the desk in front of me. 'You'll wear yourself out.'

'I'm fine.'

Jamie looks at me with a concerned expression. 'You're doing well at the moment, Sky; you're really starting to make some progress. Don't exhaust yourself worrying about the weather.'

I shake my head. *No, don't say it*, I tell myself.

'What?' Jamie asks. 'What's wrong now?'

'Nothing is wrong.'

'Maybe you should go for a lie-down.'

'I don't want a lie-down.'

'No, I know you don't. But it might do you good.'

I take a deep breath and try to remain calm. I know if I speak my mind right now, I'll definitely say something I'll regret.

'I'm only trying to help, Sky,' Jamie says when I don't speak. 'We all want you to get better.'

'Yes, I know you do. It's just … it gets a bit much sometimes … I feel smothered.'

Jamie's face falls.

'I know you're trying to help, and I appreciate it, really I do. It's just … '

'What is it just?' Jamie asks, a bit too steadily.

'I feel like you're treating me like a child sometimes – that's all.'

'I am just trying to look after you. That's what you do for someone you care about.'

'I know, and that's part of the problem – we haven't known each other that long. I really like you, Jamie, you know I do, and you've been great about my illness. But I don't want you to think about me like this.' I wave my hand over my comfy joggers and my baggy sweatshirt. 'Our relationship is so new, I want you to see me at my best, not like this all the time.'

'But that's what's so great about it,' Jamie says, not understanding. 'I've seen you at your worst and it just makes me care about you more.'

My heart lifts euphorically for a moment, and then immediately drops. 'But this isn't how a relationship should start,' I insist. 'We should go on dates, wear our best clothes, secretly wear sexy underwear underneath those best clothes … just in case.'

Jamie grins. 'If it means so much to you, we can do all that in the future when you're better.'

'But that's the problem, what if I don't get better?'

'That's nonsense. You've already improved so much in the last few weeks.'

'Yes, but it doesn't mean I'll continue to. This might be as good as it gets.'

'Then I'll deal with that. We'll take each day as it comes.'

I gaze with despair at Jamie.

'*That* is exactly my point. I don't want you to have to *deal* with anything. This illness, Jamie, is a life sentence. I might get time off for good behaviour sometimes, and believe me I relish those times. But this monster I live with is always going to be there in the background, waiting for its moment to pounce. I only have to take my eye off the ball, exert myself a tiny bit too much, and I allow myself to become weak and vulnerable to it once more.'

'What are you saying? You think I'm so shallow I'll run away the moment things get a little tough? I'd have thought you'd have realised over the last few weeks that simply isn't the case.'

'We have been trapped on an island ...' I say with a half-smile. 'Bit difficult to run across the water.'

But Jamie doesn't find this amusing.

'You think that's the only reason I've stayed to look after you? Because I couldn't escape?'

'No, I didn't mean that. I really appreciate what you've done for me – you, Talia, and Fisher – you know I do.'

'But you think that if things had been different, you wouldn't have seen me for dust? That's right, isn't it?'

'No! I don't know. I just want you to be aware of what it might be like being with me.'

'I know exactly what it might be like. Do you think I've only spent the last few weeks bringing you your meals and carrying you up the stairs? In the evenings when you're safely tucked up in bed, I've spent hours on the internet reading websites and forums about ME. I've read articles about pacing and how

323

best to help the person you're caring for. I probably know as much about your condition as you do.'

'Except what it's like to live with it,' I finish.

We both stare at each other.

'Yes, except that,' Jamie says quietly. 'I will never fully understand, just as you will never know what it's like to be dyslexic.'

I nod. He's right, of course.

'I'm so sorry, Jamie,' I say, looking up at him. 'I just don't want you to be burdened with all my baggage. I come with quite a lot, as you've seen.'

'The thing is,' Jamie says, kneeling down next to me, 'I'm like a packhorse – I'm pretty good at carrying a lot of baggage. I do it with ease and I very rarely complain.'

I smile at him. 'I don't know about the other analogy, but you certainly eat like a horse!'

'That's not where the similarities end, you know?' Jamie grins, glancing down towards his lap.

'Do you ever stop bigging yourself up?' I ask, grinning back at him.

'Do *you* ever stop putting yourself down?' Jamie counters, taking my hand in his. 'You're beautiful, Sky Matthews – even in your comfies, with no make-up on, and your hair all pulled back in that sensible ponytail you always wear it in.' He reaches behind my head to release my hair, so it cascades down over my shoulders. 'And if you want to start wearing sexy underwear in the future, I won't be averse to finding it under your clothes when I rip them off you in a fit of passion.' He winks at me. 'But for now, all that's important is that I love you, and I hope you love me.'

Jamie kisses me before I can answer him, and then he pulls away slightly to gauge my reaction.

I'm about to tell him I feel exactly the same when Jamie jumps.

'What?' I ask.

But Jamie just stares out of the window.

I turn my chair to see what he's staring at.

'Sky,' Jamie asks quietly, 'are you seeing what I'm seeing?'

'Ah-huh . . . ' I say as I stare out of the window with him.

The evening sky is blood red. It's the deepest, richest sunset I've ever seen. But that's not the only thing we're staring at, because in front of the red backdrop, floating down out of the sky like something from a Christmas card, are huge perfect flakes of pure white snow.

Thirty-one

Jamie and I stare out of the window, hardly believing our eyes.

'It's snowing,' I say eventually. 'In July.'

'I know,' Jamie says, clearly as shocked as I am. 'Today has been so hot, too. How can it be snowing?'

'I have no idea,' I say, shaking my head. 'And in front of that sunset, it's incredible.'

I whip my phone out to take some photos, then I put it down again.

'The prophecy,' I say as Jamie still watches the bright white flakes fall in front of the window. 'The one Walter told us about. How did it go? Something about winter and a red sky, wasn't it?'

Jamie gets out his own phone now; he pulls up his notes app and reads. '"If winter should fall on a blood-red summer sky, the town will flood and many will die." I wrote it down after Walter shared it with us. I hate to say it, Sky, but what's happening outside, as unbelievable as it is, is winter falling on a blood-red summer sky . . .'

'I know. What should we do?'

'I'll phone Fisher and see what he has to say. Why don't you take some photos in case it stops? Oh, and some video, too, if you can.'

Jamie phones Fisher while I record the weather. This is incredible. I've never seen anything like it. But as well as being incredible, it was also impossible; the temperature is far too warm for snow. What on earth is going on?'

'Fisher,' I hear Jamie say behind me as I film through the glass, 'have you seen it? . . . I thought you would have. Should we do anything? . . .Yeah, I know, we thought of that too.'

As I'm watching the snow still falling heavily outside, I hear the wind begin to pick up.

'I don't like the sound of that,' I say, but Jamie is still talking to Fisher. I sit down at the desk and check the anemometer, and then I check it again.

'Jamie,' I say without looking around. 'Jamie!'

'Hold on a minute, Fisher. What it is, Sky? I'm still on the phone.'

'Fisher will want to know this, put him on speaker phone.'

'I'm putting you on speaker,' Jamie says, pressing the button on his phone.

'Fisher, the wind speed is measuring on average sixty-five miles per hour.'

'What does that mean?' Jamie asks.

I don't have time to reprimand him for his lack of weather knowledge today.

'It means the wind is storm force,' Fisher says, sounding worried. 'A bad storm, too.'

'If it goes over seventy-two it's a hurricane,' I say, 'and it's pushing sixty-eight to seventy now on occasion.'

'Fisher, you've seen the snow falling, I presume?' I ask, still busily taking readings of wind speed, atmospheric pressure and temperature to see if I can figure out what's going on.

'I have, and I'm worried. It's like Zethar's prediction is coming true – the one Walt told you about. You can't see this from where you are, but the waves hitting the harbour right now are some of the biggest I've ever seen. It looks like it's caught a few people out already – there are fishing boats going out to rescue people that have been washed off the harbour wall into the water.'

'Use the new binoculars,' I instruct Jamie, my heart in my mouth. 'I'm still taking readings.' After the last time there was a storm I'd ordered us a stronger pair of binoculars, so this time we should be able to see right across to St Felix and everything that's happening.

Jamie does as I say and trains the binoculars over towards the mainland. 'Yeah, I can see. What are those idiots still doing out there taking photos if the waves are as bad as that?'

'Fisher, I don't know anything about some sorceress's predic-tion hundreds of years ago, but these winds might get worse. I think you should prepare the town for flooding if they're not already. Has someone called the Coastguard?'

'Yes, but apparently they've already been called out along the coast to rescue some of the boats caught out at sea. Our lifeboat is about to be launched in the next few minutes too. No one saw this coming; it's taken us all completely unawares. Did you forecast this, Sky?'

'No, my readings all suggested a quiet, calm, balmy evening. What about the Wave Watch, what did they say?'

'I'm not sure. I'd check for you but I think I'm going to be needed down in the town; I'm still up at Tregarlan right now.'

I feel like I'm going mad – everything I know about science

and the weather is being turned upside down. And now lives might be at stake too.

'Don't let us hold you up. Fisher, this is serious; winds of this strength aren't to be messed with. Be careful, won't you?'

'I will. Call me if you notice anything else you think might be of help.'

'We will.'

Fisher hangs up and Jamie puts his phone in his pocket. 'This is bad, isn't it?'

'If it gets worse it definitely will be. Jamie, I've been studying the weather for a long time and I've never seen anything like this. It's not just the winds, it's the snow – where has that come from? It's just not possible.'

'And yet there it is, right in front of our eyes.'

I look out of the window again and see the sky is still glowing red and the snow still falling. But now the flakes blow around in the fierce wind, like someone's just shaken a real-life snow globe, with us inside it.

'I'm going outside to have a look,' Jamie says, heading for the staircase.

'I'm not sure that's a good idea,' I say, as I hurriedly write some more readings down in our logbook. 'It's rough out there; this wind could easily knock you off your feet.'

'Don't worry. I'll be fine,' Jamie says, already halfway down the stairs.

'Don't let the dogs outside!' I warn. 'It's definitely too dangerous for them.'

'I won't!' Jamie calls back.

I sit at the desk watching the equipment, continuously noting down all the relevant figures. *This is crazy*, I think as I scribble. *None of these numbers make any sense – what the hell is going on?*

I hear the door slam as Jamie departs, and then Comet barking and scratching at it in her desire to accompany him.

Oh, Jamie, please don't go too far, I think, looking away from the instruments and out of the window once more. *It's not safe out there.*

Comet eventually settles down to listen at the door for Jamie, but Fitz decides to rejoin me upstairs. He curls up patiently beside me on a cushion while I continue to record the storm. A few minutes later my phone rings.

'Jamie, what's up?' I ask, wondering why he's phoning me instead of just coming back inside.

'Fisher just called ... says he was just heading out ... saw Gerald creeping through ... grounds of Tregarlan towards ... bunker ... going to follow him.'

'There can't be a drop going on in all this, can there?' I ask. The wind sounds so strong where Jamie is, I'm struggling to hear him.

'Yeah ... think ... is,' Jamie says, breaking up now too. 'Going to take *Doris* ... the cave ... see if I can catch ... other end.'

'Jamie, no!' I shout. 'You mustn't take the boat! The sea is far too rough, the waves are too high, the wind—'

' ... be fine ... Sky ... not far ... can make it—' The line goes dead.

My heart plummets as I remember the last time Jamie was out in weather like this. But this weather is even more dangerous. It's absolute madness to take a boat out on the sea right now.

I rush to the top of the stairs and then remember how weak I am; my muscles are already complaining and I've only gone a few steps. By the time I get to the bottom of the stairs Jamie will be long gone.

Damn you, body! I curse. *Letting me down again! What use am I stuck up here when everything is going on outside?*

I go back to the desk and pick up the binoculars to see if I can see Jamie, but he must already be around the other side of the island. I can't see anything out there but snow, waves and sea spray.

I train my binoculars back on St Felix. There are shop owners out all along the seafront, hurriedly putting out sandbags in front of their shops to try to protect them from the waves that are still washing up over the safety railings that run the length of the harbour. They're getting dangerously close to the buildings already.

People are still out taking in the storm, they're being buffeted from side to side by strong gusts of wind, but most are managing to keep themselves upright – just.

And far too many are dangerously close to the water, trying to capture this weather phenomenon on their phones and cameras.

If this wind gets any stronger Zethar's prediction will definitely come true, I think, watching people holding on to the railings, trying to make their way to the end of the harbour to get the best shots of the waves flying high over their heads, and laughing as they get covered in salty spray from the sea.

I look down at the anemometer – seventy-four miles per hour – we've reached hurricane levels.

'Jamie, why do you have to be such a hero!' I mutter, training my binoculars on the sea again in case I can spot him.

My phone rings. I grab it – it's Talia.

'Sky, you've seen the weather, have you?' she asks anxiously.

'Yes, I'm monitoring it.'

'I thought you would be. I'm worried, Sky. It's just like the prediction, isn't it? The one the sorceress gave.'

'There are some similarities,' I have to admit. 'Where are you now?'

'I'm inside watching from upstairs in my uncle's house.'

'Good, I'm glad you're not one of the fools out on the harbour. I don't have to tell you what winds of seventy-four miles per hour mean, do I?'

'Hurricane,' Talia says quietly. 'Oh gosh, that bad?'

'Yes, and it doesn't seem to be letting up.'

'Maybe I should try and warn the people still on the harbour,' Talia says. 'If the winds get any stronger, they will be in serious danger.'

'They're already in serious danger. No, you stay right where you are. Keep yourself safe.'

'I've tried ringing Fisher but he's not picking up,' Talia says, sounding worried. 'Do you know where he is?'

For one moment I think about keeping it from her, but then I realise I wouldn't appreciate it if it were the other way around.

'Fisher was just leaving Tregarlan to go and help in the town when he saw Gerald heading towards the bunker. I haven't heard from him since. Jamie, idiot that he is, has taken a boat to see if there's a drop going down in the cave.'

'In this?' Talia gasps. 'That's crazy!'

'I know, but he was gone before I could stop him.'

'I'm going to Tregarlan,' Talia says determinedly, 'to see what's going on.'

'No, I don't think that's a good idea. You stay where you are.'

'Sorry, Sky, you're breaking up ... can't quite hear you,' Talia says, her voice sounding perfectly clear to me. The line goes dead.

I try to call Talia back, but she doesn't pick up. 'Damn! I knew I shouldn't have said anything.'

I look out to sea again with the binoculars. *At least it isn't dark yet*, I think as I watch the waves once more, desperately searching for a glimpse of Jamie. *That's one thing to be thankful for.* The ominous dark sky that surrounds St Felix right now is a result of the sky's blood-red colour, the dense deep purple clouds and the heavy snow still falling, rather than the time of day.

'Wait, what's that?' I spy something in the water, not too far from the island. 'It isn't, is it?' I mutter, trying to focus the binoculars in on the object. 'Please God, no,' I say in a loud voice.

What I'm seeing in the water looks like an upturned boat, but I can only see glimpses of it as it bobs around in the waves. I quickly realise this object definitely isn't a bright purple like *Doris*'s hull; it's much duller and more of a rusty black colour.

'It's not *Doris*. Thank God.' I sigh with relief as I continue to narrate my reactions to the two dogs. Comet has now joined us upstairs, but realising something isn't right, both dogs are awake and sitting next to me, their ears pricked and their tails alert and stiff.

I look harder at the object in the water. It looks like it might be metal of some sort, and there are a lot of barnacles and the like clinging to it. 'Wait, haven't I seen something like that before somewhere?'

I rack my brains trying to remember.

'Yes, I have! In the cave when we went in search of the carving.'

I get out my phone and look back at my photos. 'There it is, and it looks exactly the same as the thing outside the window.'

I peer through the binoculars again, trying to train them on the strange object. It's being tossed about in the waves so much, it's hard to keep focused on it. But it's getting closer to me all the time, and as it does, I'm able to see it in more detail.

Contrary to what I'd first thought, the metal object is actually a sphere shape, and there are a few spikey bits on its side. It looks a lot like an old-fashioned diver's helmet, except it's a lot bigger. It does look familiar, though – where have I seen something like this before other than the cave?

Then I remember, at the exhibition Walter guided me to, the one about the history of St Felix. There was a section about the Second World War, and how it had affected the town and its residents, and there was a photo of some of the debris that had been washed up on the beaches here after the war, and one of those photos looked very similar to what I'm seeing in the water.

'Oh boy,' I say, my voice quivering a little as I talk to the dogs. 'I do hope I'm mistaken. But if I'm not, I think something that looks very much like a German sea mine is floating past us right now.'

The dogs both look up at me, not understanding.

'It's a bomb, guys,' I say, staring at them just as intently as they are staring at me. 'I think there might be a bomb right outside the island.'

Thirty-two

My breathing is heavy and my hands are shaking as I dial 999 and ask for the Coastguard.

'Yes, I know you're a bit busy right now,' I say, trying to remain calm when I finally get through to the right person. 'But a few people being washed off the harbour will be the least of your worries if this thing is still live.'

I end the call with them promising to send someone out to take a look.

I grab my binoculars again to see if it's still nearby. But it's definitely not in the area it was before. *I just hope you've not washed up on the island. If you have and you are still live, we could be blown sky high if something detonates you.*

I look down at Fitz and Comet. Comet has settled down again, clearly deciding sleep is the best option until Jamie returns. But Fitz still waits patiently by my chair, his ears pricked and his head to one side.

'Not much we can do but wait, fella,' I tell him, picking him up and putting him on my lap for comfort.

I take a look at the equipment again – the anemometer is definitely reading hurricane now.

'How did we end up here, Fitz?' I ask my little friend, snuggling my face into his soft furry coat. 'I brought you here for a quiet time. Instead, we're marooned on a Cornish island in the middle of a hurricane, with snow cascading down even though its summer, and an explosive device – that could go off at any minute – floating by outside our window.'

Fitz licks my cheek.

'Oh, and not forgetting that two of our friends have gone in search of smugglers, and the other is on their way to join them. We'll wake up in a minute, eh?'

I lift the binoculars again to see what's going on over in St Felix.

There are slightly fewer people on the harbour front now, but a lot more water as the waves crash over the top of the safety railings, each time creating a tidal river in the place where I'd sat a few days ago in the burning-hot sunshine with the dogs. If the waves get any stronger, and the sea any higher, the shops on the harbour will begin to flood soon.

This isn't looking good at all. I'm worried for St Felix, I'm worried about my friends, and I'm especially worried about Jamie.

'Please let Jamie be all right,' I pray, putting the binoculars down for moment. I look up into the clouds as I speak. 'Please bring him back safe to us. I'm sorry for doubting him, for being annoyed when he only wanted to care for me. I'm the one that's been the idiot, not him.'

Some movement in the sea makes me look back down at the waves.

'What's that?' I wonder, lifting my binoculars again. After a

336

few seconds I spot a boat flying through the water. It bounces from wave to wave as it fights its way through the rough sea. 'I think it it's the Coastguard,' I tell Fitz. 'Yes, it is the Coastguard – I recognise the orange and white of their boat.'

The Coastguard boat pulls up a little way from the island, and some of the crewmembers try to look over the side of the boat while attempting to keep their balance on the swaying deck.

What are they looking at?

I can just make out a rusty, barnacle-ravaged casing bobbing around in the water not far from their boat. *It's the mine!*

I'm pleased to see it's a lot further from the island now than it had been before, but in moving away from Aurora, it's moved closer to the mainland.

Was this really the same mine I'd spotted in the cave? I wonder as I watch the crew trying to inspect the rusty vessel. *It must be, surely. There can't be that many sea mines floating around the Cornish coast, can there?*

I watch the Coastguard struggling to keep their boat from capsizing as they examine the object in the water and I think of Jamie in *Doris* again.

How would he be managing to keep afloat in these conditions if the Coastguard were struggling? And I pray again that he got to the safety of the cave, and it protects him today like it had the first time he'd been caught in a storm.

One of the Coastguard goes back inside the cockpit of the boat and I can just make out him talking on his radio.

I desperately want to know what he's saying. Eventually he replaces his radio and relays some instructions to the others.

The boat then begins to circle around the floating mine – a big wide circle that it's difficult to keep to because the mine keeps moving in the opposite direction to the one they want it to go in, ever closer to the St Felix harbour.

And all I can do is sit and watch helplessly, while the storm still rages around all of us.

The wind speed eventually begins to drop outside almost as quickly as it had picked up. The height and ferocity of the waves start to decline, and the heavy snow changes into light flurries, eventually disappearing as the dense clouds thin out, and the angry red sky becomes a much calmer shade of blush pink, as if it's embarrassed by its earlier faux pas.

'Thank goodness,' I say as I watch the weather begin to return to something more normal for a British summer evening.

The Coastguard is now joined by a police boat, and after a brief exchange between the two, it's the police who take over the circling duties, while the Coastguard head in the direction of the island.

I watch their boat traverse the waves with a lot more ease than before, and I expect it will simply whizz on past the island to wherever it's needed next, but it doesn't, it slows up when it gets to Aurora and pulls up to our little jetty.

Shortly afterwards I hear a knock at the door.

'It should be open!' I call hobbling to the top of the stairs. 'Just give it a push. Hush, Comet,' I say to the barking dog. 'Don't you start either, Fitz.'

The door opens and a man wearing rescue gear and carrying a helmet walks cautiously through it.'

'Hello! I'm up here!' I call. 'Please come up.'

The man climbs the stairs and we go into the watchtower with the dogs, who are extremely wary of this vision in full-length padded blue waterproofs.

'I'm Ben, I'm with the Coastguard,' he tries to say, but the dogs are growling and barking at him.

'Shush, you two! Sorry,' I apologise to Ben. 'They're very protective.'

'Just doing your job, aren't you, guys?' He reaches into his pocket and pulls out a couple of dog biscuits. 'I always carry them. You'd be surprised how many dogs we have to rescue that have fallen off cliffs, or are stranded with their owners on boats.'

Ben kneels down and holds out the biscuits to the dogs, who eventually take them from him after sniffing them suspiciously first.

'Good dogs,' he says, standing up again. 'Now, I'm sorry to bother you,' he says, turning to me again. 'But were you the person that reported the explosive device earlier? They said the call came from here.'

'Yes, I was. It definitely is one, then?'

Ben nods. 'We think it's a German sea mine from the Second World War. We get them washing up around the coast occasionally. This is a particularly big one, though.'

'Is it live?'

'We're not one hundred per cent sure, but we think it might be. Bomb disposal will be here first thing tomorrow to take a look. If there's any doubt it will be towed out to sea and detonated at a safe distance from the shore. We'll put in place a maritime and air exclusion zone beforehand, though, to keep everyone safe. If it is live there will be quite an explosion – you'll see and hear it easily from here.'

He looks over at the window and sees all the equipment on and around the desk. 'What's going on here, then?'

'Weather watch,' I tell him. 'We've been keeping an eye

on the weather for a number of weeks after there were some irregular reports.'

'Nothing stranger than today, I bet. Those were some weird conditions out there.'

'I know, snow in summer? I still can't believe it myself. And that sky!'

Ben shrugs. 'If it's going to happen anywhere it will be here in St Felix. I'm not a great believer in some of the wilder tales that come from here, but I can't deny many folk are. If there's going to be weather that can't be explained it will happen here, that's for sure.'

'Will the police boat be here all night?' I ask, seeing it at the edge of the window still slowly circling the mine.

'It will. We'll make sure the tide doesn't take the mine any further inland, or close to you here on the island. I think the tide is going out, isn't it, so we should be okay. But if it begins to drift, we'll tow it out a little way under instruction from the bomb disposal boys.'

'Good, that's a relief. Thanks for letting me know.'

'You did well to spot it. When did you first see it?'

'That's a good question. I think I saw it in a cave a while ago at the bottom of the rocks just below Tregarlan Castle.'

Ben looks puzzled. 'Really?'

'Yes.' I grab my phone off the desk and show him the photos. 'I didn't know what it was at the time. But it looks very much like the same one.'

'I think it probably is. We'll check the cave, though, just in case. The storm must have dislodged it – the waves were pretty strong – and it floated out to sea. It happens, they stay hidden for decades and then some freak weather comes along, dislodges them and they become a danger again.' He hands me back my phone. 'We were lucky the police were so close, actually, or we'd probably still be waiting for them. There was some bother down in some of the caves, likely not far from where you saw this.'

'Oh yes?' I ask, my anxiety rising. What if Jamie has been caught up in it? 'What sort of bother?'

'Probably shouldn't say, but we think the boys intercepted some smuggling – accidently, too.'

'Accidentally?'

'Yeah, they'd been called out to assist us with the rescue effort. They were patrolling the coastline to make sure nobody took any vessels out in the bad weather. You'd be surprised how many do, even when the waves are as high and dangerous as they've been today.'

I try not to think of Jamie.

'Anyway, they spotted a small motorboat in trouble not far from here. There was no way a boat as small as that was going to keep afloat in a sea as rough as it was a while ago; they were on the verge of capsizing at any moment. So the boys intercepted them and tried to guide them back to the harbour. But the occupants of the boat appeared to be taking no notice of them, so they got closer and physically had to tow them back in. It was only when they got back into calmer waters that they discovered the boat was loaded with a rather large quantity of illegal cannabis.'

I open my eyes wide. 'Cannabis?'

'Yes, we're not talking small amounts, either. We think the boat was doing drops around the coast, and they got caught up in the storm. It wasn't forecast by anyone – even the Wave Watch. Did you see it coming here?'

'No, not at all. All my instruments and readings forecast a calm night.'

341

So, the Wave Watch didn't forecast the storm either, even though there was a drop going down. Interesting . . .

'Exactly, so the freak weather washed us up a couple of drugs smugglers too, as well as a bomb. Quite a productive afternoon, you might say.'

'Indeed. You don't know if there were any more boats rescued, do you? I mean, I know there were probably many, but near the caves where the other one was picked up?'

'Not that I'm aware of, but there's been so much going on, we haven't had our debriefing yet. I'll know more when we do. We're heading back to base now; we thought we'd call in here first to let you know what was happening with the mine. If that thing turns out to be live, you could have saved a lot of lives by spotting it in the water. If it had washed up on the beach and kids had started playing on it . . . I'm sure I don't need to tell you what the consequences might have been.'

I nod.

'Well, I'd better be going. Enjoy your evening. It should be a bit calmer through your window now, fingers crossed.'

I feel mixed emotions as I return to the watchtower after seeing Ben to the top of the stairs, and then apologising because I can't see him all the way to the door.

I'm relieved that the storm is over, and that someone is in control of the possibly explosive device floating close to the island. But I'm still worried for the others. I've called them several times and not one of them has picked up.

Where were they? What has happened to them, and to Gerald? And where is Jamie?

Thirty-three

I hear the door open and close downstairs.

'Jamie! Is that you?'

I rush to the top of the stairs and see the now familiar sight of a rather wet and bedraggled Jamie standing in the hall. My heart leaps.

'Yep, it's me,' he says, summoning a smile in my direction as both dogs bound down the stairs to greet him. 'Yes, yes, hello to you too,' he says, bending to fuss them. 'I'm going to get into some dry things. I'll make a hot drink and then I'll be right up.' He sounds utterly exhausted. 'Are you okay?'

'Yes, I'm fine,' I say quickly, not wanting to overload him with all my news just yet. 'I'm just relieved you're back in one piece.'

After Jamie has changed and made us both mugs of hot chocolate, we sit down together to discuss the events of the past few hours.

'...and so I really didn't do anything,' Jamie says when he's told me all about what has happened to him. 'I made it successfully across to the mainland, but I didn't go into our cave because I didn't want to scare someone away this time from dropping off whatever it is they might be carrying.'

'Cannabis,' I say, filling in the gap.

'Cannabis? How do you know that?'

'Tell you in a minute.'

'Okay . . . ' Jamie nods with a puzzled expression. 'So I hid in *Doris* in the next cave along. If you remember that was a fairly big one, too. I'm not sure what I thought I was going to achieve by that, maybe head them off as they came out of our cave – take photos of the boat or something? But the sea turned really rough then, and so I couldn't leave until it calmed down. By then I guess they were long gone.'

'Not necessarily,' I say, grinning, and I begin to tell him what happened here on the island.

Jamie listens wide-eyed when I tell him about the sea mine, and then with an open mouth as I tell him what Ben, the Coastguard, had told me.

When I've finished, he shakes his head. 'That's incredible. I saw the police boat when I came back a little while ago and wondered what was going on. I had no idea it was something to do with you, though. So it seems our friend the weather was the hero when it came to apprehending the smugglers, not me.'

'You were very brave even attempting to go out in that storm. But very stupid, too. I was so worried about you, Jamie. You really shouldn't have gone off like that. What if something had happened to you?'

'Who would have carried you down the stairs then?' Jamie says, smiling.

'You know I didn't mean that. I *was* truly worried about you. I know I've been a little diva when it comes to you looking after me, and I know you're only trying to find your way in a situation that's alien to you. But maybe we can find our way together in the future?'

'I'd like that,' Jamie says, moving closer to me on the sofa. 'I promise I'll try not to treat you like a child, or an invalid, or—'

'Just treat me like a woman,' I interrupt, covering his lips with my finger. 'A woman you care very much about.'

'I can't do that,' Jamie says, gently removing my finger, but continuing to hold my hand. 'I can only promise to treat you like someone I love. I know I've said this before, but I love you, Sky Matthews. I love you very, very much.'

'And I love you too, Jamie Sonny Samuels. Actually, maybe not the Sonny part, you can keep that all to yourself.'

We both laugh, and hug, and then we kiss, and as Jamie holds me close in his warm embrace, I glance out of the window, and see my friends the clouds have another message for me.

In the sky, which is now salmon pink as the sun fades fast, they have formed themselves into two perfectly shaped hearts. Entwined together, just like Jamie and me.

Thirty-four

'What a truly beautiful evening,' Walter says as we sit outside on Aurora watching the sun go down. Walter and I are sitting on camping chairs, Jamie is standing by my side holding my hand, and Talia and Fisher are snuggled next to each other on picnic rugs with the two dogs at their feet.

Earlier in the day we'd watched a bomb disposal unit explode the German mine out at sea. It had been a moment of elation and joy as we'd seen a huge plume of water shoot high into the air as the bomb was detonated, mixed with relief and thanks that the mine had been discovered before it had caused any harm.

'If that thing had exploded near St Felix,' Jamie had commented as we'd watched from our safe distance on the island, 'it would have done some serious damage to so many buildings and possibly to so many people, too.'

'You really did save St Felix, Sky,' Talia had said, smiling at me. 'I dread to think what might have happened if you hadn't seen it floating by.'

'I just did what anyone else would have done.'

'No, Sky,' Walter had solemnly said, 'you did it. You saved us from Zethar's prophecy. She wasn't predicting flooding in the expected sense, by sea. It was the flooding and destruction that would have taken place if that bomb had exploded near the shore. If winter should fall under a blood-red summer sky, the town will flood and many will die. Winter did fall under a blood-red sky, but luckily *our* Sky was here to save us.'

I'd simply nodded. What Walter was saying made sense, of course it did. But I still refused to believe I had thwarted a sorceress's premonition made hundreds of years ago. I couldn't deny that strange things had happened here yesterday, and I still couldn't find a rational explanation for most of them, but weather does occasionally go a bit rogue – especially with climate change, and that was what I was putting it down to this time – one of those strange blips that are sometimes recorded. The only difference was that time I'd been here to witness it myself.

Talia and Fisher had arrived back on the island not that long after Jamie, full of tales of what had happened at the other end of the tunnel.

Apparently, Talia had arrived at the bunker not long after Fisher had set off in pursuit of Gerald. When Gerald had gone through the door and down the tunnel, Fisher had decided to follow, but he'd left all the rescue equipment he'd been carrying down to the harbour outside the bunker entrance.

Talia had subsequently found his equipment in a pile, so she knew Fisher was definitely down in the tunnel. She'd then gone about securing the entrance to the bunker with the discarded ropes so no one – especially Gerald – could get out again. She'd then called Woody, St Felix's local policeman, so that when both Fisher and Gerald were ready to emerge from the tunnel, local law enforcement were there to arrest Gerald and take his latest stash of cannabis for evidence.

So I wasn't the only person being lauded a hero – Talia was too, and rightly so.

Now, we're sitting watching the sun go down together at the end of a much quieter day on the island. It's been lovely to have Walter here with us, sharing his stories of happier times here on Aurora, when he still had his beloved wife Doris by his side.

'Do you think we'll continue to experience unusual weather now the mystery has been solved?' Talia asks from her spot on the picnic rug. 'It does seem like we were all brought here for a reason, doesn't it? Especially you, Sky. Although I can honestly say I've loved every minute I've spent here this summer, even when I was trapping smugglers in a tunnel!'

'I really don't know,' I reply, watching the sun slip into the sea against the backdrop of a fast-diminishing crimson sky. 'What I have learnt since I've been in St Felix is that the weather here isn't like anywhere else I've studied it around the world. St Felix is a law unto itself in so many respects, and its unique weather is just one of its many eccentricities. There are clearly so many secrets yet to be discovered. I'm just sad I won't be here much longer to uncover them for myself.'

I look up at Jamie and he squeezes my hand. We've already discussed, somewhat bleakly, what we are going to do when we leave St Felix in a few weeks. We've even talked about moving in together, but neither of us really wants to go back to London and leave this beautiful town we've both come to love so much.

'Not necessarily,' Walter says mysteriously from his chair. 'There are a couple more secrets we might uncover in the next few minutes . . .'

'Such as?' Jamie asks. 'Come on, don't keep us in suspense, Walter.'

'Such as, what's going to happen to this island once you leave?' Walter replies rather disappointingly.

'I assume the Wave Watch will take it over again, now we're not really needed to record the weather,' I answer gloomily. 'Now Lucinda doesn't have to worry about Gerald, I'm sure she'll be super keen to get back here and carry on where she left off.'

Lucinda, as Walter had thought, was mostly the innocent party in all this. Gerald had been forcing her to give out false weather forecasts, with the threat of taking her home away from her if she didn't do as he wanted. Except yesterday Lucinda had decided to take a stand and not be pressurised this time. Instead, she gave a fake weather forecast to the harbourmaster's office predicting rough weather like Gerald wanted. He expected the area would then be clear of other craft, allowing his supplier's boat to come and go unnoticed in the calm sea. But this time Lucinda gave the correct calm forecast to everyone else, in the hope the sea would be full of boats and holidaymakers enjoying the fine weather, and the smugglers might be spotted by someone. But something went very wrong (or was that right?) with all our predictions, and the town experienced one of the biggest and strangest storms in its history.

We'd never quite got to the bottom of why our equipment hadn't predicted either of the storms, when the rest of the time it was working perfectly. But then I'd never really worked out how the clouds had managed to form into the perfect shape at exactly the right time to send us all of our messages.

Even though I couldn't make sense of it using my trusted

scientific methods, for now I had to trust in something else instead, and simply accept that like so many people had told us, strange things often happen in St Felix that can't be explained, and when they bring about the greater good, actually don't need to be.

'I have a feeling the Wave Watch will be remaining at Tregarlan for the time being,' Walter continues.

'Really?' Fisher sits up now. 'I didn't know that?'

'I don't think they do yet,' Walter says, a knowing smile on his face as he talks. 'I've not long decided it myself, and I would need to speak to Poppy and Jake first. But I'm sure they'll be fine about it – it gives them something extra to show visitors on tours of the house.'

'Why do you get to decide where the Wave Watch is based?' I ask. 'Are they letting you back in again?'

Walter shakes his head. 'No, I'm going to be busy with my own weather project, right here on Aurora.'

We all look at each other to see if anyone knows what Walter is talking about. It's clear from everyone's puzzled expressions they know nothing.

'You see, it's not just St Felix that has a way of unveiling secrets,' Walter continues with the same knowing smile. 'Aurora does, too. Secrets about caves, tunnels, smugglers, and also people – their personalities, their failings and their strengths.' He looks across at Jamie and me. 'But the one secret it's kept hidden so well, and for so long, is that the island we're all sitting on right now is actually owned by me.'

Fisher looks just as stunned by his grandfather's announcement as the rest of us.

'You own Aurora?' he asks, obviously in shock. 'Why didn't you tell me?'

'I didn't feel it necessary until now.'

'So you're the mystery person paying my caretaker wages?'

'I am,' Walter says, smiling at him. 'I wanted to keep it secret, so I made an arrangement with the council to pay you if I paid them first.'

'I thought I was getting a good deal out of the council.' Fisher grins. 'Stingy bastards most of the time they are.'

'But why?' I ask. 'Why didn't you want anyone to know you owned Aurora, Walter?'

'As you know, I had my suspicions for a long time that something was going on, not just with the smuggling, but with the unusual weather too. I wanted someone to come here who I thought might be able to help me solve some of these mysteries. And that person, Sky, was you.'

'Me?' I say, my hand on my chest.

'I was growing increasingly worried that Zethar's prediction might actually come true with the progressively strange weather I was noting. But I knew no one would take any notice of Wacky Walter Weather, so I decided I had to bring in some experts to back up my amateur projections. I thought a renowned meteorologist and a famous television forecaster would have more clout if they found something strange was going on. So that's where you two came in. When you came along too, Talia, it was a lovely added bonus I wasn't expecting.'

Talia smiles delightedly at Walter.

'Are you saying that this was all your idea?' I ask, trying to make sense of what he's saying. I wave my hand back at the house. 'None of this was anything to do with Met Central?'

Walter nods his head. 'I'm afraid so. I asked Met Central to provide me with two people fitting the description I gave them. I said I would pay your wages, provide you with somewhere to stay, and all the equipment you needed. Just as long as they kept from you who your actual employer was going to be. I also sent them some of my own reports for you to read, to pique your interest and make you think there genuinely was something odd going on – which, as you now know, there was.'

I stare at Walter, trying to digest and understand all this.

'I had to do it like that or you wouldn't have taken the job, Sky, would you?'

'Er . . . probably not,' I manage to say, my mind still trying to process everything. No wonder Gemma had been a little vague, especially about Jamie. After the trouble with Jamie's ex-wife, Walter's request must have come at just the right time.

Walter smiles at me. 'I have to say, Sky, when I found out who I had coming here, I was most impressed with your credentials. You came highly recommended.'

'And what about me?' Jamie asks jokily. 'Were you impressed by my credentials, or was I just an added bonus when I turned up, like Talia?'

'Well,' Walter says with a serious expression, 'I can't say I cared too much for Sonny Samuels . . .'

Jamie looks a little hurt by his answer.

'But,' Walter smiles warmly now, 'I've been very impressed with Jamie Samuels since I've got to know him. Very impressed indeed.'

Jamie reaches over and gives him a high-five.

'I don't think *any of us* cared too much for Sonny when he first arrived!' Talia pipes up, and everyone laughs. 'But we all love Jamie,' she finishes and she blows Jamie a kiss.

'Now my secret is out,' Walter says, 'I'd like to discuss with you all my plans for the island. Because I think it might be of interest to both Sky and Jamie now they wish to stay on in St Felix together.'

I look up at Jamie, but he shakes his head. 'I have no idea how he knows,' he says, looking as surprised as me.

'I wish to turn the island into a visitor centre,' Walter continues. 'Somewhere for people to come and learn all about the weather, both how to predict it and what's happening around them. I want it to be part scientific, which is where you come in, Sky. I'd like to use all your knowledge, expertise and experience to set up the centre, and then for the long-term running of it. I know you've got some health issues, but we can work around them so you don't ever have to do too much at once.'

'Thank you, Walter. I appreciate that,' I tell him.

'If we combine your scientific knowledge with my own ideas on how to forecast weather – a little more organically, shall we say? – I don't see why our two methods can't live in harmony when it comes to weather forecasting, do you?'

I shake my head. 'I think it sounds absolutely perfect, Walter, and I'd be more than happy to stay and work alongside you if you really want me to.'

'There's no one else I'd rather it be.'

Walter reaches out his hand to me. But instead of shaking it, he takes hold of my hand and gives it a little squeeze. Just like my grandad used to do to me, way back when in his shed, to let me know everything was going to be all right.

The past me wouldn't have been happy to tie myself down to a remote Cornish town, and a small weather project such as this. I would have thought it far beneath my qualifications and experience. But St Felix has worked its unique magic on me, just like Jack promised it would, and now the idea of staying on here yet still being able to work with the weather and share my passion with others sounds absolutely perfect.

I've not fully accepted yet that I'll never be the person I once was, but I have begun to embrace my new way of life a little better, instead of fighting it like I used too. My ME will never be all of me, but I know now it will always be an important part of what makes me the person I am.

'That all sounds great?' Jamie pipes up, looking a little lost. 'But where do I come in?'

'Alongside the management of the centre with Sky, I'd love you to be my front-of-house man,' Walter says, smiling at Jamie. 'Doing what you do best – talking to the press and the public, staging talks and tours. Perhaps we could allow Sonny out on those occasions, just for a while ... What do you say? I'd pay you both well, of course. I wouldn't expect you to do it for nothing.'

Jamie looks at me. 'By the look of you two holding hands there, I'd say the decision is already made.'

I reach up and with my other hand I take hold of Jamie's again. 'Thank you,' I tell him. 'Staying here in St Felix with you, and being allowed to visit this island as often as we like, sounds like the most perfect ending to this story, don't you think?'

'I want to be wherever you are,' Jamie says, holding my gaze. 'You know that, Sky.'

'Ahem!' Fisher pipes up. 'What about me in all these plans of yours, Walt? Only your grandson here!'

'Don't you worry,' Walter says, winking at him. 'I hear St Felix is going to be looking for a new harbourmaster very soon ... and I think you'd be just perfect for the role.'

'I've always wanted to be harbourmaster,' Fisher says

wistfully, looking back over the island to St Felix. 'Do you think I'd have a chance?'

'You'd be perfect, Fisher,' I tell him. 'No one knows the waters around St Felix better than you.'

'Can I come and visit you all in my holidays?' Talia asks, looking desperately sad she's not going to be involved in any of this. 'I've only got one more year of my degree and then maybe I can come and work at the centre too?'

'Oh, Talia, you're made for so much more in the meteorological world than this,' I tell her in what I hope is an encouraging way. 'But of course, you'd be more than welcome any time you like,' I hurriedly add when her face begins to crumple. 'We'll always have a place for you here if you want one.'

'The more often you visit the better,' Fisher says, looking lovingly at Talia and taking her hand. 'We'll all miss you when you're gone. Me especially.'

'Look!' I shout suddenly, as a strange light begins to fill the sky over the island. 'Over there!'

'What on earth is that?' Jamie asks, looking in the same direction.

The now night sky in front of us begins to fill with the most amazing light show – hues of blue, green and purple cover the sky in an incredible iridescent glow.

'It's the St Felix Aurora,' Walter says, gazing out over the sea with us. 'It seems we're not the only ones who are happy with what's taken place in the past and our plans for the future. The island is, too. This is her way of showing us.'

And as I sit watching this impossible yet magical spectacle that's happening in front of me right now, with all my friends beside me, and Fitz and Comet at our feet, I know exactly how Aurora feels.

Inspiration & Thanks

I do hope you've enjoyed my latest novel about the little Cornish town of St Felix.

It's been lovely to revisit the town once more with new characters and a new setting – the island of Aurora.

Many of you will know that I base fictional St Felix on St Ives, a small seaside town at the farmost tip of Cornwall. St Ives doesn't have an island off its coast like St Felix has. But if you venture south to Marazion, you will find the tidal island of St Michaels Mount, which, although a little bigger than Aurora, very much inspired my island.

If you've read any of my St Felix books before, you'll know that I always like to revisit characters from previous St Felix stories. This time along with a few others, the characters of Jack and Kate make several appearances. If you haven't already, you can read more about their story in *Kate and Clara's Curious Cornish Craft Shop* – my third book set in St Felix.

I've also written characters in this story who volunteer for the fictional 'Wave Watch'. This was very much inspired by the amazing members of The National Coastwatch Institution who volunteer in stations all along the UK's coastline to protect and preserve life at sea. You can read more about them at https://www.nci.org.uk

The 'Lady on a Horse' cave carvings were inspired by the very real carvings at Piper's Hole on Crantock beach in Cornwall. You can visit the beach and the cave during low tide just like Sky, Jamie, Talia and Fisher do in the story. If you'd like to learn more about the cave and the folklore that accompanies the carvings, helpful blogs such as https://cornish-birdblog.com/a-name-for-crantocks-maid-in-the-cave/ will give you much more information.

Special thanks go to Megan North who provided me with both the inspiration and facts to write about visual stress as a part of dyslexia.

And lastly, I must talk about Sky and her ME diagnosis. ME (Myalgic Encephalomyelitis) is a chronic, complex, often fluctuating neurological condition that affects the whole body. 250,000 people in the UK, and around 17 million people world-wide, suffer from ME, and I am one of them.

Everyone's story with ME is unique to them. I have tried in this book to use some of my own experiences, along with the experiences of others with the illness as a basis for Sky's story. My apologies if you too suffer with ME and this doesn't quite reflect your own journey. But I really hope reading this story will help to remove some of the stigma and misconceptions there are about ME, and more recently Long Covid – a similar post-viral condition that mirrors ME in so many ways. If you'd like to know more about ME and Long Covid, the websites *Action for ME* and *The ME Association* have lots of clear concise information.

I've thanked those that inspired the story. Now I'd like to

thank those who helped in the creation of this novel: Hannah Ferguson, my always amazing agent; Darcy Nicholson, my super supportive editor; and everyone at Little, Brown and beyond who work on my books – including Zoe Carroll and Sophie Wilson.

My family – Jim, Rosie, Tom and our three dogs: Oscar, Sherlock, and the newest canine member, Ted, who very much inspired the character of Fitz.

And to you, my wonderful readers. Thank you for all your amazing support and many touching messages over the years, they really make it all worthwhile.

Until the next time . . .

Alix

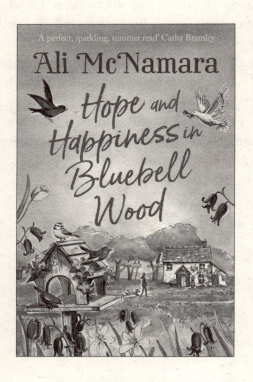

A gorgeous novel from Ali McNamara, packed with her trademark blend of humour, romance and just a little magic. Welcome to Bluebell Wood

'A perfect, sparkling, summer read' Cathy Bramley

Ali McNamara

Kate and Clara's Curious Cornish Craft Shop

Discover the glorious little Cornish town
of St Felix – where romance and magic
glitter in the summer air

Escape to Rainbow Bay, where an
inheritance and some sea air are about
to work their magic on Amelia's life